Selected Praise for

DEEPER

"Sizzling hot, but also frankly and deeply emotional, this is another star turn from Hart. The characters are wonderfully depicted—especially super-sexy hero Nick. A don't-miss reading experience."
—*RT Book Reviews*

"*Deeper* is absolutely, positively, the best book that I have read in ages! I cannot say enough about this book. The writing is fabulous, the characters' chemistry is combustible and the story line brought tears to my eyes more than once…. Beautiful, poignant and bittersweet… Megan Hart never disappoints, but with *Deeper* she went above and beyond. Fans will never be sorry if they run right out and purchase this book the day it is published."
—*Romance Reader at Heart,* Top Pick

"At first glance, it seems possible that this is all about youthful exploits and adult realities. However, there is a much more intense meaning to the overall story. While there is definitely hot, steamy sex, there are also very heart-wrenching moments of sorrow, doubt and self-discovery. I thoroughly enjoyed *Deeper*… [it] will have a special place in my reader's heart!"
—*Romance Readers Connection*

"*Deeper* is a sensual story, but there is sooooooo much more…. Bess and Nick's story makes the heartstrings hum, and the sex scenes will make your body sing…. I look forward to hearing more of Megan Hart's voice of erotica."
—*A Romance Review*

"A compelling tale of love and understanding… The story is heartbreakingly familiar in its depiction of how teenage romance can shape our lives. I found myself on the edge of my seat wondering how Bess and Nick would be able to reconcile their stormy past with their uncertain future."
—*Romance Junkies Reviews*

MEGAN HART

deeper

HARLEQUIN®
entertain, enrich, inspire™

Recycling programs
for this product may
not exist in your area.

DEEPER

ISBN-13: 978-0-7783-1521-6

Copyright © 2009 by Megan Hart

For questions and comments about the quality of this book, please contact us at CustomerService@Harlequin.com.

www.Harlequin.com

Printed in U.S.A.

This book is for a black light, a bottom bunk and a hug,
For a doorway, a pair of kicked-off shoes
and the width of a kitchen table,
And as ever and always, for a blue bathrobe,
a million miles of legs and a whole lot of hair.
Everything that came before you is a memory,
but you are the real and constant thing.

ACKNOWLEDGMENTS

Special thanks must go to the artists whose music
kept me going while telling this story. I could write without the
songs, but it sure makes it a lot more fun when I have the right ones
to sing along with while I'm typing: "Without You" by Jason Manns,
"Ocean-Size Love" by Leigh Nash, "Wish" by Kevin Steinman
and "Reach You" by Justin King.

And further thanks go to Jennifer Blackwell Yale, who was
kind enough to provide me with an accurate rune reading.

Chapter 01

Now

The sea remained the same. The sound and smell of it wasn't different, nor the push and pull of its waves. Twenty years ago, Bess Walsh had stood on this beach and looked forward to the rest of her life, and now…

Now she wasn't sure she was ready for what lay ahead.

Now she stood with cold sand scraping her toes and the salt-scented air tangling her hair. She breathed deep. She shut out the night with the darkness behind her eyelids and lost herself in the past so she didn't have to think about the future.

The night air in late May still held a chill, especially this close to the water, and her thin T-shirt and denim skirt didn't provide much warmth. Her nipples peaked, and she crossed her arms to hug some heat into herself. It seemed appropriate to shiver, remembering that long-ago summer. Remembering him. For twenty years she'd tried to forget, yet here she was, back again, and unable to forget any more than she ever had.

Bess tipped her face to the breeze that pushed her hair from her face. She opened her mouth to drink it in, to eat it like some sweet candy. The smell filled her nose and coated her tongue. It took her back more effectively than mere memory could. Transported her.

Silly. She was too old to entertain fairy tales. Time travel didn't exist. There was no way to go back. No way, even, to stay where she was. Her only option, anybody's only option, was to move forward.

Thinking this, she did move forward. One step, then another. Her feet sank into the sand and she cast a glance over her shoulder to the safety of her deck and the single candle burning there. The wind pushed the flame into flickers and she waited for it to go out, but it stayed lit within the protection of its glass container.

Back then, that house had stood apart. Now neighbors flanked it, close enough to hit if you spat in the right direction, as her grandma would have said. The house behind, four stories of million-dollar architecture, loomed over hers. Now seagrass-dotted dunes that hadn't been there twenty years ago swelled between the houses and the beach, and though a few lights shone in windows farther down the sand, closer to the main square of Bethany Beach, this early in the season most of the houses near hers were dark.

The water would be too cold for swimming. Great whites could be lurking. The undertow would be strong. Bess went to the water anyway, drawn by memory and desire.

The ocean had always made her more aware of her body and its cycles. The push and pull of the tide had seemed such a feminine thing, tied as it was to the moon. She never swam in it, but being around the sea always made Bess feel more sensual and alive, like a cat wanting to rub up against a friendly hand. The warm waters of the Bahamas, the cold Atlantic waves of Maine, the smooth, rippling Gulf of Mexico, the gorgeous blue waters of the Pacific, had all called to her, but none of them so strongly as this patch of water and sand. This place.

Twenty years later, it was stronger than ever.

Her feet found the hard-packed sand the last wave had left behind. She curled her toes into the chill. Now and then a glimmer of white foam appeared, but nothing touched her yet. She took a dragging step, letting her feet guide her so she didn't come down unexpectedly on a sharp stone or shell. Another step forward led her to even wetter sand. Squishy again. The rush and roar of the water threw up spray into the breeze, and she opened her mouth for it the way she had the scent.

The water, when at last it touched her feet, wasn't cold. The warmth was more shocking than a chill would've been, and Bess gasped. Before she took another step, another wave came. Warmth swirled around her ankles and splashed up her bare legs. It pulled away, leaving her feet buried. She went deeper without thinking. Step by step, until the water, as warm as a bath, as warm as a kiss, bathed her thighs. It soaked the hem of her skirt and splashed onto her shirt.

Laughing, Bess bent to let the water flow over her hands, her wrists. Elbows. It rolled under her touch, evading her grasp. She knelt, soaking herself in the waves.

They touched her like a thousand kisses all over her at once. Like tongues licking. Splashing higher, wetting her panties. Water covered her to the waist when she sat. Moved up over her throat when she lay back. It covered her face and she held her breath, waiting for it to retreat.

Her hair came loose, but Bess thought nothing of losing the clip that had bound it. Like seaweed, her hair swirled, tickling her bare arms and covering her face, only to be washed away by the next wave. Salt and the grit of sand painted her lips when she licked them, opened them as if for a lover's kiss. She spread out her arms, but the water wouldn't be held. Salt stung her eyes, but not from the sea. From her tears, sliding unbidden across her cheeks. They tasted bitter, not like the fish-sand-salt sweetness of the ocean.

Bess opened herself up to the water and the waves. To the past. Every time the surge came she held her breath, wondering if this next time would be the one to take her by surprise and fill her lungs with water. Or to pull her deeper, under. And she wondered what she would do if that happened. If she would care. If she would fight or let the sea take her away, if she would give up and be lost in it the way she had once been lost in him.

They'd made love on this beach with the sound of the ocean masking their cries. He'd used his mouth and hands to make her writhe. She'd slid his cock inside her to anchor their bodies, but no matter how many times they'd fucked, it hadn't worked. Pleasure didn't last. Everything ended.

Her own hands were a poor substitute, but Bess used them anyway. Sand rasped her fingertips as she slid them beneath her shirt to cup her breasts, remembering how his mouth had felt. Lower, how his hands had moved between her thighs. She parted her legs, letting the sea stroke her the way he once had. Her hips lifted, pushing against something that didn't push back. The water retreated, swirling, exposing her to the night-chilled air.

More waves came to embrace her as she caressed herself. It had been a long time since she'd taken this pleasure, done this alone. She hadn't made love to herself in so long her hands felt like someone else's.

He hadn't been her first lover or the first boy to give her an orgasm. He hadn't even been the first she'd loved. He'd been the first to turn her inside out with something as simple as a smile. The first to make her doubt herself. He'd taken her deeper than anyone ever had, and yet she hadn't drowned.

The affair had been short. A page in the book of her life, barely a chapter. Only one verse of the song. She'd spent more years without him than she had with him. None of that mattered, either.

When Bess touched herself, it was his smile she imagined. His voice, murmuring her name. His fingers linked with hers. His body. His touch. His name.

"Nick." The single word slipped off her tongue for the first time in twenty years, unlocked by the sea. This sea. This sand. This beach. This place.

Nick.

The hand that closed over her ankle was as warm as the water, and for a moment Bess thought a hank of seaweed had wrapped itself around her. A moment later another hand touched her other foot. Both slid up her legs, to her thighs. The weight and heat of a body, solid and not like the water, covered her. She'd opened her mouth to the sea as if accepting a lover, but now a real kiss claimed her. Real lips, real hands, a real tongue plunged into her mouth and stroked hers.

She should have screamed at this invasion. At this dark stranger's sudden violation. Yet this was no stranger's touch. She knew it better than she knew her own. The weight of his hands. The shape of his cock. The taste of him.

It was fantasy, memory. It was wishful thinking. Bess didn't care. She opened herself to him the way she had to the water. Tomorrow when the sun rose and her skin chafed from the sand's abuse she would call herself a fool, but here and now her desire was too strong to deny. She didn't want to deny it. She'd tossed caution aside then, and she did so now.

His hand went beneath her head to cradle it. His mouth covered hers, nibbling, before his tongue plunged again into her mouth. His moan vibrated her lips. His fingers threaded through her hair.

"Bess," he said, and then more. The sorts of things lovers said in the heat of their passion, words that didn't hold up under scrutiny.

She didn't care. Bess slid her hands down Nick's back to the familiar rounded curves of his ass. He wore denim and she pushed it down until he was naked, his skin hot. She traced the ditch of his spine with her fingers as his kiss claimed her. Water splashed and retreated, no longer rising high enough to cover them.

His hand slid between her legs and pulled at her panties. The thin material gave way at once. He pushed her skirt up to her hips. Her shirt was so thin and so wet it was as though she wore nothing. When his mouth clamped over one turgid nipple, Bess cried out and arched. His fingers found the heat between her legs. He rubbed, and her body jerked. She was ready.

"Bess," Nick said into her ear. "What is this?"

"Don't ask," she told him. She pulled his mouth back to hers. Beneath her, wet sand cradled them. She dug her heels into it and opened her thighs. She reached between them to grab his cock, the thick heat of it as familiar as everything else. "Don't ask, Nick, or it might all go away."

She stroked him gently, too mindful of the salt and sand to urge him to enter her. Not even in fantasy could she forget the agony of sand in places it didn't belong. The memory of it, of how they'd both walked bowlegged from it, made her laugh aloud.

Bess laughed again as Nick's mouth fastened on her throat. His hands roamed. The two of them writhed together, rolling in the wet sand. He laughed in turn, tipping back his head. In the faint starlight he looked no different than he ever had.

His hand moved slowly between her legs, but it was enough. Bess tensed, her fingers digging into the smooth muscles of his back. She bit back her cry as a climax filled her. Nick grunted, hips thrusting forward against her. Heat spurted against her belly, bared by his touch, and the sea smell grew briefly stronger.

Nick bent his face to her shoulder, holding her tight. The water tickled her feet but came no higher. His body, naked and smooth, covered her.

The sea had brought him to her, a fact Bess accepted without question. Without hesitation. None of this would be real in the daylight. It wouldn't be real even the moment she left the water and stumbled, soaking, to her bed. None of this was real, but all of it was, and she didn't question it for fear it would all go away.

Chapter 02

Then

"Sure you don't want a hit?" Missy waved the joint in Bess's direction, sending a cloud of fragrant smoke to tickle her nostrils. "C'mon, Bessie. It's a party."

"Bessie is a cow's name." Bess flipped the other girl the finger and cracked the top on a can of soda. "And, no, I don't need your weed, thanks."

"Suit yourself." She drew deep and coughed, destroying her carefully wrought illusion that she was some sort of druggie queen. "That's some good shit!"

Bess rolled her eyes and eyed the bowl of potato chips on Missy's coffee table. "How long have those been there?"

She coughed again. "I just put them out, bitch. Right before you got here."

Bess pulled the bowl closer and checked them carefully. Missy's trailer was consistently filthy. Seeing no bugs or garbage even when she tipped the bowl from side to side, Bess took a chance. She was starving.

"Christ, I could go for a pizza." Missy flopped onto the battered armchair and hung her legs over the side. The bottoms of her feet were dark with dirt. Her skirt rode up, flashing a hint of hot-pink lace. "Let's get a pizza."

"I have exactly two dollars to last me until payday." Bess crunched chips and swallowed them down with store-brand cola that had already lost its fizz.

Missy waved a languorous hand. "So I'll call some guys. Make them bring the pizza."

Before Bess had time to protest, Missy sat up with a grin and tossed her bleached-blond hair over her shoulder. The motion caused one unfettered breast to surge out of her tank top. Missy was built like a brick shit house, as she was fond of saying, and didn't mind showing it off.

"C'mon," she said, as if Bess *was* protesting, though she hadn't even opened her mouth. "It'll be a party. Who doesn't like a party? Well, besides you."

"I like parties." Bess leaned back against the couch Missy had stolen from outside the Salvation Army. "But I have to work tomorrow."

"Shit. So do I. So what? Let's have a fucking party, okay?" Missy jumped off the chair and settled her joint in the overflowing ashtray. "It'll be fun. You need some fun in you, Bess."

"I have fun!"

Missy rolled her eyes. "I know what kind of fun you have. I'm talking about some real fun. Get some color in those cheeks. And I don't mean the ones on your face."

"Nice." Bess laughed, even though Missy's assessment of her wasn't entirely flattering. How could she not? Missy had a way about her that didn't allow Bess to take her too seriously. "So you're going to call some boys and tell them to bring pizza. And they'll just do it."

Missy lifted the hem of her teensy-weensy skirt and flashed her tiny pink panties. "Of course they will."

"I'm not screwing some guy for pizza, no matter how hungry I am." Bess put her feet up on the coffee table without taking off her flip-flops. She would never have done that at home, God no, even in bare feet. Missy didn't seem to care. Or notice.

"What do I care who you screw?" She was already dialing the phone as she rummaged in the fridge for a beer. "I mean, do you even— Baby, hi!"

Bess listened, fascinated, as Missy finagled her way into free food. She made a couple calls and hung up, then turned back with a triumphant look on her face.

"Done. Ryan and Nick will be here in half an hour with the pizza. I told Seth and Brad to bring some beer. Heather and Kelly are coming, too. You know them, right?"

Bess nodded. She knew Ryan and had met the other girls a few times. They waitressed with Missy at the Fishnet. The other guys she didn't know, but she didn't really have to. She knew Missy. They'd either be frat boys slumming, or townies with bleached hair and permanent suntans. "Yeah."

"Don't sound so thrilled. Not everyone can live in a house on the beach, bitch."

Missy's "bitch" wasn't meant as an insult, and Bess didn't take it that way. "I didn't say anything."

"Oh, you don't have to. Your face says it all." Missy demonstrated, wrinkling her nose and thinning her lips.

"I don't look like that." Bess laughed again to cover up her embarrassment at knowing she probably did.

"Sure, right. Whatever." Missy waved a hand and returned for her joint, which she sucked greedily, coughing some more.

"Poor little rich girl. Can't your grammy and grampy fork you over some dough?"

Bess finished her soda and got up to put the can in the garbage, even though Missy would hardly have noticed if she'd tossed it onto the living room floor. "They're letting me live without rent for the summer. What more could I ask for?"

"An allowance." Missy, still puffing, went to the dresser just outside the hallway to the bedrooms and pulled out a makeup bag from the top drawer. From the bag came more jars and tubes and brushes than Bess had ever seen in any woman's arsenal. Missy already wore a full coating of cosmetics, but apparently her "at home" face wasn't presentable enough for company other than Bess.

"I'm twenty years old. I'm past the point of getting an allowance." Bess didn't point out that though her weekly paychecks were less than what Missy pulled in with her tips, Bess was saving for college and Missy was just...living.

Missy painted on a fresh set of arched eyebrows and turned her face from side to side to stare at her reflection. "I'm going to dye my hair black."

"What?" Bess was used to her non sequiturs by now, but this was a little out there. "Why?"

Missy shrugged, then adjusted her tank top to expose more cleavage. She swiped her eyelids with shadow and spoke with pursed lips as she used a brush to paint them. "Just because. C'mon, Bess, haven't you ever wanted to do something different?"

"Not really."

She turned to look at her full on. "Not ever?"

Bess chewed the inside of her cheek before remembering it was a bad habit, and stopped. "Different like how?"

Missy swaggered close enough to pluck at the collar of

Bess's Izod shirt. "I could lend you something to wear before the guys get here, if you want."

Bess glanced at her khaki skirt, bare legs and flip-flops before looking at Missy's denim mini and tiny top. "What's the matter with what I have on?"

Missy shrugged and went back to her face. "Nothing...for you. I guess."

Girls have a language in which the words have nothing to do with the meaning. Bess flushed, looking again at her clothes. She touched her hair, bound on top of her head with a spring clip. She'd showered after work and used some powder and gloss, but nothing more than that. She'd figured they'd watch TV or something, not have a party.

"I think I look fine." She sounded defensive. "I told you, I'm not planning to get screwed."

"Of course you're not." Missy sounded so patronizing and sympathetic, Bess erupted.

"What's that supposed to mean?" She strode to the mirror, pushing Missy aside to stare at her reflection before turning away to glare. "Anyway, anyone who doesn't like me the way I am can just...suck it!"

Missy's drawn-on brows rose at Bess's exclamation. "Cool it down, sugar-tits. Jesus! Fine, don't get laid. Save yourself for your lame-ass boyfriend back home."

"I'm not saving myself for anyone," Bess said. "Just because you don't comprehend the concept of being faithful doesn't mean nobody else does. And he's not lame."

And he might not be her boyfriend anymore.

Missy rolled her eyes. "Whatever. Do I care?"

"I don't know. Do you? You sure as hell keep bringing it up." Bess put her hands on her hips.

Missy glared. Bess glared back. After a second, though, Missy's lips twitched. A second after that, both of them were guffawing.

"You are such a drama queen." Missy pushed Bess aside in order to put away her makeup.

"Screw you, Missy."

"I didn't know you swang that way, sugar-tits." She fluttered her heavily mascaraed eyelashes.

Bess, as usual, had nothing wittier to counter with, and settled for trying to tidy up the disaster of Missy's living room. She'd only managed to clear piles of magazines and newspapers off the couch and chairs before the door opened and Heather arrived with Kelly in tow. Both looked pretty drunk already.

"Hey, girl!"

"Lookit you, bitch! What the hell? Who did your hair?"

"Where's the fucking pizza?"

Bess watched the interchange and wondered what it would be like to have a house where people came in without knocking and tossed themselves onto the furniture as if they lived there. She was pretty sure she'd hate it. She nodded when Kelly waved at her, but Heather, typically, ignored her. Heather didn't like Bess. The feeling was mutual, because Bess knew Heather thought she was a stuck-up princess.

People arrived for the next hour, many more than Missy had actually invited, but news of a party always spread fast. The trailer, not even a double-wide, soon became a haze of smoke, body heat and music. Bess, stomach growling, kept hoping someone would show up with the promised pizza. Bags of chips and pretzels appeared along with forties of malt liquor and bottles of every other kind of booze. At least Missy's friends brought their own with enough to share.

Bess wasn't the only one underage, but she was probably the only one not drinking. Nobody cared, assuming as long as she had a cup in her hand she was getting as wasted as the rest of them. Missy would have known, but was so busy drifting from lap to lap she couldn't be bothered with Bess.

A cheer went up when the pizza arrived, finally. Bess had met Ryan before. He fucked Missy once in a while, when they were both drunk or stoned or bored. He held the pizza boxes high, shouting out, "Two bucks, two bucks," to everyone he passed.

Two bucks. All she had in her pocket. For two bucks she could have gone and bought her own slice and a drink, but at the party she'd be able to eat as much as she wanted or could snag before it all disappeared. Ryan clearly knew what he was doing, though, because he'd brought four pizzas. The guy behind him, his face shadowed by a ball cap pulled low over his eyes, carried another three.

"Bess." Ryan winked at her as she moved aside the empty cans and paper plates already stained from previous pizzas to make room for the boxes. "How you doin', baby?"

"Good." She brushed off her hands. The table was sticky, but it wasn't worth the effort to clean it. She turned in Missy's tiny kitchen to grab some paper plates from the cupboard and set them down. Already hands were digging into the boxes and carrying away slices. She wanted to get hers.

"This is my buddy, Nick." Ryan jerked a thumb over his shoulder as his friend set down the other boxes.

Concentrating on sliding the steaming slices onto her plate, Bess did little more than flick a glance in his direction. Her stomach had sprouted the pins and needles preceding the shakes of low blood sugar, and though there'd be more than one person passed out here by the end of the night, she didn't intend to be the first. When she looked up, Nick was gone, swallowed by the mass of writhing, dancing bodies.

Ryan leaned across her to grab a napkin from the counter behind her. His arm brushed her breast. His breath wafted over her throat and cheek. Pinned between the table and the counter with no place to go, Bess flushed at the intimacy, especially when Ryan grinned and winked. His glance fell to the front of her shirt before he looked at her face again.

"Nice party," he said, and turned away to load his plate with pizza.

It wasn't the first time Ryan had flirted with her, and it wasn't even that Bess minded. Whatever arrangement he and Missy had didn't seem to be exclusive for either of them. Ryan was cute and knew it. It didn't make her feel special. Just a little off balance. It had been so long since she'd paid attention to any sort of male interest, she wasn't sure how to react.

"What are you drinking?" This came from a guy Bess didn't know by name, though she'd seen him around. He held up a bottle of tequila. "Margarita?"

Bess looked for a blender and saw none. "Umm...no, thanks."

"Okay." The guy shrugged and turned to the girl next to him, who waited with open mouth. He took the bottles of tequila and margarita mix and poured both into her mouth at the same time, stopping when the liquid started overflowing. She swallowed and choked, coughing, waving her hands, and they laughed.

Bess tried hard not to make that face, the one Missy had mimicked, but...ew. Gross. Not to mention a good way to end up in the hospital. Shielding her pizza with her body, she eased through the throng, but found no place to sit in the living room. She leaned instead against the wall in a corner. People were playing quarters already. Someone else had set up a beer bong. Bess concentrated on eating.

The problem was, once finished, she was thirsty again, which meant a return trip through the party jungle to the kitchen. She had to stop to dance a little along the way with

Brian, who worked with her at Sugarland, because he snagged her wrist and wouldn't let her pass without a bit of bump and grind. Brian liked boys, but was fond of reminding Bess frottage didn't need a gender.

"You look pretty tonight!" He shouted over the heavy bass thumping of "Rump Shaker." "Zooma zoom, baby!"

Bess rolled her eyes as he grabbed her ass and ground against her. "Thanks, Brian. You like guys, remember?"

"Honey," he said into her ear, with a lick that made her giggle and squirm, "that makes it even more of a compliment."

She could hardly deny that, so she let him feel her up and down for a few minutes while they danced.

"So, who've you got your eye on?" she shouted into his ear.

"Oh, boys, boys, boys," Brian said with a shake of his highlighted bangs. "Boys all over, honey, but sadly, most of them are straight. How 'bout you? Still remaining true to your Prince Charming?"

Bess kept herself from making a face at Brian's assessment of her love life. He didn't need to know about her problems with Andy. He'd either commiserate, which she didn't want, or give her advice, which she didn't need.

"Dish!" Brian ordered, twirling her. "Mr. Right's Mr. Wrong, all of a sudden?"

If she'd been able to get in touch with Andy more than once in the past three weeks, maybe she'd know. Bess shook her head and eased herself out of Brian's grasp. "I didn't say that."

"You didn't have to," he shouted in her ear, and she winced. "What did that bastard do?"

"Nothing!" Bess tugged her hands out of his.

Brian didn't let her go easily. "I don't believe you!"

"I'm going to get a drink."

"You have to work tomorrow!" He pretended to be scandalized, but his easy grin gave him away.

Bess laughed, shaking her head. "So do you. See you later, Brian."

Before he could protest, she kissed him quickly on the cheek and disengaged from his octopus hands so she could finish her quest for something to drink. She pushed away and through the crowd, toward the kitchen. She didn't want to talk about Andy to Brian. Or to Missy. She didn't really want to talk or think about Andy at all, because once she started, she might very well have to admit that things were going suddenly, desperately sour.

The sodas had all disappeared from the fridge, and she wasn't about to trust the open two-liter bottles littered all over the counter and table. The pizza had been completely devoured, with nothing but a few strings of cheese and some splotches of sauce left on the boxes to prove it had ever been there at all. Bess gathered up the empty cardboard and shoved it beneath the table, then searched for a plastic cup that didn't look as if it had been used. She filled it with tap water and the last couple of ice cubes, then refilled the ice-cube trays and put them back in the freezer.

"It wouldn't be a party without you, Mommy." Missy draped herself over Bess's shoulder and kissed her loudly on the cheek. "There. Now you can't say you didn't get any action tonight."

"Too late. Brian beat you to it." Bess wiped off Missy's kiss and looked out over the room. She wouldn't have been surprised if they rocked the trailer right off its blocks. Or set the place on fire from spontaneous combustion.

Missy babbled something, slurring, but Bess wasn't listening. Across the room, standing along the back wall next to the hall, stood a boy. She recognized the faded T-shirt after a second. Ryan's friend. He'd taken off his ball cap.

He wasn't doing anything notable, just tipping a bottle of beer to his lips, but he turned to look toward her just as she noticed him. Their eyes met, or she thought they did, though it was impossible to tell if he was looking at her.

That moment stamped itself into her mind forever. The smell of weed and beer, the lingering taste of pizza, the warmth of Missy's hand on her arm. The splash of cold on her calf as someone spilled a drink at that moment.

The first moment she really looked at him.

"Missy. Who is that?"

Missy, busy making fun of the guy who'd lost his cup, didn't look up at first. In the half minute it took for her to answer, Bess had already imagined herself walking across the room and taking the beer out of his hands. Putting it to her mouth. Putting *him* to her mouth.

"Who?"

Bess pointed, not caring if he saw.

"Oh, that's Nick the Prick. Dude! Wipe it the fuck up!" Missy, no longer amused by her guest's fumbling fingers, punched him in the arm. "This isn't a fucking bar!"

Bess ignored them both, just moved out of the way to let the guy get on the floor to wipe up the spill. Nick was no longer looking at her, and she was glad, because that meant she could stare all she wanted. She imprinted his profile on her mind. From this distance she had to imagine the length of his lashes, the depth of his dimple. The way he'd smell...

"Bess!" Missy shook her arm.

"Does he have a girlfriend?"

Missy gaped. She looked at Bess, then toward Nick and back again. "You're shitting me. Nick?"

Bess nodded. She'd forgotten her ice water and grabbed it up now, needing to quench the sudden dryness in her throat. *She's going to say he has a girlfriend,* she thought. *She's going to tell me he's in love with some girl with big tits and bigger hair. Or worse, she fucked him. Missy fucked him....*

Missy blew upward to move her bangs off her forehead. She shook her head. "Why do you want to know?"

Blaming the booze and weed for the stupid question, Bess shot her a look Missy couldn't possibly misunderstand. She gaped again, then laughed. "Nick? You have a boyfriend, remember, sugar-tits?"

Bess hadn't forgotten. Then again, it was sort of up in the air whether or not she still had one. She looked at Missy. "If I didn't have a boyfriend, I would be on him like butter on a cob of corn."

Missy guffawed and slapped her thigh. "Are you serious?"

Bess had never been more serious about anything in her life. "Does he?"

"Have a girlfriend?" Missy's thickly lined eyes turned calculating, and she looked over Bess's shoulder, presumably at the topic of their conversation. "No. He's into guys."

"What? No!" Bess clenched her fists, turning to stare. Nick's head bobbed to the beat, up and down, and he tipped his beer again. "He's gay?"

"Sorry," Missy said.

She gritted her teeth and tucked her fists beneath her opposite arms. "Goddamn it."

Missy's brows flew up to her hairline. "Dude!"

"I'm not a dude," Bess snapped, so disappointed she couldn't think straight.

Missy patted her arm. "Have a drink. It won't seem so bad then."

"It's not bad." Bess shook her head and gulped ice water. "Forget I said anything."

Missy ho-ho-hoed. "Have a drink anyways."

Bess lifted her glass of ice water and gulped down the rest before tossing the empty cup into the sink. "I have to get home."

Her head hurt, suddenly, and her stomach, too. All from a stupid boy she'd never even talked to. She was the stupid one. Bess shoved off her disappointment, angry at herself. Angry at Missy.

"Aww, don't leave." Missy grabbed Bess's hand. "Party's just getting started."

"Missy, I really have to go. It's late."

It wasn't, really, and she worked the late shift tomorrow. But suddenly Bess didn't want to watch everyone else drinking and smoking and making out. She didn't want to watch everyone else hooking up and having fun. Worst of all, while she'd been talking with Missy, Nick had vanished.

"Call me tomorrow!" Missy yelled after her, but Bess didn't answer.

She burst from the trailer into the welcome freshness of the cool early June air. Not much of the party had moved outside. A shadowy couple kissed leaning against the wall, their hands groping and the sound of their heavy breathing loud enough to carry. A moaning girl bent over in the bushes while her girlfriends held back her hair and urged her to "get it up." Bess reached for the pitted metal railing but tripped anyway on the last concrete step and twisted her ankle hard enough to make her curse.

"You okay?"

She looked up to the wink of a cigarette tip. "Yeah. I just tripped. I'm not drunk," she added, angry that she felt she had to explain.

"You're one of the only ones."

It was too much of a coincidence, too much like fate, but even before he stepped out of the shadows and into the streamer of light from the streetlamp, Bess knew it was Nick. He took another drag on his cigarette and tossed the butt to the dirt, where he ground it out with the toe of his boot. They both turned at the sound of vomit splattering and moans, and Nick grimaced. He took Bess by the elbow and steered her around the corner of the trailer, toward the street, so easily she didn't have time to protest.

He let go of her before she had time to protest that, too. "Some people shouldn't drink."

Bess shivered a little. The light was brighter here, and it painted his face in silver with purple highlights. He looked like Robert Downey, Jr. in *Less Than Zero,* she thought a little disjointedly. The un-strung-out version.

Nick smiled. "Hi. You're Bess."

"Yes." Her voice sounded hoarse. Her thoughts seemed fuzzy. *Contact high?* she wondered as a wave of dizziness swept her. Or Nick's smile? "You're Nick. Ryan's friend."

"Yeah."

Silence.

"I'm heading home," Bess said. Gay. Why did he have to be gay? How could he be gay? Why was every cute boy around here gay? "I rode my bike."

"That's hot," said Nick with another grin. "What do you ride? A Harley?"

Her thoughts weren't normally so slow, but somehow lust and disappointment had made syrup of her brain. "What? Oh…no. Ten-speed."

He laughed. Bess watched his throat work. She wanted to lick him, and had actually moved forward a tiny bit before she stopped herself, embarrassed. Nick didn't seem to notice.

"Where do you live?"

She hesitated before telling him, not wanting to admit she lived in one of the beachfront homes.

"Don't worry, I'm not a serial killer," Nick said. "You don't have to tell me."

She felt really stupid then. "Oh. No, it's not that. I'm staying in my grandparents' house on Maplewood Street."

There was only the barest pause before he nodded. "Uh-huh."

His gaze traveled over her, up and down, and Bess suddenly wished she'd borrowed some of Missy's clothes. Put on some makeup. Except what did it matter, when he didn't like girls, anyway?

"Nice meeting you," she said. It sounded lame, even to her. The sort of thing you said at a cocktail party, not an impromptu kegger in a trailer park.

"You work at Sugarland, right? I've seen you there." Nick thrust his hands into the pockets of his faded jeans.

"Yes." Bess looked for her bike, still chained to the hitch of Missy's trailer.

"With Brian, right?"

Bess gave an inward sigh. Of course he would know Brian. "Yeah."

"I work at the Surf Pro." Nick walked with her to the bike and watched as she unlinked the chain and wound it along the straddle bar.

One of the few stores Bess had never been in. The bathing suits were too expensive there, and she didn't surf. Or sail. She nudged up the kickstand with her foot, grasping the bike's handles, and swung her leg over the seat.

"You sure you're okay?" Nick asked. "Your ankle's okay and everything? You're okay to…ride?"

"I already told you, I'm not drunk." Her answer came out

a little more clipped than she'd intended, but it was late. She was tired. And she was trying very hard not to notice how nice his mouth looked when he smiled.

"Okay, well, maybe I'll see you around." Nick gave her a nod and waved as she pushed off and rode away.

"See you," Bess called over her shoulder, with no intention of ever seeing him again.

Chapter 03

Now

"*I* thought I'd never see you again."

At the sound of the voice in the doorway, Bess's soap-slick hands twitched on the coffee mug she'd been rinsing. It slipped from her fingers and crashed to the kitchen's tile floor. Hot water splashed her legs as she turned, gripping the counter to keep from sliding in the spill.

He stood, backlit, for just a moment before moving forward. The same dark hair, same dark eyes. Same quirked smile.

Everything the same.

Bess couldn't move. Last night she had dreamed… Oh, but it hadn't been a dream. Had it? If not, surely she was dreaming now. She curved her fingers against the sink's porcelain, finding no purchase. Nothing to grip.

"Nick?"

Now he looked uncertain. His hair dripped, and the hems of his jeans. His bare toes, coated with sand, gritted on the tile as he took a step toward her, hand outstretched but quickly pulling back when she shrank against the counter. "Bess…it's me."

Her guts tumbled inside her, and she couldn't breathe. She sipped at the air in uneven, hitching gasps. "I thought…I thought…"

"Hey." He soothed her, coming closer.

She could smell him. Salt and water and sand and sun. The way he'd always smelled, back then. Bess found more air. Took a deeper breath. Nick didn't touch her as she stared. His hand hovered an inch from her shoulder.

"It's really me," he said.

A low sob forced its way from her throat and she launched herself forward. She wrapped her arms around his waist and pressed her face to the damp fabric of his shirt. She breathed him in, deep and deeper.

It took him a second to put his arms around her, but when he did, his embrace was firm. Warm. He rubbed her back, then slid up a hand to cup the base of her skull.

Bess, eyes closed, shuddered against him. "I thought I was dreaming last night."

She remembered stumbling up the beach, peeling off her clothes, tumbling into bed without even bothering to dry her hair or brush the sand from her skin. She'd woken to find the pile of salty, sodden clothes staining the rug, and her bed a shambles. The passion of the night before had been replaced by a pounding head and slightly sick stomach.

Nick's hand rubbed a small, tight circle on her back, between the shoulder blades. "If you were dreaming, I was dreaming, too."

Bess held him tighter. "Maybe we're both dreaming, because this can't be real, Nick. It can't be real."

He put his hands on her upper arms and pushed her back

far enough to look into her face. She'd forgotten how small he could make her feel. How deceptively bigger he'd always been.

"I'm real."

His fingers on her arms felt real. Solid. Strong. Her cheek was wet from where she'd pressed it to his shirt. Heat radiated from him as though she stood in front of a furnace, and the smell of him, that lost, welcome smell, filled her head until there was nothing else inside her. Tears blurred her vision and she blinked them away. Then she pushed herself out of his arms.

Bess looked at him. Salt water had spiked his hair, but had ceased sliding down his cheeks. His clothes had started to dry, too. He took up as much space as he ever had. His touch was as warm. Time hadn't changed him, hadn't painted lines in the corners of his eyes and mouth or silver in his hair.

Bess touched Nick's cheek. "How can this be? Look at you. Look at me."

He put his hand over hers, then turned his face to press a kiss to the center of her palm. He closed her fingers over it, but said nothing.

His smile broke her.

"Oh, no," Bess said. "Oh, no. No."

She pulled her hand from his. Neither of them moved, but the distance between them grew vast. Something flickered in Nick's eyes, an emotion she couldn't read.

"How many people have a second chance?" he asked. "Don't push me away, Bess. Please."

He'd never asked her for anything. Blinking, Bess turned back to the sink. She'd left the water running, and flicked the handle of the faucet down. Without the rush of water pouring from the spigot, the sound of the ocean outside filled the space between them and brought them together.

"How?" she asked.

"I don't know. Does it matter?"

"It should."

He smiled and sent the same old twist into her belly, and lower. "But does it? Really?"

When he bent to kiss her, the taste of him chased away logic. All reason. And that, too, was the same as it had always been.

"No," Bess said, and opened her arms for him again.

The bedroom she took him to wasn't the ground-level, closet-size room next to the carport she'd used in the past. She'd claimed the master bedroom now, with its private deck and bathroom. Not that he'd have known the difference. She'd never brought him home before.

Nick seemed to hesitate in the doorway until she took his hand and led him to the king-size bed. Bess had stripped the sheets first thing this morning, but only managed to get a fitted sheet back on the mattress before the promise of coffee and breakfast distracted her. Without the mountain of decorative pillows and coverlet embroidered with seashells, the bed looked bigger. The pristine white sheet, stretched tight, begged to be rumpled.

At the foot of the bed Nick bent to kiss her, but Bess was already stretching on her tiptoes to reach his mouth. She pushed and he let her, and she was on top when they fell together onto the vast empty bed. She straddled him as they kissed, mouths opening and tongues stroking. His hands came around to grab her ass and press her to his damp, denim-covered crotch.

Bess broke the kiss long enough to reach between them and tug open the button and zipper. She reached inside as Nick lifted his hips with a groan. She found more heat, and she cupped him for a moment before working to get the wet jeans down his thighs. They didn't want to go, but she was determined. Once she got them to his knees it was easy, and she pulled his jeans off and tossed them to the floor as Nick sat up to pull off his T-shirt. He wore only a pair of thin cotton boxers, the front of which tented impressively.

Bess paused, heart pounding. She reached to fill her palm with his erection, at first with the cotton barrier between them and then skin to skin when he helped her tug those down, too. Naked, Nick lay propped on one elbow on the bed, one leg bent at the knee and the other straight. Bess knelt beside him, the hem of her shortie nightgown brushing her at midthigh.

She looked at him, then down at herself. Beneath the thin nylon gown she was bare. Her nipples had already poked out the front of the bodice. Lower, her thighs rubbed together, already slick with her arousal. She looked at him again and found the old familiarity of his body. The dip of his belly next to his hip bone and the pattern of hair leading to the thick, dark nest around his cock. She touched him again, curling her fingers around the root of it and stroking upward with a firm grasp that made him moan.

He was silk and steel against her palm. She stroked again and twisted her hand around the top of his prick before sliding down again. Nick's cock jerked under her touch, and her body pulsed in reply.

Bess looked at him. His eyes shone and a faint flush had begun creeping up his chest and throat. His mouth parted. His tongue swept his lips. His head tipped back and he sank all the way onto his back when she added her other hand to his balls, cupping and stroking. He muttered what sounded like her name, and Bess smiled.

She straddled him again, his cock trapped between the bare

flesh of her thighs. She moved, teasing him with the brush of her pubic curls. Nick put his hands on her hips, his fingers bunching the material of her nightgown as he pushed upward.

His cock rubbed her clit as he rocked against her, and Bess's lips parted in a sigh. She licked her mouth just as he had moments before. The way Nick's eyes glittered at the sight of her tongue sent shivers of pleasure dancing down her spine.

"Nick." She murmured his name, tasting it. She thought saying it might feel unfamiliar, but like the sight of his body, the sound of his name hadn't changed.

"I want you," he said in voice as rough as the grit of sand on tile. His fingers tightened on her hips as he nudged his prick along the seam of her slick folds. "I want to be inside you."

Bess nodded, unable to speak. She shifted, lifted, and he moved to help her. She bent her head, waiting for her hair to fall and shield her face as she guided his cock to her entrance. She'd forgotten she'd pulled it up to keep it from getting tangled as it dried, and with her other hand she yanked off the clip. The heavy locks, longer and thicker than twenty years ago, tumbled around her shoulders and over her face.

Nick hissed and thrust upward at the same time, and Bess didn't know if his reaction was in response to the sight of her hair falling down or the sensation of easing into her wet tightness. It didn't matter. She gave her own low cry as she settled onto him. Her thighs gripped his sides. They were connected now.

She didn't move right away. She looked up through the curtain of her hair, then pushed it off her eyes so she could really see him. Nick smiled. His grip on her hips eased, and he shifted. Bess put her hand on his chest to support herself as she leaned forward to brush his lips with hers. "If this is a dream, I don't want it to end when we're finished."

"It's not a dream." His voice was low and hoarse, but unmistakably his. "I told you that."

He lifted the hem of her nightgown to skim her thighs and belly. "Does this feel like a dream? I'm touching you."

He pushed upward. "I'm inside you."

Bess gave a half-strangled laugh. "You've been inside me before."

"Not like this." He thrust harder and she gasped at the sweet pleasure-pain of him stabbing into her.

He'd been inside her for the past twenty years, but no. Not like this, though she'd thought of it often enough. She didn't have to think about it now, because now it was happening. Bess ducked her head again as her fingers curled against Nick's chest. Beneath her palm she should have felt the thump-thump of his heart as it sped up. She took her hand away before she could notice if it was there or not. She gripped him again with her thighs and slid both her hands to the bottom edge of his ribs.

She rode him, remembering how sometimes their rhythm had faltered. She knew her body better now, and when Nick's pace began to stutter, Bess adjusted easily. She moved when he did, and when he thrust harder, biting his lip in the expression she'd never forgotten, she slowed him with a murmured word and a shift of her body. She slid a hand between them, her finger on her clit and circling just the way she needed it. She groaned at the touch and opened her eyes.

Nick's eyes flashed as he looked between them, to where her hand moved. He bit his lower lip. His grip tightened again on her hips and he ground her against him, harder and harder. Faster.

Bess closed her eyes. Sensation filled her. This moment. His touch. The sound of her breathing and the skid of his fingertips along her sweat-damp skin. She stroked her clit slowly, then faster, in time with his quickening thrusts. Pleasure built until the hard, sharp shards of it shattered inside her the way her mug had shattered on the floor. She came with a gasping cry as her head tipped back. Her clit pulsed under her finger and she pressed it, urging another wave of climax to surge forth. Nick moaned and thrust once more, his body jerking.

She collapsed on him as she got her breath back. Her face found the perfect spot in the curve of his shoulder. She kissed his neck. Nick stroked his hands down the sides of her spine before he wrapped them around her and squeezed.

"I missed you," he whispered. His arms tightened and his mouth brushed her ear.

Another spate of tears stung Bess's eyes and this time, she didn't blink them away. They mingled with the sweat on her lips and the salt tang of Nick's skin.

"You don't have to miss me," she said. "Not anymore."

Chapter 04

Then

Sugarland wasn't the worst place Bess had ever worked. That honor would've gone without a second thought to the summer camp counselor position she'd held between her sophomore and junior years of high school. The trauma of that experience had been so severe she was still convinced she'd never have kids.

Waiting on tourists wasn't as difficult as keeping twenty third-graders interested in weaving lanyards, even when the tourists got pissy about waiting for their food. Bess reminded herself over and over that not everyone in the world had been raised by apes. It just seemed like it.

"Where's my damned waffle cone?" The red-faced man pounded the counter hard enough to make the napkin holder jump.

He hardly needed any sort of cone, much less a waffle one, but Bess pasted on a bright smile for him, anyway. "Just another three minutes, sir. The machine broke down and we weren't able to prebake the cones. But yours will be fresh."

The woman with him, who'd already been handed her cone, but hadn't offered to share, stopped in midlick. "You mean, mine ain't fresh?"

Bess bit the inside of her cheek until she tasted blood, but by that time it was too late. The woman wanted her money back on a cone she'd already eaten most of, and her husband was pounding the counter and demanding two new cones. It was quickly heading into chaos, and Bess's co-worker, Eddie, wasn't much help. Only a senior in high school, he suffered from a god-awful case of acne that made him so self-conscious he never looked anyone in the eye. Plus he harbored a not-so-secret crush on Bess that rendered him nearly helpless in her presence.

Brian had called in sick, and the other counter girl, Tammy, was even worse than Eddie. She couldn't make change without a calculator, and wore her Sugarland T-shirts cut off so they'd show her tanned and taut tummy. She spent more time filing her nails and flirting with the lifeguards than anything else. If Tammy hadn't been screwing the boss's son, Ronnie, Bess would've fired her.

"Are you listening to me?" the red-faced tourist-troll hollered, while slamming a meaty fist onto the countertop.

Maybe being a camp counselor hadn't been so bad, after all.

So caught up in squaring away the greedy husband-and-wife team, who were finally mollified with two new, "fresh" waffle cones and a tub of caramel corn on the house, Bess didn't notice who else had come into the shop. Missy wasn't one to be ignored for long. She sidled up to the counter and flipped Bess a five, then pointed at the slushy machine.

She wasn't alone.

Nick Hamilton was with her. Tonight instead of a ball cap

he wore a red bandanna with tattered edges folded over his sleek dark hair and tied in the back. Among the cloying sweet odors of caramel and fudge, he smelled like fresh air and sunshine and sunscreen. His skin glistened with it, and his cheeks and the bridge of his nose bore a faint pinkish stripe. Proof of his day in the sun.

"Blue," said Missy. "Nicky, you want any?"

He shook his head and smiled at Bess. "Hey."

"Hey." She nodded, her gaze going back and forth before focusing on Missy. "What're you up to?"

Missy shrugged as she lolled against the counter. Her sly glance over her shoulder at Nick told Bess more than she wanted to know. "You know. Little of this, little of that."

A whole lot of that, was more like it. Bess forced away a frown but couldn't stop herself from looking at Nick again. Missy was eyeing him like he was a big old bowl of ice cream and she wasn't even going to wait for a spoon to eat him with. Jealousy, stupid and formless, stabbed into Bess's stomach and tightened her throat. Nick wasn't hers. From what Missy said, he wasn't going to *be* hers, either. Unless, of course, Missy had lied. It all made sense. It wouldn't be the first time Missy'd told Bess a story to get something she wanted, and Bess couldn't believe she'd fallen for it.

She grabbed up Missy's money from the counter and filled a slushy cup three-quarters full before shoving it across the counter. She made change and slapped that down, too. Rage stiffened her fingers and hooked them into clumsy claws. The coins scattered on the counter before some clinked to the floor.

"Hey!" Missy protested, bending to pick up her fallen dimes. "What's up your ass?"

Bess glanced around the small shop, but no other customers had come in. Tammy cracked her gum and looked away when Bess glared at her, and Eddie had already disappeared into the back room. Bess folded her arms across her chest.

"Sorry."

Missy looked up as she shoved her money into the pocket of her tiny jean shorts. "Yeah, well, not all of us can just go throwing our money all over the place, rich girl."

The way she said it was more insulting than being called bitch, but Bess did her best not to react. "I said I was sorry."

Missy appeared soothed, or more likely couldn't be bothered to care. She sucked suggestively on her straw, hollowing her cheeks and sliding her mouth up and down the plastic tube. "Mmmm. Nick, sure you don't want any?"

Nick hadn't been watching her display. He'd been watching Bess. "No, thanks. Can I get a soft pretzel with extra salt, though?"

He dug in his pocket while Bess reached into the hot case for an extra salty pretzel. She handed it to him wrapped in the tissue paper she'd used to grab it, took his money and made change. Sucking on her slushy, Missy watched the transaction closely. Her gaze weighed on Bess's shoulders and they hunched until Bess forced herself to stand up straight and stare her sometime friend in the face.

Missy smirked. Bess's answering smile seemed to surprise her. Bess turned to Nick. "So, Nick. I heard the Pink Porpoise is closing."

The Porpoise was the most popular local gay bar. Bess had been to it once or twice because it was one of the few bars that let underage kids in to dance. It wasn't the sort of place most straight guys went by themselves, even when they got a good band to play.

"Yeah?" He tore off a bite of mustard-smeared pretzel with sharp, white teeth.

"You didn't hear that?" Bess wiped at the counter, forcing Missy to move. "I'd have thought you would have."

Missy tugged on his sleeve. "C'mon, Nick. Let's get out of here."

Bess looked up. Nick's brow had furrowed, but he was stepping backward as Missy pulled him. Missy waved her slushy toward Bess.

"See you later!"

Nick raised the hand clutching the pretzel and followed her out of the shop. The bell jangled as the door closed. Bess slapped the counter with the damp cloth she'd been using to wipe it, and muttered a curse.

"Did you just say...pissflaps?" Tammy cracked her gum and leaned on the counter next to Bess.

"Yes, I did."

"Gross!" She made a face and angled her head to follow Bess's gaze out the door. "He's cute."

"Apparently, my friend thinks so, too." Bess dumped the rag in the sink and viciously washed her hands. Without waiting for them to dry, she pointed at the door. "Watch the counter. I'm going in the back."

Before Tammy had time to protest, Bess went to the tiny back room where they prepped food and stored extra supplies. Eddie, elbow-deep in a box of slushy mix packages, looked up when she came in. His face flushed deep crimson, making the bright red scars of his pimples stand out even more. Normally Bess tried not to look right at Eddie, because it made him blush, but at the moment she was too pissed off to care.

She grabbed up her oversize cup of ice water with the lid and sucked angrily at the straw. The cubes rattled inside the plastic. Eddie blushed harder when she stared at him. "What?"

"N-nothing." He went back to unpacking the box.

Bess had nothing to do back there, really, except get in his way, but she wanted to fume. She wanted to kick something, or break it. She wanted to slap Missy across the face and call the bitch out. Which, of course, she'd never do, because she really had no reason to.

Bess, after all, had a boyfriend.

Sort of. Or maybe she didn't. Either way, it didn't matter, because Nick wasn't the sort of guy who went for girls like her. He obviously went for girls like Missy.

"Pissflaps," Bess muttered, and wished she smoked or did something raw like that. She wanted something to do outside the back door, something that made her look cool, while she pretended she wasn't angry and aching inside at a betrayal she had no reason to feel.

From behind her, Eddie chuckled. After a second, so did Bess. It sounded a little like breaking glass, and it hurt her chest right below her heart, but she laughed just the same. She caught his eye, and the sight of his grin forced another from her, and more giggling, until after a minute they were both guffawing.

"Your friend Missy's...interesting," Eddie said when their giggles had faded. "I've never seen Nick Hamilton come into the store before."

"You know him?"

"Everyone knows Nick," Eddie said, his laughter fading. He wouldn't look at her. The pink of his cheeks had disappeared, but now crept back.

"I don't."

Eddie looked her in the eyes, a rare occasion. "M-maybe that's not such a bad thing."

"Must be nice," Tammy interrupted, sticking her head through the door. "Having time to fool around. But I'm getting slammed out here!"

Bess stood and dusted her hands on the seat of her shorts. "I'll be right there."

Tammy rolled her eyes. "You'd better. I've got three sundae cones and a jumbo tub to fill!"

As night manager, Bess could have told Tammy to suck it up and deal with it, but Tammy would take twice as long to do the same tasks Bess could do in a couple minutes. "I'm coming, I'm coming."

She didn't have time to think of much of anything after that because the store was swamped with hungry, grubby children and sunburned, cranky grown-ups begging for sweets. The last few hours before closing flew past, and by the time she was ready to close up, her mood had changed. She glanced at the clock as she shooed Tammy and Eddie out the back and locked the door, then made her way to the front to lock it, too. With any luck she'd have the bathroom to herself when she got home, and maybe a message from Andy. She'd left half a dozen for him.

"I'm sorry," she said, looking up as the bell jangled. "We're—"

"Closed?" asked Nick with a smile that turned her legs to jelly. "I hope so. I came to see if I could walk you home."

Chapter 05

Now

The sheet beneath her cheek was smooth and cool. The skin beneath her hand, warm. Nick's chest didn't rise or fall. He wasn't breathing. Was he? Could he? She spread her fingers over his nipple, but nothing pulsed beneath it. No heartbeat.

Yet he was alive. There. Solid and real, not transparent. She could touch him. God, she tasted him.

"Tell me what happened," Bess whispered. She kissed him just above his ribs and let her mouth linger on skin still tasting so much of salt.

He said nothing for so long she became certain he wasn't going to speak. His hand stroked down her hair over and over, hypnotizing her, and then stayed still. Bess pushed her fingers through the line of curls just below his belly button. The hairs tickled her palm. His body beneath her hand tensed.

"I don't think I know." He shifted and his hand took up its stroke, stroke, stroke again.

There were a hundred questions roaming in her brain, but not one to which she could put voice. If he didn't breathe, if his heart didn't beat, how could he be warm? If he was a spirit, how could he touch her? How could he fuck her?

Her own heartbeat pounded in her ears and her breath caught in her throat. A chill swept her and she turned to him, pushing closer, grateful for the warmth she couldn't seem to explain.

And really, how important was it for her to know the details of this magnificent thing, this miracle? Would the knowing of it somehow change it? Make it better?

Or make it worse?

"You don't have to tell me," Bess said.

She curled her fingers over his hip bone to press the solid curve beneath warm flesh. She'd memorized every detail of his body with her mouth and fingertips, and had forgotten nothing, but touching him now was as new as if it were the first time. Everything about him was new and old at once, and overlaid with memory.

"I was gone," he said simply. Three small words with such complication in their meaning. "But now I'm back."

Bess nuzzled his side, then pushed up on her elbow to look at him. Nick's fingers tangled in her hair before he let go. She leaned close enough to kiss his mouth, but didn't. She waited for the puff of his breath on her face, and of course it didn't come.

"I don't want to know," Bess told him. "It doesn't matter. Does it? You're here now."

He put his hand on the back of her neck and pulled her down for the kiss. Mouth to mouth, lip to lip, tongue to tongue. Their teeth clattered briefly, and Bess pulled away to look again into his eyes. They were the same. She traced the line of his brows with her fingertip and buried her face into the solace of his shoulder.

"No," he said after a few seconds. "I guess not."

He held her for a minute while her shoulders shook with the sobs she tried without success to bite back. "Why are you crying?"

She held him tighter, her laughter mingled with tears. "Because…I just found out you were gone and I didn't even know, and now you're back. You're here and I'm here, and it's like…"

"It feels different, too," Nick said. "It feels…deeper."

Bess laughed and looked into his face. She touched it. Solid and real. "I'm going crazy."

"You're not. I'm real." He put her hand on his crotch. His penis stirred beneath her touch. "Does that feel like you're crazy?"

Bess rolled her eyes a little, but didn't pull her hand away. "Same old Nick—"

"Thinking with my dick," he finished for her. "Yeah. Some things don't change."

"And some things do," she told him. Still in her shortie nightgown, Bess got up from the bed and went to the window. Her thighs felt a little chafed and she ached between her legs from the unaccustomed rough treatment, but though they hadn't used a condom, nothing trickled down her thighs.

Apparently, just as he didn't breathe, Nick didn't ejaculate, either. There was heat, and she smelled him on her body, but no…evidence. This thought strangled her with the half laugh stuck in her throat. Bess rested her head against the cool window glass and closed her eyes, listening for the sound of the ocean she couldn't see.

His bare feet whispered on the carpet and his heat reached her before his hand did. She didn't shrink from his touch, but neither did she go to him. When she opened her eyes, he was looking out the window, too. He turned to her. He ran a hand down her hair.

"It's longer," he said.

He was the same, but many things about her had changed. "Yes."

"I like it." He tugged the ends and slipped his hand up to cup the back of her neck. "It's pretty."

She didn't think he'd ever said she was pretty. The compliment nearly overwhelmed her with emotion, and she chewed the inside of her cheek until she got herself under control. "Thanks."

"I mean it."

Her laugh tasted bitter. "Right. Two kids and a lot of years later, I'm still the same."

"You are to me." His voice gained a hard edge that made her look at him.

Bess lifted her chin, then pulled off the nightgown and dropped it to the floor. In the bright and unforgiving early afternoon sunshine, she wanted to cringe and hide behind her hands, but she straightened her back and let him see her. All of her. The scars, the marks, the places where her body had changed. She'd kept in shape and actually weighed less now than she had then, but…she didn't look the same.

She gestured at her body. "I'm not a girl anymore, Nick."

His gaze traveled over her from head to toe, so slowly she wanted to squirm, but Bess kept herself still. When at last he raised his eyes again to her face, she braced herself for the look of disgust, or worse, mockery.

This time when he reached for her hand, she let him take it. He pulled her two small steps into his arms. Their bodies still fit as perfectly as they always had. Against her belly, his penis thickened, not quite erect. His hands found the curve of her ass and pulled her closer.

"I don't know what you're worried about," Nick said. "To me you look the same as you always did."

She laughed. "You don't have to flatter me."

He pursed his lips. "Yeah, 'cuz that's really my thing. Flattery."

"I have gray in my hair. And…" She didn't want to catalog all her flaws for him when he could so easily see them for himself, but at his still-curious gaze, Bess couldn't stop herself. "And crow's-feet and laugh lines…you don't see any of that?"

He shook his head. Andy had often claimed the same thing, but Andy was also the first to remind her that if she ate too many cream puffs her ass would spread. Bess let her head rest against Nick's chest for a moment before looking at his face again.

"Tell me what you see."

"You're beautiful," Nick said.

He'd never told her that, either. She wouldn't have believed he meant it then, anyway, if he had. She believed him now.

Chapter 06

Then

*B*ess kept her bike between her and Nick, as though that small barrier there made any sort of difference. He was still so close she could smell him. Close enough for their arms to brush every so often. She tried ignoring the tingle that shot up and down her arm every time his bare skin connected with hers, but it wasn't easy.

"You don't have to walk me the whole way," she protested when they got closer to her house. "Really. It's late."

"Which is why I should walk you." Nick grinned.

They stopped under a streetlamp. His pirate bandanna held his dark hair off his face, but Bess remembered the way it had fallen across his eyes the night of Missy's party.

"You really don't have to," she said.

It would be hard to explain to her aunt and uncle or cousins or any of the half-dozen other people staying in her grandparents' beach house exactly why she was being escorted home by a young man. A townie, no less, and definitely not Andy. They all knew Andy. They all loved Andy.

She loved Andy.

"Fine. Okay." Nick shrugged and pulled a pack of Swisher Sweets cigars from his pocket. He lit one with the lighter he pulled from his jeans pocket. The fragrant smoke swirled between them, and Bess, who normally would have coughed, sucked it in.

The circle of light was a wall around them, keeping out the night. Bess heard the low mutter of voices and the jangle of a dog's leash, but she didn't turn to see who was walking by. The soft and never-ending roar of the ocean was muted here, just three blocks back from the beach. She'd taken him the long route home.

"It's a crazy house," she explained, though Nick hadn't asked her to clarify. "It's my grandparents' house and they let everyone in the family take turns with it. They could get more money if they rented it, but they said they'd rather know who's sleeping in their beds."

And who was shitting in their toilets, according to Bess's grandpa, but she didn't say that.

"Makes sense." Nick nodded and sucked in smoke, his eyes squinted.

"They let me stay there," Bess continued, half hating the eagerness in her voice and what she knew had to be a transparent attempt at keeping the conversation from fading away. "I get the crap room, but it's a place to stay. So I can save money for school."

Again, Nick nodded, though this time he didn't add anything. Bess waited, watching the smoke so she didn't have to look at his face and see if he was looking at her. Or if he wasn't.

"I go to Millersville University," she said. "Do you go to school?"

"Nope." Nick tossed the butt down and ground it with the toe of his sneaker. "Not that smart."

She laughed at that. Nick's smile said he hadn't been kidding, and she stopped laughing. "Oh, c'mon. I'm sure that's not true."

Nick shrugged. "Being a smart-ass isn't the same thing, Bess." The way his voice wrapped around the single syllable of her name gave her a thrill. "Being smart isn't everything."

"Says the girl who's smart."

"Like I said," Bess repeated, looking away, "smart isn't everything."

Nick shoved his hands in his pockets and rocked back and forth on his feet. "How long have you known Missy?"

"For about three years. Since I started working down here." Bess toed the gravel and leaned on the handlebars of her bike. "You?"

"Just met her. She's Ryan's girl." Nick gave a low, amused snort. "Sometimes."

"Yeah. Other times she's everyone's girl." Bess surprised herself with that bit of mockery, but Nick didn't seem shocked.

"Yeah," he agreed, with another of the slow grins giving Bess a fever. "Not mine, though."

"It's not any of my business."

Nick said nothing. Finally, unable to bear the silence, she looked at him. He wasn't smiling.

"She tell you I'm queer?"

Bess's mouth parted but she didn't quite find the words right away. The longer she didn't answer, the worse it seemed, until finally she said, "Yes."

"That little bitch." Nick scowled. Bess had fallen hard for

the grin, but the scowl made her heart pound like the surf. "What the fuck's her problem with me? If she's not telling everyone I screwed over Heather, she's making shit up about me being queer."

It didn't take Bess long to figure out what he was saying. Nick looked up at her rueful laugh. "I don't think it was about you, really," she said.

"No?" He put his hands on his hips and scowled harder. The light overhead cast his eyes in shadow, but Bess caught the flash of anger, real anger, in his gaze. "What, then?"

"Um…" Bess had been dating Andy for as long as she'd known Missy, but there had still been plenty of rivalry, never actively acknowledged. "Missy likes to prove guys like her better, or something. I don't know. If I say I like a guy, she's suddenly going after him."

That little revelation hung between them and Bess wished she could take it back. Nick grinned slowly, looking even more like a pirate than ever. Bess smiled, too, a bare second after he did. She couldn't have stopped herself even if she wanted. They shared a look and something unspoken passed between them. An understanding. At least, that was how it felt to her, and when Nick spoke he proved her right.

His scowl softened to a frown. "I thought she was your friend."

"Yeah. Well." Bess shrugged. "She is. Sort of."

"Girls," said Nick with a shake of his head. "Jesus." He gave her a sideways glance and an equally sideways smile. "So…she didn't tell you I wanted to ask you out?"

Bess's heart lodged so firmly in her throat she was certain she couldn't speak…until the words came. "No. Did she tell you I have a boyfriend?"

"No." Nick eyed her. "You do?"

Bess nodded after a moment's hesitation, not trusting herself to speak. "Sort of" seemed a dangerous answer to that question. Nick scuffed the gravel.

He stopped, head cocked. "What a fucking bitch."

Bess shrugged again, though he was only voicing what she'd thought earlier. She shouldn't have cared about sounding disloyal. Missy obviously didn't care about the unspoken rules about poaching.

"We really should mess with her a little," he said. "Give her a taste of her own medicine."

Bess had often thought of doing just that, but had never quite figured out how. "Oh, yeah?"

Nick nodded. "Yeah."

"And how do you think we should do that?"

It was as if he'd opened a hinge on top of her head and poured her full of heated honey, thick and sweet, easing its way into every crevice from her toes to her scalp. It made her feel languid, that look. And naughty.

"Don't tell her anything. Just let her think something's up with us." Nick grinned again. "Drive her a little crazy, wondering. Right?"

Bess shivered at the idea, the crazy rightness of it. The dangerousness. Yet there was no question of what her answer would be. None at all. "Right."

Nick held out his hand. "It'll be fun."

Bess slid her palm against his and curved her fingers around his. Nick had big, strong hands, a little rough. His fingertips brushed gently at the back of her hand, the sensation magnified by sudden anticipation.

He would pull her closer, just then. Maybe kiss her to seal the deal. Bess's mouth parted and her body tensed, but Nick let go of her hand and left her yearning.

"Fun," she agreed hoarsely, and cleared her throat. She stepped back, the bike once again a barrier. "I've got to get going. Thanks for walking me."

"I'll see you, right?" Nick didn't move.

Bess didn't dare turn to look at him fully, but settled for a forced-casual glance over her shoulder. "Sure. Come by the shop tomorrow."

"Bess!"

She stopped. Turned. Smiled. "Yeah?"

"Good night." Nick saluted her, then spun on his heel and shoved his hands in his pockets.

He walked away, whistling, and Bess watched him until he left the circle of light they'd shared, and disappeared into darkness.

Chapter 07

Now

"Mom! Are you listening?" Connor's voice snapped Bess back to attention.

"Yes. Of course I am. Graduation is June 13. The invitations for the party already went out, honey. I got it covered." Bess cradled the phone against her shoulder as she bent to search inside the fridge. She'd been forgetting to eat for the past two days. She was ravenous. "And you guys are leaving right after that with Dad for the Grand Canyon."

"Yeah." He didn't sound as excited about the trip as he had a few months ago when they'd been planning it.

"You'll have a good time, honey." Bess ducked to look for something in the back of the fridge. "What time is everyone coming over today?"

"They're not."

"Why not?"

Connor, her oldest, grunted into the phone. "Dad didn't open the pool."

Bess paused in her rummaging. "He didn't?"

Andy had always been so adamant about opening the pool for Memorial Day. Having a party for their friends and neighbors. The boys had always invited tons of kids over for burgers and dogs and swimming.

"No."

Bess really didn't want to ask, but Connor's sullen answer prompted the question. "So you're not having a picnic today?"

"No, Mom, God. Weren't you listening? No party today! Dad didn't open the pool!"

"So," Bess said calmly, to fend off any further histrionics from her easily annoyed oldest son, "what are you going to do?"

"I'm going over to Jake's house."

"What about Robbie?"

"What about him?"

"Is he going with you?" The question came by rote. Bess found a jar of jelly and one of olives and pulled them out. She really needed to get to the grocery store. It had been on her list of things to do, but her priorities had...changed.

"How should I know?"

"Well," she said patiently. "You could ask him."

"Robbie's got his own friends," Connor said coolly, as though putting on a sophisticated tone could change the fact that at eighteen he was still complaining like an eight-year-old about having to take his younger brother with him.

"I know he does. But Jake is his friend, too. I just wondered if he was going with you, that's all."

"I don't know."

Bess sighed as she pulled out bread and a knife and found a plate in the cupboard. "Where's your dad?"

Silence. Connor breathed into the phone. Bess stopped making her sandwich. "Connor? Something wrong?"

"No."

Bess put the knife down and sat to give this conversation her full concentration. "Is something going on with your dad?"

"I said nothing's wrong! I gotta go."

"How's studying for finals coming?"

"Fine. Mom, I gotta go. Jake's waiting."

"Are you driving or is Dad dropping you off?" Connor had had a few fender benders since getting his driver's license, and though he insisted he was a more careful driver now, Bess wasn't as comfortable with him behind the wheel as Andy was.

"I'm driving."

She bit her tongue against an admonition. "The Chevy?"

"As if Dad would let me take the BMW."

"I thought the Chevy needed new brakes."

"Dad says he's taking it in next week."

A vision of crumpled metal and blood spattered on the highway turned her stomach to ice. "Wear your seat belt. Make sure Robbie does, too."

"I gotta go."

Without waiting for her to say goodbye, Connor hung up. Bess stared at the phone for a second before replacing it in the cradle. She remembered a sweet, affectionate child who'd never hesitated to hug and kiss her. Who'd been unrelenting with his affection as a matter of fact, to the point of being overwhelming. When was the last time he'd hugged her? When had he been replaced by the sullen, combative young man who locked her out of his life?

"Mmm, jelly sandwich." Nick, wearing only a towel tucked low around his hips, sauntered into the kitchen. He glanced at the phone. "Everything okay?"

Bess nodded as she spread the bread with jelly and used a fork to scoop out some olives. "That was my son. Connor."

She deliberately didn't look up as she said it. They hadn't talked about why she was at the beach house, or her life now. For the past two days, she and Nick had done little else but screw and sleep. Well, she'd slept. She didn't know what he did, only that she'd woken more than once to find him gone. Each time, she'd been convinced she'd dreamed it all, and he wasn't coming back. So far, he always had.

"Want a sandwich?" She gestured at the plate and then looked at him.

Nick put a hand flat on his belly. "I don't think so."

He didn't breathe or sleep, so he probably didn't eat, either. Bess shoved away that detail. Thinking too much about stuff like that made all of this seem too much like a dream when she wanted…no, needed…it all to be real.

She pulled out the chair and sat to bite into the sandwich with a small sigh. Her stomach rumbled and the hunger she'd been ignoring roared to life. Jelly had never tasted so sweet.

Nick leaned an arm against the door to the deck and stared out at the beach. Bess liked watching him like that, with the late-afternoon sun dappling him with gold. He stood with un-selfconscious ease, unaware of or unconcerned with her scrutiny. She could count his ribs, though he wasn't thin, just lean. The jelly coated her tongue and she swallowed against the sudden rush of saliva. She wanted to press her face to the tuft of hair under his raised arm and nuzzle him. Smell him. She wanted to tug the carelessly knotted towel and reveal all of him to her hungry gaze. She wanted to get on her knees and take him in her mouth and have him fill her up all over again.

He turned and caught her looking. She saw no surprise in his gaze, just the same heat that was burning in hers. Nick didn't move toward her, though. He stayed silhouetted in the doorway and watched her eat. His eyes took in each movement of her hand to her mouth, each bite, each time she swiped her tongue along her lips to lick away the jelly. He watched her eat as if he was eating, too, only his meal was made of desire and not bread and jelly.

Bess finished her sandwich and licked her fingers, the touch of her tongue on her skin as sensual as if Nick had taken her hand and licked it himself. She picked up an olive and popped it into her mouth, where the tangy, sharp taste contrasted with the jelly's lingering sweetness, making her eyes water.

The front of Nick's towel bulged, and still he didn't move. Bess turned sideways on the straight-backed kitchen chair to face him. She parted her legs, giving him a shadowed glimpse of her thighs below the hem of her nightgown. Nick swallowed. She watched his throat work. She watched his mouth open, his tongue creep out, and she inched up the hem of her gown with a slow, purposeful curling of her fingers in the fabric.

Higher and higher the material crept as Bess clutched it. Her thighs trembled. Her clit throbbed as she parted her legs still further. What did he see now? The first hint of dark blond curls? The shadow of her cleft? The smoothness of her inner thighs?

She shifted soundlessly on the chair and tilted her pelvis just slightly. Offering herself to him. He still didn't move, though now the front of the towel bulged even more and his fists had clenched at his sides. His chest hitched. His jaw tightened, and Bess watched the small muscles of his cheek leap.

She pulled the gown higher and let the cool breeze from the ceiling fan wash over her bare skin. Without looking away from his eyes, Bess ran her other hand over her breasts until her nipples poked the front of the lace. She didn't have to see herself to know how she looked; his gaze reflected her. She licked her fingers and slid them under her gown. She used her own wet heat to stroke her rigid clit.

Nick groaned.

Bess, smiling, opened her legs wider to show him exactly what she was doing. No more hiding. She rubbed herself in small, tight circles until her inner muscles clenched and she had to bite her lower lip on a groan of her own.

At the noise, Nick's hands moved as though he wasn't exactly sure what to do with them. He took one step and stopped. He put a hand to the place where the towel tucked against his body, but didn't open it. The pale blue cotton was too thick to outline the shape of his stiffening cock, but there was no doubt he was getting hard.

Bess's gown now bunched up around her waist. The cool, slick, white-painted wood slipped beneath her bare ass as she moved on the chair. She let go of her gown to grip the seat, her other hand moving faster between her legs. Her toes pointed and she pushed upward a little. The back of the chair dug into her shoulder blades. She wanted to close her eyes, but didn't.

"Take off the towel and come here," she ordered.

Nick did with a simple jerk of his wrist. The towel fell unheeded to the floor and he stepped over it. Without stopping the slow circle of her fingers on her clit, Bess let go of the chair to reach for him. She pulled him closer. Her fingers dug into his ass. She kissed his belly and his muscles jumped. She licked him, and his hips bumped forward.

She put her hand at the base of his prick, holding him still while she feasted on the warmth and salt tang of his skin. She nibbled his hip as her hand worked faster between her legs. Nick gathered her hair at the base of her neck and kept it from tangling around her wrist or his cock, wet now from her mouth. She took him in deep, down the back of her throat, gratified at his grunt of pleasure and surprise.

New tricks.

She slid her first and middle fingers inside herself and used the heel of her palm to press against her clit in the same rhythm she was using to suck him. Up, down. She used her tongue to swirl along the rim of his cock head as she brought her curled fist up to meet her mouth. Hand and mouth in tandem, other hand between her legs. She fucked him and she fucked herself. Nick pushed forward as his hand tightened in her hair. Bess opened her mouth at the sting as he pulled, but didn't protest.

She was already close, her body primed rather than depleted by the past two days of near-constant sex. Pleasure swelled inside her. It would have been easy to lose herself in it and forget what she was doing for him. Easy to stutter. She was so close she almost couldn't care.

Nick mumbled encouragement as he pumped forward, and she took him all the way in. Stroke, lick, suck, rub. Bess shuddered and had to move her mouth away in order to breathe. Her hand slid up and down along his length while the one between her legs slowed. Slower. Slower… She pressed her body forward into her palm and took him in her mouth again.

She came. The world got dark for a moment, closed to all but the climax washing over her and the taste of Nick. He cried out, something incoherent. Heat flooded her tongue. The memory of his taste and smell, but only the memory. He came in her mouth but only memories filled it.

It didn't matter. Was, in fact, better that way. A bonus. She'd go down on him ten times a day if she didn't have to actually swallow.

Her clit pulsed against her hand in the sweet aftershocks of coming. Bess kissed Nick's stomach and reached behind her head to loosen his fingers from her hair. She looked up at him with a smile.

He stared down at her, face slack in the aftermath of his pleasure, but then smiled back. "Holy shit."

She laughed and kissed his stomach again, then pushed him gently away so she could stand and go to the sink, where she washed her hands and splashed cool water on her face. Rinsing her mouth was habit rather than necessity, but the cool water tasted good and she cupped a couple handfuls to her mouth.

He was still staring, still naked, when she turned from the sink. "Wow."

Bess raised an eyebrow and leaned against the counter. "Wow?"

Nick bent to grab the towel and wrap it around his waist again. "You're fucking amazing, you know that?"

She grinned, pleased. "Thank you."

"No…" Nick shook his head. "I don't mean that."

This wasn't quite as nice to hear. "No?"

"No." He shook his head again, so that his hair fell over his eyes. "I mean…you didn't used to be like that."

That was both true and not. She hadn't been like that with him. "I'm not sure what you want me to say, Nick."

"I don't want you to say anything." He crossed to her and took her in his arms, but didn't kiss her. "I just wanted you to know you're incredible."

"Thank you." She poked his chest. "Better than you re-membered?"

He laughed. "Just different."

She ran a finger around his nipple and watched it tighten. The past two days had proved his cock would do the same if she stroked it, though they'd just finished. Bess looked up at him. "Comes with the territory, Nick."

Age, she meant. Nick brought her hand to his lips and kissed the fingers, then nibble-kissed up her arm until she laughed and squirmed away. He let her go, but his eyes gleamed and his smile sent warmth oozing all through her.

"Amazing, that's all."

Bess curtsied. "I'm going to take a shower, and then I have to go to the store."

Nick had already showered, but he followed her into the large master bath. Bess started the hot water, then quickly brushed her hair and pulled it into a loose bun on top of her head to keep it as much out of the spray as possible. She pulled off her nightgown and tossed it into the laundry. The scent of sex had thoroughly saturated the fabric. Hell, it had probably saturated the entire house by now.

Nick leaned against the sink, watching. Bess tested the water with her hand before getting in, giving him a glance over her shoulder. "You coming in again?"

"I'll wait until you're done."

Even before, when they'd spent every spare moment they could together, it hadn't been like this. She'd eaten at his table and brushed her teeth in his sink, slept in his bed and watched TV on his couch, but she hadn't lived with him. They hadn't been together for so long without a break, the way they'd been here.

Bess ignored him as she ducked under the water and let it hit the sore spot between her shoulders. Her entire body ached here and there, and bruises had blossomed in strange places. She and Nick hadn't been rough, just frequent and abandoned. She touched one spot, an already yellowing rose on one hip, and remembered Nick's teeth had put it there. She filled her palm with shower gel and scrubbed her skin, reminding herself to pick up a net sponge at the store. Her knees and calves prickled with hair she'd been too busy to shave, and she reached for her razor. The shower had a built-in seat and she used that to prop up her foot as she scraped the blade along her soap-softened skin.

The shower door slid open and she jumped, cutting the back of her ankle. The water stung and she looked up, annoyed. "Ouch!"

"You okay?" Nick leaned in the opening.

Bess touched the wound. It left her fingers briefly crimson, but the water quickly washed away the blood. "I'll be okay."

"Can I watch you?"

Refusal rose to her lips, but she shrugged. "Sure."

Self-conscious from his attention, Bess fumbled through the rest of her routine. She'd been looking forward to a long, hot shower, but finished quickly instead and turned off the water. Nick handed her a towel matching his. Bess wrapped it around her chest and stepped out onto the bath mat.

"I never watched a girl shave her legs before."

She thought about telling him she wasn't a girl, but didn't. "Was it everything you ever dreamed of?"

Nick chuckled and moved out of her way as Bess went to the sink. "Sure."

She brushed her teeth and rubbed her skin with lotion, then hung up the towel. He was still wearing his towel. "Are you planning on getting dressed at all?"

"Sure." Nick glanced into the bedroom, then back at her. "My clothes…"

"Oh. Right. You can toss them in the washer while I'm gone. We probably should do the sheets and towels, too." Bess pushed past him and into the bedroom, where his clothes lay in the same pile they'd stayed in since she'd first stripped them off. Behind her, Nick came into the room.

"Yeah," he said. "Well, it's not just that."

He toed the pile. Bess looked up from the drawer where she was pulling out a pair of panties for the first time in two days. She stepped into them, then reached for a bra.

"Oh," she said, feeling really stupid. "They're all you have."

Nick nodded. The breath suddenly wheezed out of her, and Bess had to sit on the edge of the bed. Her stomach tumbled and she pressed her hands to it. She tried to take slow, even breaths, but heard the whistle of her own gasps anyway.

One set of clothes. This seemed more important, somehow, than the fact that he didn't sleep or eat or breathe. One set of clothes only, nothing more, because Nick had nothing more. Was it what he'd been wearing when he…? Bess shuddered and clapped her hands over her eyes.

The bed dipped beside her. Nick put his arm around her shoulder, and though she meant to resist his touch, Bess turned and buried her face against him. She didn't weep. This wasn't grief rearing up inside her, stealing her breath and turning her guts. It was something else. Fear, maybe, that she was insane. Fear of the unknown. Fear he'd go away again without letting her know, and this time she'd have no secret hope harbored within her of ever seeing him again. If he went away this time, she'd never be able to convince herself he would come back.

"I'm sorry," Nick said.

She released her grip on him and looked up. "Don't be sorry."

He touched her softly under the chin. "Believe me, Bess, it freaks me out a little, too."

"I'll buy you some more clothes when I go out." She got up, needing action to force away emotion. "You're about Connor's size."

She turned, to see him looking stunned. She paused with one arm through the sleeve of her blouse. "Nick?"

"How old's your kid?"

"Connor's eighteen," she said. "Robbie's seventeen. They're what my grandma called Irish twins. Eleven months apart." Her old habit of babbling caught up with her, and the wider Nick's eyes got the faster she spoke. "Nobody would ever mistake them for twins, though. They barely look like brothers. Connor's dark and Robbie's light, like me…."

She trailed off. Nick had stood and gone to the window to stare out. His shoulders hunched as he gripped the windowsill. Tension vibrated in every line of his body.

"Nick?"

"I didn't think," he said. "I know you said it, but I really didn't think about it."

Instinct told her to go to him, but old habits couldn't completely change. She imagined, instead, the silk of his skin beneath her comforting touch. Nick bent his head, his voice a low rasp.

"Tell me how long it's been," he said.

How could he not know? She had counted every day since the last time she'd seen him, one by one like bricks in a wall. How could he not remember, unless the passage of time had meant nothing?

"Twenty years," she told him without pause. There was no point in trying to soften it.

Nick's body jerked before he got himself under control. He half turned toward her, a tight smile pulling at his reluctant mouth. "So he's not mine, at least."

"Not yours?" Bess's breath skipped in her lungs. "Oh, Nick. No. He's not. Did you think he might be?"

Nick shook his head. "No. I don't know. When you said you had kids, I thought… I mean, I knew you might. I thought you must have gotten married and stuff. I just didn't think... Twenty years..." He trailed off and his mouth twisted again. He blinked rapidly.

The sight of this breakdown, however valiantly he fought it, destroyed the old reserve. She went to him and took him into her embrace. He buried his face against her neck and clutched her so tightly she thought her ribs might crack. She held him while he fought the sobs.

"Shh," she soothed, her hands rubbing his back comfortingly. "It's all right."

Nick shook his head against her. Heat pressed her skin, but though his shoulders heaved, apparently he could no more shed tears than he could sweat or ejaculate.

"I don't know where I was," Nick moaned, so low she could barely hear him. "Where the fuck was I, Bess? For twenty fucking years?"

"I don't know, baby," she whispered. "But you're here now."

He pushed away from her and stalked the room, stopping to grab up his boxers from the pile and shove his legs into them. He turned as she watched, and his face had gone dark. Storm dark.

"Didn't anyone look for me?" he demanded, throwing out his hands. "Didn't you care where the fuck I went?"

She blinked, trying not to be offended by his sudden wish to blame her. "I cared. But I didn't know you were...gone. Not like that."

"Why not?" He advanced on her to grab her by the shoulders and shake. His fingers dug into her skin. He'd leave more bruises.

She couldn't explain to him how hard it had been to find out where'd he'd gone or how easy it had been for her to believe he didn't really want her. "I asked about you, but nobody knew anything. I waited for you, but when you never came I thought you didn't want to. I didn't know you couldn't. Nobody knew."

He let go of her and paced as she watched. He turned to look at her, answering his own question before she had the chance. "You mean, nobody cared."

She'd cared, but Bess said nothing.

"I was that much of an asshole, huh?"

"I never forgot you."

"That's supposed to make me feel better?" He shook his head.

"No. It's just the truth."

"Did you want to forget me?" he asked her after a moment.

Bess sighed, but answered. "After a while. Yes. After a while I just put that summer behind me."

Nick shook his head, turning. He sank onto the bed, his arms crossed low over his stomach as if it hurt. He rocked a little and groaned, then looked up, face bleak. His cheeks and the bridge of his nose bore the same faint sun-kissed blush of pink, and the rest of his skin was as tawny as it had always been, but dark circles had lodged beneath his eyes. Lines that had nothing to do with age bracketed his mouth.

"I wanted to come to you," he whispered in a soul-sick voice. "I remember, now. I said I'd find you. I wanted to. But instead—"

She shook her head and went to him. Their knees touched when she sat next to him. She took his hands from their grip on his stomach and put them around her, and she pulled him close. His face nestled with perfect precision into the hollow of her neck and shoulder, and hers found the same place on him. She closed her eyes. She breathed him in. She touched him. Once upon a time the sun hadn't risen without her thinking about Nick's smile, and the wind hadn't blown without it whispering his name.

"You're here now," she said. "And that's all that matters."

Chapter 08

Then

"What's going on with you and Nick?" Missy wasn't subtle enough to pretend she didn't care.

Bess, on the other hand, was clever enough to pretend she didn't know what Missy was talking about. "Nick?"

"You know who I mean." Missy jerked a thumb toward the living room, which bounced with the usual party.

Bess let her gaze follow. Nick leaned against the wall near the hall, tipping a beer to his mouth and talking to Ryan. It was a near mirror of the pose in which Bess had first seen him. It affected her even more this time, but she kept her expression bland when she looked back at Missy.

"What about him?"

Missy scowled. "What's going on with you two, that's what."

Bess shrugged and tipped the glass blender container—God knew where it had come from, or even if it was clean—toward her cup. Brian had made frozen margaritas. She sipped and her eyes watered instantly at the burn of tequila. "Holy shit."

"Holy shit is right," Missy said, her own eyes narrowed.

Bess sipped a bit more to hide her smile. "This is strong, that's all."

"Especially for a Miss Goody Two-shoes who doesn't drink." Missy crossed her arms and leaned back against the counter. The position shoved her cleavage out of her tank top. "Don't change the subject."

"Nick?" Bess looked again. This time, he was looking back. And smiling. It was the smile that got Missy, Bess was sure of it, and she smiled, too. "Nothing's going on with him."

"I saw you," Missy hissed. She was on her way to being drunk, but not quite there.

Bess flinched as a fine spray of margarita-scented spittle flew from Missy's lips. "Saw me what?"

"When you went to the bathroom," she said. "You walked past him!"

Bess laughed and inched away to get out of the soak zone. "Oh, c'mon. So does everyone who has to go to the bathroom, Missy. He's standing right there."

Missy shook her head. "No. No, you—" she stabbed her finger toward Bess "—you...*sidled*."

Bess burst into laughter that turned a few heads, even over the sound of the Violent Femmes pounding from the speakers. "Look who got herself a Word of the Day calendar."

Missy didn't appear insulted, but she did look crafty. She gulped the final dregs of her margarita without even a grimace. "I saw you touch him when you went past."

She hadn't, actually. Over the past week, as he'd managed to stop in almost every day to see her, Bess had thought about touching Nick. She always thought about it, but never did it. "You're drunk. You didn't see anything."

"I saw you," Missy insisted. "I saw you thinking about it, Bessie."

"How the hell do you see anyone thinking about anything?"

Missy made a face. "Just because you're pissed I told you he's gay…"

"I think he's the one who's pissed about that. Not me." Bess couldn't help looking for him again. Touching him with her eyes. Now he was deep in conversation with Brian, whose hands were waving, but while Bess missed the sizzle that came from Nick's gaze meeting hers, she also liked watching him when he wasn't looking. She could drink him in that way.

"I'm talking to you!" Missy snapped her fingers in front of Bess's face.

She heaved a sigh and gave Missy her attention. "Nick and I are just friends."

Missy spluttered into laughter. "Oh, right. Nick? You and Nick the Prick? He's not friends with any girl unless he's fucking her."

"Whatever, Missy." Bess tried to pretend hearing that didn't bother her, but her friend wasn't too drunk to know when she'd struck a direct hit.

"Yeah, yeah. You say whatever." She pointed across the room. "Ask Heather about him. She'll tell you."

Bess wouldn't ask Heather for a glass of water if she were on fire. She looked up, though, to see Heather standing with her hip cocked, talking to Nick. Heather flung her fall of long blond hair over her shoulder and twirled a piece of it around one finger. If she pushed her boobs any closer to him she'd be holding his beer in her cleavage, Bess thought, and turned away.

Missy looked triumphant, then put on a mask of sincerity

that might have fooled someone as drunk as she was, but didn't convince Bess. "I was only looking out for you, Bessie. Nick's bad news. And you have a boyfriend, remember?"

As if Bess could forget. She hadn't told Missy about the sort of. "We're just friends." She tried to make the words taste better by swallowing them with a swig of margarita. It didn't work, and made her cough. Missy pounded her on the back.

"I'm just saying," Missy said, but nothing else, as if those three words were explanation enough.

Across the room, Bess watched Heather lean in close to Nick, who didn't pull away. And why should he? The blonde had big tits and a small ass and a flat stomach. Heather could suck the chrome off a truck hitch. She didn't "sort of" have a boyfriend.

"Slow down with that drink," Missy advised as she poured herself another. "That bitch Brian's a fiend for the alcohol."

For maybe the first time in her life, Bess wanted to get drunk. Instead she put down the cup and left the party. At home she declined an offer by her older, married cousins to join in on a game of gin rummy. She stretched the phone cord as long as it could reach, out onto the deck, and though it wasn't their appointed time she called Andy, anyway. The phone rang for a long time before his brother answered.

"Andy's not home."

"Do you know when he'll be back? It's Bess."

Did she imagine Matt's hesitation? The sympathy in his voice? Would Andy's brother tell her the truth if she asked him to, about the other girl whose letters Bess had found in Andy's desk drawer?

"I don't, Bess. Sorry."

He sounded sorry, but that didn't do her any good. Bess thanked him and hung up. She looked out at the black ocean but could see no waves.

She hadn't meant to look in Andy's drawer, hadn't been looking for something she wasn't meant to see. He'd asked her to grab a package of snapshots he wanted to show his parents, and Bess, who liked Mr. and Mrs. Walsh but wasn't sure if they really liked her, had been all too happy to escape the dinner table to get them.

She'd been in Andy's room quite a few times and knew what drawer in his desk he meant. The pictures weren't there, but there was a rubber band-bound package of envelopes addressed to Andy in a looping, unfamiliar hand. A girl's handwriting. Men didn't dot their *i*'s with little flowers.

She hadn't meant to find them, but once she had there was no question of her not reading them. She'd eased the first from the envelope and glanced at the salutation, skimmed the body of the letter and went straight to the signature.

Love, Lisa

Love? What the hell was some girl doing sending Andy, Bess's Andy, letters signed with such a word? At the sound of footsteps in the hall, Bess had crammed the letters back into the rubber band. If it had been Andy in the doorway she'd have confronted him then, not left it a secret dissolving them like acid.

But it had been Matty, Andy's younger brother, who'd come to see what was taking her so long. Bess saw on his face he knew what she'd seen, or guessed, but Andy was Matt's brother and Bess was just some girl who might or might not someday be part of their family. Matt had said nothing, so neither had she. Not to Matt, and not to Andy himself.

She'd left the next day for the shore with Andy's promises ringing in her ears. He'd write. He'd call. This year, he'd visit. So far he hadn't kept any part of his promise.

So far, Bess had stopped expecting him to.

Chapter 09

Now

The Surf Pro still sold overpriced bathing suits, but like so much else time had changed, money was no longer quite the issue it had been when she was younger. Bess perused the racks of clothes, knowing she wouldn't find much of anything Nick really needed—jeans, T-shirts, boxers, socks. Her fingers drifted through racks of baggy surf shorts and wetsuits. It didn't escape her that she knew just what a twenty-one-year-old guy needed, or what one would like.

She'd only stopped into the shop on a whim because Nick had once worked there. She wasn't sure what she'd expected to find. A plaque? A shrine to his memory? She doubted there'd even be anyone working there who remembered him. That, more than anything, and hearing him ask why she hadn't known he was gone, pushed her out of the shop and back onto Garfield Street. She'd driven into town to hit the small grocery store, Shore Foods, because it was what she knew. A lot had

changed since the last time Bess had been to Bethany Beach.
More shops, for one. She'd have to look for something like a
discount store to find everything she really needed, but for
now Nick would have to deal with wearing shorts and T-shirts
she picked up from the Five and Ten.

Across the street from where she'd parked was Sugarland. Or
rather, where Sugarland had once stood. The storefront had
changed, nearly swallowed up by a bunch of newly constructed
specialty shops and an arcade, but the store inside looked mostly
the same. Cleaner and with updated decor, but not much different than it had been when she'd been a slave behind the counter.

On impulse, clutching her plastic bag of gaudy, tie-dyed
clothes, Bess crossed the square and went into the shop. The
bell jangled on the door the way it always had, and she couldn't
help smiling. The bored teenager behind the counter barely
glanced up. She looked about sixteen, with dark, thick hair
pulled into a ponytail, and rectangular glasses perched on the
end of her pierced nose. She yawned as Bess came up to the
counter.

"Help you?"

"I'd like a large tub of the caramel corn." Bess hadn't bothered reading the menu, but surely Sugarland still sold the
gooey, secret-recipe caramel corn that had been so popular.

The girl waved a languid hand toward a small pyramid of
tubs. "We only have small right now."

Bess couldn't forget the hours she'd spent bending over the
hot vat of sugar, corn syrup and melted butter. Mr. Swarovsky, Sugarland's owner, had insisted on fresh caramel corn
every day. "Is it fresh?"

Bess winced the instant the words slipped from her mouth.
She sounded just like every uptight tourist who'd ever made
her crazy. The girl didn't react much, just shrugged.

"Sure, I guess. Hey, Dad!" she called over her shoulder toward the back. "Dad!"

The man who ducked out of the back room took up a lot of vertical space. His broad shoulders and lean hips gave the illusion he was taller even than he was, though Bess estimated him at over six feet. Dark thick hair spiked off his forehead, and glasses nearly identical to the ones the counter girl wore would have hinted at the family relationship even if she hadn't called him Dad. The man's smile stretched across his face and revealed straight, gleaming teeth. It transformed him instantly from geeky to gorgeous, and Bess wondered what she'd done to deserve such a look.

"Bess? Bess McNamara?" The man came around the counter, oblivious to his daughter's goggling stare, and reached for Bess's hand.

She gave it, and he pumped it up and down. "Yes? I mean, yes. I'm Bess."

"Bess." The man held her hand tight in both of his for a few minutes longer than necessary before letting go. "It's me. Eddie Denver."

It was rude to gape in disbelief, but Bess did anyway, scanning him up and down while he laughed. "Eddie? Oh my God, Eddie…wow!"

He laughed and ducked his head, and that gesture cemented it for her. "Yeah. Times change, huh?"

Bess wouldn't have recognized him if he hadn't introduced himself. Gone were the acne, the braces, the scrawny, perpetually hunched shoulders. Eddie Denver had grown up. "How did you know it was me?"

Eddie's smile brought a twinkle to his eyes evident even from behind his Elvis Costello-style glasses. "You haven't changed at all."

Bess laughed, feeling self-conscious. Her turn to blush. "Oh, sure."

Eddie shook his head. "No, I mean it."

She touched her hair, left loose around her face today. She wasn't going to point out the silver threads there, or pat the extra curves in her thighs and ass. She looked around Sugarland. Eddie's daughter was still goggling.

"What are you doing here, Eddie? Don't tell me you're still working for Mr. Swarovsky!"

Eddie tipped his head back to laugh, and Bess marveled at his easy self-confidence. "No. I bought the place from him about five years ago. Oh, this is my daughter, Kara."

Kara wiggled a few fingers and went back to looking bored. Eddie laughed. "She's thrilled to be here, can't you tell?"

Kara rolled her eyes. Bess gave a commiserating smile. "Your dad and I used to work here together."

The teen nodded. "Yeah. He told me all about it, oh, about a million times."

Bess and Eddie laughed together at that.

"Tell me what you've been doing with yourself," Eddie said. "I haven't seen you since that last summer you worked here."

Bess started to speak, stopped, laughed. "Oh, you know. The usual. Married, kids. Nothing exciting."

Eddie glanced around the empty shop, then back at her. "Hey, let me buy you a cup of coffee and we'll catch up. Can you? Do you have time?"

For an instant Bess caught a glimpse of the old Eddie, the one who'd never been able to look her in the eye. It was endearing, that hint of times past, and she nodded. "Sure. That sounds great."

"Watch the shop, Kara. I'll be back."

Kara rolled her eyes again and shooed them with her hand. "Whatevs, Dad. Go."

Eddie gave Bess an apologetic look as he held the door open for them both to leave. "Sorry about Kara. She's not too thrilled about having to work in the shop."

"Don't worry about it." They paused to let a car go by before crossing the street to the coffee shop. "I've got two boys. I know how teenagers can be."

Eddie opened the door for her at the coffee shop, too. His manners gave Bess both a little thrill and a pang of regret that such courtesy should be somehow notable. He even stepped back to let her choose the table, and asked her what she wanted, then went to the counter to order for both of them. It seemed a little old-fashioned but definitely flattering. Bess couldn't help studying him as he gave his order to the counter staff with confidence. Not much like the stammering, blushing Eddie she'd known back then.

"Thanks," Bess said when he brought her café mocha and a plate of chocolate-dipped biscotti. Her stomach rumbled and she bit off the end of a dry, crumbly cookie. "Wow, good."

Eddie dipped his into his coffee before nibbling. "Yeah. I swear I should buy stock in this place. I'm here every day."

"Maybe you could set up a trade agreement. So many cups of coffee for so many tubs of corn."

Eddie gave that infectious laugh again. "Yeah, sure. Except sadly, nobody's interested in my popcorn since Swarovsky's opened up down the street."

Bess hadn't followed, and her face must have shown her confusion.

"When I bought the place from old Mr. Swarovsky," Eddie explained, "I wanted the rights to the secret recipe, too. The old man was willing to sell me the store because Ronnie supposedly didn't want to take over, but when it came time to give up the family recipe, the old man hemmed and hawed. I tried telling him Sugarland wasn't worth much without the caramel corn. He died while we were in the final negotiations. I got the store for a song...but not the recipe."

Bess made a face. "Ouch. And then Ronnie opened up his own place?"

"You got it. Just down the street." Eddie shrugged. "Apparently he had plans to do it for a while, but he and his dad didn't see eye to eye on it. When his dad died, Ronnie got the recipe and I got the old shop."

"Eddie, that's too bad. I'm sorry." Bess reached automatically to pat his arm. He glanced up at her touch, for another fleeting instant looking the way he used to. She took her hand away.

"It's okay. I'm doing a nice business with the ice cream, and I do sell a couple different varieties of popcorn, but we can't really compete with the genuine Swarovsky's. Even if I wanted to be a jerk and use the recipe...which would be stealing. You know how people are about that stuff, Bess. You remember."

"Loyal," she said with a nod. "Yeah, I remember."

Eddie rapped the table with his knuckles. "Hey, enough of that. Tell me about you. Your life. What grand and exciting things did you go on to do?"

Bess's laugh wasn't quite as vibrant as his. "I wish I had a lot of stories to tell you, but I don't, really. I went to school. Got married. We had two boys, Connor and Robbie. Connor's eighteen. Robbie's seventeen. They're going to be coming down here in about two weeks, as soon as school lets out."

"If they need jobs, send 'em my way," Eddie said seriously. "Right now it's me and Kara, but once the season really gets going I'll need a couple other kids."

Bess smiled. "I'll let them know. Thanks."

Eddie sipped more coffee and eyed her over his mug. "What about your job?"

Bess turned her mug around in her hands. "Oh, that. Well, I worked for a little while, but when I got pregnant with Connor I quit and just never managed to go back."

"You were going to be a counselor," Eddie said. "That's too bad you had to quit. Not that staying home to raise your kids isn't an important job," he added hastily. "God knows someone should stay home and raise the children. I just meant…"

"I know what you meant," Bess said quietly. "I wanted to do a lot of things I didn't. Having Connor changed a lot."

She and Eddie stared at each other over their cooling coffees and biscotti crumbs. He sent her another smile, not so broad or wide, but sweeter for being so tentative.

"Kara's mother, Kathy, and I never got married. We, umm…well, I can't even say we dated," Eddie admitted. "The year after your last one here, I shot up about four inches, lost the braces. My face cleared up. I wasn't Quasimodo anymore."

"Oh, Eddie."

He shook his head. "I know what I looked like, Bess. Anyway. I guess the sudden transformation sort of went to my head. I got cocky. A little careless. Kathy was the daughter of one of my mom's friends from church. Both our moms tried to hook us up, but I wasn't really interested in marrying a preacher's daughter."

Bess swept biscotti crumbs into a pile. "But you had a baby with her?"

She hadn't meant to sound judgmental, and Eddie didn't seem to take it that way. He gave her a rueful grin and crunched the last of his biscotti.

"She wouldn't marry me. We both should have been more

careful, but Kathy was the one who said she wasn't going to spend the rest of her life married to the wrong person just because she'd made a mistake. We share custody of Kara. Kathy married an accountant from New Jersey."

Bess wiped her fingers free of chocolate with a paper napkin. "And you?"

"Never got married." He leaned back in his chair to study her, his head tilted. "Never found the right woman, I guess."

Heat tickled Bess's cheeks. "You look good, Eddie. I'm glad to hear you're doing well. Really. Even if you are still a townie."

They both laughed.

"With beachfront properties selling in the millions, being a townie isn't quite a slap in the face, you know. Not that I have a beachfront house," he amended. "Kara and I have a place in Bethany Commons. The condos. It's not so bad, even if we do have to share it with you tourists."

"Hey," she protested. "I'm officially a townie now!"

Eddie gave her the familiar head tilt and an entirely unfamiliar slow, assessing grin. "Cool."

"What about everyone else?" she asked, looking away. "Have you kept in touch with any of them?"

"Ah, well, obviously I don't hang out with Ronnie Swarovsky at the country club."

"Obviously." She laughed. "Did he and Tammy get married?"

"They did, actually." Eddie filled her in on twenty years worth of gossip and news. Bess was surprised at how many of the people they'd known back then still came back for the summer, or lived here year-round.

"Melissa Palance lives over in Dewey." Eddie crunched biscotti between his white, even teeth.

Bess gave him a questioning look, but figured out who he meant a few seconds later. "Missy?"

"She goes by Melissa now." He laughed. "She's got four kids and is married to some real-estate bigwig."

"Wow. Four kids?" Bess shook her head. "I can't believe it."

"She stops into the shop sometimes. You wouldn't even recognize her, Bess. She's not blond anymore, for one thing."

Bess twirled a strand of her shoulder-length hair. So far the silver wasn't overpowering the gold, but in the next few years she figured she'd have to decide whether or not to go gray gracefully or start coloring. "Who is?"

Eddie ran a hand over his dark, shaggy hair, where no signs of white glinted. "My dad's in his seventies and doesn't have a gray hair."

"Wow! Good genes."

Eddie laughed. "He's bald."

Bess eyed Eddie's thick hair. "You don't look like you're in any danger of that."

"Let's hope not. How about you? Do you keep in touch with anyone? Brian?" Eddie paused, sounding casual. He sipped coffee and settled back in the booth. "Nick?"

"I..." Bess stopped to drink some coffee. "I lost touch with Brian after college. And Nick...no. I never kept in touch with him."

"You didn't?" There was no mistaking the sound of pure pleasure in Eddie's voice, even if he did try to mask it with surprise. "You guys were pretty hot and heavy. Weren't you?"

He knew they'd been. "Yes, but...it didn't work out."

"So he's not the guy you married."

Bess looked up, shocked that Eddie might have thought so. "God, no! Can you imagine?"

She couldn't, actually. Married to Nick? How her life would have changed.

Eddie shrugged. "I didn't know. He up and disappeared.

Missy said she thought he joined the army. I thought maybe he went with you."

"No. I married Andy." She paused. Eddie had only met Andy once. From what she could remember, Andy hadn't been too nice.

"Ah." Eddie didn't ask any more questions. "Sounds like you've been doing well. I'm glad for you," he added, though something in his face told her he hadn't quite been convinced she was doing as well as she pretended.

Of course, maybe she was just projecting the truth she knew onto him.

"I should get going," Bess said. "Thanks so much for the coffee. It was great seeing you."

"Tell your boys about the job offer." Eddie stood, too. "And don't be a stranger, Bess."

"I won't." This time, she held the door open for him.

Eddie paused on the sidewalk. "You're staying at your grandparents' house?"

"It's mine now. But, yes. Same old place."

"Yours?" Eddie whistled low, then grinned. "Nice."

Bess laughed. "By default. I lucked out. Mom and Dad didn't want to deal with the hassles and the taxes."

"Even so. It's a great property. They had it up for sale for a while, didn't they?"

She nodded. "Yep, but then decided not to sell."

"I know." Eddie grinned. "I tried to buy it."

"Eddie Denver," Bess said in admiration. "You really are a mover and a shaker, huh?"

He laughed and made the same sort of shooing motion Kara had given them in the shop. "I wish. Someday, maybe."

Bess joined his laughter and looked toward her car, still parked close to the market. "I've really got to go. I need groceries."

"You know there's a Food Lion now, right? It's bigger than Shore Foods."

"There's a lot of stuff that wasn't here before," Bess told him. "It's like I've got to relearn the whole town."

"If you ever want a tour," Eddie offered, "you know where to find me."

She smiled. "I'll keep that in mind."

"Well. See you." He waved and loped across the street, back to his shop.

Bess watched him go, trying to fix the memory of the old Eddie over this new version, and pleased to find she couldn't.

Chapter 10

Then

*B*ess wanted a shower. She wanted to wash away the smell of sticky sweets from her hair and skin, and stand under pounding hot water until the faint headache behind her eyes went away. That was all she was thinking about, a shower and bed, when she closed up Sugarland and found Nick waiting for her again.

"Hey," he said as casually as ever, as if there was nothing odd about him showing up there.

"Hi." Bess made sure the doors were locked, and tucked the keys into her backpack. "What's up?"

Tonight he wore the bandanna again, along with a black, tight-fitting T-shirt with white letters that read Better to Be Dead and Cool Than Alive and Uncool. Somehow Bess doubted Nick had ever been uncool in his life.

"Nice shirt."

Deeper 87

He glanced at it, then gave her a grin that squinted one eye. "Thanks. They sell them at the Surf Pro."

"I'm sure they do." Bess laughed. "I'm sure they're very popular, too."

Nick shrugged. They stared at each other. The orangeish light from the streetlamp made his eyes look more gray than brown, and she wondered what it did to her blue ones. Probably turned them some nasty color the way it did her skin.

"So…" Nick got off the bench where he'd been lounging and shoved his hands in his pockets. "You going home?"

Bess nodded. "I was planning on it."

"Want to walk along the beach?"

"With you?" The question blurted out, potentially insulting, but Nick didn't seem offended.

He looked from side to side and held out his hands. "I'm the only one asking."

She crossed her arms. "How do you know that? Maybe I have tons of offers for moonlit walks along the beach."

Nick saluted her, mocking. "Maybe you do. But you also have a boyfriend."

"Sort of." This blurted out, too, and she frowned.

Nick's eyes gleamed. "What does 'sort of' mean?"

She waved a hand. "Nothing."

Nick the Prick is only friends with girls he's fucking. Missy's warning should've meant less than nothing, but Bess couldn't forget it. Nick wasn't fucking her. But they weren't friends, either. Were they?

"Is that like sort of being pregnant?"

Bess laughed. "No."

Nick grinned again. "C'mon. You have to walk home. Why not walk with me along the beach?"

"What about my bike?"

"Leave it here." He nodded toward her ten-speed, chained safely to the rack. "You don't have to work too early tomorrow. You can walk."

"How do you know what time I work?" Bess asked suspiciously, but she was already slinging her backpack over her shoulders and facing toward the boardwalk rather than the street.

"I just know." Nick wiggled his hand and made a "woowoo" noise. "Like a psychic."

"Uh-huh." She hooked her fingers into the straps of her backpack just below her armpits. The sidewalk wasn't deserted even this late, but it was far less crowded and she and Nick could walk side by side.

She paused when they got to the ramp leading to the boardwalk next to the Blue Surf Motel, toeing off her sneakers and pulling off her socks. She tucked the socks inside the shoes and put them in her backpack. She wiggled her toes on the wood, still warm from the summer sun though it had set a couple hours before. She sighed.

Nick laughed. "Long day?"

"A lot of standing. You have to stand at work, too, don't you?"

They walked together to the stairs leading down to the sand. Streetlamps lit the beach here, turning it to stark whiteness but leaving the sea itself in shadows. The sand was still kicked up, not yet smoothed by the grooming trucks. She spied more than one half-destroyed castle.

"Yeah." Nick bent to untie his boot laces and pulled his boots off. He staggered, off balance.

Bess laughed when he fell, and he grinned up at her, his eyes flashing. He got up, brushing the sand from his rear and dangling his boots from his other hand.

"You're lucky I don't get easily insulted," he told her.

"Sorry," she said without remorse.

Nick snorted. "Uh-huh. Right. I know how girls are."

"That's what I heard." Bess scraped one foot along the chilling sand as she walked and left a line behind them. In the morning it would be gone.

Nick turned around to face her, walking backward. "Heard what?"

Bess looked sideways at him. "That you know all about girls. A lot of girls."

He turned again, still walking. "Who told you that?"

"Who do you think?"

He shot her a glance. "Same bitch who told you I was queer? She's a real reliable source."

Bess feigned nonchalance. "I'm just saying what she said."

"Which is what, exactly?"

They'd reached an outcrop of rock, big slabs of it poking from the sand like the back of an alligator, or a dinosaur. The jetty. The waves crashed louder here. Bess hopped up on the rock and Nick followed.

"Well, after I told her I knew you weren't gay—"

"Jesus." Nick snorted. "Ryan really reamed her for that, by the way."

"Did he?" Bess hopped onto the sand on the rock's other side. The lamps had ended with the boardwalk. Light still shone behind them but in front the only glow came from the windows of houses lining the beach.

"Yeah. He was pissed."

This was interesting. "Because she said you were gay?"

"No." Nick snorted again, laughing. "Because she tried to get me to fuck her."

"Oh." Bess wished she hadn't asked. It wasn't as if she hadn't known, but she didn't want to hear it.

"I didn't." Nick stopped walking, and so did she. "If you care."

Bess shrugged. "Why should I care?"

He stared at her. The wind came up and tugged at the tied ends of his bandanna. He reached up to slide it off his head, and the wind played then with his hair. After what felt like a very long time, he smiled. "You tell me."

"According to Missy you fuck a lot of girls."

"I didn't fuck her."

Bess started walking again, her stride determined. Light behind, darkness ahead. She didn't need the light to know where she was going.

"It's not my business, Nick."

"So Missy told you I'm what, some sort of big slut?"

It wasn't a word Bess had often heard used for a boy, and she laughed. Nick didn't. "Are you?"

"I thought it wasn't any of your business."

"It's not!"

"I'm not queer," Nick said, "and I've screwed pretty many girls. Just not Missy."

He'd stopped walking again, and Bess did, too. She turned to face him. He'd linked his boot laces together over one wrist and shoved his hands into his pockets again. She crossed her arms, wishing she'd taken her sweatshirt out of her backpack before hitting the beach.

"I'm sorry," she said after a minute stretched out with nothing but the sound of the waves between them. "It's really none of my business."

"What else did she say about me?"

From farther up the beach came the sound of laughter and the sudden bright flare of green glow sticks being activated. Bess watched them circling through the air, tossed by unseen hands, before looking back at Nick.

"That you used to go out with Heather."

Nick's breath hissed out of him and he glanced away. He pulled the package of Swisher Sweets from his pocket and lit one, cupping it to keep the wind from blowing out the lighter's flame. The fire lit his face briefly, casting it in red and gold. When he clicked the lid shut, everything seemed blacker until her eyes adjusted.

"And let me guess. I screwed around on her, right? Broke her heart? Oh, I was so eeevil, right?"

"Is that what happened?"

"She cheated on *me,* that's what happened."

"I'm sorry." Bess wasn't surprised. She didn't ask if Heather had broken his heart.

Nick shrugged. Fragrant smoke tickled her nose. "Shit happens."

"Even so. That sucks."

He looked at her. "Yeah. Whatever. That was the last time I'll ever be someone's 'boyfriend.'"

Bess paused as a group of teenagers ran past them, tossing their glow sticks and shouting.

"You make it sound like a bad thing," she said when they'd gone.

They started walking again. Every now and again Nick's cigar would glow as he drew in a breath. Bess watched the cherry tip get brighter and fade as she waited for him to answer. They were almost at her house.

"Yeah," he said finally.

"So…you just…fuck them?" She stumbled on the word even though it wasn't as if she was a prude. No matter what Missy said. "What kind of girl puts up with that?"

"The lucky ones?" He grinned, but when she didn't smile in return, it faded. "Hey, I was kidding. I didn't screw Missy. She's Ryan's girl. I don't poach."

That term, the one she used herself, set Bess back a step. "Well...good to know."

She pointed up ahead to the deck of her grandparents' house. Lights blazed from inside the kitchen and living room, and several candles burned on the railings. The wind brought the sound of laughter. Probably her aunt Linda. The little kids would be in bed, but the nightly game of rummy would just be getting under way.

"That's mine," she said.

"Nice." Nick stopped when she did.

"It's okay. Crowded but...yeah, it's nice." Bess was tired of defending where she lived. Missy usually made it into such a big deal.

Nick looked up at the house, then at her, and finally down to the water. "I guess I'll head back, then."

"Oh...okay."

"Unless you want me to stay? Invite me up to meet the folks?" He grinned at her.

"Umm..."

"Nah." He cut her off before she could answer. "I've got to get going."

"Thanks for walking me home." Bess wanted to explain it wasn't that she didn't want to invite him in. She never invited anyone in. But it wasn't anything about Nick in particular....

"No problem." He bent to pick up a stone or a piece of shell, and winged it into the waves. "I wanted to tell Missy we spent the night together and my mama didn't raise a liar."

Bess startled into laughter. "Oh...!"

He turned to her and smiled. The light from the deck fell across his face, maybe even blinded him a little. Bess's hair flew across her eyes and she pushed it away. When she finished, he was closer. Close enough to murmur in her ear, "Tell me something."

If Bess turned her head, their cheeks would touch. She'd be able to brush his skin with her mouth. She could breath him now, smell him, the scent of sun and sand and sunscreen. Her heart tried to jump out of her chest. She felt its pulse in her throat and wrists, between her legs. She didn't turn her head.

"What?" she whispered.

"What does 'sort of' boyfriend mean?"

She swallowed hard. "It means...I'm not sure. It means I think he's cheating on me."

"But you don't know, for sure?"

When she shook her head, the soft brush of his cheek on hers made her knees weak. "No."

"Maybe you ought to find out." Nick breathed this last directly into her ear.

His arm brushed hers, and his hip. If anyone were to look out and see them, she knew it would look as though they were kissing. If he moved even a fraction of an inch, or if she did, they would be.

"Maybe I should."

He took only one step away, but it might as well have been a million. Bess blinked rapidly and drew in a deep breath, trying to seal the smell of him inside her but finding only the smell of the ocean. Without saying anything else, Nick backed off and left her there.

She had to wait a long time before her legs stopped shaking, so she could go inside.

Chapter 11

Now

"Where were you?" Nick came out of the shadows between the living room and kitchen. He still wore only boxers, and his hair was spiked and rumpled.

His sudden appearance and the loudness of his voice so startled Bess she dropped one of her bags. Hoping it wasn't the one containing the eggs, she bent to retrieve it before she answered. "I told you I was going to get some groceries and buy you some clothes. They're in that bag on the table."

"You were gone for hours." Nick didn't sound appeased.

Bess looked up. His mouth had turned down at the corners. She glanced at the clock. He was right. "I'm sorry. I ran into Eddie Denver in town and we got to talking."

Nick sneered. "Eddie Denver, that punk?"

"He's not a punk!" Bess unpacked milk, eggs, bread, peanut butter, lettuce. "You didn't even know him!"

Nick hitched himself up on top of the counter, legs dangling, and snagged her wrist as she leaned past him to put away some boxes of chai. "You used to work with him. I know who he was."

"Yes, well, you don't know who he *is*," Bess said with a pointed glance at his hand on her. "And he is not a punk."

Nick didn't let her go. He tugged her between his open legs and used them to hold her tight against the counter. "Fine. He's not a punk. You were still gone a long time. I missed you."

He put her hand on his back and grasped her shoulders. He kissed her, though it took a bit of contorting to do so. Bess opened her mouth to his urging, her annoyance fleeing in favor of arousal.

"You taste good," Nick murmured against her mouth.

"Ugh. I'm sure I have coffee breath."

He anchored his fist at the back of her neck and put his face close to hers, then sniffed so audibly she giggled and tried to pull away. "Everything about you smells good," Nick said. "Tastes good. Feels good."

His hands moved over her body as they kissed. Bess put her palms on his thighs, her fingertips just beneath the hem of his boxers. The coarse hairs on his legs tickled her fingers. She stroked her thumb over his skin and was rewarded by the prickle of gooseflesh.

Nick took one of her hands and put it to his groin. "See what you do to me?"

He stroked her hand up and down along his prick, which poked through the front of his boxers. His mouth claimed hers, tongue probing and stroking at the same pace as their joined hands. The fingers on the base of her skull tightened, squeezing gently, and Bess moaned at the pressure.

"Tell me I do the same to you," Nick demanded, his mouth next to her ear now.

"You do."

"Tell me I make you wet."

"You do, Nick. You know you do." Bess closed her eyes as his hand gripped hers, up and down, up and down along his erection. "You always did."

"Always?" He sounded amused. His tongue flicked her earlobe, followed a moment later by his teeth, and she shivered. "You like the way I touch you?"

"Yes." She opened her eyes and pulled away enough to look into his face. "I like the way you touch me."

"Do you want me to touch you now?"

"Yes."

Gone were thoughts of making sure the ice cream made it to the freezer, of putting away the grocery bags to save for use another time. Nothing else mattered just then but the way Nick's dark eyes held hers and the feeling of his cock in her palm. Bess shivered again, experiencing her own gooseflesh.

Nick's hands were hot, and more heat radiated from his bare chest when she bent her head to kiss him just above his left nipple. Bess pressed a kiss there, leaving a faint smudge of lipstick. She licked his nipple, smiling when it tightened and when he moaned as she sucked it gently.

The fist at the back of her head moved up to pull her hair from its coil. Nick's fingers tugged through the length, tangling and pulling, but Bess didn't wince. She stroked him as she licked and kissed his skin. The handle of the drawer in front of her dug into her just above her pubic bone. She didn't wince at that, either.

"I love your hair." Nick wrapped his fist in it and tipped her head back. Too hard, too rough, but it didn't matter. The suddenness of the gesture left Bess gasping. He pulled her away from the counter as he pushed himself off it and onto the floor, which vibrated as he landed. He was already kissing her by the time he did.

He backed her up, step by step, without letting go of her mouth. When her ass hit the edge of the kitchen table, Bess yelped. The table scraped across the tile. She put her arms down, fingers curling around the edge.

Nick's hand dived under her long cotton gypsy skirt. His thumb hooked her panties and yanked them downward. The material caught on her thighs, but he slid his palm against her anyway. His fingers slipped through her curls and found the waiting wetness.

He drew his fingers up and centered one on her clit, then he pressed. Bess twitched. She couldn't open her legs wide enough, bound as they were by the elastic around her thighs. Her skirt cushioned her ass but the table edge still dug into her flesh.

Nick's tongue flickered over her lips before he kissed her hard again. His fingers curled against the base of her skull while the other hand moved between her legs. He held her like that, in two places, and though she could have pushed him away, she didn't.

"I feel your heart beating here." Nick jiggled his finger against her clit. He nudged her chin up so he could fasten his mouth on her throat. "And here."

Bess took a deep breath. Cobwebs laced the ceiling corners and stirred in the breeze from the fan. That same breeze made the heat of Nick's tongue all the fiercer.

She put one hand on his shoulder, digging when he bit and sucked on her neck. Her hips moved against his hand. He pulled away to look at her face.

"You like that?" He wasn't smiling. His mouth had pursed in concentration.

Bess jumped at the sudden crack of thunder, but Nick didn't flinch. His eyes were darker than usual. Like a storm.

"Yes," she whispered past dry lips. She licked her mouth and his gaze fastened on the swipe of her tongue before capturing her eyes again. "I like it."

"Did you think about me while you were away?"

She didn't know if he meant this evening or the longer time when she'd been gone, but the answers to both were the same. "Yes, Nick."

His fingers slowed on her clit. Teasing. He'd learned her body in the past two days better than he ever had. He paused until her muscles tensed, and then he started again.

"Did you think about me touching you?"

"Yes."

"Fucking you?"

"God, yes." Bess groaned as his hand between her legs made it impossible to imagine thinking of anything else.

"Tasting you?" He pulled his hand up and swiped his tongue along his fingertips.

She shuddered, unable to answer.

Nick smiled, his eyes as dark as the storm outside. Thunder boomed again. He put his hand back between her legs. His fingers slipped faster, coated with his saliva and her own wetness. Bess gripped the table and his shoulder hard enough to cramp her fingers.

"I want to watch your face when you come," Nick said. "I want to see you looking at me."

She could look nowhere else.

Nick's hand moved a little faster. Bess tensed. Lightning lit the window and thunder followed closely after. The first spatter of rain hit the glass like the sound of marbles clattering into a jar.

Her inner muscles fluttered. Her feet skidded on the tile. The elastic of her panties, stretched to the limit, crackled in protest, but Bess couldn't care about ruining them. The world had become Nick's hand between her legs.

She swam inside the pleasure as it swelled and finally over-flowed. Her eyelids fought to stay open, and she bit her lower lip hard enough to sting, only to open her mouth wide in a gasp the next second when Nick's touch sent her over the edge.

Thunder drowned out her strangled cry. All she could see was his face, serious until he smiled and chased the darkness from his gaze. Bess put the hand that had been gripping the table over his to still it, her body pulsing faster than her heart-beat. She relaxed her grip on his shoulder, too, and felt the in-dentations her nails had made in his skin.

The phone rang.

Both of them startled and looked toward the sound, which was somehow more invasive than the fading thunder. Neither moved. The phone rang again, and again. Bess meant to move toward it, but her legs had grown so stiff she couldn't at first straighten them. By the time she got to the phone, the ancient corded handset that had been part of the house forever, she was sure the person on the other line would have hung up.

No such luck.

Her skirt fell to her ankles but her panties were still bunched around her thighs as she snatched up the receiver. "Hello?"

Behind her, Nick blew out a long, slow breath. She didn't look at him, but cradled the phone between her ear and shoul-der as she eased up her panties.

"Bess?" He sounded as if he'd expected someone else.

"Andy." The scrape of a chair behind her distracted her, but Bess kept her eyes on the refrigerator and the takeout menus hung there by magnets shaped like flip-flops. "What's up?"

"It's about the boys."

Bess stifled a groan. That long-ago summer when she'd talked with Andy on the phone, she'd sometimes stretched the cord as long as it could go in order to speak to him with some semblance of privacy. She was tempted to do that now, too, but didn't.

"What about them?"

"They're going to have to come to you earlier."

"But…I thought you were going to take them to the Grand Canyon!" The words slipped out, sounding more petulant than she'd intended, and Bess cursed herself for giving Andy any reason to use his favorite patronizing tone with her.

Which of course he did. "Bess, c'mon. You know they'll have a better time at the beach."

"That's not the point, Andy."

Andy gave a deep, long-suffering sigh. "What is the point?"

Bess dug her fingernails into her palm and mentally counted to five before answering. "The boys are going to finish out the school year with you and then you'll take two weeks for that rafting trip. Then they'll come here, with me, after the Fourth of July. That's what we talked about, Andy."

"Yeah, well, about that…"

Bess waited as anger boiled up her throat like bile. Worse than bile. Worse than acid.

"I was thinking they could get out early. Skip those last couple of days. They've only got half days anyway."

"Absolutely not!" Bess forced her fingers to uncurl. "Whose idea was that? Theirs or yours?"

His silence told her it was neither, and her stomach lurched along with the anger. "Never mind. No. The boys will finish school there. Connor's got his graduation, Andy. You're not going to take that away from him, are you? What might be his last chance to see his friends?"

Andy sighed. "Fine. But the trip will have to be postponed. I got offered the chance to go to a conference in Palm Springs, and I really need to go."

"Need to? Or want to?"

"Bess, be fair. What do you care, anyway? I thought you'd love to have the boys earlier."

Bess glanced at Nick, who watched her without expression. "They're looking forward to that trip, Andy. You can't disappoint them that way."

"I already talked with Connor about it. He's fine. Says he wants to get down there and start earning some money."

"And Robbie?" Robbie was the more sensitive of her sons, the one who strove more valiantly and with less success for his father's approval.

"He'll be fine with it, too."

Of course Andy hadn't talked to Robbie about canceling the trip. And it would be canceled. Bess knew her husband too well to know any different. She put the phone against her forehead for a moment while she tried to keep her cool.

"Obviously you've made up your mind," she said after a moment. "Fine. The boys will come here to me after Connor's graduation party instead of the end of June. You're right. I'll love to have them."

"Good. I'll let you talk to Robbie."

Before Bess could protest she heard Andy yelling Robbie's name. A minute after that, her son said, "Mom?"

"Hey, honey."

"What's up?" He sounded worried. He sounded that way too much, and Bess's heart hurt at having to disappoint him again.

"Honey, Dad just told me he's got to go to a conference in Palm Springs. So you and Connor are coming to me right after school lets out."

Silence. Robbie breathed into the phone. Bess tapped her forehead with the phone again, fighting the thickness of emotion in her throat.

"I'm sorry, honey. I'm sure Dad wouldn't cancel the trip if this conference wasn't important."

"I'm sure he wouldn't cancel our trip if she wasn't going to the other one." Robbie's voice dripped acid.

That her son knew about the "her" was worse than Bess finding it out herself. Her fingers clenched into her palm again, finding the grooves left from her nails still there. "Robbie—"

"Never mind, Mom." His voice shook a little bit, but he got it together. "It's okay. Me and Conn'll be down after school. Right. Fine. Cool."

Bess forced her voice to brightness. "Hey. Remember I told you about the place I used to work? Sugarland? Well, I know the owner and he said he'd be glad to give you and Connor jobs this summer. So how about that?"

Robbie made an effort at sounding pleased that didn't fool her. "That'll be good. Conn was worried about finding something if we didn't get there right away this summer. Me, too. You know, for college and stuff."

"Don't you worry about college, Robbie. Connor, neither. Okay?" Bess glanced at Nick again, but he'd left the table with the chair pushed back. Her stomach dropped, but in the next second she heard him moving around in the living room. So he hadn't completely gone. "Sorry, honey?" Robbie had said something while she was distracted.

"Never mind."

"No, Robbie. Tell me. It's just there's a storm here and I didn't hear you."

"I said, can't I come earlier? Like Dad wants. Can't I skip the last few days of school?"

"No, Robbie. You can't." Bess glanced into the living room and saw Nick's shadow stretching long. "You have to finish up."

Another long beat of silence moved through the telephone line, until Robbie sighed loudly. "Okay."

"I miss you," Bess said. "You and Connor both."

"How about Dad?" Robbie asked astutely. "Do you miss him?"

"I miss you and Connor," Bess repeated, and when Robbie hung up she wondered who'd taught him to be so cruel. If he'd learned it from Andy…or from her.

Chapter 12

Then

It was Andy's turn to call Bess, but so far the phone hadn't rung. She'd told him what time she'd be home from work, and warned the family members staying in the house that week she was expecting a call, but though she'd kept her shower brief and dressed quickly, the phone hadn't rung. He was only twenty minutes past the time she'd expected him, but that was long enough.

Bess joined the rummy game and played without paying much attention, thus actually coming out ahead in the end. Since they were only betting pretzel sticks it wasn't a big deal, but her uncle Ben kept calling her a card shark and that led to many impressions of the old *Saturday Night Live* skit "Land Shark," which in turn led to more recent imitations of Chris Farley's "in a van down by the river!" which in turn had Bess laughing so hard she snorted soda through her nose and had to leave the table.

She really had a wonderful family, and it was great she didn't have to pay rent, she thought as she washed her face in the kitchen sink. But she did wish there weren't always so many of them. She was waiting for the day when they told her she was going to have to share her room and bed with someone because of overflow, but so far it hadn't happened.

She went to sleep when they all did, even Uncle Ben, who claimed insomnia and liked to fall asleep in front of the TV instead of in bed. Andy still hadn't called. She'd left three messages over the past two weeks. She'd sent a letter, too, and a postcard. Andy had sent nothing.

When the phone did at last ring, Bess had fallen into a sleep so deep she dreamed about alarms blaring, and knocked her clock from the nightstand trying to turn it off. Blinking, she rose up in the darkness, muttering, and tore herself free from the tangle of sheets and blankets to get to the phone before it woke anyone else.

"Bess?"

"Andy, what time is it?"

"You sound out of breath." Andy…giggled?

"You sound drunk."

"Nah. Naw. No." Andy snuffled into the phone.

"I thought you were going to call me earlier." Bess wound the cord around her finger as she pulled it out onto the deck and closed the sliding-glass door behind her. She shivered and yanked up a blanket from a deck chair. Bundling herself, she tried not to think about what time it was.

"Me-n-Matty went out."

"I can tell." Bess yawned. "Where did you go?"

"Persia's."

"Is that a club? Or a person?"

Silence.

"Andy?"

"I meant we went to Hooligan's. Hooligan's, Bess. You know. Pool and stuff. Me-n-Matty."

Andy was fucking a girl named Persia. Bess tried to laugh, but all that came out was a strangled snort. Who the fuck named their daughter Persia? And what was worse, the fact that Andy was cheating on her or the fact that his brother, who Bess had thought liked her, knew about it and wouldn't tell her?

"I left messages for you. Why didn't you call me back?"

"I'm calling you back right now."

Bess listened to the ocean's purr, which was more soothing than the snorting sort of snuffle Andy had going on. "It's the middle of the night."

"I couldn't wait until morning. Had to talk to you."

She wanted to believe that, but couldn't quite manage. "You're drunk, Andy."

"I'm not drunk," he said, which meant he was.

She heard more shuffling. "I have to go to work in a few hours. I'm hanging up—"

"Don't!"

She paused, halfway out of her chair, and sank back into it. She waited for Andy to speak, but he wasn't talking. Bess closed her eyes, throat tight, and wondered if he was going to tell her the truth now. If this was it.

The end.

"I love you," Andy said. "Do you love me?"

She could say yes, but knowing she was not the only girl to love Andy kept her mouth from cooperating. "I'll talk to you tomorrow."

"Don't hang up," he pleaded. "I want to know."

Bess had twisted the phone cord so tight around her fingers they'd gone numb. She released them and rubbed them against the blanket to get some feeling back. "Yes."

Andy laughed. It wasn't his normal hearty chuckle, but a sort of sly, slippery, smirking sound that turned Bess's stomach. "When'm I gonna see you?"

"When are you coming down?"

"Ah, ah, ah," Andy said. "You said you'd come home."

Which made no sense at all to her and hadn't when she'd agreed to it. "Andy, you're the one with weekends off."

"Come up during the week, I don't care."

"So I can do what? Hang around your parents' house while you work? Come down here on the weekend. At least you can go to the beach."

Andy grunted. "C'mon, Bess."

She wanted to yell in frustration, but kept her voice down. "Let me guess. Your weekends are all tied up."

The silence went on so long she was sure he'd passed out.

"Bess, Bess, Bess," Andy slurred, finally. "'M gonna go to bed."

"You do that," Bess said, voice tight. "Tell Persia I said hi."

More silence. Maybe Andy wasn't drunk enough to miss her clear message. She heard him breathing, hard.

"Don't be like that, Bess."

"Like what?"

"Jealous like that. You're always so jealous."

"Do I have a reason to be jealous?" She ground out the words.

"No, no. No, Bess."

She didn't believe him. There had been others. The letters, for one. Photos of him with his arm around a girl whose name she didn't know. Maybe that was Persia. The real question was, why shouldn't she be jealous?

Except she wasn't, really. She had been, there was no doubt of that, but now, here, Bess only felt tired.

"Go to bed, Andy," she told him, and hung up the phone.

He didn't call back.

Chapter 13

Now

*N*ick came up behind her without saying anything, and slipped his arms around her waist. Bess had been staring into the darkness and listening to the ocean. He rested his chin on her shoulder, and she leaned back into his embrace.

She didn't want to know, but the words came, anyway. "What was it like where you were?"

His fingers tightened briefly on her shirt, bunching it before relaxing. "Gray."

She turned her head a little, though his face was too close to be more than a blur. "Gray?"

Nick let go of her and stood beside her to lean his elbows on the railing. "Yeah. Not black or white. Just…gray."

Bess looked across the beach, lit here and there but mostly dark. Beyond lay the waves she could hear, and smell, almost taste…but not see. Nothing about any of it seemed gray to her.

The questions she'd successfully fought down before tried

to rise to her lips, and she bit them back again. Ignorance truly was bliss. If she didn't know the truth of where he'd been, what had happened, she wouldn't have to wonder how he could be here, now.

"Until I heard you say my name," he whispered.

Her breath snagged in her throat. She linked her fingers through his, pulling him to her. He came willingly enough. She tucked herself against him again.

"I missed you so much. It was all I could think about once I got here," she murmured.

"You never came back in all these years?"

She shook her head. "No. I never did."

Nick's lip curled and he looked at her with half his face illuminated from the golden light spilling from the kitchen windows, and the other half dark. "You married that asshole."

Bess nodded.

Nick ran his hands through his hair before turning back to grip the railing. "Why?"

"Because I loved him."

Nick laughed. "Yeah, I think I remember you saying something like that."

She rubbed her bare arms and wished for a sweater. "It was true at the time."

"Sort of," Nick said with a mocking grin she only glimpsed, since his face was still turned away.

"A lot happened after that summer," she said quietly. "It didn't change all at once. We had to work on it, Nick. Andy was there. You weren't."

"It wasn't my fault!" The wind turned Nick's shout to confetti, but it was still loud enough to attract attention, if anyone else was outside on a deck. Before Bess had the chance to shush him he'd taken her by the upper arms and said, from deep in his throat, "It wasn't my fault. I wanted to."

"I didn't know that," she told him, without softening or bending. Without apologizing.

Nick let her go and paced the smoothly worn boards of the deck. His hands went to the pockets of his jeans, washed and dried now, but he pulled out nothing. Bess had brought him a toothbrush and toothpaste, clothes, but no cigarettes.

"How long?" Nick asked, his back to her. His bare feet paused on the boards.

"I told you. Twenty—"

"No." He shook his head but didn't turn to look at her. "How long did you wait before you decided to marry him?"

"It was six months before we got back together for good." Then, it had seemed an interminable amount of time, fraught with angst and anxiety. Now it was no more than a blink.

Nick turned, mouth bracketed again by lines. "So you married him? Because you didn't believe I'd do what I said? You didn't believe me?"

"Did you ever really give me any reason to believe you, Nick? Did you ever give me anything?"

He flinched. "Don't be a bitch."

"You can call me a bitch if you want, but you know it's true." Tears burned her eyes and slid down her cheeks. She didn't bother dashing them away. "I asked you, flat out—"

"I didn't mean it!" His voice rose again. "Jesus, Bess, didn't you know I didn't mean it?"

"I didn't know anything!" She still didn't, actually. "I don't know anything now! All of this is crazy, Nick. It's insane!"

He crossed to her in two steps and took her in his arms. It was the action of a man, not a boy, and though she didn't remember him ever acting that way back then, it seemed perfectly suited to him now. He looked down into her face and brought their bodies close together. As it had since the first night of his return, heat radiated from him like a small sun. Her own personal sun, around which she orbited the way she always had.

"I know I was an ass back then, Bess. I know you hated me."

She shook her head. "No. I never thought you were an ass. A lot of other things, but not that."

A small grin touched the corners of his lips. "I know I lied to you, but not about coming to find you. I meant it. And now, this…it's not crazy. Why do you think I came back? Why was I able to, after all this time?"

She shook her head a little. "I don't know."

"Because of you." He pulled her closer and bent to brush his lips across her cheek and nuzzle her neck. "Because when you went down to the water and wanted me, the gray went away."

His hands were hot on her, his mouth hotter. When he slid his palms up to cup her breasts through her T-shirt, Bess's lips parted in a silent sigh. Her nipples tightened at once and the beat of her heart stepped up. Under his touch, she melted again, the way she always had.

Maybe always would.

"This is crazy," she whispered again, but it didn't feel crazy.

It felt right. It felt like she had waited her entire life to feel Nick's hands on her, like she'd been born to fit his touch. It felt like nothing else had ever mattered or ever would but his mouth moving over her skin and his hands holding her.

"Everything was gray until I heard you say my name." Nick kissed her throat and nudged her backward, his hands guiding her so she wouldn't fall. "I didn't know where I was, but it didn't matter anymore because I heard your voice and knew where I wanted to be."

It was a more poetic speech than any she could remember

hearing from him, but like the rest of this, it didn't seem out of place. Bess let Nick guide her through the sliding-glass doors, across the linoleum, through the living room and into the bedroom. He kissed her mouth when they got to the bed, and she pulled away to catch her breath.

They looked into each other's eyes, both breathing hard. Nick licked his lips and passed a hand over her hair, then cupped her cheek for a moment before finally resting his hand on her shoulder.

"What?" he asked.

"You didn't used to…"

He kissed her mouth again, hard, before gentling the pressure. He pulled away just enough to say against her lips, "I didn't used to do a lot of things."

He nipped at her bottom lip, not hard enough to hurt, then ran his tongue over it. Her mouth parted for him and his kiss took her breath away, not from its harshness but from the uncommon tenderness.

"Stop thinking about the way things were," he murmured as he lifted her shirt over her head. His palms skimmed the lace of her bra, then unhooked it and tugged it off, too. "Just think about the way things are now."

It was so much easier to do that with his mouth tracing the slope of her breasts. When he suckled gently at one nipple, Bess cringed, pushing his mouth from her skin even as they both moved onto the bed. Nick lifted his head.

"No?"

She shook her head a little, not wanting to explain about nursing her boys, how things had changed for her since then. Not wanting to think about it, actually. She wanted to do what he'd said. Think about now.

Nick studied her for a moment, but said nothing, just

moved to her ribs and belly. His kisses left a trail of tiny hot spots that faded slowly, only to ignite again when he retraced his path. His fingers toyed with the snap of her denim skirt, but before he undid it he sat up to pull off his T-shirt. Bare-chested, he knelt next to her.

Bess studied his body, more familiar to her after the past week than it had ever been. She reached to circle his nipple with a fingertip, then traced the line of dark hair on his belly to where it disappeared into the waistband of his jeans. Her hand fell away and he covered her with his body, bare flesh to bare flesh. The button of his jeans was a small, sudden chill on her hot skin and she wriggled under him as he kissed her mouth again.

They turned to face one another, legs entwined. Bess ran her fingers through his hair, relishing the silk of it. She cupped the back of his neck to pull him closer. Farther down, his shoulder blades jutted like the stumps of shorn wings. She traced the lines of his bones, and he shuddered against her.

"Tickles," he murmured into the hollow of her throat. His hand slid up her thigh, beneath her skirt. "Why do you bother putting these on when you know I'm only going to take them off you again?"

He stroked her panties, then rolled her onto her back and knelt again. He used both hands to push up her skirt and hook her panties down. They slid without resistance over her thighs and knees, and Nick followed them all the way down to her ankles, where he tugged them off and tossed them away. His hands slid up again, over the same places, and his mouth followed. He nudged her legs apart with his head and settled between her legs.

Bess undid the snap and zipper, but with her skirt bunched around her waist there seemed little need for her to take the whole thing off. Nick's mouth caressed one of her knees, then the other, and he looked up at her.

"Take it off," he ordered, changing her mind about the necessity of being totally naked. "I want to see you."

He got out of his jeans while she slid out of her skirt. He wore no briefs, was bare beneath the denim, and Bess licked her lips at the sight of his cock growing thicker as he pushed the material down his thighs and stepped out of it. He crawled up the bed to cover her again.

She thought he would slide inside her at once. She was wet enough for him. Ready. Aching, in fact, for him to fill her, a term she'd often read in books but had never understood could be true.

Nick didn't do so. He kissed her mouth and looked down into her eyes. His hand slid between them and his fingers found her clit without hesitation. His gaze flared when she gasped at the touch.

"I could fuck you a million times and never get tired of it," he told her. "There's always something new about you."

Bess didn't believe that could possibly be true, but she believed he meant it. There didn't seem to be an answer to it, nor did Nick seem to expect one. He stroked her gently until her hips moved and her hand gripped his arm.

Then he moved. Without ceasing the slow, steady circling of his fingers on her clit he moved his mouth down her body. His breath flickered over her nipples, but he didn't pause there. The muscles of her belly trembled, but he didn't stay there, either. Once more he settled between her legs, and Bess half sat, propped on her elbows in immediate reaction.

"Nick—"

She quieted at once when, without preamble or hesitation, he kissed her. His thumbs parted her swollen, slick folds and his mouth fastened onto her sweetly throbbing clitoris. His lips pressed her and a moment later the point of his tongue took up the pace and motion of his fingers. Bess couldn't think of anything else. He licked her slowly, then faster when her hips lifted to meet his mouth.

She was close already. Not ready to tip into orgasm yet, but the pleasure building between her legs had moved from simple to complex, leaving no question about where it would go. Many times over the past twenty years, her body had stuttered or stalled when presented with pleasure. Her mind had over-ruled the simplicity of climax and left her tense with frustration.

Not tonight.

Nick slid one, then another finger inside her as he used his tongue to caress her. A third stretched her—not as much as his cock would, but she moaned anyway as he fucked her with his hand and mouth. Her fingers gripped the sheets of the bed she hadn't bothered making. Her heels dug into the mattress as her hips tipped upward.

Climax danced out of her grasp, and her head fell back, eyes closed and jaw clenched in concentration. Nick's hand slowed. His tongue followed suit. He blew heated breath across her wet flesh, and Bess let out a sigh.

He did it again and she tensed, hovering, ready to crash, but again the pleasure eluded her. Nick withdrew. Bess opened her eyes.

He rolled onto his back, pulling her by the hip to straddle him. She thought he meant for her to slide onto his prick, and though the thought of it sent a fresh burst of arousal through her, part of her sighed with disappointment at not being able to finish beneath his tongue.

"No," Nick said hoarsely when she gripped his cock. His hands held her hips as she looked at him curiously. He pulled her forward. "I still want to lick you."

Her entire body flooded with fire. It had been different, somehow, with her on her back and him between her legs. Passive, as if that made a difference. Now he wanted her to move over his body, to straddle his face the way she straddled his hips. Her first inclination was to refuse, and she shook her head, but Nick's tug on her hips inched her forward on her knees. Her hands found a place to grip the headboard.

Now he held her ass, still urging her to slide her knees forward. When she got close enough, he wrapped first one arm and then the other beneath her thighs to push her body toward his face. It was the longest second Bess had ever counted, that moment between the time her clit brushed his chest and the one when his hands on her ass pressed her body to his face.

In this position she could move as easily as she desired, and Nick could either direct her movements with his grip on her hips and ass, or he could stay still. She could grind down on him, if she wanted, or pull away so only his breath tickled her. Caught between the extremes, Bess hovered until he smoothed his hands over her rump and eased her onto his waiting mouth.

A breath sobbed out of her and she closed her eyes. It was silly to be embarrassed now, after everything else, and it wasn't quite shame that made her block out the sight of things. It was more to keep herself from being overwhelmed by all of this, so new. He'd told her not to think so much and to focus on the now, so that's what she did.

At first, his hands rocked her hips, but after only a moment or two of feeling the intense pleasure of his lips on her clit, Bess started the motion on her own. Not the same, exactly. He'd been too timid. She added a small twist to the action that soon had her shuddering with need.

Bess knew her body well and had shed many of the inhibitions that had plagued her when she was younger, but she'd never been in control of her pleasure in quite this way. She could pull away or move closer, rock her clit against his tongue, even move up and down if she wanted.

Her fingers gripped the headboard harder, tighter, as the coil of desire twisted low in her belly. Her body shook with it. Her hair fell over her face, tickling, but she ignored it as she tried to remember to breathe. The roar of the ocean sounded loud in her ears, drowned out only by her cry of joy when, at last, she came.

The world spun until she remembered to breathe. Bess unhooked her stiff fingers from the headboard and moved down Nick's body to find his mouth with hers as her hand guided him inside her. They joined with a mutual groan. She tasted herself on him, for the first time not put off by the thought of it. She opened his mouth with her tongue, stabbing it deep as she took his cock all the way into her. Nick was pushing upward as she pressed down. They moved together, at first raggedly until they found their rhythm.

Her fingers clutched at his shoulders, gouging. Bess kissed Nick hard enough to bring the taste of blood to her tongue, and broke off with a gasp, only to dip her head and bite again at the smooth column of his throat. He fucked into her harder. Pounding. His hands held her tight against him.

It no longer mattered who was in control.

The sheer roughness of his thrusts gave her another orgasm, less liquid than the first. Her body tensed and released. Nick growled. His body arched. He shouted when he came, and that sound of his pleasure filled Bess with such relief, so much pleasure of her own, that she laughed. A small giggle at first, followed by a heartier chuckle.

Nick's thrusts eased, and he opened his eyes. His grip on her hips loosened. He grinned and joined her laughter, and they laughed together until the bed rocked with it as much as it had from their fucking.

The Nick she'd known would have been put off at her laughter, but now he only drew her close to swallow up her giggles with his mouth. His hands smoothed over her back, over her ass, and rolled them both until they could lie on their sides, their heads on the same pillow.

"Why are you laughing?" he asked when his kisses got interrupted by her guffaws.

"Because I'm so happy." Bess hadn't known the answer to his question until she answered.

"Ah," he said, and kissed her softly on her bruised lips. He stroked her hair and looked into her eyes. "Me, too."

Chapter
14

Then

$\mathcal{N}$ick lounged against the counter looking like seven different kinds of sin, and Bess was doing her best to ignore him. He wasn't making it easy. The constant in and out of customers hadn't deterred him from his place on the shop's single high stool, or urged him to finish his obscenely large ice cream sundae. He caught Bess looking at him from around a couple of teenage boys trying to see if the accumulated contents of their pockets could support their slushy habit. Nick, his dark eyes alight, licked a hunk of dripping fudge from his spoon.

Slowly. With his tongue. Then he did it again.

"Sorry?" Bess snapped back to reality, her throat and cheeks heating, and paid attention to the boy at the counter in front of her. "You wanted a blue raspberry?"

"Two." He pushed the small pile of coins and crumpled dollars toward her. "Four straws."

"Mmm-mmm, Daddy oughta be spanked for wanting to

watch them suck those straws," Brian muttered when Bess jerked her thumb toward the slushy machine next to him as she passed on her way to the back room to grab up a new box of soft pretzels for the oven.

"I don't know what's more disturbing," she said on her way back through. "The fact you're calling yourself Daddy or that you're perving on a bunch of skaterpunks."

Brian laughed as he slipped the clear domed lids over the plastic cups and stuck two straws in each. "Honey, those boys are plenty old enough. I'm twenty-one. Only a year older than you."

Bess snorted and started hanging the pretzels on their small, rotating hooks inside the glass warming case. "They might be over eighteen, Brian, but I'm not the one drooling over them."

As all of this exchange took place sotto voce, it didn't make Bess too happy when Brian sent an unmistakable glance to Nick's end of the counter. "Not over *them,* anyway."

"Shut up," she muttered, and elbowed him in the side as she snagged the slushies and sent the teenagers on their way.

"What?" Brian's look of mock innocence might have fooled a nun.

Bess, fortunately, wasn't a nun. "Just shut up!"

For the first time in over an hour, the shop had emptied. Nick dug his spoon into the Sugarland Special, a concoction of four scoops of ice cream, hot fudge, peanut butter sauce, whipped cream, sprinkles, crushed chocolate cookies and a pretzel rod. He lifted the spoon again and let the oozing ice cream drip onto his tongue.

This time, damn him, he grinned.

"Mmm, mmm, mmm," said Brian with a hand on his hip. "You keep doing that, Nick Hamilton, and I'm gonna think you have a crush on me."

Nick laughed and didn't seem to care if the corners of his

mouth gleamed with hot fudge. He pursed his lips. His air kiss sent Brian into a shimmy of giggles. Bess had to turn away to hide her smile.

"He's got a crush on someone, anyway," Brian muttered in her ear when she tried to get past him on her way to the back room.

Bess, unable to help herself, looked at Nick again. He was swirling the long-handled spoon through the remains of his sundae and scooping up bits of chocolate cookie. Her stomach rumbled, but even she couldn't convince herself her hunger for ice cream was the only thing making her mouth water.

"Hey, Bess," Nick said, destroying her illusion that he'd really come in here to eat ice cream. "I'm having a party tonight."

"That's nice." With a glare at Brian, she went to the back room to see how Eddie was doing with the latest vat of caramel corn. Mr. Swarovsky only let the Sugarland managers make the syrup, based on a family recipe, but Bess had finished the last batch a few hours before and had set Eddie to packing it up into the refillable plastic tubs.

"How's it going?" She swiped a hand across her forehead at the swell of hot air. The back room wasn't air-conditioned.

Eddie glanced at her, but didn't make eye contact. "Good. I'm almost done."

He was, too, with a task that would've taken Tammy twice as long to finish. Brian, as well, not because he was incompetent, but because he would have kept popping into the front of the shop to see what was going on. He was too much of a social butterfly to be stuck in the back, and Eddie preferred it. Bess was thankful, and not for the first time, that Mr. S. had hired such divergent employees. It made her job a lot easier.

Well, aside from the errant Tammy, who bragged about blowing Ronnie Swarovsky, the boss's son, and couldn't be fired no matter how many times she screwed up.

Bess realized she was shifting from foot to foot as Eddie worked, probably making him nervous, and that she really had nothing to do back there. Eddie didn't need her supervision. Brian, on the other hand, did.

She didn't want to go back out there. Almost a week ago, Nick had walked her home along the beach. Their conversation wouldn't leave her. He'd told her she should find out what "sort of" a boyfriend meant.

If her last conversation with Andy was any indication, "sort of" meant not at all. Bess still wasn't sure how she felt about that. She'd been with Andy for four years. Four good years. He seemed bent on throwing them all away, and she didn't know why. She only knew she was far less upset about the prospect of being suddenly without a boyfriend than she'd been a month ago.

"I'm going to step out back for a few minutes," she told Eddie, who nodded without looking away from the vat of coated popcorn and the spatula he used to scoop it.

The air outside wasn't much cooler, and it stank of garbage, but since she'd discovered even the smells of sweet treats could turn toxic from overexposure, the slightly sour odor emanating from the garbage cans was something of a relief. She leaned against the warm bricks and pulled a pack of gum from her pocket. She didn't smoke, but she could chew gum.

Andy had been so much a part of her life for the past four years, Bess had no idea how to imagine herself without him. They'd started dating her senior year of high school. Andy, who'd graduated two years ahead of her, had come back for Homecoming. He and some friends had crashed the Homecoming dance. The staff had turned blind eyes to the former football heroes and prom kings, who'd then demanded dances from all the girls in the Homecoming court.

Bess would never forget the feel of Andy's hand in hers as he'd helped her down from the stage and onto the dance floor. She couldn't remember the name of the Richard Marx song that had been playing, or what flowers had been in her corsage, but she'd never forget how blue Andy's eyes had been, or how wide and white his smile when he asked her name.

She knew who he was, of course. All the girls would have. Andy Walsh had made quite an impression on the sophomore girls when he'd helped out with the football unit in gym class his senior year. Ms. Heverling had never had a class so interested in the sport before she used Andy as her assistant.

He didn't remember Bess from that year, and she didn't remind him that once he'd told her she'd thrown a perfect spiral. She never told him the only reason she knew anything at all about football was because of that year in gym. She let him believe she knew how to follow the game because she liked it. It had seemed a harmless enough lie. Important, even. She wanted to like what Andy liked. She wanted him to like her.

By the end of her senior year, Bess wanted Andy to love her.

They'd dated through the mail, infrequent phone calls and even more infrequent school breaks during her senior year. Looking back, she realized it was that distance that had made it all seem so great. The less she saw him, the more important it became to do so.

She'd looked at half a dozen schools because she knew her parents wanted her to explore all her options, but there was no other choice for Bess than Millersville University, where Andy was entering his junior year.

The relationship had stepped up quickly after that. Away from home for the first time, she'd found nothing seemed as scary or intimidating as it might have, with Andy there to ease her way. She'd lost her virginity to him within the first week of her freshman year, in the narrow single bed in his dorm room while his roommate studied down the hall.

Part of her had been afraid things would crumble when they saw each other so often. They'd spent more time together in the first month of school than they had for the entire first year they'd dated. Andy seemed to think nothing of it, though, accepting her into his circle of friends and his routine as easily as if she'd always been part of them. He'd told her he loved her before she said it to him, and had played the part of the doting boyfriend so convincingly she'd never doubted him.

So what had changed?

"Bess?" Eddie poked his head out of the back door. "Brian needs some h-help up front."

"Be right there." She spat her gum into the garbage and went back inside with a sigh.

Brian was getting slammed, but diva that he was, had managed to get the crowd mostly under control. They milled around the small seating area, but nobody was kicking up much of a fuss. Nick still reigned from his corner chair, though the ice cream had vanished. He wasn't in the way or anything, but seeing him there put a frown on Bess's face, anyway. He was a distraction she still didn't have time to deal with.

She and Brian served the customers as fast as they could, but it was another forty minutes before the last of them left the bell jangling as the door closed behind them. Brian collapsed against the counter with an exaggerated sigh and begged a break, which Bess had no choice but to give him. With Brian gone out the back faster than a frat boy chugging a beer, Bess was once more left alone with Nick.

"So," he said with a grin as sweet as the sundae he'd finished. "Party. My place. Tonight."

Chapter 15

Now

"Hi, Kara. Is your dad here?" Bess leaned on the counter to talk to Eddie's look-alike daughter.

"Hey." Kara lifted a hand but barely glanced up from the tabloid paper spread out in front of her. "Nope. I think he ran to the coffee shop or something. You want me to call him?"

Bess didn't take the girl's lack of enthusiasm as an insult. "Sure, if you don't mind."

Kara shot her a grin. "Nah. He told me if you stopped by I had to let him know, like, right away."

This scrap of information might have made Bess feel self-conscious, but for the fact that she stood in Sugarland, where years ago Eddie Denver had had a crush on her. There was something comforting in thinking he still might. She laughed and drew a chair up to the counter.

"Thanks."

Kara shrugged, already pulling a bright pink cell phone

from her pocket and keying in a number. "No prob. Dad? She's here. Where are you? Want me to ask her to wait?"

Kara held the phone away from her face to turn to Bess. "He's not at the coffee shop, he ran to the office supply store. Can you wait for him? He says it'll be about half an hour."

"Sure." Half an hour was longer than she'd planned to spend, and Bess's thoughts went at once to home and Nick waiting for her. But she really needed to talk to Eddie.

"She'll wait. Yeah, whatever." With a roll of her eyes, Kara disconnected the call and shoved the phone back in her pocket. "He says he's hurrying. Do you want anything while you wait?"

"Lemonade," Bess said. She was already salivating at the thought of the tart liquid.

She looked around the small shop while Kara cut the lemons and used the press to squeeze the juice, adding it to the sugar and water and shaking it. Eddie had changed the decor a little, but not much. The equipment looked newer, the menu a little more extensive, but so much was the same that Bess felt she was sitting on the wrong side of the counter.

The season hadn't really begun, which made the sudden swell of customers a surprise. Kara blinked as the bell over the door jangled and a crowd surged inside, all of them lining up at the counter, jostling, to point out what they wanted from the menu board.

The line was long enough and the customers boisterous enough to fluster anyone, but Kara kept her cool. She took orders and filled them as fast as she could, while the noise and heat level inside the small shop grew to oppressive levels.

"Bus tour," explained one of the women to Bess.

Five minutes passed while Bess sipped her lemonade, with no sign of any decrease in the crowd. Despite the nose ring and blasé attitude, Kara had an easy way with the customers that kept them from getting too rambunctious. Bess saw a lot of Eddie in Kara's efficiency, but even so, it was clear the girl was getting overwhelmed, after all. Bess recognized the clenched jaw and clumsiness as Kara tried to take orders faster than one person could do alone.

"You need a hand," Bess observed when Kara came her way to grab the last soft pretzel from the warmer.

Kara paused to flash her a grin so much like Eddie's Bess had to return it. "Think you can handle it?"

"I think I remember how." Bess flipped up the hinged counter—God, the same squeak!—and stepped behind the counter.

"You run the register," she told Kara, after a glance showed her there was no way she'd figure out how to operate it in the next five minutes. "I'll take orders."

They worked together with only the most minor of mistakes, until the crowd, with food and drink in hand, at last disappeared. As the door jangled behind the last customer, Bess saw Eddie watching them through the front window. Then he ducked inside.

"How long were you standing out there?" Bess laughed.

Kara gave a disgusted snort. "Gee, Dad, thanks so much for helping!"

"You two had it under control." Eddie grinned. "Not so easy to forget, huh, Bess?"

She shook her head and gave him a rueful smile. "No, apparently not."

"You were doing great."

"Dad," Kara interjected. "Enough with the goggle eyes, okay? It's creeping me out!"

Eddie laughed but didn't duck his head. "Bess, you wanna grab a cup of coffee?"

"You're going to leave me here all alone again?" Kara crossed her arms and huffed.

Eddie looked out the front of the shop, where there were more empty parking spots than full. "We're just going across the street. If you get swamped, call me."

Kara grumbled a little, but sighed. "Fine. Whatever."

"It's why I pay you the big bucks, remember?"

At this, she burst into laughter that completely unraveled her carefully woven persona of rebellious teenager. "Oh, sure, Dad. Suuure!"

He blew her a kiss. "Be back in a few. Bess? Ready?"

He held the door open for her as she came around the counter. On the street, she squinted against the bright sunshine. The breeze tangled her hair across her face and she pushed it back.

"Summer's here," she said as they crossed the dual one-way streets. "I wasn't sure it was ever going to come, with all the storms we'd been having."

"It always gets here, sooner or later." Eddie held open the coffee-shop door for her and Bess scooted through. "And it always ends, too."

She glanced at him over her shoulder. "That's pretty deep."

Eddie laughed. "Oh, yeah. That's me. Deep as the ocean."

She shook her head a little, smiling, but his words made her think again of Nick, and she glanced at her watch. Eddie saw the look, but led her to the counter. He waited until they'd both ordered and taken seats at a table before asking, "Do you have someplace to be?"

"Oh…not really." Bess shrugged off his scrutiny. "It's a habit, I guess."

Eddie held up both his wrists, bare except for the dark hair of his arms. "That's why I don't wear a watch. I used to always be checking, checking. I didn't pay enough attention to where I was. I was too worried about where I was going."

Bess got up to grab the coffees before Eddie could, and she brought them over to the table. "See what I mean? That's deep."

"Yeah. Who knew?" Eddie dented the foam on his coffee with a breath.

"I mean it." Bess didn't bother trying to sip her drink. Too many burned tongues had taught her patience. At least when it came to coffee.

Eddie looked up at her. "Do you?"

"Yes."

His smile grew slowly but was all the more powerful for it. "Thanks."

"You shouldn't sound so surprised," Bess said. "I always knew you had a lot going on inside."

"Had a lot going on outside," he said. "All over my face."

She didn't act as if what he said wasn't true. "Everyone has an awkward stage."

"Yeah. Mine lasted, oh, nineteen years." Eddie chuckled and sipped his drink.

Bess braved a taste of hers. The barista hadn't used enough syrup, but otherwise it was good. Still a little too hot. "But look at you now."

Eddie didn't say anything at first, and Bess thought maybe she'd hurt his feelings somehow. Meaning to apologize, she gazed at him. Eddie was staring out the window to the sidewalk.

"You know," he said quietly, "no matter what else happens, a big part of me is always going to be that shy, terrified kid with the pimples."

"Lots of people feel that way, Eddie."

He looked at her. "Do you?"

Bess opened her mouth to say no. Time had changed her.

She understood, but didn't share his sentiment. "Yes. I do. I swear to you, the face in the mirror surprises the hell out of me some days."

"You weren't a big geek, though." Eddie smiled. "What do you see? What do you remember yourself as?"

It had been Eddie who told her Nick wasn't good for her. That being with him made her doubt herself. "I still see a woman who doubts herself."

"You shouldn't."

"You—" she pointed at him "—shouldn't think of yourself as a big nerd, either."

Eddie held up both hands in surrender. "Fair enough."

Bess looked outside at a passing couple, each holding a funnel cake. Her stomach grumbled at the sight of the fried dough topped with powdered sugar. One of them even had a glop of syrupy cherries on top.

"God, that looks good." She sighed.

"So go get one." Eddie swirled his coffee, the foam now gone. "The first one of the season's the best."

Bess shook her head. "The last thing I need is a funnel cake. Besides, I don't really want the whole thing. I just want a bite."

"That's it?" He laughed, craning his head to stare after the couple outside.

"Yes. That's enough. You're right, that first bite is always the best." She glanced across the street at Sugarland. She couldn't see Swarovsky's from here, but she'd passed it on the way into town. Original Secret Recipe! screamed the sign in front, and she'd wanted to throw cotton candy at it, just for Eddie's sake.

"Mini funnel cakes," Eddie said thoughtfully.

They looked at each other for two beats of silence, then both began talking at once.

"What if you sold miniature funnel cakes!"

"We could do all kinds of good stuff…"

"Fried candy bars," Bess said, with a shiver at the thought of such decadent sweetness. "And Oreos! I mean, those things are killers and you really only need one!"

"If you kept the prices reasonable enough so that people wouldn't feel like they were getting ripped off—" Eddie interrupted himself. "Fried pickles!"

Bess made a face. "Ew."

"They're delicious," he insisted. "What about mini corn dogs?"

"Soft pretzel eggs!" Bess cried, so loudly everyone in the coffee shop turned to look at them.

"What the heck are soft pretzel eggs?" Eddie asked.

"It's something I used to make for my boys. You take a soft pretzel and crack two eggs into the holes. It's kind of like a breakfast sandwich. They love them." Eddie gaped at her until Bess ducked her head. "What?"

"It's brilliant."

"Oh, stop it." She laughed.

He shook his head. "No, I mean it. This coffee shop and the burrito joint are the only two places serving breakfasty type stuff. I'm always at the shop early, anyway. It wouldn't be hard to have an early shift. We could get a new piece of the market."

"Do you think so?" Bess gulped her coffee, now the perfect temperature.

"I really think so. And we won't need Swarovsky's caramel corn anymore. We'll make our own niche." Eddie grinned and slapped the table hard enough to bounce the napkin holder.

"You could call it Just a Bite," Bess offered.

"We," Eddie said.

Bess didn't get it, at first. "Hmm?"

"We," he repeated. He leaned forward slightly. "We'll call it Just A Bite. You have to be in on it."

Bess held up her hands and shook her head. "Oh, no. No, that's not what I meant—"

"C'mon, Bess. Do you have a better offer? Are you going back to work?"

"I'd thought about it, but…"

"You'd be great. You always were full of great ideas. And you really know how to keep up with a business like the one we're talking about. Hey, I saw you today. You were having fun."

"Sure I was. I knew I could leave whenever I wanted."

Eddie charmed her with a tilted smile. "That's the best part of being the boss, Bess. You get to leave whenever you want."

She knew that wasn't really true. A business like Sugarland was a lot of hard work. Long hours. The food industry was a tough one in which to succeed. "It's not really what I envisioned myself doing with my life, Eddie."

"Right." He sat back in his chair, the gleam in his eyes undimmed. "What do you see yourself doing with your life?"

"I haven't thought that far ahead."

"So think about this. If I want to make Sugarland into Just A Bite, I'm going to need more than what I've got. I'm going to need an ideas partner, at the very least."

She suspected he was flattering her. "You're going to need money, is my guess."

"That, too." Eddie didn't look daunted. "But that, I can get. Someone with real creative vision and the skills to put it to work is harder to find."

"You're serious about this." Bess finished her coffee. The last dregs of it were cold and a little bitter.

"I'm serious."

"A partnership is a lot of work! We could hate working with each other!"

"I never hated working with you."

Bess had to look away from the intensity of Eddie's gaze. "I never hated working with you, either, Eddie, but that was a long time ago."

"Don't forget, I'm still the same crater-faced geek underneath, Bess."

She stopped herself just in time from chewing at the inside of her lip, a bad habit she'd worked hard to break. "And I'm that girl who doubts herself."

Eddie leaned toward her again. Bess was glad for the barrier the table and their cups made between them. She thought if there'd been nothing keeping them apart, Eddie might have reached for her hand, or shoulder. She wasn't sure what she'd have done.

"Think about it," he said solemnly. "Promise me you'll think about it?"

Bess dipped her head to give him a tilted grin of her own. "You don't take no for an answer, huh?"

Eddie shook his head. "Not usually."

"See? You're not the same, after all."

He got up to gather their garbage and toss it into the can next to their table. "If I'm not, maybe you're not, either."

Bess stood and looked at her watch again. Time had once again flown while she talked with Eddie. "I really have to get going."

He nodded. "I have to get back to the shop. Thanks for stopping by, though."

She was already outside when she remembered she hadn't had a purely social reason for visiting him. "Oh, I almost forgot. I wanted to tell you that my husband's not taking the boys on the trip they'd planned. So they'll be able to start sooner than I thought. They're coming the thirteenth of June now instead of the beginning of July."

"Great." He grinned. "I'll need new helpers."

"Even if you decide to change Sugarland into a mini funnel cake paradise?" she teased.

"Especially if I do."

They stood across from each other at her car. Bess held the keys tight in her fist and had already used the remote to unlock the driver's door. Yet she lingered, not getting in right away, though by now the ticking of passing time had become as noticeable to her as the beat of her heart.

"We'll have to do this again. Coffee, I mean." Eddie shoved his hands deep into his khakis, a stance Bess recognized from when he was younger. Now, though, even with hunched shoulders, he towered over her.

"Yes. It was nice."

"And think about Just A Bite," he said, backing up without looking away. "You promised."

Bess cringed, waiting for him to trip and go sprawling, but Eddie managed to get all the way to the curb of the concrete island and the forest of parking meters without incident.

"I'll think about it."

"Great!" He grinned and took one hand from his pocket to give her a salute. "See you!"

He didn't go any farther, just stood there with one hand on a parking meter, watching her pull out. He waved as she started to drive away. Bess waved back.

She liked Eddie. Always had. She liked talking with him even more now that, as adults, they weren't caught up in the awkward melodrama of teenage crushes and working together. Becoming Eddie's partner might bring all that back. On the other hand, as much as they'd remained the same, they'd both also changed. A lot. She'd said she'd think about it, that was all, and that's what she did all the way back to the house.

She'd had a good time with Eddie, but by the time she pulled into the carport, her entire world had once again become Nick. Every breath, each pulse, every step took her closer to him. By the time she got to the door she could already taste and feel him, and she wondered how she'd ever managed to spend even one minute without him next to her.

Chapter 16

Then

"I know he got home from work hours ago." Bess didn't wait for Matty to try to cover for his brother. "Matt. Please. I need to talk to him."

Andy wouldn't be expecting Bess to call him tonight. They usually phoned each other Mondays at ten, unless she was working late. Andy didn't like her to call after ten, saying he had to go to bed in order to be up on time for work.

He'd snagged a final internship in a comfy law office ten minutes from his house. He worked nine to five and had an hour lunch, when one of the partners usually treated him at a nice restaurant, and they'd already started talking about finding him a permanent position when he officially graduated at the end of the summer. It was as different from her job at the Sugarland, and would be as different from her future career in social work, as mushrooms from Mozart.

"Bess..." Matty sighed. He had been in her grade at school,

though they'd never really hung out much until she started dating Andy. "He's in the shower."

Bess paused. At nine o'clock on a Friday night, chances were good Andy wasn't in the shower getting ready for bed. "Did he tell you not to let me talk to him?"

Matty made an uncomfortable noise.

"Matty? Did Andy tell you he didn't want to talk to me if I called?" The need to know burned inside her.

Something shuffled on Matty's end of the phone. "He's my brother, Bess."

"So that gives you an excuse to be as shitty to me as he is?" She should've felt like a bitch for saying it, but Matty sounded guilty, not offended.

"I'm sorry." His voice dipped low. "He really is in the shower."

"Getting ready to go out?"

"Yeah, I guess so. It's not like he runs his agenda past me for approval," Matty said. "He goes out a lot. I don't always know who he's with."

"Sometimes you do," Bess muttered. She looked into the living room, where her aunt Jamie and uncle Dennis were busy laying out a new game of Monopoly. They'd just arrived for their week's vacation and always played a marathon game. Bess turned her back and twirled the phone cord around her finger. "Is he out of the shower yet?"

Matty sighed again. "Yeah. Let me get him."

"Thanks."

Matty said nothing, but Bess heard the clatter of the phone, more shuffling, and a muffled, "Here. I'm fucking sick of being your messenger boy, Andy."

"Fuck you, Matty."

"You, too, bro. You, too."

Usually Bess would have smiled at the banter between

brothers, something so foreign to her as an only child. Tonight she only stared hard at the linoleum, counting the flowers in the pattern while she waited for Andy to get on the phone.

"Yeah? What's up?"

"Hi. It's me."

"Yeah. I know it's you. What's up?" Andy sounded distant and distracted.

"I miss you." Bess, mindful of the house always full of people, pulled the phone with her into the small broom closet. She sank onto the floor with her back to the door, which didn't close all the way because of the cord, and pulled her knees to her chest. "I miss you, Andy, that's all."

"You just talked to me a few days ago."

Bess tried to keep her voice light. "Yeah, I know, but I still miss you. Isn't that okay?"

"Sure." She could picture his shrug and his frown. He was probably looking in the mirror, brushing his hair. Flexing his biceps. Typical Andy.

"Where are you going?"

"Out."

Don't ask with who. Don't ask him. Don't be the jealous girlfriend he accuses you of being.

"With who?"

"Some of the guys. Dan. Joe."

She'd never met either of them. "From work?"

"Yeah."

"I'm going out, too." Bess gnawed her cheek but stopped when it stung. She put her fingertips to the spot and they came away bloody. "To a party."

Andy's voice sounded faraway, then got closer, and she imagined him putting aside the phone to pull a shirt over his head. "Have fun."

"Yeah, this guy…Nick. He invited me."

"Have a good time." More muffled shuffling. She heard the clatter of something metal. His watch, maybe. "Bess, I gotta go. The guys are waiting for me."

"But I'll see you next week, for the concert, right? I got the weekend off." Andy had scored tickets to see Fast Fashion at the Hershey Stadium. It was supposed to be one of the biggest shows of the summer.

"Yeah, about that…"

Bess's stomach sunk. Laughter reached her as her aunt and uncle and the couple who'd joined them for the week started mixing drinks and serving food. They were having a party of their own.

"What about it?" It couldn't be good.

"I don't have a ticket for you."

"What?"

"I don't have a ticket for you," Andy repeated. It had been bad enough the first time. Hearing it a second twisted her stomach into knots.

"What do you mean you don't have a ticket for me? We talked about it. I got the weekend off—"

"I could only get five tickets, Bess." Andy sounded annoyed, but not defensive. "You said you weren't sure about getting the time off. I asked some people from work to go."

Bess chewed on her answer instead of her cheek before she spoke. "Who?"

"Dan. Joe. Lisa. With Matt and me, that's five."

The name, the same as in the letters, stabbed her in the stomach. "Who's Lisa?"

"We all work together. She likes Fast Fashion. I told her she could come along."

Bess chewed her words harder this time, tattering them.

"So...what you're saying to me is that you're going to take some girl from work instead of me? To a concert we've been talking about all summer long? You're going to take some girl you just met, instead of me. Your girlfriend."

"I knew you'd be like that."

"Like what? Upset?" She spat the words like gristle.

"Why do you have to be like that?" Andy sounded disgusted. "Shit, Bess. It's just a fucking concert."

"Forget it." She got to her feet. The air in the closet was stifling, but she felt cold. "Never mind, Andy. I've got to get to my party."

He sounded relieved she was dropping it, not concerned. "We'll see Fast Fashion another time—"

"Don't." It was all she could manage to say through the ribbon drawing tighter and tighter around her throat.

"Be careful at that party. You know you're not a big drinker."

Bess said nothing.

"I'll call you tomorrow, okay?"

"Tomorrow isn't Monday, Andy."

He gave a long-suffering sigh. "Goodbye."

He hung up.

"I miss you, Andy," Bess said again, and closed her eyes against a spate of tears. Maybe if she kept saying it, it would be true.

Chapter 17

Now

*B*ess leaned into the spray of hot water and let it pound her back and shoulders. Eyes closed, she put a hand on the shower wall and sighed. Most every part of her ached, not just her shoulders, but though it was the sort of tenderness a massage might have alleviated, the thought of someone touching her wasn't appealing at the moment.

As infants born only eleven months apart, her boys had clung to her like limpets. Connor had still been nursing right up until a few weeks before Robbie was born. Bess had had nightmares about tandem nursing or forcing Connor to start taking a bottle, but he had given up the breast on his own and started drinking from a cup. He'd been a little jealous when Robbie came and took his place on Mama's lap, though, and Bess had lost track of the hours she'd spent on the couch watching hour after hour of daytime television while one baby nursed and the other demanded her attention.

Andy hadn't understood what she meant when she'd told him she was "touched out." He'd come home from work expecting the house to be clean, the children fed and put to sleep, and a warm and willing wife lounging naked in their bed. He didn't understand how Bess could be so tired from doing "nothing" all day long, or why the thought of sex had lost its appeal for a woman who'd once had a libido to rival his own. The days had long passed since caring for babies had sapped Bess of her desire to be touched, but the past week had seen a small revival of it.

It was more than the sex. Fucking Nick was even better than it had been before. She was more confident now, knew her body better, had no trouble telling him what she liked and how to do it. They'd always had fun together, but it had been tempered by a certain aloofness from both of them. Neither had been willing to admit what they were doing was any more than a casual, summer thing.

It was different now.

She couldn't begin to imagine how he must feel, being brought back from *the gray,* as he called it. It was hard enough for her to accept without hurting her brain, and it hadn't happened to her. For the most part they spoke of his time away as if he'd been on a trip. Or in a coma. Neither of which would explain how he could look exactly the way he always had, or why his heart didn't beat or why he didn't breathe. Why he didn't sleep.

Bess couldn't imagine what it must be like for him, so when he needed her body, she gave it to him. When he wanted her to sleep next to him tangled limb to limb, she allowed it even though she hated to be touched while she slept. When he asked her to tell him how much she'd missed him, she told him. When he turned off the television or put aside the newspapers so she could focus on him and he could ignore the changes the world had made, she did that, too.

She gave him what he wanted because she couldn't imagine how it would feel to have died and returned, and because giving in to him was easier than having him tell her how it felt.

The water hadn't yet run cold when she decided to get out, but she knew if she stayed in much longer Nick would come looking for her. Bess turned off the spray and stepped out, dried off and pulled on her lightweight silk robe. Andy had brought it back from Japan, teasing her about being his geisha. Now the silk clung to her damp body as she tied the belt at her waist. At the sink she brushed her teeth and flossed, then spread a thin layer of expensive face cream over her skin. She looked at the fine lines around her eyes. Andy called them crow's-feet, but Bess preferred to think of them as laugh lines. At least she'd had a life filled with enough laughter to line her face.

"Hey, baby." Nick reached for her when she came into the living room, where he was dealing out a game of solitaire. He settled her onto his lap and slid a hand between her thighs, frowning when she tensed. "What's up?"

The pet name still sounded odd coming from him, even as his casual affection thrilled her. Bess kissed him, then ducked her head against his shoulder. "Nothing. Just a little sore."

Nick's fingers gentled against her thigh. "From me?"

Bess rubbed a fingertip over the letters on the front of his T-shirt. "Don't worry about it."

He cupped his hand between her legs. "You're so hot down here." He didn't move his fingers, though, just held her. "I'm sorry if I hurt you."

Bess laughed. "We've just been having a lot of sex, that's all. I'll be okay." She sat up to look at him, and when he kissed her that fact, like the pet name, sent a chill of pleasure through her. "I do have to run out to the store, though. Get some things."

Cranberry tablets, for one, to fend off any potential problems from all the action. Food and some real clothes for Nick, for another. Essentials. She'd been here for two weeks and aside from a few quick trips into town, hadn't been shopping.

Nick frowned. "Yeah. I guess you do."

She cupped his cheek and turned his face to look at her. "I'll bring back whatever you want. What do you need?"

Nick nudged her to get off his lap, leaving her in the chair while he got up to look out the sliding-glass door to the deck. "You could get me some cigarettes."

He didn't eat or drink or breathe, but he could smoke? "Anything else?"

His too-casual shrug told her more than he probably wanted to. "Couple of long-sleeved T-shirts. Boxers. Pair of sweats."

"Okay." Bess went to him and put her arms around his waist to rest her cheek on his back. They stayed that way for a few minutes until he turned to hug her.

"Don't be long," he said gruffly, and Bess smiled despite herself, her face hidden against his chest.

It used to be that all she wanted was to know Nick wanted her. They were still feeling their way, and neither had spoken about what would happen next week when her boys came to stay, but there was no doubt in Bess's mind that Nick wanted her. He hadn't said he loved her. She hadn't said it, either.

She tipped her face for a kiss, which he gave, then went to the bedroom to dress. She pulled on panties and a bra, then a flowing summer dress and matching cardigan, and slipped her feet into sandals. Grabbing her sunglasses and keys along with her purse, she kissed Nick goodbye and went downstairs to the carport.

She hadn't asked him to come with her, and he didn't ask to go. Bess thought, like his avoidance of TV and newspapers, it might be that Nick didn't want to see the changes in the town. Or maybe he didn't want to run into anyone who might recognize him, anyone to whom he'd have to explain his miraculous return.

Taking Maplewood Street to Route 1, Bess thought about Nick's family. She didn't know much, just that he'd been raised mostly by an aunt and uncle who lived in Dewey Beach. She'd never met them. Nick had barely talked about them, but chances were good they still lived there. But what purpose would it serve them to see him?

Could they even see him?

Bess pulled into the vast parking lot of the huge grocery mart but didn't get out of the car. A sudden, racking set of chills swept over her and she shuddered. Though it was the first week of June, she turned the heat on high and clenched her jaw to stop the clattering of her teeth. Her stomach churned, and she swallowed hard, over and over, to force back a gag.

Her separation from Andy, even though it had been her choice…coming back to the beach house…had it all triggered some sort of breakdown? She'd spent so many years remembering Nick Hamilton, she'd manufactured him, along with an explanation about why he hadn't come to her the way he'd promised. Her life had been turned upside down. Was she now grasping at anything to make it somehow better?

Her teeth stopped chattering under the force of dry, heated air, but gooseflesh still pimpled her arms and thighs. Bess slid up the hem of her dress. A paling bruise on one knee could have come from an encounter with a coffee table, not from giving Nick head on the kitchen floor. The twin dark circles on the inside of her thigh could have been mosquito bites, scratched open, and not the prints of his fingers. She pressed herself through her panties. There was no pretending away the ache there, from being so thoroughly, deliriously, incredulously, marvelously and constantly fucked.

Bess moaned and dropped her skirt back to her knees. She gripped the steering wheel with both hands. Sweat dripped down her cheeks, though she still felt chilled, and she turned off the heat. Around her in the parking lot, people in T-shirts and shorts went to and fro with their packages. The sun shone. Summer.

It was summer, and Bess had lost her mind.

She fumbled in her purse for a package of mints to take away the sour taste on her tongue. She sucked one slowly. The air in the car was too hot now, and she cracked open her window. From outside, the normal, common sounds of cart wheels squeaking, traffic and conversation settled her stomach better than the mint. Bess took another, crunching it. She breathed deeply.

Just because she didn't know if anyone else could see Nick didn't mean he existed only in her mind. She'd touched him, felt him, smelled and tasted him. He was real. How he was real was a question for which she had no answer, but the explanation could not be that she was insane.

She'd never forgotten him, but neither had she spent the past twenty years pining for him. Her life with Andy hadn't been all trials and tribulations. She'd married him with the intent of loving him forever. They'd had two sons who would bind them together forever even if their marriage ended. Bess took another slow, deep breath. Her marriage *was* ending, but that didn't make her crazy, either.

She forced herself out of the car. The cooler air outside helped settle her, too. She had to catch the hem of her dress to keep it from flipping up in a sudden breeze, and that simple touch of air on her bare legs further convinced her of her sanity.

Inside the superstore Bess stacked up purchases. New beach towels, soap, shampoo, laundry detergent. A folding beach chair with backpack straps. A kite. Cigarettes for Nick, along with clothes. A new pair of flip-flops for herself. Groceries.

The bill was higher than she'd expected, but even in the superstore, prices were higher at the beach. She paid with her credit card, thinking about the irony of buying her lover clothes with her husband's money, but then not caring. After all, Andy paid for his lover's trip to Japan, and other things, too. And in a few months, Bess would be paying all her own bills. She had money from her grandparents and parents, but she'd have to get a job, too.

Somehow, that final thought convinced her more than anything else had that she wasn't losing her mind. How could she be crazy when she was so practical?

Nick was real. The question wasn't why, for that she could guess pretty well. She'd come back to the beach house, and so had he. They were tied together, even after all this time. Unfinished business. Or something else. Some emotion she didn't want to admit. Something stronger than lust.

The question wasn't why, but how. For the first time since Nick had come out of the water to kiss her, she thought she might be ready to think about how it had happened.

She'd never been inside Bethany Magick, but the sign caught her attention on the way home. Bess pulled into one of the narrow parking spaces in front of the shop. The outside was painted red and purple, with gilt-edge windows and doorway. Glass witches' balls hung in the windows above displays of candles, tarot cards and other mystical paraphernalia. Books, too, and that was what she was interested in.

Inside, the shop smelled like rosemary, and Bess took a deep, long whiff. Small pots of it grew along a sunny windowsill behind the cash register. She wondered if she could grow some in her living room.

"It's rosemary," said a voice from behind Bess. "For remembrance."

Bess turned to see a woman about her own age. She didn't wear the expected flowing gypsy skirts or dangling earrings, but rather a pair of faded, comfortable-looking jeans and black flip-flops, along with a form-fitting T-shirt with a skull on the front. The skull's eyes were hearts outlined in glittering rhinestones.

"Yes," Bess said. "It's one of my favorite smells."

The woman beamed. "I'm Alicia Morris. Have you been to Bethany Magick before?"

"Hi. Bess Walsh, and no." She glanced around. "Is this your store?"

"Yep." Alicia smiled proudly and moved behind the counter. "Look around. If you have any questions, let me know."

"Thanks." Bess had plenty of questions, but she wasn't quite sure how to ask them. "I'm just browsing right now."

"Sure. Go ahead."

Bess had no idea what she was even looking at, much less what she should be seeking for, but she made a slow circuit of the shop. Comprised of two rooms with an open arch between them, Bethany Magick had something, it seemed, for every taste. Close to the front of the shop and the cash register were shelves holding Magic 8 Balls, Ouija boards and inexpensive novelty items like unicorn-shaped candles, plastic gnomes and boy wizard glasses.

"The good stuff's in the other room," said Alicia from behind the novel she was reading. "I keep that stuff around for the looky-loos and tourists. But you're not either, are you?"

Bess put down the feather-topped pen she'd been examining. "You can tell?"

Alicia grinned. "I had a fifty-fifty chance of being right, didn't I? I couldn't lose. If you really are a local you'll be glad I didn't confuse you with one of those dad-gum tourists, and if you're a vacationer you'll be flattered I think you're a townie."

Bess laughed. "I'm sort of both, actually. I used to live here during the summers years ago, and now I have my grandparents' old house, but I haven't been back in about twenty years."

"Twenty's a nice round number." Alicia's eyes sharpened with interest. "Which house, if you don't mind my asking? By *old* you must not mean one of those mondo-mansions going up all over."

"No. It's on Maplewood. The one with the wraparound deck. Gray shingled siding. There's a huge new house just behind it, so you can't really see it from the street anymore."

"I think I know which one you mean. You can see it from the beach."

"Yes." Bess touched the fuzzy, brightly colored hair on a small plastic troll. It was cute, but wouldn't help her. "So what do you mean by the good stuff?"

"Let me show you." Alicia put down her book, a romance by the look of the cover, and led Bess through the archway. The beaded curtain clicked like whispers as they brushed through it.

This room was dimmer and lit by fiber-optic lights set into the ceiling. Shelves and small tables draped with velvet held an array of interesting items. Sacks of smooth stones, packs of cards, gleaming pendants on chains.

Books filled one wall floor to ceiling, and a small waterfall splashed and tinkled in the corner. A curtained doorway led to another room not visible from the front.

"I do readings back there." Alicia pointed. "Tarot, palm, runes. By appointment only, though, since I can't leave the shop unattended."

"Of course not." Bess had heard of tarot and palm readings, but not runes. She lifted a sack of stones from one of the tables. "Runes?"

"Runes are a system of divination. Like tarot cards." Alicia demonstrated, shaking out a number of small, smooth stones from a velvet bag onto the table. She lifted one, marked with what looked like an upper-case *P.* "This is the Wynn rune. Usually symbolizes joy or luck, or something being resolved happily." She gazed at Bess evenly. "Ring any bells?"

Bess laughed, self-conscious. "I'm not sure. I'm in the midst of a divorce, actually. That doesn't seem to fit."

Alicia rubbed the rune between her fingers and studied her. "Are you sure?"

Bess laughed again. "It's a situation being resolved, anyway."

The woman grinned and pulled another rune from the bag, holding it up. "Wyrd."

"What's that one mean?"

"Fate. Destiny. An unknown outcome." Alicia clinked the stones together in her palm.

Bess swallowed hard. "That's..."

"Incredible?" Alicia shook her head and slipped the runes back into their small velvet bag. "You should have me read for you sometime. Really read for you. I'll give you the local discount."

It was Bess's turn to grin. "Really? Thanks."

Alicia tipped her head to study her for so long it should have become uncomfortable, but Bess didn't feel that way. "What did you come in here for?" she asked at last.

"I'd never been in. It looked interesting. And," Bess admitted, with a smile designed to downplay her answer, "I thought I might like to learn about…spirits."

"Spirits?" Alicia's smile again thinned, but didn't disappear. "Why?"

Bess stumbled on her answer to the blunt question. "I'm interested?"

The shopkeeper nodded and went to the bookshelves, where she pulled out a thick hardcover volume. "*The Other Side* is a good reference source without being too heavy."

"Ghost stories?" Bess laughed awkwardly as she took the book.

"Some. More like encounters. Theories. Experiences of trained mediums, trying to explain why some people can't seem to leave this plane."

Bess flipped through a few pages. "What about those who…come back?"

She looked up when Alicia didn't answer. The other woman stared, mouth slightly pursed. "Come back?"

Bess shrugged hastily. "Do they ever come back?"

"Do you mean a near-death experience? Tunnel of white light, that sort of thing?"

"No. I mean someone who's died but their spirit doesn't come back right away. Maybe not for a long time." Bess closed the book but grasped it tightly.

"I'm not an expert on spirits," Alicia said thoughtfully, "but I'm sure there are accounts of spiritual manifestations taking place over long periods of time that would make it seem like the spirit went away, only to return. But I'm not sure if that's what you mean."

"Oh, I don't really mean anything." Bess laughed and held the book to her chest. "I'll take this one. Do you have anything else?"

Alicia tapped a few volumes, then pulled down one more. She didn't hand it to Bess right away. "Is the spirit malevolent?"

"Malevolent? Oh, no! Oh, wow. No." Bess shook her head vehemently. "I'm just interested—I don't actually, you know...*have* a spirit."

Alicia didn't laugh, though her faint smile remained. She handed Bess the book, called *Beyond the Grave.* "You might still find this one interesting."

The cold shudder from earlier crept down Bess's spine, but she took the volume. "What's it about?"

"Harmful spirits." Alicia smiled then, a real smile, and the tension eased. "Read it with the lights on."

"Thanks." Clutching both books, Bess followed Alicia to the cash register. "Are you a trained medium?"

Alicia looked surprised as she rang up the purchases. "Me?"

"You said that *The Other Side* had experiences from trained mediums in it. I didn't know you could train to be a medium."

Alicia laughed and bagged the books in a shimmery silver sack, tucking Bess's receipt inside. "You can train to be anything, I'm sure. But, no. Not exactly. I've been practicing Wicca for about fifteen years now, and I've had training in that."

"You're a witch?" The word sounded funny.

"Yep." Alicia reached behind her to break off a long twig of rosemary from one of the pots. She sniffed it, eyes closed, then smiled as she handed it to Bess. "Here. Rosemary. For—"

"Remembrance," Bess finished with her. "I didn't forget." They both laughed.

"Come back again. Get that reading."

"I will," Bess promised as she took her bag and headed back outside.

The air had cooled considerably since she'd entered the shop. Clouds now danced across the sun, not all of them dark, but enough to turn the sky from blue to gray.

Gray.

Bess put her bag in the car and drove home faster than she knew was safe, but even so the first boom of thunder was already cracking overhead when she pulled into the carport. Rain lashed the earth a moment later, and she sat in her car for a minute after keying off the ignition, just watching the sheets of water turn the sand to mud.

The wind whipped at her dress as she opened the trunk and pulled out bag after bag, running to put them safely in the small hallway at the bottom of the stairs. Only when she'd unloaded everything did she go inside herself, locking the door behind her and grabbing as many sacks as she could carry. She dropped them at the top of the stairs, which emptied directly into the living room, but she didn't bother going back for the rest.

"Nick?"

There was no answer but the rain on the deck outside, and the rumble of thunder. She went to the sliding doors and pressed her face to the glass. Rain had already sliced the beach and churned the waves. An abandoned umbrella tumbled end over end and hit the water. She watched it move farther out, pulled by the waves, before she turned to the living room again.

"Nick? Where are you?"

Stay calm.

"I'm sorry I was so long. I had to get a lot of things."

He wasn't in the kitchen, which she could see from where she stood. He wasn't downstairs in the small laundry room or the smaller bedroom that had once been hers. That left the three upstairs bedrooms.

"Nick! This isn't funny!"

But would she laugh if he popped out from a closet, shouting "Boo!"? Yes, she would, if only because it meant he was still there. Bess called his name again, her voice hoarse and drowned out by the rain.

She flung open the door to the smallest of the upstairs bedrooms. Two sets of bunk beds, one either side of the window, made a narrow path and reminded her of summer-camp cabins. The closet door hung open, the space inside empty.

"Nick!"

The second room had a double bed and full-size futon. Nick wasn't in either one of them. Not in the closet there, either, though when she flung the door open her heart stopped in preparation for the scare. It started beating reluctantly when she opened the door to the bathroom the bedrooms shared. The room was only big enough for the tub and shower, sink and toilet, and had no place to hide. She pulled back the shower curtain, getting ready to scream. No Nick.

That left her bedroom and its attached bath. She wanted to see him so badly that at first, she did. The glare of lightning lit the rumpled mess of her bed, making her believe the pillows and blankets were a body. She was already flipping on the light switch and striding to the bed before her eyes adjusted and she saw the truth.

Bess let out a low, sobbing breath and then stood straighter. She shook herself. Bathroom. He had to be in the bathroom. Except he wasn't. He wasn't anywhere, and as she went back to stand in the middle of the living room, Bess listened to the silence even the storm couldn't deafen.

Nick wasn't there.

Chapter 18

Then

"*W*ant a drink?"

Bess had been scanning the room for the sight of Nick, but the hand holding out a plastic cup aslosh with beer didn't belong to him. She shook her head. The boy offering her the beer shook his head, too, and handed the cup to the girl who came in behind her. Turning back to the keg on the floor just inside the door, he pumped the handle up and down and held the small black hose over another cup.

Bess moved away from the door to make room for more people coming in. Nick's apartment wasn't very big, and it didn't take many guests for it to feel crowded. Even so, though she knew he had to be here, she didn't see him.

The music thumped, loud enough to make speech worthless. She stood at the short end of a rectangular living room. Two couches, a desk and a weight bench lined the walls. Directly in front of her was an opening through which she could see a table with chairs, and directly behind that, the open door to a small bathroom. She presumed the kitchen was that way, too.

"Bess!" Brian, giggling, blundered away from a group of girls playing quarters, and grabbed her hand. "Hey, honey! You made it! I told Nick you'd come."

"He asked?" Bess let Brian drag her toward the coffee table, around which a bunch of people sat watching a girl and a boy with their hands on the planchette of an Ouija board.

"You're pushing it," the girl complained, and took her hands away, while her partner protested he wasn't.

"They're fucking with the spirit world," Brian said. "Come sit with me on the couch! Don't you need a drink? Hey, someone get Bess a drink!"

"I'll get my own drink." She tugged herself from Brian's octopus grasp. Fortunately, his attention span seemed pretty limited at the moment, and she had no problem getting away.

She found Nick in the kitchen, holding court for a bevy of giggling girls with bikini-top tans and drinks in their hands. He looked up when she came in, and raised his bottle toward her.

"Hey! You made it!" He didn't hop down from the counter, but pointed toward the fridge. "I've got soda in there, if you want."

She ought to have been pleased he knew her that well, but all at once Bess didn't want to be so predictable. So good. She looked at the bottles of vodka, rum and tequila on the counter. Usually these parties were BBTS—bring booze to share. She'd picked up a box of buttered crackers on the way over, more to make sure she had something in her stomach than anything. She put the box on the table among the detritus of chip bags and empty cups, and helped herself to a can of cola, a cup and a healthy shot of rum.

She looked up before she took the first sip, to find Nick watching her. His dark eyes gleamed as he grinned and tipped his beer toward her in a silent toast over the heads of his admirers. Bess raised her cup to him and drank.

Her eyes watered and her throat burned, but the second sip went down much smoother. The taste of it wasn't so great, especially not mixed with store-brand diet cola, but though she wasn't much of a drinker herself, Bess had been around plenty of people who were. The more she drank, the better it would taste.

There was no place for her get close to Nick, but somehow that didn't matter. The look he'd given her had told her that. She was here; that was what mattered. Taking her drink, Bess left the kitchen and went back to the living room.

The crowd was still gathered around the Ouija board. The planchette moved faster than it had before, so fast Bess didn't see how anyone could believe it was being moved by spirits. She couldn't see what it was spelling out, but from the awed looks it must have been something interesting.

"I'm telling you," Brian said. "They are fucking with the spirits. That is not good, Bess. Not good."

"You're drunk." She sipped more rum and coke.

"Honey, yes I am!" He snapped his fingers in the air and burst into a flurry of giggles, then tried to kiss her.

Bess turned her head at the last minute, so his mouth landed on her cheek, but she did suffer his full-body hug without trying to get away. Brian snuggled against her. After a minute, his mouth moved along her neck, though, and she jerked back.

"Brian!" She had to fight not to laugh; he'd never stop if she did that. "Jesus, I'm your boss! And a girl!"

"I know, I know." Brian looked unapologetic. "But you're just so yummy, honey, and nobody else here is as accommodating."

"That's a big word. I'm surprised you can say in your intoxicated state."

"Oh, ho, ho!" Brian wagged a finger. "Look who's talking?"

"Dude. Are you hitting on Bess?" Nick's amused voice slipped straight to Bess's gut, and lower. "Don't you know she sort of has a boyfriend?"

Brian snorted, but backed off. "That asshole?"

"Is he?" Nick and Brian both turned to look at her.

Bess shrugged, but said nothing.

"Interesting answer," Nick murmured.

Brian, for once, seemed without words. He looked back and forth between the two of them, shook his head and moved off toward the kitchen.

Bess turned to Nick. Tonight he didn't wear a ball cap or a bandanna. His hair fell slightly forward over one eye and lay in shaggy feathers over his ears and the back of his neck. Bess wanted to run her hands through it.

"Nicky! Come play!" Missy had shown up, sans Ryan, and was already pulling Nick toward the other side of the room, where a group of boys and girls sat in a small circle. "Truth or Dare, c'mon!"

"C'mon." Nick grabbed Bess's hand and pulled her along, too.

They all sat down, the circle widening to fit them. By now the edges of Bess's vision were pleasantly blurred, but the warmth in the pit of her stomach came from Nick's fingers linked with hers more than the booze. He didn't let go of her hand even when they sat and someone handed him a plastic cup of beer. Then he squeezed her fingers once, twice, and let go, but they were sitting hip to hip and thigh to thigh, which was almost as good as him holding her hand. The game was already in progress when they sat. Someone had put an empty bottle in the center of the circle.

"It's Spin the Truth or Dare," Nick leaned in to say into her ear. "If the bottle lands on you, you get to pick one or the other."

Bess nodded, half disappointed it wasn't simply Spin the Bottle. When it was her turn, she picked truth and had to tell everyone how old she was when she lost her virginity. Eighteen, an easy answer. When she spun, it landed on Missy, who picked dare. Figuring it was a no-brainer, Bess dared Missy to flash her boobs, which she did before Bess even finished the question. The game got rowdier and rowdier as it went on, as those sorts of things usually did. Someone dared a girl named Jenny to kiss Bess on the mouth, which they did to the accompaniment of hoots and shouts.

Bess, laughing, excused herself when they'd finished. She needed to use the bathroom and get another drink, though she planned to have straight soda this time. She wasn't drunk and didn't want to be. Even so, giddiness swept over her as she washed her hands at the bathroom sink.

Why had she been so worried about coming to Nick's party? It was fun, that was all. Just fun. Andy went out and had fun. Lots of fun. Why shouldn't she go out, too? It was summer fuhgodsakes. Didn't she deserve a little—

"Fun," Bess said to her reflection.

She was a little drunker than she thought. Sort of. The thought made her laugh.

When she came out of the bathroom, the people fucking with the spirit world had abandoned the Ouija board and joined the other circle. Bess stood in the doorway for a minute, watching, but instead of going back, took a seat by the abandoned board.

"Have you tried it?" a girl with long black hair tied in a high ponytail asked from her spot on the couch. "The Ouija?"

"No. You?"

The girl shook her head. "No."

"Hey, Alicia." Nick waved a hand at the girl, who waved back at him as he sat at the coffee table. "Do it with me, Bess."

"Oh, I don't know." But she was already sitting, so she put her drink to one side and placed her hands on the plastic planchette.

Their fingertips touched. Bess licked her lower lip at the imagined tingle she got from touching him. It was imagined, wasn't it? People didn't tingle in real life. Did they?

"Do you know how to do this?" she asked Nick.

"Nope." He grinned at her and leaned forward a little to look down at the board. "Is anyone here?"

"Don't you have to have a quiet place, or light a candle or something?" The girl he'd called Alicia leaned forward, too.

"People were doing it before." Bess blinked and lifted her fingers for a second before putting them down again. Definitely a tingle.

"*You* ask it something." Nick lifted his chin to her. "Make it work."

"Is anyone there?" Bess asked.

The planchette slid to YES.

"Holy shit, that's freaky." Alicia scooted back and put her feet up on the couch, as if something might reach out from underneath and grab her.

Nick didn't seem perturbed. He grinned. "Ask it something else."

"What's your name?" The alcohol was beginning to wear off, leaving Bess owl-eyed and sensitive to sound.

The planchette moved without hesitation. "C–A–R–E. Care?"

YES

"Is that your name?"

YES

"Where are you, Care?" Bess glanced at Nick, who stared at the Ouija board.

I AM A GHOST

"Shit," cried Alicia. "Seriously, that's freaking me out! Are you pushing it?"

"Not me." Nick looked at Bess.

"Not me, either."

I AM A GHOST

I AM A GHOST

I AM A GHOST

The planchette moved faster now, sliding easily from one letter to the next without stopping, a cycle of words. Then it stopped in the center of the board. Bess noticed she was breathing hard. Nick, too.

"Are you a good ghost?" The line from *The Wizard of Oz* rose in Bess's mind, but this wasn't Glinda talking to Dorothy.

The pointer spun slowly, twisting their hands with it.

YES

"He didn't seem so sure." Nick looked at Bess. "Maybe he's a bad boy."

The planchette moved so quickly Bess's fingertips nearly slipped off.

NICK

"What about him?" Bess asked.

BAD BOY

Nick laughed. After a minute, so did Bess, though ruefully. "You're doing it, Nick. You're moving it."

NO

I AM A GHOST

She knew before the pointer stopped moving what it had said. "And Nick's a bad boy?"

YES

BUT U LIKE IT

Nick laughed again, and so did Alicia, but Bess only smiled self-consciously.

"How much does Bess like me?"

ALL

"All what?" Bess asked, before she could stop herself.

ALLOT

"He might be a good ghost, but he's not a good speller." Alicia still watched the proceedings avidly, though she hadn't put down her feet.

BAD BOY

"You're a bad boy?" Bess watched Nick watch the pointer move.

WAS

"He's a ghost, now," Nick pointed out in a low voice.

YES

They all laughed.

"How'd you die, dude?" Nick asked.

The pointer didn't move. A small vibration rumbled through it, as though it were trying to skid across the board, but it stayed still. After the way it had fairly flown along the curved alphabet to spell out its answers before, this was the same as silence.

"Awkward," Nick said.

"Maybe that was a rude question." Bess looked at him.

YES

She gazed at the board. "Do you have anything to say to us, Care?"

MISTAKE

Nothing more. "You made a mistake?"

NO

"One of us made a mistake?"

WILL MAKE

Bess looked at Nick. He looked at her. She had to swallow slowly before she asked the next question. "Which one of us?"

The pointer spun to her, then immediately to Nick.

"Okay, this is just too freaking weird." Alicia got off the couch. "Later, guys."

A burst of laughter rumbled up from the group still playing with the bottle. The thump of the music reverberated. Bess and Nick stared at each other.

BAD BOY

MISTAKE

I AM A GHOST

"Yes," Bess murmured when the planchette stopped. "We know."

"Does Bess want to be with me?" Nick asked.

Bess held her breath.

YES

Nick smiled. "Is that her mistake?"

NO

It was a stupid, silly parlor game, and she'd been drinking, but the sight of those two letters seemed more important than logic or anything else.

"Should Bess break up with her sort of boyfriend?"

MISTAKE

"It's a mistake for her to break up with him?" Nick didn't look away from Bess's eyes. "Or to stay with him?"

Bess took her hands off the planchette. "This is silly."

Nick hadn't taken his hands away. He looked at the pointer. "Don't you want to know what the spirits say?"

"No." She got up on shaking legs. "This is dumb."

Nick stood up, too. "Hey, don't be upset."

But suddenly, she was. Tears fought for freedom and won, slipping down her cheeks to paint her lips with bitterness. Bess pulled away from Nick, away from the party. Away from everything.

She fled outside. On the porch, more people hung out, drinking and smoking. They blocked the steps to the street, but she pushed through them, not caring if she was being rude.

Her feet hit the sidewalk, then the street. She'd forgotten about her bike, tied around the side of the house Nick had the bottom half of. She clenched her fists and swiped away tears, heading back for it.

He found her there, fumbling with her lock. "Bess."

She stiffened and stopped trying to turn the small, stubborn dials to the correct combination. "It's just a game."

Nick moved closer. Bess turned, but the house met her back and he was in front of her. She had no place to go.

"I didn't mean to make you upset." He looked as if he wanted to touch her shoulder, but didn't.

Bess took a deep breath. "It's not you. It's me."

"I've heard that before." His grin tried to tempt her into answering.

More tears threatened. She wanted to blame the booze, but it was more than that. It was Andy. And Nick. All of it. Everything.

"I just don't understand," she said, her vision blurring again, "why, if I love him, all I can think about is you?"

Once said it was too late to take back the words. She didn't want to. Truth lifted the weight from her shoulders.

Nick said nothing.

Bess looked away. She should have known it. He wanted

what he couldn't have, and when she told him the truth, he didn't want it anymore.

It was wrong to want this. Bess stood on the edge of a cliff and stared into the murky waters of moral ambiguity, waiting for Nick to push her. He didn't.

So she jumped.

When she kissed him, she put her hands up to press his shoulders back against the house. He did nothing at first, just moved at her touch, but then one hand slid around to cup the back of her neck while the other went to her hip. She pinned him to the wall with her body. His mouth nudged hers open, but his tongue didn't slip inside. He pulled away, just a little, the slight pressure of their lips touching making an unbearable tickle. Bess thought he might speak, but the only whisper came from their mingled breath. She leaned forward and kissed him again. Her tongue darted into his mouth, stroking tentatively and then harder when he did the same.

Their mouths met, slanting, and parted, only to come together immediately. She breathed him in and held the scent and taste of him in her lungs. His body pushed against hers, her tight nipples and the heat between her legs. Heat throbbed through his jeans against her belly.

Nick was the one who broke it, pulling away to stare into her eyes. "This isn't a mistake, Bess."

"No," she said, surprised she could speak. "It's not a mistake."

Chapter 19

Now

*T*here was no way Bess could sleep in her bed, which still smelled of their lovemaking. She sought the overstuffed couch in the living room. The denim slipcover hid what had once been a floral-print sofa, and while it had done much for the room's decor, it made the cushions stiff and slippery and cold. She grabbed up a throw from the back of a chair and wrapped it around her.

Her eyes hurt from holding back tears, and so did her throat. She couldn't allow herself to weep, fearful she'd dissolve into hysteria and be unable to stop. Instead she bundled herself in the afghan her grandma had knit, and curled on her side to stare through the sliding-glass doors. The deck railing hid most of the beach from her, but she glimpsed whitecaps as the tide drew them higher up the sand. There'd be an undertow tonight, she was sure of it.

Bess had never been much of a swimmer, despite spending

every childhood summer at the beach. She liked to build castles or lie in the sand, though now the memory of all those sunburns had her compulsively checking every freckle and mole on her fair skin. She liked to pull her chair up to the ocean's edge and let the water tickle her feet while she lost herself in stories of other worlds. If the day grew hot enough she might go in for a brief dip to cool off, but she didn't really like to swim in the ocean.

Because once she'd almost drowned.

She didn't remember much about it, just that she'd been small. With Grammy holding one hand and her mom the other, little Bess had kicked and splashed, until a rogue wave had pulled her from their grasp and tumbled her, head over foot, beneath the water. She could recall the tug of the tide and the scrape of sand on her back and face as she rolled. She'd held her breath instinctively, and closed her eyes against the sting of salt. Her lungs had hurt within moments, worse than the scrapes on her knees and elbows. A rough slice of broken shell cut her hand as she scrabbled for something to hold on to.

Just before they pulled her out of the water, the pain had stopped. And she'd seen...

"The gray." Bess gave a start, the words on her lips tasting like blood from where she'd bitten her tongue.

They'd pulled her out of the water and she'd vomited up the sea, and until now she'd forgotten all about how the world had turned to gray. Until now. Bess sat up straighter, her heart pounding. The afghan tangled around her feet.

She smelled salt water and seaweed, and, blinking, turned to the doorway, where a dark figure stood silhouetted.

She heard the soft plink-plink of water dripping onto the hardwood floor. She heard the sound of her own breath. She heard the rush and roar of the ocean outside.

She opened her arms.

He knelt at her feet and buried his face in her lap. His shoulders heaved. His hair, soaking, wet her skirt, and his skin beneath her palms was hot and wet. He was naked. Bess ran her fingers down the individual bumps of Nick's spine, the sleek curve of his ribs. He'd always been lean, but now he seemed fragile, too.

He sobbed once and grabbed her thighs. The odor of the ocean overpowered everything else, his usual sensual smell of soap and cologne with a hint of smoke gone. Nick moaned low in his throat, and broke her heart once more.

"Don't leave me again." Each word sounded as if it tortured him. His fingers curled into the folds of her skirt.

Though he radiated heat like sun-baked sand, Bess gathered up the blanket and wrapped it around him, then eased herself onto the floor beside him. Nick buried his face against her neck. His wet hair tickled her cheek. Bess held him tightly, the two of them wrapped in the afghan, and wondered what to say to make all of this better.

"When you're gone, I think you won't come back."

Bess rubbed her cheek along his wet head. "I came back, Nick."

His arms tightened on her. His shoulders heaved a time or two more, but then he pulled away. His eyes flashed in the stripe of light from the window. She saw no tears.

"I had to go out," she said softly. She pushed his hair, drying now, off his forehead, and cupped his cheek.

She'd always imagined Nick as fearless. She'd been the one to doubt. The benefit of hindsight showed her he'd been as afraid as she had. Maybe more. Even so, seeing him this way disconcerted her.

"I know you did." Shaking off her touch, he sat with his

back against the couch. The blanket fell around his waist. "Forget it."

"When I came home, and you were gone…" Bess hesitated, but she'd already decided the second verse was going to have a different chorus. "I thought you weren't coming back. I thought I'd lost you, Nick. Forever, this time."

He turned to look at her, the mouth that brought her such pleasure turned down at the corners. After a moment he reached to cup his hand behind her neck. She thought he might kiss her, maybe pull her onto his lap and start to fuck her there on the floor, and despite the bruises and the chafing, her body responded at once.

But Nick didn't kiss her. He only looked at her. "I don't want to go back. Not ever."

Bess shook her head a tiny bit, not dislodging his grasp from her neck. "And I don't want you to."

Shadows bisected his faint smile. "No?"

"No."

"What are we going to do?" His fingers curled and his thumb pressed against the beat of her pulse. She leaned toward him, letting his heat wash over her. "When your kids get here? What then? You gonna tell them I'm your boyfriend? Tell 'em you're fucking me, and oh, by the way, I'm not…I'm—"

She put her mouth on his to silence him. He let her kiss him, but he didn't kiss her back, and after a second she pulled away. "Shh. I'll think of something."

Nick got up. The blanket dropped. She'd been on her knees for him before, but this time it didn't feel right, with him looking down on her. Bess stood, too.

Nick stalked to the wall and turned on the overhead light. Bess threw up her hand to keep away the glare, and blinking, didn't see him grabbing her wrist until he was already pulling her toward the large mirror. He stared at their side-by-side reflections.

"What do you see?" he asked.

Bess's eyes had adjusted now to the brightness, but she blinked a few more times. "Me. And you."

Nick gazed hard into the mirror. "I look the same to you. And you look the same to me. But not to yourself."

"I don't remember what I looked like then," she said. "Unless I see pictures. I can't remember what it was like to stare at my face in the mirror, Nick. I look the way I look. I look my age."

He turned to her. "You're afraid of what people will say."

"There's more than one reason to be afraid of that," Bess told him, not meaning to be cruel, but hearing it sound that way.

Nick gazed again at their reflection. "Do you think anyone would recognize me?"

"I did."

He smiled. "How about someone I wasn't fucking?"

"Gee, Nick," she said, stung. "Was there anyone you weren't fucking?"

"Hey." He caught her arm as she pulled away. "Bess. Don't. I'm sorry."

She let him draw her close, her face against his bare chest. She slid her hands down his back to fill her hands with the firm, smooth cheeks of his ass. He nuzzled her hair.

"I just wonder," he whispered. "If there's anyone beside you who would remember who I am."

"Your family."

A minute tension built in his body, then relaxed. "Most of them didn't know me back then. I doubt any of them would know me now."

The ocean tang had faded, replaced again by Nick's special scent. Bess breathed him in. Between them, his cock stirred.

"I know there are people in town who might remember you. But memory's a funny thing, Nick. Unless they had a picture of you to compare it to, I'm not sure they'd believe you were you. They might think you looked familiar, but who'd believe you hadn't changed at all in twenty years?"

"Maybe they'd think I'm my own son."

She tipped her head to look up at him. "Maybe they would. If they thought about it at all."

Emotion flickered across his face before fading. "This is fucking complicated. I keep waiting for it to turn out to be a mistake."

Mistake.

Bess shook her head at a sudden memory, gone wispy with time. "No, it's not a mistake."

Nick slanted his mouth over hers, his tongue slowly probing inside. He lifted the hem of her shirt and took it off. He settled his hands on her bare skin and kissed her once more. His erection pressed heat to her belly.

"I want to fuck you again."

The crudeness of his words made her arch back. His hand slid over her ribs to toy with the lace of her bra. The other reached around to grab her ass and pull her tighter. He ground himself slowly against her as his kiss left her breathless.

"Tell me you want it, too," he ordered. His eyes flashed when he pulled away.

"I want you." Bess licked her mouth, watching his eyes go to her lips, her tongue, before meeting hers again. "You know I do."

He took her there on the floor. She came, hard, with the nubbly rug biting into her shoulders and ass. Nick came moments later, shouting her name. When it was over he cradled her under the afghan, and though the floor was hard and uncomfortable, Bess was too boneless to immediately get up.

"Don't you want to know where I was?" he asked.

"If you want to tell me."

"I went swimming," Nick whispered.

Bess tucked his arm tighter around her. "Weren't you afraid?"

"Of what? Drowning?" He linked their fingers together.

Bess kissed his hand, joined with hers. She'd meant hadn't he been afraid of being sent back to the gray, whatever that was. But she said nothing. Nick pulled her closer, her ass nestled into the cup of his groin. He kissed the back of her shoulder.

"No matter how hard I swam," he whispered, "I couldn't get anywhere. I couldn't get away from you."

"Did you want to?"

"I just wanted to know if I could," Nick said, which answered a question, but not the one she'd asked.

Chapter 20

Then

There was a message she hadn't noticed the night before pinned to the bulletin board by the phone when Bess got up the next morning: "Andy called," written in her aunt's rounded hand. Dishes piled high in the kitchen sink and the Monopoly game still laid out on the coffee table were the only other signs of occupation. Aunt Lori and Uncle Carl weren't early risers on vacation. Bess wished she didn't have to be.

Her head throbbed with exhaustion as she poured a tall glass of water and took out a slice of pizza from the box in the fridge. Pineapple and ham weren't her favorite toppings, but beggars couldn't be choosers. One of the main benefits to sharing the house all summer with a revolving group of family members was that they all, by tacit agreement, fed her on occasion. The food knocked back the lurching in her stomach, but her head still ached. Pressure throbbed behind her eyes, but she took a long, hot shower without interruption, and that helped.

Down in her tiny room, getting ready for work, she finally looked in the mirror. Her wet hair clung to her cheeks and neck, darker than when it was dry. Her freckles had come out across the bridge of her nose, brighter today against skin paled by weariness. Her mouth was what caught her attention, though.

Her mouth. The lips Nick had kissed. She bared her teeth, viewed her tongue. The tongue that had been in his mouth.

Bess had to sit. Fast. Dizziness swept over her and she put her face in her hands, her elbows resting on her knees, waiting to see if her pizza was going to come up.

Her stomach, though jumpy, didn't fly out her throat. Her eyes throbbed, but she didn't want to cry. In fact, all she could do was grin, wide and wider.

She'd kissed Nick Hamilton.

He'd kissed her back. He'd touched her, and she'd touched him. Gasping laughter burbled out of her, and she stifled it behind her hand. Another look in the mirror showed the same sight. Her mouth, still swollen from Nick's kisses.

They hadn't done more than make out. With so many people in his apartment there'd been no chance for privacy, and with an early shift for both of them in the morning, the night had already gotten too late. Bess had been the one to stop, to leave, though he'd followed her to her bike and kissed her breathless there, too.

Shit. A glance at the clock told her she was going to be late. Bess tied up her hair, slipped into the white polo shirt and short khaki skirt she wore as a uniform, grabbed up her backpack and headed off to work. By the time she got there, the early morning air had whisked away her headache. She still couldn't stop grinning.

"Don't look at me like that, you bitch." Brian, head in his

hands, moaned from the back step of the shop. "Fuck it all, I'm hungover. Why aren't you?"

"Because I'm not stupid enough to get drunk on a night before I work the early shift," Bess said. She nudged him with her toe. "Up and at 'em, boy toy."

Brian shuddered, but rose. "It's too fucking early. Why isn't Tammy here?"

"Because," said Bess patiently, as she unlocked the door, "it's you and me and Eddie today. Tammy's got the late shift along with Ronnie."

"Of course." Brian snorted. "The lovebirds."

Eddie strolled up the walk just as Bess got the door open. "M-morning."

Brian waved a hand. "Eddie, how's about you take care of the counter today while I sit in the back and count slushy cups?"

Eddie looked so alarmed Bess took pity on him. "Shut up, Brian. Drink some water, take some aspirin."

Eddie eyed Brian as they all went inside, and watched him disappear at once into the tiny bathroom. "What's the matter with him?"

"Hangover." Her earlier headache seemed like a faraway dream, thank God, replaced by the memory of Nick's taste. "He'll be okay. We were at a party last night."

"Isn't he always?"

Today Eddie wore a polo shirt much like Bess's, only his was navy blue. The collar hung down on one side and flipped up on the other. Without thinking too much about it, Bess smoothed them both down flat. Eddie froze at her touch, and she tried to pull away without making it seem as if she knew she'd freaked him out.

"You were uneven," she said. "Your collar."

"Thanks." Eddie's blush could've baked a pretzel. He wouldn't meet her eyes.

Bess knew how he felt, but being the one on the opposite side of the adoration made her feel awkward. "I'll be out front."

They both nodded uncomfortably, and she left him. This early there wouldn't be any customers, but there was a lot of prep work to be done. The store would open in an hour, and though Bess didn't understand how anyone could stomach ice cream or popcorn before noon, once she switched the sign to Open there'd be a steady stream of customers all day long.

The best part about working so early was that she'd get off early, too. Which meant she could see Nick that much sooner. Which meant they could…well, what, exactly, could they do?

Andy called.

Bess's good mood plummeted. There hadn't been a time on the note, but since she knew her current roommates had stayed up late, it could have been anytime before three, when she'd got home. A tight, hard smile, nothing like her earlier grin, pulled her mouth. So Andy had called and she wasn't home? Good. Let him be the one to wonder where she was, who she was with.

Again, the memory of the night before hit her in the gut and she had to put out a hand to steady herself.

"You okay?" Brian asked. His face gleamed pink, and his hair and the collar of his pink polo shirt were damp. "Don't tell me you're hungover, too. If you have to yark, do it in the back."

"No. I'm fine." Bess straightened, trying to take a few deep breaths.

If Andy found out she'd kissed Nick, he'd break up with her.

Was that a bad thing?

And hadn't she already decided she wasn't with him anymore?

"You look bad." Brian stuck a cup under the soda fountain and filled it, then pressed it into her hand. "Drink this. Maybe you need something to settle your stomach."

"I told you, I'm not hungover." Bess gulped the soda anyway and held out the cup for more.

He filled it and watched her sip at it more slowly the second time. "Uh-oh."

Bess put the cup down by the sink and started flicking the switches on the pretzel case and slushy maker. She didn't look at Brian. Despite his consistently flamboyant behavior, he was observant and smart. And blunt.

"You fucked him?" Brian breathed this like it was a state secret. "Holy shit, Bess, you fucked Nick Hamilton."

"No!" She shook her head. She saw Eddie watching them from the doorway, but if he'd had a question he swallowed it and disappeared again into the back room. "Shut up, Brian!"

"Ooooh, honey!" Brian clucked his tongue. "What happened to your boyfriend?"

"Nothing happened to him. I didn't have sex with Nick." Bess busied her hands so she could feign disdain.

"You did something with him. Damn, girl. Missy told me the two of you had something going on."

Bess turned. "Oh, so we're an item in the gossip column now?"

Brian held up his hands. "Chill, sister golden hair. Missy doesn't usually know what the hell she's talking about."

Bess glared. "Even if she did, it's not any of her business. Or yours."

"Point taken." For once, Brian seemed serious. He came up behind her to rub her shoulders with strong fingers that found the knots of tension without any effort. "Just be careful, sweetie."

Bess let herself relax under his massage for a minute. "I'm a big girl, Brian. I'll be okay."

He worked at a knot at the side of her neck. "Nick's a player, honey. That's all."

Bess's back stiffened, destroying the benefits of Brian's massage. She went around the counter to fill the napkin holders on the café tables. "I said I'd be fine."

Brian didn't answer at first, and Bess looked up.

"You have it bad for him, huh?"

It was her turn to say nothing. She bent back to her task. "It's nothing."

"That's not nothing." Brian came around the counter to touch the side of her neck. "That's a big old hickey."

Stunned, Bess put her hand to it. She hadn't seen it, but now, pressing, she felt the small soreness there. "Oh, shit."

Brian laughed. "Boyfriend'll eat you up, sweetie. I know you can handle him, but just…be careful."

Bess lifted the napkin holder to try and catch a glimpse of the bite mark in its metal reflection. "Damn it."

"I have some foundation in my backpack. I'll get it for you."

She looked at him. "Brian, I love you."

"Story of my life, honey. Story. Of. My. Life." Brian sighed. "Now if only I could find *my* Prince Charming…"

Nick wasn't her Prince Charming, Bess thought as she finished filling the napkin holders. In the tiny bathroom, daubing makeup on the mark he'd left on her skin, though, she knew he was…something.

But what?

There wasn't time to think about it, because the rush of the day began. She and Brian and Eddie kept things under control, and if Eddie seemed quieter and Brian just a little sassier, Bess barely noticed. Every time the door bell jangled her heart stuttered and she looked to see if it was Nick, but it never was.

She didn't even have his phone number to call him, she thought, as her workday neared its end with no sign of him. She knew where he lived and worked, but could she just go find him without an invitation, the way he'd come into Sugarland to seek her out? Should she?

She still hadn't decided by the time Ronnie showed up to take over. Bess hadn't decided by the time she packed up her bag and unlocked her bike. At the end of the alley, she had two choices. Turn left to make her way home, join in the Monopoly game, eat pizza and hang out with her aunt and uncle and their friends. Call Andy. Suffer through another painful conversation, or make it official. Tell him the truth and let him break up with her.

Bess turned right.

It had been less than twenty-four hours since she'd ridden this same route, but it seemed to take a lot longer than it had at three in the morning. Her courage nearly failed her when she locked her bike to the railing of Nick's deck.

Bess knocked on his door before she could stop herself. It took him forever to open it, but it was worth it when he did wearing a towel and nothing else.

"Bess." Nick sounded surprised. He slung a hand through his wet hair, pushing it off his face.

"Hi."

He stepped aside to let her in. He was naked under that towel, and her skin tingled in response. Suddenly she wished she'd gone home to shower, change her clothes. Put on make-up. She reached to unclip her hair, at least, let it hang around her shoulders. She turned to face him.

"About last night," she started.

Nick grinned.

"I know you like to fuck around."

His smile melted like a dropped ice-cream cone.

Bess took a deep, courage-making breath. "And I just wanted to tell you…it's okay. If that's all you want."

Now his lips thinned. His dark brows furrowed as he crossed his arms over his chest. The towel slipped a fraction of an inch on his hips, and Bess couldn't stop herself from wishing it would fall all the way off.

"It is?"

"Yes." She nodded.

Neither of them moved closer to each other. She wanted him to kiss her the way he had last night. She wanted him to pin her up against the wall, put his hands on her. She wanted him inside her.

"I know you're not looking for anything serious." Her voice shook—no surprise, since she'd forgotten to breathe again. "And that's okay, because I'm not really in a position for anything serious."

Nick watched her. His chest rose and fell, faster than it had a moment before. Because of her?

"No?"

Bess shook her head and wet her lips. She lifted her chin. Her hands had clenched at her sides and she forced them to open, relax. She hadn't thought about what she was going to do when she got here, but now that she stood in front of him all she could think about was fucking him until they both were sore.

"I want you," she whispered. "Now."

Nick didn't pin her against the wall. He didn't move. His chest rose and fell and his eyes, impassive, regarded her.

Finally, he smiled again, with one side of his mouth. "You're sure this isn't a mistake? Last night we were both drinking. It could've happened to anyone."

That he wanted to pretend that's all it had been should've stung more, but Bess didn't let it. She pulled her shirt over her head and thrilled to the way his eyes flared. His smile froze. His hands, tucked beneath his opposite elbows, twitched, but otherwise he didn't move.

"It didn't happen to anyone. It happened to us." Her fingers slid open the button on her skirt and she stepped out of it. Her matching bra and panties covered more than some bikinis she'd seen, but it wasn't the same. Not at all.

She knew that through the lace he could see her nipples, now hard, and the darkness of the hair between her legs. Nick made a small, strangled noise in the back of his throat. Bess didn't dare look away from his face, not even to see if the front of his towel was lifting. She reached behind her to unhook her bra, and took that off, too. Neither of them glanced at it when she tossed it to the pile on the floor. Nick didn't look away from her eyes.

They stayed like that for longer than it took to breathe in and out five times. She knew because she counted each breath. When Nick parted his mouth to speak and nothing came out, Bess moved toward him.

Two steps took her to him. Another two pushed him against the wall. He hit it with a thud and a rush of breath that became a groan when she tugged away the towel. Bess slid her mouth over Nick's collarbone, the highest point on him she could reach without him bending. Down, lower, to one copper-colored nipple. She licked it, her hands going to his waist and holding him. Lower still, fast, her mouth skimming his side to the curve of his hip. She bit at the bone there, lightly, and he muttered a curse. His hands went to the wall, flattened.

She moved up his body with her mouth until they stood

belly to belly. He was hard, his cock trapped upright between them. She still wore her panties. His thigh was between her legs, and she slid her satin crotch along his skin.

When she bit at his biceps, Nick cursed again and wrapped his arms around her. He bent, his mouth finding her throat. He put a hand between her legs, and Bess gave a soft cry.

She took him in her hand and stroked. Their mouths covered inches of open skin. Their hands stroked and roamed. Perhaps only a minute or two had passed since she'd pushed him against the wall, but she didn't need more. She was ready for him and didn't want time to stop and think.

"Condoms?" she murmured into his ear, assuming he'd have some.

"Bedroom."

It took more than two steps to get there, but they managed quickly enough. She hadn't been in his bedroom before, which was off the kitchen. He had a dresser and an ancient TV on a stand and a wall of CDs and videos, but the only thing Bess cared about was the king-size mattress and box spring on the floor.

Nick slid open his top drawer and pulled out a handful of square foil packages. They fell in a rainbow of colors to the bed. Bess was already pushing him down onto his back and crawling up over him. She straddled him, his cock hot against her crotch through her panties, and sifted through the pile.

"Black Jack?" She lifted the first she came to. "Interesting."

Nick lifted his hips, rubbing himself against her. His prick whispered on the smooth fabric of her panties, and Bess had to put a hand on his chest to steady herself at the sudden, exquisite shudder of sensation.

It was wrong to be here, and she didn't care, and that not-caring was almost as much of a turn-on as Nick himself. She tore open the package and sheathed him, only a trifle awk-wardly, with shaking hands.

Nick watched her without moving as she got up and stripped off her underpants, then straddled him again. She took the base of his cock in her hand, but didn't move right away. Bess breathed, slow and deep, her courage not quite fail-ing her.

Nick said nothing, but his dark eyes gleamed. His mouth had parted, his lips moist from the swipe of his tongue. He was breathing fast. He made no move to force her, not even a ges-ture. In his cock, the pulse beat hard and fast, like her own.

She was going to do this. She was doing it, before she thought anymore. She lifted herself to guide him inside her, and slid slowly down. She gasped. Nick's eyes closed and his back arched, pushing his cock deeper inside her than she'd been prepared for.

It wasn't perfect, but fantasy always boosts reality. Bess put both her hands on Nick's shoulders, angling her body to put pressure where she needed it most. She was intent more on maximizing any position that felt good rather than concen-trating on coming. She didn't expect to have an orgasm.

The small, sharp climax took her by surprise. Her eyes flut-tered as she leaned forward. Her hands gripped his shoulders as his gripped her hips. She blew out a small moan as the pleasure coursed through her.

She glanced at his face. Nick looked as surprised as she did, but only for a moment, because then his eyes closed and his face twisted in his own climax. He thrust once more, groaning, and stopped moving. He licked his lips and opened his eyes.

They stared at each other in silence broken only by the sound of their breathing. Bess swallowed, aware of the clutch and grasp of her thighs, sweaty against his sides. She relaxed her fingers from his shoulders and rubbed the small spots she had left. She rolled off him and onto her back.

Nick said nothing, and Bess wasn't sure what to say or what to do. If she could do anything, that was, aside from try to catch her breath and return to being rational.

She waited for guilt to stab her, but it didn't.

After a while the pattern of Nick's breathing changed, got softer and more regular. She turned to look at him. Outside the window, it wasn't even dusk. His profile was not yet familiar to her, and she studied it carefully. The slope of nose and chin, the shadow of dark lashes on his cheeks. The dark silk of his hair falling over his forehead.

He was the loveliest sight she'd ever seen.

Without looking at her or even opening his eyes, Nick said, "Bess?"

"Hmm?" Languid from the sex and a little overwhelmed with emotions she hadn't expected to feel, Bess rolled onto her side to face him.

"Don't ever think you know what I want."

It wasn't until later, when beneath the hot water of her own shower Bess tried and failed again to find the guilt she knew should belong to her, that she realized something. They'd put their hands and mouths all over each other. They'd licked and stroked and sucked and bitten.

But they hadn't once kissed.

Chapter
21

Now

*B*ess was used to the low mutter of the television plaguing her dreams. Andy had long been in the habit of falling asleep in front of the set, the volume turned low but still loud enough to carry through the house when all else was silent. Maybe that had been the first sign their marriage was failing, when Andy'd started choosing late-night talk shows instead of bed with her.

Now she clawed her way up from a nightmare and woke, wide-eyed, without knowing at first where she was. Bess blinked rapidly and ran her fingers over the sheet half tangled around her waist. The pillow beneath her cheek was damp— whether with sweat or tears, she couldn't be sure. The doorway, through which she glimpsed the blue-white flicker of the TV, was in the wrong place. So was the bed. She turned to look at the ceiling as waking finally claimed her.

The beach house.

She was at the beach house, and the man in the living room

watching something with a canned laugh track was not Andy. Bess pushed herself onto one elbow and stifled a yawn with the back of her hand. Her dreams, as awful as they'd been, had fled, leaving behind nothing but a slightly sour stomach.

She untangled herself from the covers and slipped on her nightgown, then padded into the living room. Nick sat, elbows on his knees, staring at the tube. He didn't look at her when she came in, nor when she sat next to him, thigh to thigh. He wore only boxers.

"Hey." Bess kissed his bare shoulder.

"Hey." Nick blinked, then looked at her. "Jesus, Bess."

She rested her head on his shoulder as she looked at television. He'd been watching the news channel. "Turn that off."

Nick didn't move. "So much stuff…"

Bess grabbed up the remote from the coffee table and clicked off the TV. The darkness fell around them, and she closed her eyes to help them adjust. Next to her, Nick still didn't move.

"I know what you said, about the time. But I just didn't think about it." Under her cheek, his shoulder lifted and lowered with his sigh. "Damn it, Bess."

"Shh. You'll get used to it." She took his hand, linked their fingers. Squeezed.

Nick didn't pull away, but he didn't squeeze back. He shook a little, and Bess put her arm around him. She held him tight, but he didn't soften to her embrace.

"I'm going to make some toast," she said after a few minutes had passed in silence.

She kissed his shoulder again and got up. In the kitchen, the light seemed too bright, hurting the back of her eyes until they adjusted. She pulled soft white bread, a guilty pleasure, from the freezer, where she kept it to protect it from the constantly damp sea air. She put two slices in the toaster and rummaged in the fridge for real butter and strawberry jam. By the time the toast popped up, beautifully golden, she'd poured a mug of orange juice.

Nick came into the kitchen as she was buttering the toast and spreading it with jam. He hopped up on the counter to watch her. Bess stood to eat, the formality of a chair somehow ridiculous for a simple piece of toast.

"The smell of toast makes me think of sex." Nick grinned faintly.

She tucked a bit of crust into her mouth and licked her fingers. "I seem to remember you telling me that." She held up the last crust. "Want a bite?"

Nick shook his head. "What's the point?"

He was right, but Bess didn't pull back her offered crust at once. She didn't eat it when she had, but instead tossed it into the garbage pail. She'd lost her appetite, too.

Nick slid off the counter and put a hand on her shoulder to turn her toward him. "I'm sorry."

"You don't have to be sorry." She shrugged, not looking at him. "You shouldn't do something you don't want just to—"

"To seem normal?" Nick spoke softly. His fingers curled, bunching the fabric of her nightgown on her shoulder. "Would it make you feel better if I pretended to eat? Maybe I could lie all night beside you like I'm sleeping, just so you don't feel you're fucking a freak."

"I don't think you're a freak!" She glared at him.

There was always heat between them. Heat from Nick's skin, the heat of their passion, the heat of anger. Now the heat of his fingers burned her through the flimsy material of her nightgown, and Bess jerked away. She swept the crumbs on the counter into her cupped palm and dusted her hands into the garbage pail.

Nick was there when she turned. "I'm sorry."

Bess looked at him then, her chest heaving from breathing too fast. Nick's gaze was dark and solid, unreadable but familiar. He'd looked at her that way before, as if he were dissecting her inch by inch and giving her nothing in return.

She'd hated it then and hated it more, now. "Don't put words in my mouth."

His direct gaze faltered a little as the corners of his mouth tilted. "How about if I put something else in your mouth, instead?"

Bess crossed her arms over her chest and backed up a few steps. She didn't smile at him. "You can't have it both ways, Nick."

This seemed to set him back. "What's that supposed to mean?"

"It means," Bess said unevenly, "I can pretend there's nothing strange about this. About us. You. I can pretend without a problem that you're my much younger lover. Or I can acknowledge that this entire situation is fucked up, that you came back from...from somewhere—"

"From the gray," Nick interjected in a low voice.

"That you were gone and came back," Bess said more loudly. "You were my lover twenty years ago and you've shown up out of nowhere—"

"Not out of nowhere!" Nick snapped, advancing on her. "Fuck, Bess! How can you pretend anything when you know where I was? What I am? How can you just act like that doesn't matter?"

"Because I love you!" she cried.

The words spun into silence. Outside the windows, the sun was rising. A new day. New waves would rise from the same old sea and break upon the same old sand.

"I love you," Bess repeated, and took Nick's hands.

She'd never said it to him before. He'd never said it to her, and she didn't expect him to now. His fingers tightened on hers, but he didn't surprise her with words. His mouth thinned, clamped shut, but his eyes no longer held a wall between them. Plenty of emotion swirled in his gaze, and though much of it might still be unreadable, none of it was unreachable now.

"I love you," she whispered, and pulled him two reluctant steps closer to her. She put a hand on his cheek. Her thumb caressed his mouth. "I always did."

Nick closed his eyes and turned his face just enough to kiss her hand. He put his arms around her and held her close to him. They stayed like that for a long time, though Bess didn't bother counting the minutes.

Pressed to Nick's chest, his skin hotter than her breath, she closed her eyes.

"I don't care what you are," she said. "I'm just so happy you're here." She pushed away from him to look at his face. She took a deep breath. "But if you're not—"

"No." Nick shook his head and pulled her to him for a long, slow, deep kiss. "No," he said again. "I want to be with you. I just needed to know you were sure about me. No matter what."

"I'm sure." Bess kissed him. "If we have to pretend to the world we've just met, I don't care. If we have to say you're something else, I don't care about that, either."

Nick smiled. "What about your kids?"

Bess sighed. "They don't need to know we're sleeping together. Not right away."

She hoped he'd understand, not take it the wrong way, and to her relief, Nick nodded.

"Sure. I get that. Don't want to freak 'em out. But what will we say I am?"

"A boarder." Bess ran her hands down his ribs. "You can have my old room. You'll have your own bathroom and entrance. If they ask, I'll tell them the truth. It costs a lot of money to keep up this place, and my financial situation is more precarious than I'd like."

Nick waggled his eyebrows at that last bit. "Ooh, fancy. Will they buy it?"

The way he put it made it sound like a worse lie than Bess wanted to admit it was, but she nodded. "Yes. They'll buy it."

Nick slipped his hands around to her ass and squeezed as he bent to nibble at her neck. "So, will you sneak down at night to my lonely slave quarters and have your way with me?"

Bess giggled as his lips and teeth found sensitive spots. "We'll see."

"And when the summer's over?" He asked the question almost lightly, but Bess didn't mistake it for anything but serious. "What happens then?"

She put her fingers in his hair and made him look at her. "I'm not leaving at the end of the summer."

Nick straightened. "You're not?"

Bess shook her head slowly. "No. I'm not."

"You're sure?"

"I'm not going back to my husband. We're officially separated." It was the first time she'd said the words aloud. She was surprised at how they could still hurt. Bess swallowed hard and cleared her throat, tipping her chin. "Connor goes to college in the fall. Robbie will stay here, with me. Andy's staying in the house in Pennsylvania. He hasn't admitted it, but I know he has a mistress."

Nick scowled. "Fucker."

His indignation on her behalf lifted some of the weight from Bess's shoulders. "As if what I'm doing is any better?"

Nick gave her a solemn look before taking her face in both

his hands. He'd kissed her many ways before. Tenderly, roughly, passionately. This was the first time he kissed her thoughtfully. When he pulled away, Bess's heart had begun its familiar hammering as her body responded.

"Do you feel bad?" he asked her.

She shook her head. "No, Nick. I should, but I don't."

Just as she should've felt guilty back then, but never had.

"Good." He kissed her again, then rested his forehead against hers. "So. What's the story?"

"Morning glory?" Bess teased. He didn't get it. "Sorry. It's from *Bye, Bye Birdie*. What story do you mean?"

Nick kissed her lightly and stepped back, then around her into the living room. "My story. What's my name? What do I do? If we're going to keep this up, I need to have a name."

She hadn't thought of that. "What's wrong with Nick Hamilton?"

"Junior," Nick said with a grin over his shoulder. "I'm my own son? Daddy-O ran off and left me and my coke-whore mama when I was a kid?"

"Maybe he didn't leave you," Bess said quietly. "Maybe he died."

Nick turned, grin fading. "You think so?"

She nodded after a moment. "Just because I didn't know doesn't mean nobody else did, Nick. I…I could find out. If you wanted to know."

Nick said nothing. He went to the sliding-glass doors and out onto the deck. The bright morning sun cast glints of gold along his skin, tawny and not pale no matter what his corporeal state. Bess followed to lean on the railing. The breeze ruffled her hair.

Nick stared out to the sea. The Atlantic would never compare with the placid blue of the Caribbean, but today the water looked less green. The whitecaps were frilled lace along the edges of the waves. Even the sand seemed to shine brighter.

"And I came back to town to work for the summer." The hitch in Nick's voice was the only indication of emotion.

Bess put her hand on his shoulder. "Yes. And you needed a place to stay. And I…"

He turned to look at her. "You're renting me a room in your house because you knew my dad."

She nodded. "Yes."

"And anything else we're doing isn't anyone's goddamn business."

She smiled at that. "Exactly."

Nick looked back out to the water. "I'll have to get a shit job. I don't have any ID. Get paid under the table until I can get hooked up with something."

She wasn't surprised he'd know how to get a fake identity. She reached to squeeze his arm, which was as solid as anything. Since the moment he'd come back, he'd been nothing less than fully real, even if he didn't eat, sleep or breathe.

"It will be all right," she told him.

Nick smiled, still looking out to the ocean. "Yeah. I guess so."

It would have to be. Who would believe anything else? Who would believe Nick Hamilton had died and come back from the dead to spend his time fucking her?

"Why don't we get dressed and walk into town? We'll go along the beach. You can ask around. I know those places hire kitchen staff under the table. We can do a little shopping. Make a day of it."

"Make a date of it?" He shot her a grin she felt all the way down her spine.

"Oh, yes." Bess wiggled her eyebrows in an imitation of his earlier expression. "A date. How scandalous."

"It's the shore. Nobody'll be scandalized. They'll all be jealous. I've got a smokin' sugar mama and you've got yourself a hot superstud."

"Well, when you put it that way, I don't see how anyone could possibly be scandalized."

Nick laughed. "Have I ever cared about that?"

"I don't think so." She had. Quite a bit. But maybe not so much anymore. "C'mon. Day's wasting."

"It can waste a little longer," Nick said, the swipe of his tongue across his lips leaving no question as to what, exactly, he meant.

He took her into the master bath shower, where he pushed her up against the back wall. He unhooked the handheld showerhead and passed the spray of pulsing water over her entire body. Kneeling in front of her, he lifted her foot to prop it on the shower's built-in seat. Then he moved the stream of water back and forth over her clit.

Bess had used the showerhead before, but the sensation of warm water, like a hundred flickering tongues, under someone else's control became immeasurably more erotic. She pumped her hips forward, seeking to capture the elusive tickle, and was rewarded with a spurt or two before Nick shifted the stream. Her clit pulsed as she looked down at him, kneeling with his cock in his fist.

He pumped himself slowly as he passed the water again over her clit, then down. She wanted him inside her, but the water had brought her so close she couldn't speak, not even to ask for what she wanted. She couldn't stop her hips from rocking against the spray. Her orgasm swelled inside her, refusing to be denied or put off, not even in the pursuit of what she knew would be equally as pleasurable.

Bess gave a low, guttural cry as her entire body contracted

and her wet skin skidded on the tiles. She cried out again as he directed the water onto her pussy, just below her clit and over it to just above. Nick jiggled the showerhead and Bess came, arching her back.

He was on his feet before the final spasms had finished surging through her. He turned and bent her, her hands going to the bench where her foot had been a moment before. Nick parted her folds with his cock and pushed inside slowly, then began thrusting almost at once.

It felt so good she cried out again, pushing back against him and tilting her body to open deeper for him. Her feet slipped a little on the shower floor but her grip on the bench kept her steady. Nick fucked into her, hard, as the pulsing water beat against her back. A moment later it was replaced with the swipe of his hand down her spine as Nick angled the showerhead below her. The water spurted up, coating her breasts and belly, but also hitting between her legs. Bess let go of the bench with one hand just long enough to push the showerhead lower against her clit.

Nick gasped out something incoherent, probably when the water hit his balls, and thrust faster. Bess rocked against his cock and the water, biting her lip and finally giving in to the desire to moan and cry out his name, over and over.

He answered, murmuring and then gasping a mingled stream of curses and endearments that tipped her over the edge into orgasm again. He followed with a shout and dropped the showerhead, which writhed at the end of its hose, whacking her in the ankles.

Bess gasped for breath in the steamy air, and Nick withdrew slowly. He helped her up, the took the water and dialed the massage function to the gentlest spray so he could wash her all over, taking his time until at last he reached her still-tender places. Bess jumped when the water sprayed her there, but Nick didn't let it linger long enough to hurt.

"Guess I can cross that off my list," he said when it was time again to speak.

Bess laughed and reached around him to turn off the water, which was growing chilly. "I might have a list of my own, did you think of that?"

"Bring it on."

He handed her a towel and took one for himself, rubbing at his hair until it stood on end. Their eyes met in the mirror.

"I'll never get tired of you," he said suddenly, and with such sincerity Bess blushed.

"I hope not."

"No." He shook his head, reaching for her. "I mean it, Bess."

"Okay." She kissed him, hugged him, held him tight against her with nothing but the towel between them. "I believe you."

Chapter 22

Then

"So, when am I coming down?" Andy's voice sounded tinny with distance.

Or maybe just wishful thinking.

Bess didn't have a calendar in front of her, as if that would have mattered. "When do you want to come, Andy?"

In the past three summers she'd worked in Bethany Beach, the same three summers she'd been dating Andy, he'd only visited her twice. He said it was because, though he had the weekends off, she usually didn't, and he didn't want to hang out by himself. He didn't want to sleep on the couch, or worse, the floor, and since Bess's family was always occupying the rest of the house, sharing her bedroom was out of the question. Bess, who thought a free stay at the beach would have easily trumped any of those insignificant inconveniences, had stopped pushing him to visit.

Now, of course, when she no longer wanted him to, he'd decided it was time.

"I work every weekend," she added before he could answer. "And the house is booked for the rest of the summer, too. You can have the cot on the screened porch, I guess."

"Very funny."

She hadn't been joking. "It just seems sort of silly, Andy, to drive all the way down here for two days when I won't even have the time off."

"Can't you get the time off?"

"I'm a manager," she explained for probably the fourth time. "And I really need the money."

"Yeah, right. The money." Andy hadn't ever suffered for money in his life. "I guess I thought since I haven't seen you since May, you might want me to visit."

"We were supposed to see each other for the Fast Fashion concert," she reminded him. A week ago she wouldn't have dared bring it up. Now everything he said made her want to fight him. "How was that, by the way?"

"Is that what this is about?" Andy's laugh curled her toes— and not in a good way. "Are you still mad about that?"

"About the fact you gave another girl my ticket to see my favorite band? Why should I be mad about that, Andy?"

"Don't be such a bitch."

"Why is it that whenever I call you out on something you've done, you call me a bitch?" Bess looked into the living room, where a new set of relatives were happily making themselves at home.

This week it was her cousin Danielle and her husband, Steve, with their three adorable but exhausting kids. Bess had already promised to babysit one evening, an offer that was less generous when you considered Danielle and Steve were offering to pay her almost as much as she made at Sugarland.

"Do you want me to come or not?"

"I wanted you to take me to that concert," Bess said in a low voice.

"Jesus, can't you let it rest?"

"No," she said. "I guess I can't."

Andy gave a heavy, long-suffering sigh. "If I'd known you were going to be such a pain in the ass about it, Bess—"

"I think you might have guessed, Andy," Bess interrupted. "It's not like I didn't tell you how I felt. It's not like I said it was okay with me if you went without me. You knew, and you did it anyway."

That was what bothered her more than the fact he took some other girl. The fact she'd told him how she felt, and he'd disregarded it. Now she couldn't stop remembering all the other times he hadn't paid attention to her, or what she wanted. What she said.

Andy was quiet. "I'm sorry, okay?"

"It's not okay!" she cried, her voice high and thin.

"What do you want me to do about it now? It's over! I went, okay? There's nothing I can do about it now!"

"No. You're right. There's not."

"I said I was sorry, Bess."

It would've been easier to forgive him. Put it aside. Make it all right again. But Bess said nothing, and the silence between them grew and grew while she couldn't guess what Andy was thinking, and couldn't stop imagining Nick's face.

"I love you," Andy said.

"Do you? Really?"

He hung up on her. She stared at the phone for a few seconds before hanging up herself. *Bastard.* Her stomach churned and her hands felt shaky, but she didn't cry.

Leaving the cacophony above, Bess retreated to her room. It was clean because she couldn't afford to let it get messy. She had barely enough space as it was. At the wooden desk, she pulled out a box of stationery. Embossed with her initial, *E* for Elisabeth, it had been a Christmas gift from a maiden aunt a long time ago. Bess never used it because she didn't equate herself as an *"E"* and writing on the stationery had always felt like putting on a costume. Now, she pulled out a piece along with a pen and the matching envelope.

Dear Andy,

I don't love you anymore.

Andy. I'd hate you but I can't even care enough about you to do that.

Andy,

I fucked someone and he made me come so hard I went momentarily blind, and I think I'm falling in love with him. So you can keep your little twat from work and all the concerts you want.

Dear Andy, I'm not sure how to tell you this, except to tell you the truth. I don't think I love you anymore. And I'm pretty sure you don't love me, either, because if you did you'd have taken me to see Fast Fashion instead of some girl you just met. And I know you think being mad about a concert is stupid, and maybe you're right, but it's not the concert. It's the choice you made, choosing someone else over me.

Bess scratched out line after line. She chewed the end of her pen. And at last, she put all the scribbled-on pages back into the stationery box and slid it into the drawer again, without addressing the envelope.

Chapter 23

Now

"Ready?" Bess had tugged on a light sundress and a matching cardigan. Lacy bra, filmy panties. She carried her sandals rather than wore them for the walk to town along the beach. Nick and she had finally gotten around to heading there.

He was staring out the windows toward the ocean again. "Yeah."

The shops would barely be open by the time they got to town, but the sun had risen higher than she'd expected while they dallied in the shower. She'd lost count of how many times they'd made love.

Bess locked the door behind them and tucked her keys in her bag, then followed Nick along the narrow, sandy path between the dunes to the beach proper. The sand was already hot on her toes, but it felt good. She lifted her face to the breeze, fresh against her cheeks. It fluttered her hair.

"I think I'm going to buy a sun hat."

Nick, hands in the pockets of his jeans, glanced at her. "Then you won't get freckles."

"Or skin cancer, hopefully."

He turned to walk backward, watching her. "I liked your freckles."

She laughed. "Oh, sure, because freckles are so sexy."

"Sure they are. Right across your nose."

Bess laughed again. "If you say so."

They veered closer to the see to walk on the wet coolness and to avoid the scattered blankets and umbrellas from the few souls hardy enough to brave the water, which was still chilly this time of year. Nick bent to pick up a black, fan-shaped shell, perfect without chips or cracks. It fit neatly into his palm, and he passed a thumb over it before handing it to her.

The beach house had jars stuffed with shells of all shapes and colors, but Bess tucked this one into the pocket of her cardigan anyway. It was the first thing Nick had ever given her that she could hold or keep.

She was still smiling when he dropped to his knees.

"Nick?"

He hunched, shoulders heaving. One hand dug into the sand, while the other clutched his stomach. A wave rushed up and swirled around his fingers, leaving behind a curl of seaweed and a lacy froth of bubbles that popped and broke.

Bess knelt beside him and put her palm on his shoulder. "Nick, what's wrong?"

Nick shook his head. His dark hair fell forward, hiding his face. He groaned. Another, bigger wave came and wet the legs of his jeans and splashed Bess's dress. She put her arm around his rigid shoulders.

Nick pushed against the sand and crawled backward a few inches. He stopped, shaking, then pushed again. The trail he

left looked like the scuttle marks of a crab. His first attempt
had pulled her arm away from his shoulders, and Bess followed.
Her dress dragged in the wet sand and slapped at her bare legs,
scratching them, but she ignored the sting.

"Nick," she murmured. "Tell me what's happening?"

He looked up at her, his face pale. "It hurts." He let go of
his stomach and straightened, still on his knees.

Bess helped him get to his feet. They stood facing each
other, his hands in hers and their heads bent, as if they were
studying something they'd found in the sand. Bess watched his
fingers curl over hers.

Sand had grimed the creases of his knuckles. A small white
scar bisected the base of his right thumb. Dark blue veins made
a map of the back of his hand. These hands were real, and solid.

She looked at his face. "What happened?"

"I couldn't go on. It was like being gutted."

She couldn't pretend to understand what that felt like, but
nodded anyway. "Are you...sick?"

His mouth twisted and she felt instantly stupid. "No."

She squeezed his hands. "Then what?"

Nick shook his head. Around their feet the waves advanced
and retreated. She'd dropped her sandals, but didn't turn to
check if they were being sucked out to sea.

Nick's mouth thinned. His back straightened further.
"Come on."

He turned, now holding only one of her hands, and stalked
back across the sand. If any of the other beachgoers had noticed
anything wrong, they didn't seem to be paying much attention. Nick strode through the waves thinned by their reach up
the sand, and pulled Bess with him. She looked back at her
sandals, safe higher up on the beach, and saw the water erasing
their footprints as though they'd never walked there at all.

They passed her house and the square of beach in front of it that would've been a yard in a traditional house, and went beyond.

"Count." Nick dropped her hand.

"What?"

He stepped forward. "Count them."

Ten paces from the boundary beach in front of her house, he doubled over with a grunt, both hands on his gut. Eleven, and he staggered. At twelve he let out a low growl that raised the hair on the back of her neck.

"Nick, don't, for God's sake!"

At thirteen steps, Bess realized she could see through him. She hadn't been walking with him, but now she flew across the sand to grab at him. She reached for the back of his shirt to yank him back, the way she'd once yanked Connor from the path of an oncoming car he'd stepped in front of. Her heart had hammered then, too, her vision narrowed to nothing but her hand, grabbing and finding. She'd pulled her son to safety that day, but now her fingers slipped and scrabbled on the fabric of Nick's T-shirt. Her fingers clutched and grabbed... and slid through.

"Nick!"

The wind whipped his name from her lips. He staggered back. Her hand filled with solid, soft fabric, and she pulled. His shirt tore with a purr. He fell onto the sand with her standing over him, and he rolled to his side, groaning and twitching, but he was there. He was solid. He was still real.

He did that scrabbling crawl again, then curled into a ball in the soft, dry sand as Bess knelt beside him and cradled his head in her lap. A shadow fell over her, and she cringed.

"Is he okay?" A girl with blond pigtails and a blue bikini offered a Thermos jug. "Does he need some water?"

Nick rolled to his feet, crouching, then got up. Bess followed. Though coated with sand, he nevertheless gave the girl
a grin of such stunning beauty Bess could see the blonde fall
instantly in love.

"I'm okay. Pulled a muscle at work." Nick grimaced, stretching his leg out and twisting a little at the waist. "It's a killer."

The girl looked faintly dubious, but another grin from
Nick flustered her enough that she stepped back. "Okay. I just
wanted to make sure."

She looked at Bess with none of the interest she'd shown
Nick. Bess understood. She smiled and nodded at the girl, who
took another step back, then another, and finally walked off
with a few backward glances. She sat down on her blanket,
settled the Thermos in the sand and picked up her book, but
kept looking over at Nick.

His grin faded and he turned toward Bess's house. Without
speaking to her, or even waiting for her to follow, he stalked
again across the beach. His footprints dug shallow graves in the
dry sand, with nothing to make them disappear but time.

After a minute, Bess followed. "Nick. Wait."

He didn't stop until he'd ducked under the stilts of the carport and leaned against the wall by the door. His shoulders
heaved again, but he got himself under control faster than he
had before, and he didn't go pale. He pounded the wall.

Bess, silent, watched him. Nick punched the wall hard
enough to split the skin of his knuckles, but when he pulled
his arm back, the only sign of injury was his grimace of pain.
He shook his hand, muttering. "Fuck, fuck, fuck."

"Nick. Look at me. Talk to me."

"I can't sleep, but I feel pain." His smile looked more like
a rictus than an expression of humor. "How's that for fucking
hilarious?"

Bess reached for him, but he shrank from her grasp and yanked at the door. It wouldn't open, of course—it was locked—and he moved aside for her to open it. Again without waiting he pushed inside and stomped down the short hall into the small bedroom next to the laundry room. He knocked over the desk chair and went to the window. This one didn't look out over the ocean, but rather directly into the board fence separating the house from the one next door.

The room was only large enough for the desk and chair, the lamp in the corner and the daybed that, opened to its full size, left no space to walk in. The tiny closet had no door because the desk had been pushed right up against it.

Bess, shaken, stood silent in the doorway. Nick pounded the window frame hard enough to rattle the glass, then again more softly. He turned to her.

"I can't leave."

"I don't understand." She didn't want to understand. She picked up the chair and settled it back against the battered desk.

"The night I went swimming. I told you I couldn't leave. Today, I couldn't get more than twelve steps away from your beach."

"It's not my beach—"

"This house!" Nick threw out a hand. "The beach that goes with this house! And I goddamn guarantee that if I tried to go out to the road I wouldn't get any farther that way before it's like something's tearing my guts out through my throat! Before I—"

"Stop it!" Bess clapped her hands over her ears, then her mouth. She drew in a shaky breath. "Nick. Stop."

They stared at each other like circling wolves until Nick sagged and sat on the bed. He put his head in his hands. Bess sat next to him to drape her arm around his shoulders. He didn't pull away.

"We'll figure this out." It was what she'd always told her

boys whenever they faced a problem they couldn't immediately solve. It seemed to be the right answer now, too.

Nick's fingers tightened in the hair at his temples and he answered in a muffled voice. "There's nothing to figure out, Bess. I can't leave. If I try, it kills me all over again."

She didn't think he knew he'd started to vanish in front of her eyes. She wasn't sure she wanted him to know. "I'm sorry."

He pulled his face from his hands to look at her. "Are you? Really?"

"What's that supposed to mean?" Her retort stung her tongue.

"I think you know what the fuck it means."

She refused to blanch at his language or his anger. Besides, she knew, even if he didn't or wouldn't admit it. "Of course I don't want you to leave. But if you're saying I'm happy that you can't go beyond the beach—"

"You don't want me to leave," he said in a low voice, without looking at her. "I get it. I know, Bess."

She was not the one who'd done this…was she? She would never have wished him pain. Her voice, when it came, sounded faraway. "I'm sorry it hurt you."

He shrugged wordlessly. She put her head on his shoulder. Nick stiffened at that but relaxed a moment later. Bess felt a small but certain victory when he turned to her, put his arms around her and buried his face in the side of her neck. When he kissed her mouth.

When he told her he didn't want to leave her, anyway.

Chapter 24

Then

*T*he next time Nick had a party, he seemed to think there was no question about Bess attending when he showed up at Sugarland to tell her about it. And, in fact, there wasn't any question in Bess's mind, though apparently Missy had a few.

She was there, eating a soft pretzel dipped in mustard, when Nick came in. He tossed a few words her way, but unlike the one he gave Brian and Bess, his invitation to Missy was less than enthusiastic. He even called back to Eddie, though everyone knew Eddie didn't go to parties. Then Nick winked at Bess, flipped Brian the finger and sauntered out, leaving the shop desolately empty.

Brian fanned his face. "Damn, that boy makes a sex vacuum wherever he goes."

Bess laughed. "A what?"

Missy glared. "If you're saying Nick Hamilton sucks, Brian, you're right."

"Don't I wish," Brian declared with a simper. "But what I meant, Miss I'm-Not-Queen-of-the-Science-Fair, was that he makes a sex vacuum—you know. An empty space. He sucks all the sex right out of the room when he goes... Oh, forget it." Disgusted, Brian stomped into the back room.

Bess's grin faded as she turned to Missy. "What's the matter with you?"

"Nothing's the matter with me. But don't you think Andy might have a problem?"

"Andy's none of your business." Bess wiped down the tables and ignored her.

"I can't believe you're going to dump your boyfriend for a fling with Nick the Prick, that's all." Missy's softened tone didn't lend any sincerity to her words.

Bess straightened and fixed the other girl with a steady gaze. "Don't call him that."

"What, Nick the Prick? How about Nick the Dick?"

"I refuse to discuss this with you." Bess went back around the counter to rinse out the washcloth.

"You'll see. Don't say I didn't warn you." Missy hopped off the high stool to toss her trash. "Nick fucks around. He fucked around on Heather—"

"First of all," Bess interrupted, "I'm not Heather."

She didn't expand on that, just allowed Missy to figure out the comparison.

"Second," she continued, "he's not my boyfriend. I'm not his girlfriend. What we're doing isn't anyone's business but ours, and it's between us, okay? Third, he says Heather cheated on him."

Missy flipped her hair back over one shoulder. "Well…"

"Yeah. Well." Bess rolled her eyes. "Whatever, Missy. Really. Lay off. Just because you're jealous—"

Missy gaped, then flushed, then tossed her hair again. "Oh, right!"

Bess glared. Missy glared. Missy looked away first.

"Whatever," she muttered. "He's a prick and you're my friend. I just don't want to see you get hurt."

"Nobody's going to get hurt, Missy."

Missy stepped aside to allow a pack of ice-cream-addicted zombies get to the counter, and by the time Bess had finished waiting on them, she had gone.

Bess took more care with her hair and makeup and clothes for this party. She even put on matching underwear, a pretty emerald-green satin set she'd bought herself for her birthday.

"You look pretty." Benji, her cousin Danielle's oldest son, poked his head into the laundry room. With just a sink, mirror and toilet it wasn't as nice as a fully equipped bathroom, but it was private. Mostly.

"Thanks." Bess touched up her eyeliner, a smoky gray that made her eyes look much bluer. She glanced at Benji, who wore a pair of Spiderman pj's and had chocolate fudge smeared at the corners of his lips. "What are you guys doing?"

"Mama and Daddy said we have to go to bed." The affront he felt was clear.

Bess smiled as she smoothed gloss over her lips. "You'd better listen to your mama and daddy then."

"Do you have a boyfriend, Bess?"

She capped her gloss and tumbled her scant makeup supplies back into their bag, then turned to look at her small relative. "Sort of."

He laughed. "Gross!"

She ruffled his hair. "Someday, Benji, you're going to have so many girlfriends you won't know what to do with them."

He squinched up his face. "Why won't I know what to do with 'em?"

Good question. "Trust me," Bess said. "You'll see."

Déjà vu struck her as she biked to Nick's place, but it faded as soon as she went inside his apartment. This party was like a night at the opera compared to the bass-thumping, booze-riddled bash of last time. Bess saw a couple familiar faces, Brian, Missy and Ryan among them, but the other few guests were strangers.

Nick greeted her at the door. "C'mon in."

"Wow. You have real food?" She looked at the kitchen table, set with a platter of subs and a few bowls of chips.

Nick laughed. "Yeah. Hungry?"

She was starving, actually, but felt shy at first about helping herself. Nick led her to the table and filled her plate with food. She stared at him across the table as he layered chips on top of the sub.

He caught her looking and grinned. The moment broke a second later when most everyone else from the living room pushed into the kitchen, which wasn't big enough for them all.

They ate, they laughed, they played an ancient game of Trivial Pursuit. The drinking was kept to a minimum. It took Bess until halfway through the game to realize this was a couples party. She counted mentally, blanking out the sound of Missy asking another girl a question about the Soviet Union. One boy for every girl. Or in Brian's case, one boy.

She was Nick's date at his own party.

For some reason this caused her palms to sweat and her lips refuse to do anything but smile. She didn't win Trivial Pursuit. She also didn't care.

The party ended earlier than the other had, too, at some hour late enough to officially be morning, but which still felt like the middle of the night. Nick waved goodbye to the last of his friends, then shut the door and turned to look at Bess, still sitting by the coffee table.

"I'll help you clean up," she offered. It wouldn't take long, and she didn't want to leave. She didn't know how else to suggest she could stay.

Nick didn't turn down her offer, but pulled out a bag of white bread from his fridge and popped some into the toaster. "Want some toast?"

"Are you still hungry?" Bess couldn't have eaten a thing.

He hopped up on the counter, his feet dangling. "Yeah."

Bess leaned against the counter directly opposite him. His kitchen was so small his foot brushed the bottom of her denim shorts. When the toast popped, he pulled out one piece and crunched it, dry.

"Toast smells like sex," he said from around a mouthful of crumbs.

Bess laughed. "What?"

Nick wafted the slice in front of her face. "Doesn't it?"

"If you say so."

He finished the piece and didn't eat the other. Bess leaned to brush some crumbs from his lips. Tension as thick as honey swirled between them.

She'd been bold before, but despite Bess's scoffing Missy's warning still rang in her head. She wanted to step between his legs and pull him down to her for a kiss, but hesitated.

Nick's eyes gleamed. "Sure you don't want any toast?"

"I don't want toast." Surely she didn't have to spell it out?

"Really." He cradled his elbow in one hand and used the other to tap his chin. "What could you possibly want, instead?"

She laughed and moved closer. "It's no fun if you don't want it, too."

"If I don't want it, I'll make sure you know."

Encouraged, she stood on her tiptoes to offer her mouth, but Nick put a hand on her shoulder. The gesture was subtle, but there was no doubt he was pushing her away.

Bess took a step back, the smile sliding from her face. "No?"

Nick was off the counter and guiding her backward before she had time to ask again. Three steps took them through his bedroom door, which he kicked shut. She was on the bed with him on top of her one second after that.

His mouth fastened on her throat as his hands started on her shirt. Bess spent less than a minute stunned into passivity before lifting her arms so he could pull off her shirt. They were both naked in moments.

She took him in her hand and stroked. Nick shuddered against her neck, his fingers sliding between her legs. He hissed a little when he found her wet and ready. More than ready. He pressed his finger to her clit, and Bess cooed with pleasure.

Nick reached in the drawer for a condom and gave it to her. She stared at it for a second, then at him.

"You put it on. I'll help you." He dropped his hand over hers and moved it up and down his erection. He bit his lip when she palmed the head and twisted on the downstroke.

"I've done this before," Bess whispered, with another laugh.

"Still helping." Nick's voice had gone husky. He took her other hand, the one with the condom, and positioned at his prick so the latex ring settled around the head. Then, together, his hand over hers, they unrolled it all the way down.

Bess stared, mouth dry, the sight more erotic than she'd ever have expected. Each motion, every movement, seemed like almost too much to endure. This simple act, sheathing him so he could go inside her…inside her!

Her nipples throbbed, hard and tight. Heat swelled in her belly and her cheeks and along the column of her throat. Bess looked at Nick as he leaned back on the pillows, then she took her hand off his cock.

She dropped onto her hands and knees beside him, then flipped onto her back. "This way."

Nick rolled on top of her and guided himself inside her. He pushed himself up on his hands to look down into her eyes. He moved, and she moved with him.

She caught her breath at the pleasure as they rocked, getting closer. "Say my name."

Nick blinked and shook his head minutely. "I won't…"

"You will," she breathed.

The corners of his eyes tightened, and so did his mouth as he fought against doing what she asked. She tilted her hips, taking him in deeper. He didn't look away from her eyes, and in that moment, just before he gave her what she wanted, she felt somehow she'd won something precious.

Her name whispered out of him, low and hoarse, and he squeezed his eyes shut as he came. She followed at once, her body tightening around him, but she didn't look away. Later, condom disposed of and visits to the bathroom taken care of, she lay next to him, sharing a pillow and staring at his ceiling.

"Are you going to tell him?" Nick asked quietly.

"I don't think so."

Nick shifted. "Pretty ironic, don't you think?"

She looked at him. "What?"

He gazed at her. "That you're the first girl I've really wanted to be with in a long time, and you have a boyfriend."

"Sort of," she said, unable to hide her smile.

Nick didn't smile. "Listen. I can't promise you I'll be with you forever or anything like that—"

She sat up. "I don't expect you to."

Nick sat, too. "But I can promise you you're the only girl I'm fucking right now."

Bess blinked rapidly, surprised and pleased and scared. "I'm not sleeping with anyone else, either."

Nick grinned. "No?"

"I broke up with him." She smiled, pulling her knees to her chest and resting her chin on them. Andy didn't know it, maybe, but she did.

"So you have lots of time then. To spend with me." Nick slid a hand up her thigh.

"Yes. I guess I do."

"Good," he said, as if they'd settled something important.

Bess wasn't sure exactly what it was.

Chapter 25

Now

$\mathcal{F}$or the first time in nineteen years, Bess had opened up her own checking account. It hadn't taken long. Half an hour at the bank and another fifteen minutes at home to set up the new account on her laptop's accounting software program. She should've felt empowered, or at least reassured by the numbers in the columns, but as she stared at this, one more proof of how her life was changing, all she felt was sad.

"What's up?" Nick leaned over her shoulder to stare at the screen, but kissed her cheek and moved away before she could comment. "Put that away and come to bed."

"We just got out of bed," she murmured. Her fingers stroked the keys, scrolling through the numbers in the columns. She'd entered her projected bills for the next few months. "I'm going to have to get a job."

She looked at Nick, who'd gone to look out the sliding-glass doors. He glanced over his shoulder at her, then turned. Bess shut down her program and closed the laptop.

"Yeah," he said after a moment. "I guess I'm not going to be much help, there."

She didn't point out that it wasn't as though he was going to cost her a lot, either. "I'm not worried about that."

He gave her a half nod and looked back out through the glass. "What sort of job do you want to get?"

Bess laughed a little. "I've been thinking about it, actually. I've had an offer."

"Yeah?" Nick glanced again over his shoulder. "From where?"

"Eddie. We came up with a great idea for a new shop and…I think I'm going to tell him I'm interested." She hadn't been positive she meant it until she heard herself say so, but once the words came out Bess knew it was the right decision.

Now Nick turned, hands on his hips and face pulled into a scowl. "What sort of shop? With Eddie? That—"

Bess gave him a warning look, and he stopped. "Eddie's a business owner, Nick. He bought Sugarland. He's got the experience to run a shop, and we decided this was something new and unique. Not just another popcorn palace."

Nick's mouth worked, but he looked away without saying anything. He was jealous, Bess realized, and couldn't help but smile. She went to him and slipped her arms around his waist. Her cheek pressed sweetly between his shoulder blades. She breathed in and out against his warmth.

"It's just a job," she whispered.

"He's in love with you," Nick said, not whispering.

"Oh…no, he's not." Bess sighed. "That was a long time ago."

"Not to me," Nick told her, not moving.

She turned him gently until he faced her. "It was a long time ago."

He frowned, then sighed, then shrugged and tucked her against his chest. "Fine. If it's what you want to do."

She didn't need his permission, but she didn't point that out, either. "I think I want to give it a try, Nick. It's a great idea, and if we can get it off the ground, it'll be better than working for someone else."

He stroked a hand over her hair. "I don't want you to work. I want you to stay here with me all day long and never get out of bed."

"Oh, wouldn't that be nice?" She laughed. "Too bad this is real life."

She heard a smile in his voice. "Yeah. Too bad."

Bess tipped her head back to look at him. "I want to go talk to Eddie. Tell him I'd like to go ahead with the idea. Will you be all right for a while?"

Darkness flashed in his eyes for just a second. "Sure."

"I don't have to go now…."

"No." He shook his head. "You do have to go. You can't stay here all the time. I'll be okay. I'll watch a movie or something. No big deal."

"Are you sure?" Yet she couldn't pretend she wasn't itching to get out of the house for a little while. The ideas for Just A Bite were beginning to bubble up and up, and she wanted to talk to Eddie about them. "I won't be long."

"I said I'll be fine," Nick snapped, and pushed her out of his arms so he could stalk to the couch, where he stabbed the remote with one finger and turned on the sports channel.

"Fine." Bess refused to argue with him. "Can I get you anything while I'm out?"

"No."

She didn't push him further, just went into the bedroom and dressed quickly. She made sure to check for marks, too, but found none that anyone would be able to see. She pulled her hair into a topknot, grabbed her purse and paused to kiss Nick as she left.

"I'll be back soon," she said.

"Take your time." He didn't make it sound like a generous offer.

Bess bent to kiss him again. "I will think of you every second I'm gone."

A reluctant smile tugged his mouth, even if he kept his gaze glued to the television. "Sure you will."

Her hand crept lower, to stroke his stomach. "Be ready for me when I get back."

He pushed her hand lower, over his crotch. "I'm always ready for you."

This time when she kissed him, he kissed her back. They wrestled for a moment until he pulled her over the back of the couch and onto his lap. He kissed her harder, then pulled away to look into her face.

"Don't be too long," he said in a low voice.

"I won't," she assured him. She kissed him again, and he let her get up. By the time she left, he'd turned his attention back to the TV.

Eddie was more than happy to leave Sugarland under Kara's capable eye and walk down the block to the Frog House, where they ordered omelets and home fries and coffee.

"I could eat breakfast anytime," he said with a satisfied sigh when their plates arrived. "Gosh, that looks good."

The very fact he said "gosh" made Bess feel suddenly bubbly toward him.

"So," he continued, unaware of her sudden reaction, "what's on your agenda for today? Are you going out to look for a job?"

She shook her head and stabbed at her eggs, though she was so excited she could hardly eat a thing. "Actually, that's what I'm here to talk about."

"Yeah?" Eddie grinned and set down his fork. "Tell me."

Bess laughed. "I've been thinking about Just A Bite—"

"Woo hoo! I knew it!" He pumped a fist in the air.

Bess expected embarrassment at the way heads turned to look at them, but her cheeks didn't burn. She laughed again. "I have no money, Eddie. I need a job. I'm not even sure—"

"I told you. I can get the money. How's your credit?" His grin softened, still tweaking the corners of his eyes, but he looked more serious.

"Fine, I guess." Bess's heart thumped a little faster. They were really going to do this. "Will that matter?"

"If your name's on the line of credit, sure." He looked her over. "This is going to be great."

Then she did blush. "I'm glad you think so."

Eddie beamed. "I mean it."

"I have to do something," she said. "My last job was as an addiction counselor. They don't even have the same drugs now, Eddie. I mean, people are snorting and shooting stuff I never heard of. I'm not sure I could get back into it."

"You could." Eddie made it sound so easy, Bess believed he was right. "But I'm glad you're not going to!"

Warmth flooded her at his enthusiasm. "The bills won't pay themselves. And after this summer, when Connor goes off to college and Robbie gets settled into school, and when the divorce goes through…"

She trailed off, but Eddie didn't let the silence become uncomfortable. "Fall will be the perfect time to start making the renovations. It will all work out, Bess. You'll see."

There was something so comforting about the way he said it. "I know."

Eddie's phone beeped and he pulled it from his pocket with a glance at the screen. "That's Kara. I guess I should head back."

"I should get home." Bess grabbed up the check before he could. "I have this."

"No." Eddie made a play for the slip of paper, "I asked you. It's my treat."

"Nope." Bess clutched it close to her chest, out of reach. "I got it."

He held up both hands in surrender. "Fine. But then I owe you one."

"No, you don't!" She laughed. "You bought coffee the last time!"

Eddie shook his head. "I asked you, I should pay. Anyway. Maybe I could take you to dinner, sometime?"

Dinner was not breakfast, and they both knew it. Knew what the question was really asking. Bess opened her mouth to answer, but Eddie cut her off gently.

"If it's too soon, I understand. I mean…with the divorce and everything. It could just be a friendly dinner."

"I didn't think it would be anything else," Bess said.

Eddie had a lovely smile that made his blue eyes twinkle from behind the dark-framed glasses. "Too bad. Because I was really asking you for a date."

She shifted, uncomfortable not because she didn't think the idea was appealing, but rather because suddenly, it was. "Eddie…"

"Just think about it." He leaned forward a little bit.

Bess looked into his eyes. "I can't, Eddie."

She hoped he wouldn't take it the wrong way, but what would the right way be? She couldn't tell him the truth, and leaving him to think he understood her reasons seemed more dishonest than he deserved.

Eddie nodded as though he'd expected her answer. "Fair enough." He smiled. "But if you change your mind, the offer still stands."

Bess cocked her head to look him over. "You've really changed, haven't you?"

"I hope so." Eddie passed a hand over his hair and looked self-conscious for the first time since they'd met again. "I grew up, I guess."

"It suits you," Bess said, though once the words were out of her mouth she thought she'd regret them.

Eddie's smile didn't let her. "Thanks."

They looked at each other for half a minute or so, smiling, and Bess stood. "I've got to get back to the house. Thanks, Eddie. For…everything."

For giving her sons jobs. For asking her on a date and proving she wasn't just someone's mother or a soon-to-be ex-wife. For being her friend, even after twenty long years had changed them both.

"Anytime," Eddie said, and Bess believed him.

Chapter 26

Then

The ease with which they'd fallen into familiarity amazed her, but Bess didn't admit it to Nick. He seemed to assume this was the natural course of things—initially casual but smoking-hot sex, followed swiftly by spending every moment of free time together. Every time she closed Sugarland and he was there waiting for her, her stomach swooped and dipped in the roller-coaster rush of first attraction.

Of course, it had only been three weeks.

They didn't walk hand in hand along the beach cooing poetry, and he didn't bring her flowers. Nick was more likely to feed her pizza and a milkshake at his apartment than buy an expensive dinner. A trip to the movies meant a drive, and since neither of them had a car, it meant relying on the generosity of friends. Missy was ignoring them both and Ryan did whatever Missy wanted, so Nick and Bess's dates were restricted to what they could do in town.

She didn't care. Most times after working a full day she really only wanted to crash on the couch, anyway. She'd been picking up as many hours as she could, which sometimes meant working a closing shift and then getting up early the next morning to open, taking a four or five hour break, and going back to close again.

They didn't give what they were doing a name. Didn't even acknowledge it to anyone, though it couldn't have been a secret. Brian had stopped teasing Bess about it, which proved to her how serious it must seem to anyone observing, but between themselves neither of them talked about the "we" or the "us."

Bess hadn't spoken to Andy since the night he'd hung up on her. Every day that passed without her calling him or him calling her made it harder to imagine doing so. She tried to feel sad, or guilty, or even to be angry about the way things had happened, but there frankly wasn't much room in either her head or her heart for wishing or moping. Nick had filled her up, every crack and crevice.

She hadn't moved into his apartment and rarely even spent the night, trying at least for an attempt at propriety. She did hang a toothbrush in his bathroom and kept a small bag of toiletries there, and that seemed so significant to her she made sure never to mention it.

The sex got impossibly better each time they did it, which was every time they saw one another. Which was at least once a day, sometimes twice, and once a memorable four times that had left her wincing for a day or two when she rode her bike. This, too, they didn't talk about. Not about how he liked to pin her hands above her head or wrap his fingers in her hair when she got on her knees, and not about how there were days when he opened the front door and fucked her up against it within minutes of her arrival. Not about how they were naked in every way two people can be with one another, but since the first night they'd been together, they'd never kissed on the mouth.

Tonight, Bess flopped on Nick's bed in front of the rotating fan pushing swirls of hot air around the room. Her own tiny room had central air-conditioning, but she didn't mention that. She never took Nick there. She didn't want to have to explain him. Andy had been a fixture at family functions for so long there was no way her relatives wouldn't ask questions she didn't want to answer. She yawned, curling one of Nick's pillows beneath her cheek while he flipped lazily through the channels. They'd already eaten. Already fucked. She was only trying to rouse enough energy to take a shower and ride home.

Nick stopped at a scene on the TV of a woman with long, dark hair throwing snowballs at a boy with blond hair. They fell down in the snow, laughing and kissing.

"Want to watch this?" He tossed the remote onto the dresser without waiting for an answer.

"*Love Story?* Sure." She'd seen it half a dozen times, which meant it was perfect for a night when she didn't want to concentrate.

As naked as she was, Nick moved behind her to share the mound of pillows. One hand rested familiarly on her hip. His pubic hair tickled the small of her back, and Bess shifted a little against him. Their legs twined. She yawned.

"I should go."

Nick's hand tightened a little on her hip before relaxing. "In a while."

Too lazy from two orgasms, and not wanting to face the bike ride home on hot streets, Bess said nothing and didn't move. The movie played on, and though she had seen it so often she could quote some of the dialogue, for some reason tonight it made her more melancholy.

"What a bunch of crap." Nick's breath ruffled the back of her hair. "Love means never having to say you're sorry? C'mon."

"It's romantic," Bess said.

"It's lame."

She sat to look at him. "Why is it lame? They love each other."

Nick stared. "You think that's love?"

"I didn't say it was real," she said scornfully. She drew away from him a little bit. "I just said it was romantic. Some people like that."

Nick sat, too. "Like you?"

She lifted her chin. "Maybe I do."

Nick's laugh for once didn't urge her to join him. "Well then, you're fucking the wrong guy."

It wasn't anything she didn't already know, but Bess looked away. Nick scooted closer, nudging her shoulder with his chin and putting his arms around her. She didn't even glance at him.

"Hey," he said quietly. "I'm going to get a drink. Do you want one?"

She shook her head silently. Before he got up, she grabbed his wrist. When he looked at her, she leaned in, just a little, lips parted.

Nick didn't kiss her. The moment stretched between them until it broke, and he got up and left the room.

She was sitting in the same position when he came back and made a flying tackle onto the bed. Nick cuddled her, his mouth pressed close to her ear.

"You think too much," he said. "Don't think so much."

Bess, who spent way too much time thinking, pushed slowly away from him and started hunting for her clothes. He sat up to watch her, at first silently, but when she slipped her legs into her jean shorts and buttoned them, he stood and grabbed her arm.

"Don't leave."

"I have to work in the morning, Nick."

"Stay here tonight. Sleep here."

She shook her head. His fingers dug a little deeper into her skin, the sort of reaction she welcomed most other times, but now seemed only to make her want to cry.

"So…you can stay when you're fucking me, but when that's done you can't sleep next to me?"

"So," she said evenly, looking into his eyes, "you can put your dick inside me but you can't put your mouth on mine?"

He let go of her arm. Bess bent to pick up her shirt and pull it over her head. Nick didn't move.

"Is that what you want?" he asked. "You want flowers and long walks in the park? I don't do that."

"That's not what I'm talking about."

He followed her through the kitchen to the living room, where she hunted for her backpack. "What are you talking about?"

She whirled. "Are you ever going to kiss me when we're not fucking?"

Nick scowled, but strode to her and kissed her cheek with a loud smack.

Bess shook her head. "Are you ever going to kiss me on the mouth?"

"Maybe for Christmas or your birthday."

"Fuck you, Nick," Bess said, wondering how this conversation had begun and why she was making so much of it. She turned on her heel and left.

He caught up to her when she was only a few steps from his place. His bare feet slapped the pavement. He'd pulled on a ragged pair of shorts from God-knew-where, but at least he wasn't naked.

"Christmas is months away," Nick said. "So's your birthday."

Bess stopped and turned her bike back, leaning it against his porch. "Yeah? So?"

He crossed his arms over his chest. "So...months from now, Bess."

She mirrored his position. "And? Months from now I won't be here anymore."

He unhooked his arms to brush her hair off her shoulders. "I'll come see you."

She laughed humorlessly. "Oh, yeah? Will you?"

It was Nick's turn not to laugh. "Yeah. I will."

Bess didn't know if she wanted to bend or break. "And you'll kiss me on the mouth at Christmas?"

He nodded. His hand slid down her arm to tug at her wrist. To pull her closer.

"What about between then and now?" she inquired suspiciously.

"Is that what you really want?" he asked softly into her ear.

She shivered at the whisper. "Just because I don't want to be your girlfriend doesn't mean...it doesn't mean..."

His mouth moving on her skin made it hard to speak.

"Doesn't mean what?" Nick murmured.

"Doesn't mean I don't care about you," she finished, and pushed him away with a hand on his shoulder.

Nick looked at her, then nodded slowly. "Come inside with me."

She shook her head. "No. I have to go home."

His hands crept to her waist. "Come inside with me, Bess."

She wanted to, more than anything. "No."

Nick brushed his lips along the dip of her collar, then up

her neck to her ear again. "Come inside and I'll kiss you wherever you want."

"I don't want you to do it if it's not what *you* want!" Stubborn and hating herself for it, Bess tried not to be wooed.

"And I told you not to think you know what I want. Come inside."

She'd gone two steps toward the porch with him when her emotions made her clumsy and she stumbled on the steps. Nick caught her with a hand beneath her elbow.

"Be careful," he said.

Bess looked at him. "I think it's too late for that."

He smiled. Then he kissed her, right there on the porch where the whole world could see. Right on the mouth. Right where she wanted.

Chapter 27

Now

"You'll be all right?" Bess couldn't stop herself from asking the same question she'd asked less than half an hour before, but now that she was actually getting ready to leave it had risen to her lips and refused to be restrained.

"What am I going to do? Throw a party?" Nick looked up from his place on the couch, where he'd been reading a yellowed and sea-swollen copy of *Brave New World*.

"It wouldn't be the first time." Bess found a smile.

Nick snorted lightly and tucked a finger between the pages to mark his place. "I'll be fine. You're only going to be gone for two days."

"It's going to be a long two days."

"So come over here and kiss me goodbye," he said. "Because when you come home with your kids, we won't be able to fuck in the living room anymore."

She crossed to the couch and bent over the back to kiss him, but Nick tossed the book aside and captured her. He pulled her, laughing, over the top of the couch and onto him. His arms pinned her, not that she was struggling. He kissed her slowly and thoroughly.

"You'd better get on the road," he said, but neither of them moved.

Bess looked into his eyes, so dark there seemed almost no delineation between the iris and the pupil. Today he wore a bandanna tied around his hair to hold it off his face, and the sight of it was sweetly nostalgic. Bare-chested, wearing jeans lower than sin, he had to know how sexy he looked. He always had.

Against her belly, even through the denim of his jeans and the cotton of her sundress, Nick's cock bulged. He'd woken her this morning with his hand between her legs, made her come twice before he'd even entered her. He'd rubbed up against her while she'd been packing the small overnight bag she was taking, and kissed her so frequently throughout the morning, her lips were puffy.

"Again?" she murmured against his mouth.

"I don't want you to forget me."

"As if I could."

His hand slid her dress up and over her ass. He rubbed her lacy panties as he kissed her. His thigh thrust up between her legs and he pushed down on her butt to press her against it.

"I can feel how hot you are, even through my jeans."

Bess shifted to put her hand between them. "I can feel how hard you are."

Nick slipped a palm beneath her panties to caress her bare skin. He traced the seam between her buttocks, making her squirm, and pinned her still with his other arm.

"I want to fuck you so hard you can't stand," he whispered

into her ear. "So every time you take a step, you think about me inside you. I want you to spend the next two days wishing I *was* inside you."

Bess had no doubt all of those wishes were going to be true, but his mouth on hers prevented her from answering with anything but a groan. Nick's tongue swept inside her mouth over and over, arousing her mercilessly.

"You know what I love most off all?" she asked when he at last pulled away to let her breathe.

His hands roamed her body, tugging at her panties. "What?"

"Kissing you."

He stopped moving and looked into her eyes. Then he kissed her again with a soft brush of lip on lip that promised more. When she opened for him, he gave it. Nick made love to her mouth until her head spun.

"Like that?" he asked.

"Yes."

He smiled and hooked his thumbs into her panties and eased them off her ass and down her thighs so she was bare. His hand moved between her legs and found her clit. She jumped a little when he rubbed it.

"I know what else you like, too," he said, and then, caught up in the intensity and ecstasy of their lovemaking, Bess forgot everything else.

She was late leaving, which meant she was late getting to the house she'd shared with Andy for the past thirteen years. As she pulled into the driveway, Bess's heart thundered in her ears. She had to forcibly uncurl her fingers from the steering wheel, and getting out of the car left her so light-headed she had to close her eyes lest she faint.

"Mom!"

She blinked and pasted on a smile as Robbie barreled out

the front door. He was too old to hug her now, but he danced in front of her the way he had since toddlerhood, bursting with something important to tell her. "Hi, honey."

Robbie reached into the backseat to grab her suitcase without being asked, and that small gesture shot fierce pride through her. He slung the strap over his shoulder and followed her toward the front door. He'd grown even in the few short weeks she'd been gone, and Bess's heart ached afresh for the dissolution of their family.

"I'm pretty sure I aced all my finals," Robbie was saying as she opened the front door.

Inside, the house no longer even smelled familiar. Robbie dropped her suitcase on the floor by the door and Bess picked it up to set it by the stairs. Her son, still talking, was already heading down the long hall toward the kitchen, and Bess followed because she could think of no other place to go.

Bags of chips and pretzels, hot dog and hamburger buns and jars of pickles and dips covered every inch of counter space. Bess sighed, but at least Andy had bought the food for Connor's graduation party the next day. They planned to have it out back, by the pool, and had hired a disc jockey to come. The yard would be overflowing with friends and family, and with any luck, Bess wouldn't have to talk to Andy at all.

"Where's your dad?"

Robbie, waist-deep in the fridge, pulled out a long, wrapped submarine sandwich. He set it on the counter and took out a knife from the drawer. "Oh…working?"

On a Friday night? Not likely. "How about your brother?"

"Oh." Robbie shrugged. "He's out with Kent and Rick and those guys."

"Ah." Bess tried not to feel stung that Connor hadn't

stayed home to hang out with her. "You don't have any big plans for tonight?"

Robbie held up the huge hunk of sandwich he'd cut for himself. "This and the entire first season of *The X-Files*. You up for it?"

She hadn't eaten since breakfast that morning and her mouth watered at the sight of thick slices of turkey and salami and the smell of the sub dressing. "Yeah. Cut me a piece."

She grabbed one of the bags of chips and tore it open, putting handfuls on their plates. She and Robbie ate in the den in front of Andy's big-screen TV, polishing off half the huge sub and most of the bag of chips between them, along with a two-liter bottle of soda and a pint of ice cream. Robbie went to bed at midnight, with Andy and Connor still not home, and Bess puttered around the kitchen, cleaning up crumbs and scrubbing nonexistent dirt.

The kitchen remodel had been Andy's idea, though he'd said it was for her. When they'd added the in-ground pool in the back, Andy wanted sliding-glass doors to the backyard. That had meant ripping out most of the counter space along the rear wall. The project had snowballed, and now the kitchen gleamed with marble counters and every appliance anyone could possibly desire, plus a few Bess had never even used. She wouldn't miss it, not any of it, and this more than anything else brought the tears.

She swiped them away quickly enough when she heard the front door open and close, and the slow, steady footprints of someone coming down the hall. She braced herself to face her husband, but it was Connor who swerved into the kitchen and went immediately to the cupboard for a glass he filled with water from the sink.

"Hey, honey," Bess said.

Connor gulped down water and wouldn't look at her. "Hey, Mom."

"Are you all ready for tomorrow? It's late." She glanced at the clock. Connor hadn't had a curfew for the past year or so, because he hadn't needed to be told when to come home. Now it was after one in the morning.

"It's just a stupid ceremony. We don't even really get our diplomas." He set the glass in the sink and turned as if to go.

"Connor."

He stopped in the doorway, finally, and looked at her. There was no mistaking his red eyes or too-careful gait for anything else. The question was, should she address it?

"Did you have fun tonight?"

He nodded.

"Listen, Connor…"

He held up a hand. "Mom, spare the lecture, okay? I just want to crash so I'm not dead tomorrow morning."

"What were you doing, out so late? I was worried."

Connor's glance flickered. "I'm fine."

"I can see that." She crossed her arms.

"Why don't you worry about Dad, if you want to worry about something? He's not home, either."

"Your dad is an adult—"

Connor snorted loudly, and with unmistakable derision. "Yeah. Sure."

"Go to bed, Connor," Bess said sternly. "Sleep it off."

She waited until he'd left before she went into the den to make herself a bed on the couch, but though she waited up for what seemed like forever, she didn't hear Andy come home.

Whatever Connor had been doing the night before, he was up and in the shower when Bess finally trudged up the stairs to her bedroom so she could sneak into her own shower before either of the boys found her on the couch. They knew she and Andy were separating, but she hadn't told them it was going to be permanent. She didn't want to ruin Connor's party...or their summer.

Andy, with damp hair and a towel around his waist, stood shaving in front of the mirror. He looked over at her when she came halfway through the door and stopped as though she were stuck. Then he looked back to the mirror.

"Sleep well?"

Bess glanced over her shoulder at the bed, which didn't look as though it had been slept in at all. "Fine."

Andy wiped his face clean of foam and splashed himself with cologne. Bess edged past him and rummaged for a clean towel. She took her time because though she'd been naked in front of Andy hundreds of times, she didn't want to get naked in front of him now. Thankfully, he left before she had to. Maybe he didn't want her to be naked in front of him, either.

The graduation ceremony was longer than it had to be, but years of attending school plays and concerts had prepared Bess for that. Robbie sat between her and Andy, and instead of sighing over yet another speech, Bess soaked in every moment. It would probably be one of the last times they ever spend together like this. As a family.

Nobody else seemed to notice that Bess felt out of place in her own backyard. Unbeknownst to her, Andy had hired a caterer to come in to cook the hot dogs and burgers and do all the serving and cleaning up. Bess tried to assume he'd been trying to be thoughtful, but without the usual tasks of fetching food and washing dishes, she wasn't sure what to do with herself.

They'd sent out so many invitations she'd lost track of how

many people to expect, but as more and more guests poured into the backyard, dived into the pool and overflowed into the kitchen, Bess didn't feel overwhelmed. Again, this would be the last time they'd all be together like this. After today, things were going to change.

Bess hadn't ever been good with change. She'd never been good with taking leaps of faith, or risks or chances. When something worked, she tended to stick with it.

Even when something didn't.

"Hey, Bess!" Ben, Bess's second cousin on her dad's side, waved at her from the table holding the cake. "Great party! My mom and dad are over there."

He pointed, and Bess waved. Relations had been a little strained among some of the family members when her grandparents had been deciding what to do about the beach house, but her cousin Danielle and her family had never made things awkward.

"You'll have to come down sometime this summer," she told Ben. "The way you used to."

He laughed, a tall, broad-shouldered man who looked a lot like her grandpa. She still remembered him as a little boy with chocolate on his cheeks. "If I can get some time off work, sure. Thanks."

Bess waved at him again as he headed off through the crowd with his cake. She checked automatically to see if she needed to cut more, but the caterer was already on it. Ditto for the napkins and plasticware.

"Don't look so worried. Everyone's having a great time."

Bess turned and broke into a broad smile at the sight of the familiar face. "Joe!"

The man beside her could have stepped off the cover of a men's fashion magazine. He should've looked overdressed compared to the rest of the crowd, but something about his clothes suited him so perfectly Bess couldn't have imagined him in denim shorts and a T-shirt with Kiss the Cook on it. Joe and Andy had worked together before Bess and Andy were married, but though the men had eventually ended up at different law firms, they'd always kept in touch. Joe had been to the boys' christenings and birthdays for years, so it was no surprise seeing him now. Yet tears sparked behind Bess's eyes at the sight of his smile, anyway.

"Little Connor all grown up," Joe said mildly. "I see he towers over you and has a bevy of giggling beauties at his beck and call."

"Yes. That's Connor." Bess laughed, some of her melancholy fading. Joe grinned, his gaze flickering past Bess to a woman standing by the pool. Bess, watching him, smiled, too. "How's married life treating you?"

Joe's smile got wider. "Can't complain."

"Lucky you." Bess looked automatically for Andy, though she couldn't see him.

This time, Joe didn't look away. "Hey, Bess, about that…"

She waved a hand. "Hush. It's not your problem."

Joe's brow furrowed. "Yeah, I know. But…"

"I said hush," Bess repeated. "You're Andy's friend. I don't expect you to take sides. Besides, it's for the best."

Joe nodded. "How are the boys?"

Bess looked toward the pool, where Robbie and Connor, on opposing teams, played water volleyball. "I hope they'll be fine, but really…how can I expect them to be fine when I'm changing everything they've ever known?"

"Bess." Joe's voice, low and firm, was as welcome as the pressure of his fingers on her shoulder. "Kids are resilient, and believe me, it's better they learn how to make a relationship work rather than watch one that's broken. Better for you, too."

Bess caught sight of Andy at last. He was talking to a woman by the buffet table. Bess didn't recognize her, but she didn't have to. She turned, her stomach sinking.

"Thanks, Joe." Her voice gave no indication of the turmoil within, but Joe's gaze followed the path hers had taken.

He squeezed her shoulder again as the woman he'd married arrived with two drinks. Bess had met Sadie only once before, at their wedding. She didn't have the strength for small talk, so she excused herself on the pretense of checking something in the house. In the kitchen, Andy's kitchen, she wove through the throng and went upstairs to her bedroom, where she lifted the phone and dialed an almost-forgotten number.

She closed her eyes, picturing the beach house. The outdated yellow phone with its stretched-out cord, ringing and ringing. Nobody answered.

Finally, she hung up. She tensed at the sound of soft voices in the hall, and went to the bedroom door, meaning to close it. Through the crack she saw Andy and the woman standing in front of one of the multi-photo frames Bess had filled with snapshots over the years. Andy was pointing out different pictures of Connor and Robbie, and his companion listened intently.

They weren't touching, but they didn't have to. Bess closed the bedroom door with a subtle click she knew they'd have to hear, and waited. It took Andy only half a minute to come in.

"Bess—"

She said nothing, and he stopped himself. Andy closed the door tight behind him and approached where she sat on the end of the bed. When she didn't move, even to flinch, he stopped moving as abruptly as he'd stopped speaking.

She stared at him, the man she'd married with the best intentions. Andy stared back. Time had been harder on him than it had been on her, though she shouldn't have been pleased to notice. Andy's hair had begun to thin and his waistband expand, but he was still a good-looking man.

"So," she said. "We'll be leaving when the party's over."

"You don't have to. You know you can stay overnight. Get an early start."

"No. I think I want to go. It only takes four hours. The boys want to get there, too. I asked them."

Andy nodded slowly. "Bess, listen…"

She waited, but he trailed off and shifted uncomfortably. "Don't, Andy. Okay? Just…don't. We don't need to go over old ground."

"Just like that?" he asked, harsher than she expected. "You're done?"

"Aren't you?" This was harder than telling him she was leaving had been.

Andy sighed, mouth pursed in the expression she'd always hated because it made him look so old, and Bess gave him the courtesy of looking away so she wouldn't have to see him that way.

"I don't want you to think I'm not willing to try, that's all."

"We've tried," she said.

"But we could try again."

Once, his smile had meant everything to her. She'd believed him when he'd said it would all work out, it would be all right. For a long time it had been…and for a long time, it had not.

"Let me ask you something," Bess said, her voice clear and without tremor. "Do you love her?"

Andy coughed. "Who?"

"Don't insult me. Or her. Do you love her?"

His refusal to answer was more than enough reply for Bess, but she didn't get up. She looked at him, though, her expression effortlessly smooth. "You'll be all right, Andy."

"That's a trite answer!"

"It's a true answer. You'll be all right." She got up then, though there was still a lot of distance between them. "And now you have the chance to find something really wonderful. Don't throw it away."

"Like I did with you?" His wry response twisted his mouth, and the honesty in it surprised her.

She gave him honesty, too. "I'll never regret marrying you, Andy, because we have two beautiful sons I love more than anything in this world. But I think it's time to stop fooling ourselves."

"Let me ask you something, Bess."

She waited patiently for him to say what he needed to say.

"Was it all a mistake?"

"No, Andy," she whispered, at last losing her composure. "It wasn't a mistake."

When he hugged her, Bess didn't have to fight so hard to hold on to every sensation. She wouldn't ever forget how it felt to be in his arms that one last time.

Chapter 28

Then

"*H*e's not here, Bess."

Bess ground her teeth in frustration. "Where is he, Matt?"

"He's out."

"With her?" Bess tapped her fingers on the counter, then twisted the phone cord in her hands.

"I don't know what you mean," Matty said.

She sighed and contemplated anger, but to her surprise, the frustration seeped out of her and left behind only a sense of relief. "Can you leave him a message?"

Andy's brother paused, then sighed. "Yeah, sure. Let me get a pen."

"You don't need a pen," Bess said.

Matty made a soft, low noise. "I'm really sorry, Bess."

"It's not your fault." She closed her eyes and slumped a little. "Just tell him…goodbye."

"That's it?"

"If he doesn't get it," she said, her voice a bit bitter, "maybe you can explain it to him."

"Yeah. Okay." Matty sighed again. "For what it's worth, I think he's being a real jerk."

Bess smiled at this. "Thanks."

"No problem."

She put the phone back in its cradle. She waited for tears, but like the anger, they'd fled. She looked up to see her aunt Trish paused in the doorway.

"Bess, you have a friend here to see you."

Her aunt's expression left no doubt that it was a friend of the male persuasion. Her heart leaped. Nick? Here? "Thanks."

Eddie waited for her on the deck. If the scrutiny of her family unnerved him, he didn't show it by shuffling or ducking his head, but when Bess appeared at the sliding-glass doors his cheeks flushed. "Hi, Bess."

"Eddie?" Bess carefully didn't meet the curious gazes of her family. "Is everything okay?"

"Sure, it's okay."

Some sort of explanation seemed necessary. "Eddie works with me at Sugarland."

That seemed to satisfy everyone. Eddie smiled. Bess smiled, too, still not sure why he was there.

"I was taking a walk," he said. "And I thought I'd stop by to say hi."

Bess had worked with Eddie for the past three summers, and he'd never stopped by to say hi. "That was nice."

Eddie shifted a little. "Want to take a walk with me?"

This earned them both another set of looks, so to fend off questions, Bess nodded. "Sure."

Eddie let her go first down the set of splintery stairs to the sand below. Bess waited at the bottom. She found she couldn't quite look at Eddie as they walked side by side toward the water, and for the first time, understood how it must be for him to be near her.

"So…how are you?" Eddie scuffed some sand.

He couldn't have known she needed a friend just then, and yet there he was. "I'm okay."

He nodded, not looking at her. "Good."

Bess slipped off her sandals and walked to the water's edge. The cool waves tickled her toes as she stood, staring out at the sea. She thought there should be something to say, some conversation to be had, but nothing seemed to come. Eddie didn't seem inclined to say anything, either. Together they stood at the edge of the waves and watched them go in and out.

They stood there for a long time.

"Thanks, Eddie," Bess said finally.

"Sure," he said, and looked at her. She looked back. "Anytime."

Now

Neither of her sons seemed to care when Bess told them she had a boarder. They'd hosted exchange students in the past, and this didn't seem too different. They were both a lot like their father in that way, not caring about things that didn't have much to do with themselves. Connor had only grunted, staring out the window, and from the backseat Robbie hadn't said much more.

Bess stopped herself from talking more about it, though her mouth wanted to keep running. Something in her words or the tone of her voice would give her away if she spoke too much. If the situation had been different, she told herself, she'd have been honest about Nick's presence in her life in the way Andy hadn't been. But things weren't different; Nick still looked twenty-one and he wasn't quite alive. It would be asking a lot for her boys to accept him as her lover.

She didn't want to admit she was afraid about telling the truth. If Andy was the only one with a lover, she'd shine so much more brightly in comparison, wouldn't she? If the finger of blame were pointed it would be at Andy, not her. She was ashamed to realize how important that felt.

The closer they got to the beach house the faster her heart beat. By the time they pulled into the carport beneath the house, she was sweating. Her back ached from sitting so stiffly behind the wheel. Her stomach dipped and dived with anticipation.

Love and food poisoning, strikingly similar.

Connor and Robbie got out of the car before Bess did, and both had grabbed their duffels from the trunk before she'd even closed her door. She'd given them both their own keys, and Connor unlocked the door. They were both inside, the door hanging open behind them, while she still stood by the car.

The longer she waited to go inside, the higher the anticipation built. The longer she could convince herself he'd be there, that all would be well. If she didn't go inside, she'd never have to find out if he'd left her while she was gone.

"Mom!" Robbie's voice drifted down the stairs. "Can you grab my pillow?"

Bess unlocked the trunk again and pulled out Robbie's pillow. With no more excuse to linger, she went inside. Directly ahead of her down the short hall were the stairs. Immediately to her right was the door to the laundry room, and next to it the door to Nick's room. It was closed. Had it been open when she left? She couldn't remember.

"I get the big room!"

"No way!"

"I'm older!"

"Mom!"

"Coming!" She navigated the stairs, gave Robbie his pillow and went to her bedroom to put away her purse. Her heart lifted and fell when the room was empty and silent.

No Nick.

He was gone. She knew it. She'd left him for two days and it hadn't been enough to keep him here. He'd gone away again—

The rumble of voices in the living room caught her ear and an undertow of relief tumbled her around for a minute before she went out to see them all. Connor had already raided the fridge for soda. Robbie was pulling out the video game console Bess had brought on an earlier trip but had never hooked up.

And Nick…oh, Nick stood in the living room wearing a pair of jeans and a button-down shirt over a plain white T-shirt. She'd bought him those clothes based on her memories of his taste, and they fit him as well as if he'd picked them out. The sight of his bare feet had her wanting to get on her knees to kiss them.

"Hey, Bess." Nick's casual grin and wave were not the sort of greeting she'd grown used to from him.

It took her too long to answer, and before she could, Nick had already bent over the video game system Robbie was untangling.

"Sweet system," he said.

It was the perfect thing to say. Robbie beamed. "Thanks. I got the new Bounty Hunter game. Want to play?"

"Sure."

Connor hollered from the kitchen, "He sucks, man! You'll kick his ass."

"I doubt it," Nick said.

"So, you've met N-Nick." She stuttered a little on his name

and earned a curious glance from Robbie and a more intense one from Connor. "Nick, these are my sons, Robbie and Connor."

Robbie grinned. "And I don't suck."

Connor wandered into the living room with the bag of chips and the drink and plopped onto the couch. He put his feet up on the coffee table and tossed the chips there, too. "You do, dude."

"Whatever." Robbie dismissed him. He finished untangling the myriad of cords and handed one game controller to Nick. "My mom says you're staying for the summer, huh? In the little room?"

"Yeah. Got a job at the Rusty Rudder, tending bar. So I won't be around that much." Nick took the controller and passed his thumbs over the knobs and buttons. He didn't look at Bess.

None of them looked at her. She'd experienced this before, the Invisibility of Motherhood. She shouldn't have been surprised or disappointed. She wanted her boys to accept Nick as part of the household. She wanted him to like them.

So why did it feel as if they'd automatically formed some sort of club in which she was not welcome?

Bess went to the kitchen to put away the bottle of soda Connor had left on the table. The blips and buzzes of the video game filtered into the kitchen from the living room, punctuated by Connor's taunts and Robbie's retorts. A quick check of the fridge and cupboards told her she needed to buy groceries. What had sustained her for the past few weeks was going to last no more than a day or two with the boys in the house.

She looked out into the living room. Nick's dark hair contrasted sharply with Robbie's blond shag. The three of them laughed. Boys playing. How could she have thought he wouldn't get along with them? He was only a few years older than they were, after all.

Her gaze caught the framed reproduction of a map of the world hanging on the living-room wall. *Here There Be Monsters,* indeed. She didn't want to stand in her kitchen, feeling old and comparing her lover to her sons.

"Guys, I'm running to the grocery store for a few things. Any special requests?"

"Froot Loops," Connor called over his shoulder without turning around.

"Ho Hos," Robbie added.

Nick said nothing, just manipulated the three-dimensional character on the TV screen.

"Nick? You want anything?" Jesus, now she *sounded* like his frigging mother.

"No, thanks."

Bess left them to their game and went to the grocery store. Unlike the last time she'd been here, she didn't have to sit in the parking lot and wonder if she'd lost her mind. The girl on the beach had seen Nick, and so had her boys. He did exist, even if she still hadn't figured out how or what they were going to do for the rest of their...her...life.

She hadn't had time yet to read the books she'd bought from Alicia at Bethany Magick, but a thick paperback caught her eye at the checkout counter: *Spirit Guides.* She scanned the back cover copy, expecting some New Age or Native American text, but the blurb seemed to cover a more extensive topic, and on impulse she tossed the book onto the conveyer belt with the rest of her purchases.

Back home—and it did not escape her that she'd begun thinking of the beach house as home—Connor and Robbie helped her unload the groceries, but Nick was nowhere to be found.

"He said he was going to bed," Robbie replied to her too-casual question.

There was no good reason for her to see if that was the case, and when all the bags had been emptied and everything put away, Bess went to bed herself.

She didn't think she'd fall asleep so fast, but she must have dozed off almost at once because she was dreaming when her eyes flew open when she heard the creak of her door. She sat up, instantly on alert, the knowledge that her children were in the same building having infiltrated her subconscious responses.

Her door closed again with a click. The dark figure moved at once to her bed. By the time he got to her, Bess already knew it wasn't one of her sons. She threw back the covers and shifted over to make room for him, and Nick slid between the sheets wearing nothing but boxers and a T-shirt she stripped him out of quickly.

They didn't speak. It had been a long time since she'd had to do this in silence—so long Bess couldn't recall the last time she'd had to be so quiet when making love. As Nick's tongue found her breasts, her belly and thighs, when his mouth moved over her body and began to lick, she fisted her hand against her mouth to keep from crying out. The whisper of the sheets might have given them away, but when he finally moved up her body to slide inside her, his thrusts were so slow and deliberate the bed barely creaked.

They moved together, mouths sealed so no noise could leak out. His body pressed hers as his cock filled her and withdrew, over and over. They'd never fucked so slowly. While normally she needed a finger on her clit to help her along, this time the easy pressure of his body against hers built the pleasure with excruciating slowness. Her thighs trembled as she locked her legs around him. The stroke of his tongue in her mouth echoed what he was doing with his prick. Slow and easy. Sweat covered her and her fingers dug into his back, then his ass, pushing him harder against her.

Her orgasm happened in small but growing ripples, each beat and pulse larger than the next as her body jerked beneath his. She came and came again, or maybe she never stopped. Even after the initial climax eased, the nudge of Nick's pelvis against her clit sent waves of pleasure throughout her.

He was still kissing her when he shuddered into his own orgasm. He sucked in a gasp, stealing her breath so she could make no noise even if she'd wanted. The darkness spun with stars. Pushing against it, Bess tried to breathe, but with Nick's mouth slanted so tightly across hers the effort was impossible.

He broke the kiss and rasped out the breath he'd stolen. She drew heated air into her lungs with a sudden, grateful mewl. It was the only sound they'd made, and she tensed, listening for any sign they'd been heard.

Nick rolled off her but kept close, his hand on her belly. Bess stared at the ceiling, where stars no longer danced. After the heat of Nick's body covering her, the room's chill pimpled her arms and legs and perked her nipples, but she didn't yet reach for the sheet to cover herself.

She turned to look at his head, so close to hers on the pillow. Nick smiled. His teeth flashed white. Bess cupped his cheek and smiled, too.

"This was risky," she murmured.

"I know."

"We really can't do it like this."

"I know." He kissed her hand and tucked it between his.

Bess linked their fingers. "I don't want to have to hide, but—"

"I know." He stopped her with a kiss to her mouth. "I know, I know, I know."

She felt worse about his acceptance than if he'd fought her about it. "It won't be like this for always."

Nick didn't say he knew. He kissed her and crept from her bed. He left her in the dark, staring at the ceiling. It took a long time before she fell back to sleep.

Chapter 29

Then

*N*ick didn't say a word when he opened the door to find her on his porch. Bess gave him no time to speak. She pushed him back and closed the door behind them.

She kissed him, hard, on the mouth. Then she hugged him, just as hard. It took Nick a few seconds to wrap his arms around her, but when he did she sank against him with a small sigh. His hand came up to stroke the length of her hair.

"You okay?"

She nodded against him, not trusting her voice. His arms tightened around her again. Beneath her cheek, his heart provided a steady thump-thump that threatened to hypnotize her. They were swaying, just a little, to some unheard music.

He made no protest when she hooked her fingers into the hem of his white T-shirt and eased it up over the flat plane of his belly, or when she bent her mouth to kiss his bare skin. He said nothing when she tugged the shirt off over his head and tossed it to the floor, or when she tucked her fingers in his belt buckle and pulled it open. But when she made to undo the button and zipper, Nick put his hand over hers.

"Bess."

She looked up, vision blurred. Nick took her hand and linked their fingers. He didn't move, and neither did she.

"Are you sure this is what you want?" he asked.

She drew a slow, deep breath and blinked away the blur. "Yes."

She led him to his bedroom, where she pushed him gently back onto the bed, stripped of everything but a sheet. She straddled him, her hands on his chest, and looked down while he gazed up. Under her, his erection nudged her, but Bess didn't do anything just yet. She looked, instead.

"What are you waiting for?" Nick asked at last, his voice raspy.

"I just want to remember this," Bess said.

"Why are you afraid you'll forget?"

She shook her head and small tendrils that had escaped her ponytail tickled her cheeks. "I don't know. I'm just afraid I will."

Nick half sat to capture her and bring her down to his mouth. "You won't forget," he murmured against her lips. "You couldn't ever forget this."

She laughed at this show of ego and let him roll her onto her back. "You're pretty sure of yourself."

He nipped at her jaw and throat. "Yep."

She pushed him gently until he looked into her eyes. "What about you?"

"What about me?"

Bess turned her face so his kiss landed on the corner of her mouth. "Will you forget about me?"

"Bess," Nick said as he ran a hand down her body to center it between her legs. "I don't intend on having to."

She kissed him fiercely then, her fingers digging into his hair and holding him tight to her mouth. He groaned when she tipped his head back to bite the curve of his shoulder.

They rolled again until she was on top and could pull her shirt off. Her bra went next. His hands came up to cup her breasts. Bess hissed when his palms skidded over her nipples, already tight. She'd never liked a rough touch, but with Nick she craved it.

They got the rest of their clothes off with avid hands. Naked, she lay against him, their breath coming faster. Bess licked her lips and thought of speaking, but words might have ruined it just then. She stayed silent, hoping her eyes and hands and mouth told him what she felt. Wishing she could know for sure what he did.

She thought he would fuck her hard and fast. She thought it was what she wanted. She should have known by then she couldn't ever tell what Nick wanted. He made love to her slowly, slowly, looking into her eyes the entire time.

And Bess discovered that was what she'd really wanted, after all.

Now

Through the big glass windows at the front of the shop Bess saw Eddie waiting for them, and smiled. "There's Eddie."

Robbie, scrubbed and shaved and smelling of some cologne that made her want to cry a little at how grown-up he'd become, nodded. "And you're sure he's going to give me a job?"

"Positive." Before they got to the shop, Bess stopped to look at him. "But I don't want you to think you have to take it."

Robbie rolled his eyes. "Relax, Mom. I'm not going to be

a douche like Conn, okay? If he wants to turn down a sure thing, that's his problem."

Bess didn't reprimand him for his language, which also made her want to weep for her baby's childhood. "I won't be upset if you decide to get something on your own, that's all I'm saying."

Robbie's quick and unselfconscious hug reiterated how tall and broad he'd grown, and how precious he still was to her. "I told you, I want to."

By this time Eddie was opening the front door and waving them in. He greeted Bess with a surprising hug and kiss to the cheek, a gesture she didn't know how to return without feeling foolish. Eddie didn't bother giving her the chance to worry about it. He held out his hand to Robbie.

"You're Robbie. God, you look like your mom."

Robbie laughed. "Not really."

Eddie laughed, too. "That's a compliment."

"In that case," Bess said, "thank you."

Eddie gestured for them to sit at one of the café tables, where a folder of paperwork awaited. "So, Robbie, you're ready to work for me, huh?"

Robbie sat obediently. "Yes, sir."

Eddie looked faintly surprised and grinned at Bess. "Nice manners."

"Mom's a drill sergeant," Robbie said.

They all laughed. Eddie pushed the papers and a pen toward Robbie. "I just need you to fill out all this stuff, and you can get started today. Kara will be here in about an hour and she'll be able to walk you through all the major tasks. But I'm sure you'll do great."

"Robbie worked for two summers at Hershey Park in their foods department," Bess offered.

Robbie rolled his eyes, and she stopped herself from bragging about him more.

Eddie moved to the counter, which now boasted six high stools instead of the lonely one from times past. He'd set out two mugs and had a Thermos of coffee waiting.

"Are you sure your other son doesn't need a job?" he asked as he poured.

Bess didn't see the point in being coy. "Connor wants to make his own way, Eddie. I appreciate the offer, but he wanted to find a job on his own."

Eddie nodded as he added cream and sugar to his mug. "I can understand that."

"Conn's got a stick up his...shirt," Robbie said from the table behind them.

"Connor's always been a little more stubborn," Bess stated.

Eddie grinned. "Well, if he changes his mind, let me know."

"I will. Thanks."

Her friend leaned a little closer. "So, after Kara gets here and takes over, want to go grab some breakfast? We have a lot to talk about."

Bess's stomach rumbled at that moment. She'd be a liar if she said she wasn't hungry, but she couldn't exactly tell Eddie she was yearning to get home so she could have hot supernatural sex. Not to mention that Connor would most likely still be there, since his interviews weren't scheduled until later in the day. "Sure."

"Good."

They chatted while Robbie filled out the paperwork. Bess wondered if Eddie had always had such a charming sense of humor, or if he'd grown into it the way he'd grown into his broad shoulders and long legs. She'd always known he was smart, but he was funny, too.

Leaving Robbie to Kara's tender mercies, they headed down the street to the Frog House again, where another breakfast awaited. Eddie had done a lot of preliminary work regarding the mechanics of starting a new business, creating spreadsheets about what equipment they could keep and what they'd need to buy. He sifted through a sheaf of papers, explaining his thoughts, while Bess listened, blown away at his expertise.

"And we'll have to get the paperwork for a partnership," he said with a glance. "You'll want a lawyer to look at it. What?"

She shook her head. "You're sure you want to add me as a partner, Eddie? I'm not bringing much to this."

He sat back in his seat. "Would you feel better if you were a silent partner? Not on paper? No risk?"

"Oh, it's not that." Bess touched the folder of documents. "It's more your risk than mine. Do you really want to make me a *partner?* I mean—"

"I trust you." Eddie smiled. "But if you don't want to do it—"

"No. I do want to do it." She meant it, too. She nodded and looked again at the papers. "I really do."

"Well, then. I want you."

Heat flushed her cheeks and throat, but the blush was welcome. So was the smile that followed. "It's scary, isn't it?"

"It doesn't have to be." Eddie closed the folder. "I think it's exciting."

"It can be scary and exciting, too, can't it?"

He looked thoughtful. "Sure."

"It's a big change for me," Bess said. "I haven't worked in years."

The quaver in her voice embarrassed her, and she wished

she hadn't said anything. "I haven't really done anything but be a wife and mother for years," she blurted, making it worse.

Eddie smiled. "Then maybe it's time for a change, huh?"

It wasn't that simple or easy, but Bess smiled, too. "Yeah. Maybe it is."

Chapter
30

Then

"I have to get back." Nick gathered up the paper from the wrapped sandwiches he'd brought to share, and tossed it in the Dumpster. "Lou called in sick today so I only get half an hour."

Bess sucked the last bit of soda through her straw and tossed the paper cup in the garbage. Nick wiped his hands on his jeans before putting them on her waist and pulling her close, a gesture that had her giggling even though she appreciated it.

"What? Those chips were greasy," Nick said. "You'd rather I got your shirt dirty?"

Bess, allowing herself to be pulled against him, shook her head. "No. I was just thinking how I'm glad I don't have to do your laundry."

Nick snorted. "I wish I didn't."

She fit in his arms just right, her own arms around his neck. "We can do it later, when I get off work, okay?"

Nick, bending to nuzzle into her neck, murmured, "We could just go naked. Set a trend."

She laughed breathily as his lips made a moist pattern on her skin. "Oh, sure. That would go over really well."

His hands drifted from her waist to her ass, rubbing. "I'd like it. If you were naked all the time—"

"B-Bess?"

She looked over her shoulder. Eddie stood in the doorway, cheeks crimson and eyes averted. She stepped out of Nick's arms and turned to the door. "Yes?"

"I n-need some help with the inventory."

"Oh. Sure. I'll be right in."

Eddie didn't go at once. His gaze rose to take in Nick, then Bess, before he ducked back inside the shop. Bess turned to face Nick, intending to get in one last kiss before he left her, but his scowl stopped her.

"What's the problem?" she asked.

Nick jerked his chin toward the doorway. "He's in love with you."

Bess laughed, self-conscious, because Nick wasn't wrong. "Oh, he's not."

Nick's lip curled. "He is. Little nerd's got the hots for you. Big-time."

"So?" Bess slipped her arms around Nick's waist, but holding him was like holding wood. "Why does that worry you?"

His scowl didn't soften when he looked at her. "I'm not worried. Why should I be worried? You have something going on with Eddie the dork?"

The vehemence in his voice stunned her, and she stepped back. "No. Of course not. God, Nick. What's your problem?"

"I don't have a problem," he said. "I have to go."

"I'll see you tonight, right?" Their relationship seemed

suddenly far more of a slippery slope than it had a few minutes before.

"Yeah," Nick said as he threw a black look toward the doorway. He stalked away down the alley without kissing her. Without looking back, either.

With a sigh, Bess went inside. Eddie had piled a few boxes of paper cups on the floor and pulled out the packing slips. He was supposed to count the sleeves of cups and match them to the packing slips before putting the cups in the supply closet. A simple task he'd performed a hundred times already.

"What's the problem?" She sounded grouchy, but didn't care.

"These cups aren't the ones we usually order," Eddie explained. "And also, there aren't enough in the boxes. I mean, there aren't as m-many as there are listed on the sheet."

Bess peeked into the box and checked the sheet. "Five sleeves in the box, five on the paper."

"But there are supposed to be fifty cups in a sleeve," Eddie told her. "There are only forty-seven in three of them."

Bess looked again, half-torn between admiration at his attention to detail and still annoyed at how this stupid problem had caused, however indirectly, friction with Nick. "So…mark it down and I'll leave a note for Ronnie. He can deal with the supplier."

Eddie nodded and scribbled some numbers on his list. "Okay."

"Is that it?"

He nodded again without looking at her. Bess heard the buzz and hum of conversation out front, and though she knew Brian and Tammy both needed supervision, she wasn't quite ready to get back out there and deal with the public. She watched Eddie go through the remaining boxes. She knew she was making him nervous, because his fingers fumbled and his cheeks got redder and redder through the fringes of black hair hanging over them.

"He's not good for you."

For a second Bess wasn't sure she'd heard Eddie say anything at all, much less those actual words. "Who?" was a stupid question to ask, because she knew exactly who Eddie meant, but the word rose to her lips anyway, as though she meant to pretend she didn't.

Eddie straightened, giving her a rare look in the eye. "Nick. He's not good for you."

She crossed her arms. "Oh, really?"

Eddie shook his head but didn't glance away even as his face flamed impossibly redder. "No."

Bess felt the inexplicable hitch in her chest that meant she was moving toward tears. "It's not any of your business, Eddie."

"I'm just saying, that's all. Maybe nobody else will, but I will."

"Oh, really?" she repeated. "For your information, you're not the only person to warn me away from him, okay? And it's not any of their business, either. I don't care about his reputation, Eddie. I don't care what he's done before. What Nick and I are…what we do, isn't anyone's business but ours."

They'd both kept their voices pitched low, and Eddie didn't raise his now. "I'm not talking about his reputation. Most of it's just talk, anyway."

Before this conversation began, Bess would have said Eddie didn't know anything about the local singles-scene gossip. The way he spoke now told her that, though he might not be in the party crowd, he knew everything about them all. The look in his eyes told her he wasn't much impressed, either.

Bess set her jaw. "Then why's he so bad for me, if his reputation's a bunch of crap?"

"Because," Eddie said quietly, "he makes you doubt yourself."

Bess couldn't speak. Her lips parted, but her tongue cleaved to the roof of her mouth and her throat closed as tight as a fist. She drew in one gulp of air that stuck, burning, before she managed to swallow it back.

"He does," Eddie said.

Then he went back to his counting, and Bess, still left with nothing to say, went to the front of the shop to get back to work.

Chapter 31

Now

"Connor?" Bess called as she climbed the stairs. "I'm home!"

Connor was just coming out of his bedroom when she got to the living room. Wearing a clean blue polo shirt and khaki cargo pants, his hair still wet around his collar, he headed for the kitchen, where he pulled open the cupboards to take down a box of cereal and a bowl. He glanced at Bess but didn't do much more than that.

"You look nice," she said anyway. "Why don't you have a sandwich? I bought turkey and coleslaw. It's lunchtime."

Connor looked up from the bowl of fruity colored rings now floating in milk. "I want cereal."

"Right." Bess gnawed the inside of her cheek for a moment. "Of course you do."

Because if she'd said, "Why not have a bowl of cereal, Conn?" he'd have gone at once for the bread and mustard. She watched her older son consume the cereal with the efficiency of a high-powered vacuum, then get up and put the bowl and spoon in the dishwasher. He left the cereal and milk on the table, but Bess didn't point that out.

She recognized the signs. He was looking for a reason to argue with her. Andy was the same way, and she wondered if the trait was inherited or learned.

"Where's your interview?" she asked.

"Office Outlet."

"The office supplies store?" Bess couldn't hide her surprise.

Connor's jaw set, and she recognized that, too, though this time it came from her. "Yeah. What's the problem?"

Her own pet phrase, echoing back at her. "No problem. I just thought you'd get a beach job."

"It is a beach job, Mom," Connor said in a voice pretending to be patient. "We're at the beach. It's in the outlet mall."

"But that means you're going to have to use my car," Bess said.

Connor gave her a look. "Yeah."

Bess sighed, seeing where this was going and not looking forward to it, at all. "Connor, I thought you'd get a job in town here, so you could walk or ride your bike."

"I don't want to scoop ice cream or wait tables or sell souvenirs." His voice rose the tiniest bit. He was getting ready to defend himself with righteous indignation, and Bess didn't feel ready for it. "Office Outlet pays a dollar above minimum and will give me a bonus if I stay until the end of the summer. Then I'm out of here, anyway. It's only a couple months."

"It's going to be a very long couple of months," Bess said without thinking about it.

Connor's face darkened. "Maybe I should've stayed with Dad. He said he'd buy me a car to use."

"Did he?" Bess faced her son, though now that he towered

over her by five or so inches it was more difficult for her to seem intimidating. "Did your dad say you could stay there?"

The look on Connor's face was answer enough. Bess sighed. Connor scowled.

"Honey, I'm not pretending this is going to be easy for any of us," she began.

"So make it easy for me," Connor retorted. "Let me use your car, Mom! Just let me use the goddamn car, okay? Let me take this frigging job!"

Bess's silence, for once, was not because she couldn't think of what to say. Plenty of retorts arose, but she held them back as she gazed steadily at her son. Connor, to give him credit, looked guilty, though he clenched his jaw and didn't say anything more.

"We'll work this out," she said finally. She meant more than the car or the job, and she was pretty sure Connor knew it.

He nodded, looking so much like Andy in his sullenness Bess had to glance away. "Okay. Can I take it now?"

"Yes. But call if you get the job. I need to know when you'll be home. And," Bess added, cutting him off when he tried to answer. "You're not always just going to be allowed to take the car. I may have to drop you off and pick you up. I can't be without my car all the time, Connor."

"Yeah, I know." He moved a half step toward the stairs. "Can I go, now?"

"Yes."

Bess moved aside to let him pass. She didn't watch him go. When she heard the door slam downstairs and the car rev up and drive away, she sat at the kitchen table and put her head in her hands.

"Hey." Nick's soft voice prompted her to look up.

She didn't know how long she'd been sitting that way. "Hey."

He rubbed her shoulders, his fingers working at knots of tension she didn't even realize were there until his touch started to melt them. "C'mere."

She let him take her hand and lead her to the bedroom, where he pulled the shades and locked the door. In the dim coolness, Nick undressed her slowly, his hands rubbing over her goose-pimpled skin. He moved her to the bed, where he stripped back the comforter and pushed her to her stomach on sheets that quickly warmed beneath her.

"Close your eyes," he said, and she obeyed.

She waited, listening, the small ease in her tension rebuilding at the small noises magnified by her darkened vision. The subtle shush of material moving over skin, the rasp of a zipper. The soft pad of bare feet on the carpet and the small whine of the springs as he got on the bed next to her.

When he touched her, Bess sighed. Nick's hands, as warm and smooth as heated oil, slid over her shoulder blades and down her spine, all the way to the curve of her ass. Again and again he stroked, stopping sometimes to knead the tightness in places she didn't know could get tight. He used his knuckles, fingers, thumbs and palms. He swept her hair to the side and found the trigger spots at the base of her skull, manipulating them until she whimpered with the exquisite, painful pleasure.

It took her a few minutes to notice when he'd stopped massaging and merely stroked her skin, over and over. Hypnotically. Bess opened her eyes and turned her head to look at him. Nick stopped stroking, his hand resting at the base of her spine.

"Thank you," she whispered in a voice hoarser than she'd expected.

Nick slid down next to her and took her into his arms. Hugging him was like bringing in an armful of sun-warmed sheets. Soft, hot, smooth. Bess leaned forward to breathe him in. Fresh.

"You always smell so good," she murmured, tucking one leg between his thighs. Her cheek rested on his chest.

Nick pressed her head beneath his chin and anchored her against him with a hand on her waist. "That's better than smelling bad, huh?"

"Much better."

Content for the moment, Bess closed her eyes again. She'd never been one for napping, but now she couldn't help the drowsiness stealing over her. Tucked up against Nick this way, her muscles looser than they'd been in months, and nothing but the purr of the air-conditioning to distract them, Bess thought a nap seemed like the best of ideas.

"We don't do much of this," she murmured.

"Much of what?"

"Just…being." That's what she meant to say, anyway, though she wasn't sure if that's what came out.

Nick's soft chuckle let her know he'd heard her. His arms tightened around her slightly. "You mean, we're usually screwing our brains out."

Bess yawned and blinked, then pushed away enough to look up into his face. "Yes. I guess so."

He shifted to look at her. "I'm happy to oblige, ma'am. If that's what you want."

Bess couldn't deny the tingle zapping through her body, her instant reaction to Nick's innuendo. She smiled slowly. "I'm not saying I don't love that, too…."

Nick kissed her mouth, then said against her lips, "I know. I know what you mean."

"How?" she asked seriously, pushing away just a bit more to see straight into his eyes. "How do you know?"

"I just do." He shrugged. His toe stroked along the back of her calf.

Bess ran a hand down his chest and tucked it against his hip. "It's just different, that's all. Everything is with us this time, isn't it?"

Nick rolled onto his back, an arm cradling his head, but his other hand was still close enough to hold hers. He squeezed her fingers gently and rubbed his thumb along the back of her hand. But he didn't answer her.

Bess stayed on her side, studying him. "It's not a bad thing."

He turned his head to face her. "I didn't say it was."

"You didn't say anything," she pointed out.

Nick gave her a small smile. "It's different. Is that what you wanted me to say?"

Bess sat, the earlier, luxurious languidity fading. Now the room seemed too cold, and she got up to push the floor vent closed with her toe. When she turned back to the bed, Nick had sat up.

Bess gathered her clothes to begin dressing, but before she could even step into her panties, Nick was on his feet, his hand on her wrist. The suddenness with which he'd moved startled her, and she cried out. His kiss swallowed the small noise.

Bess froze under Nick's mouth, but his kiss gentled and soothed, urging her lips to open. His tongue dipped inside and stroked in and out as his fingers slid between her legs to do the same. Bess gripped Nick's shoulder, her clothes falling forgotten to the floor.

He backed her up a couple steps until her butt hit the edge of the dresser. This was the Nick she remembered, the one who touched her in all the right places. The one who didn't use pretty words. His fingers slid inside her and she gasped, then again when they withdrew and he slid her wetness up and over her clit.

He curled her fingers around his prick and they stroked him to full erection together. His kisses got harder, his grip tighter, but she loved it. She always had. She loved how he made her body respond.

He nudged her thighs open wider and guided his penis inside her. The dresser was just the right height, and Bess used one hand to hold herself steady, the other to grab Nick's shoulder as he pushed forward. The mirror rattled and so did the small glass dish of earrings and change she kept on top of the dresser. Nick grabbed the hand gripping his shoulder and slid it between them. As he'd used his hand over hers on his cock, he did the same now with hers on her clit. When she was circling it with her fingers, he let go and used both hands to grip her hips so he could thrust into her harder and faster.

Harder. Faster. Each time Nick fucked into her, Bess's fingers slipped on her clit until all she had to do was press them to her body and allow him to move her. She tipped her head back, her lower lip caught between her teeth as she tried hard not to moan too loudly. The edge of the dresser cut into the back of her thighs and Nick's hands squeezed so fiercely she wanted to writhe.

She came like fireworks, bright sparks of pleasure against the dark sky of her emotions. His name caught in her throat and snagged her tongue, scraped past her lips and left a taste like blood. Her fingernails dug into the wood of the dresser. She opened her eyes. Her orgasm manifested itself in her vision with more bright streaks of color, swirling as she blinked.

"I love you." The words whispered out of her just as he closed his eyes and tipped his head, grunting in his climax. She wasn't sure he heard her. After a second, she wasn't sure that mattered.

Nick thrust and shuddered. When he looked at her again, slowly blinking, then smiling, it was as if her heart started beating and she hadn't noticed it had stopped.

"Not everything's different," he said. "Some things are the same."

He kissed her then, but it didn't take away the taste of blood.

Chapter 32

Then

The summer was more than half over. Normally at this time of year Bess would be counting the days until she could hang up her polo shirt and leave Sugarland behind. Leave the beach. Get back to school. To her life. To Andy.

This year had been different in so many ways already she shouldn't have been surprised that her feelings about staying and going were different, too, yet when she flipped the calendar from July to August the tears rose in her throat. Bess sniffed them back and stabbed the pin into the corkboard to hold the calendar in place.

Usually the board would be abristle with tacked up photos, copies of her schedule, messages and pay stubs. This summer all she'd stuck into it was the calendar, each day crossed off in red ink when it was done, and a few takeout menus that were probably out of date.

And why?

Because of Nick.

The days she'd have spent hitting the boardwalk with friends were spent with Nick. The nights she'd have spent going to the underage clubs or simply hanging out with her family…the same. Nick had consumed her summer. And summer was almost over.

"Bess?" Her aunt Carla's voice drifted down the stairs. "You want to come have something to eat?"

"I'll be right there!" Bess swiped at her face to rid it of any tears that had managed to slip past her defenses. Aunt Carla had eyes like a hawk.

This week's beach-house crew consisted of Aunt Carla, Uncle Tony and their three daughters. Angela, Deirdre and Cindy were typical beach bunnies, heading out to the sand as soon as they got up, and spending every day broiling themselves into wrinkles and skin cancer. They stalked the boardwalk at night, on the hunt for cute boys, and pretty much ignored Bess unless they wanted some free diet sodas from Sugarland.

Aunt Carla, on the other hand, had made a mission out of taking the place of Bess's mom. It didn't seem to matter that Bess spoke to her parents once a week, without fail, or that she'd been working at the beach for the past three summers and going to college for the past three years, and therefore hadn't actually lived at home with her parents since she'd been eighteen. Aunt Carla had a habit of mothering everyone, so Bess shouldn't have been surprised her aunt was doing it to her. But considering she allowed her own daughters to stay out until all hours, Bess thought it was a little unreasonable of her aunt to expect Bess to check in with a daily schedule.

The food was good, though. Unlike most of the other family members who came for vacation, Aunt Carla didn't believe in eating out for every meal. Not even at the beach. Breakfast and lunch were casual, but she cooked dinner almost every night. Tonight it was steaks on the grill and baked potatoes, corn on the cob, green salad and fresh biscuits.

Bess's stomach was already rumbling as she followed the good smells up the stairs and into the living room. Uncle Tony snored on the recliner. Bess heard the muffled chatter of her cousins in their room, along with the blare of a radio. They'd be getting ready to go out right after dinner, while Uncle Tony and Aunt Carla read books on the deck or went for a walk along the beach.

Bess, on the other hand, had no plans.

She hadn't seen Nick in three days, not since Eddie had interrupted them behind the shop. Nick hadn't been home that night when Bess stopped by after work. He hadn't come by the next day, either, and she hadn't gone to his apartment again. She wasn't stupid, or so desperate she had to chase him down wherever he might have gone.

All right, so she wasn't stupid. After three days without Nick, desperation didn't seem so…desperate.

"You look pretty, honey." Aunt Carla, her curly blond hair piled high on top of her head, beamed as Bess came in. "Can you grab that bowl of coleslaw? I thought we'd eat on the deck. Tony! Get up!"

Uncle Tony, snorting and blinking, lumbered out of his chair. "Huh? What?"

Aunt Carla rolled her eyes as Bess grabbed the bowl of slaw. "Tony, dinner. Call the girls."

Bess took the bowl to the picnic table out on the deck, where her aunt had already laid out plates and silverware. The napkins fluttered under the weight of a large shell. She put down the bowl and looked through the glass doors, behind which she could see her aunt, uncle and cousins getting the rest of the food and bringing it out. She could see herself, too, with clouds and sky behind her. Her reflection shimmered, like an illusion. Blink, and see the family inside. Blink again, see the girl standing in front of the window. It was a mind-fuck, truly, and she turned away from the sight of her own ghost.

That's when she saw him, on the sand. Nick, hands in his pockets, staring up at the deck. Bess had raised a hand to him, her heart skip-thumping and her lips spreading into a grin, before she realized it. He didn't wave back.

"Bess, honey?" Aunt Carla's voice hovered so close to Bess's ear she jumped. "Is that a friend of yours? Why not invite him up for dinner? We have plenty."

Bess had gripped the railing to keep herself from waving again after Nick hadn't. Now he'd turned to face the ocean, his arm swinging back and then releasing. Bess watched the small stone skip out onto waves placid with the low tide.

"Oh…no." She shook her head. "No, that's okay."

It was bad enough she hadn't seen him for three days, but now to know he was stalking her at her house but ignoring her? Bess turned her back firmly and smiled at her aunt, who gave a dubious look over Bess's shoulder, but seemed appeased enough to let it go.

There was no room in Bess's stomach for dinner, not around the stone lodged there. She forced herself to eat anyway. Tiny bites of steak, a half a potato, a nibble or two of corn. It had been weeks since she'd had anything this good, and she cursed Nick for being the reason she couldn't enjoy it.

"You're going to waste away to nothing," Aunt Carla chided as Bess helped her clear the table.

The cousins had already escaped to freshen their lipsticks

and style their hair. Uncle Tony had retired to the master bathroom with his newspaper. Bess didn't mind helping with the dishes, actually. She had no place else to be.

She read for a while in her room. The book, a tattered paperback about twin boys with a secret, had been part of the house's library for as long as she could remember. Bess had read it every summer for as long as she could remember, too, but this year the familiar scenes had, for the first time, ceased to thrill or chill her. Part of it was her age. Tittered commentary about freak-show hermaphrodites and severed fingers kept in ring boxes had seemed shocking when she was younger, but cable TV had shown her more disturbing things.

She tossed the book onto her desk. Her bed was lumpy. Her sheets needed washing, and her comforter, too. Her pillow had flattened. She grumbled, she sighed, she contemplated soothing herself with the familiarity of her own hand, but couldn't muster the enthusiasm for it.

She didn't bother with shoes or even a bra. Nobody would see her breasts bouncing in the dark, and she wasn't planning on walking very far. She just needed to get out of the room. Grabbing up a zippered sweatshirt, Bess let herself out into the carport, then followed the sandy path through the dunes to the beach. The flicker of the television made dancing shadows in the windows of the house, and the night wasn't so black she couldn't see. A fire burned in front of the house a few down from hers, and she heard the rise and fall of laughter over the sound of the waves, but down by the water's edge she could be as anonymous as she wanted.

Except she wasn't alone down there.

Nick sat at the edge of the wet sand, his arms locked around his legs. He had a six-pack of beer nestled next to him, and his bandanna next to that, like maybe he'd used the cloth to cover the beer when he was walking. He didn't look at her when she sat next to him. The cold sand made her shiver and she pulled her sweatshirt closer around her.

"I'm sorry," he said before she could speak, and those two words thoroughly stole any answer she could possibly have given. "I was an ass."

Bess ran her fingers through the soft sand and found a smooth stone, a rough shell. She rubbed the edges of each and then allowed them to clack together in her palm when she closed her fingers overtop.

"I don't understand why you got so mad, that's all. It's not like Eddie is anything but a friend to me."

"He doesn't like me."

Bess laughed softly. "You don't like him, either. So what?"

Now he turned to look at her. "He's tried to tell you not to be with me, hasn't he?"

Bess bit her lower lip for a moment before answering. "Yes."

"And he's your friend." Nick cracked open one of the beers. "Maybe I'm afraid you'll listen to him."

"Oh...Nick." Bess put her hand on his shoulder. "I make my own decisions. Don't you know that by now?"

He drank and set the beer back into the sand. When he kissed her, she tasted the bitter, yeasty tang on this lips and her stomach suddenly rumbled. His hand came up to slide beneath her hair and cup the base of her skull as his tongue toyed with hers.

"Would you really care?" she asked when he pulled away. She pitched the question low so he could ignore it, pretend as though the rush and tumble of the waves had hidden it.

"The summer's not over," Nick said.

It wasn't the answer to the question she'd asked. "We have another month. I go back just after Labor Day."

Nick drank again. Set the beer down. This time, he didn't kiss her.

"Four weeks, and you'll be gone."

"Yes."

Does that bother you? She wanted to ask, but fearful of not hearing the answer she preferred, did not.

"Are you going to tell your boyfriend then? When you go back?"

Bess shook her head.

Nick snorted under his breath. "Yeah. Probably not."

"Were you sitting here all night?" She moved a little closer to him, and though he didn't pull away, neither did he put his arm around her.

"No. I took a break. Went to get the beer. Came back."

"To see me?" She sounded too hopeful and hated herself for it.

Nick looked at her. "Maybe."

"Would it kill you," she said stiffly, "to just say yes?"

"Yes," Nick said. "I came to see you."

He'd given her what she wanted, but it didn't satisfy her. "This isn't any of Andy's business."

"Because he'll break up with you." Nick sounded smug.

"Maybe I'll break up with him," Bess retorted. "Maybe I already have, Nick, and just didn't tell you."

He looked at her again, assessing. "Why wouldn't you tell me?"

"Because if I didn't have someone else…if I was suddenly available, you'd run so far and so fast I'd never hear from you again." She believed this.

Nick looked out to the ocean. "That's not true."

"No?" Bess got on her knees in front of him, heedless of the fact she knelt in cold wetness. "Look at my face and say that."

Nick stared, then smirked. "That's not true."

"No." She shook her head. "Not good enough. Tell me that if I didn't have a boyfriend anymore you would still be interested in me."

"Bess," Nick said with a sigh. "I'd still be interested in you."

She blinked against the sudden up-and-down tilt of her emotions, and reached for him. His arms went around her. She kissed his mouth, soft at first and then harder. She straddled him, forcing his legs to straighten to give her a place to sit. She took his hands and put them beneath her sweatshirt, under her cotton T-shirt and on her bare breasts.

Nick moaned into her mouth. Bess licked his lips with slow flickers, teasing him to move forward to capture her kiss. She threaded her hands through his hair and held his head to keep him still.

She looked into his eyes, flashing with silver in the night. She kissed him again. "A month can be a long time."

His palms cupped her and her nipples rose, tight and turgid against them. She rocked her crotch forward on his belt. Her legs closed around his waist, squeezing.

She wasn't quite sure how she unzipped his jeans and how they wriggled her out of her shorts, but she knew exactly when she slid onto his erection. Nick moaned into her mouth. His hands on her bare ass were chilly, but she didn't care. She just wrapped her legs tighter around him and rocked.

A shout went up from the bonfire and something flat skidded into the sand a few feet from them. Their mouths unlocked and both turned to face the guy running to grab the flying disk. His footsteps threw up sand, which stung Bess's hands and shins, but he barely gave the two of them a second glance.

This excited her no end, fucking on the beach, and she dug her nails into Nick's back when she came, with her face buried against his neck to muffle her shout. He pulsed inside her harder than she'd ever felt, but it wasn't until she'd moved off him that Bess remembered the condom.

Or rather, the lack of one.

She said nothing about it, just gathered up her clothes and wriggled back into them while Nick zipped and buttoned. She sat next to him again, but this time he put his arm around her. The night wind had turned colder and she undid her sweatshirt to give him some.

"What are you so afraid of?" she whispered, when it seemed as if the night was going to go on forever, like the ocean, and neither of them would say anything again.

"I'm not afraid of anything."

He was lying, and they both knew it. Bess rested her head on his shoulder and took his hand, linking it with hers in his lap. She timed the rise and fall of her breath to his.

"Do you trust me?" Nick asked after a moment.

Bess didn't hesitate to answer. "Yes."

"You shouldn't," he said. "I'll fuck you over like I fucked over everyone else."

"I don't believe that."

His fingers squeezed hers. "I don't trust *you,* Bess."

She tried not to be hurt. "Do you trust anyone?"

He shook his head after a second. "No."

"You can trust me, Nick." She kissed his hand and tucked it between both of hers. "You can."

He laughed low, under his breath. "Yeah. Because everyone else has been so trustworthy. I trusted my mom when she promised not to get high again, or not to bring home strangers she'd fuck to get a hit. I trusted the social worker who told me my aunt and uncle would take good care of me. I trusted Heather when she said she wasn't going to fuck around on me, too."

"I'm not any of those people."

Nick got up and strode down the beach, Bess a few paces behind him. She caught up to him, taking his hand though he tried to pull it away. She stopped him. Turned him until he looked at her.

"I'm not those people!" she cried, not caring if the shout carried.

Nick turned his head and spat into the sand before looking back at her. "I don't want your fucking pity."

"I don't!" His accusation had shocked her. "I don't pity you, Nick. God! If what you say is true—"

"Why would I lie?" He gave her a shark-toothed grin. "Unless I'm just messing with you."

"No wonder you don't have an easy time trusting anyone, is all I'm saying." Bess let go of his hand to put hers on her hips. "But it's not an excuse to be an asshole."

"I *am* an asshole," he said, as if it were his astrological sign.

"I don't care," Bess insisted.

Nick shook his head. "You should."

"I don't!" She laughed, suddenly, and tipped her face up to the night sky and the stars sprinkled there. "I don't care if you're an asshole, I don't care what anyone says, okay? I don't care!"

Nick laughed, too, after a minute. "You're out of your fucking head, you know that?"

"I know it." Bess leaped into his arms and covered his face with kisses, but it was all right, because Nick caught her. He caught and held her and they both twirled around until he lost his balance and they fell in a tangle of arms and legs onto the sand. "I'm out of my fucking head, Nick."

For you.

She didn't say it aloud, but not because she didn't trust him.

Because she wanted him to trust her, and something like that couldn't be forced. It would come or not come.

He kissed her, rolling, and she didn't care about the sand in her hair or in her clothes. She kissed him back and held him close, and they laughed as they looked up at the stars.

"Orion." Nick pointed. "That's the only one I know."

"The Big Dipper." Bess scanned the sky, then pointed. "And the little one. You know what the best part of the stars is?"

"What's that?"

She rolled on her side to face him, and he did the same. Nick reached to tuck her hair behind her ears. Bess took the chance to kiss him again, just because she could.

"They're the same no matter what sky you're standing under. I mean…yeah, they might move or look like they're in a different place, but they're the same stars."

Nick tilted his head to look up. "Yeah? So?"

"So even if you're apart from someone you want to be with, you can look up at the stars and know they're looking at the same ones."

Nick blinked and gazed at her, his face solemn. The bonfire had died down and the moon was no more than a fingernail, so not all of his features were clear, but Bess didn't need to see every line of his face to picture it.

"That is such a bunch of romantic crap," he said, but laughed and pulled her closer when she tried to pinch him.

"There's nothing wrong with romantic crap every once in a while," she retorted.

Nick buried his face in her hair and breathed deep. "Your hair smells good. I can smell you on my pillow when you're not there. When I'm not with you, I can't stop thinking about how good your hair smells."

A spate of shivers tickled her, but he wasn't finished.

"I think about you when I hear songs on the radio, too."

Bess burrowed into his arms, her face against his chest. Under them, the sand was chilly, and above them, the ocean breeze, but in Nick's arms she wasn't cold. He squeezed her.

"And fine, now I'll think about you when I look at the stars, too. Are you happy?"

She pulled away to look at him. "Yes."

"Jesus. Girls," he said in a disgusted voice.

"Boys," she said with a roll of her eyes.

He kissed her until she couldn't breathe. "It's getting late. You'd better go home. I've got to work early tomorrow."

"Me, too." They climbed to their feet.

He walked her back to her house, stopping to pick up the plundered six-pack along the way. At her door he set down the beer and tied the bandanna around her hair. He kissed her, pressing up against the stucco wall, his hand going easily beneath her knee to lift it so he could move against her.

"Go inside," Nick whispered hoarsely into her ear. "Before we do it again, right here. We already took a stupid chance tonight."

So he had been thinking of it, too. "I know."

He let her go. "I'll see you tomorrow."

"Nick!" she called after him.

He topped and turned.

"You can trust me," Bess told him. "I mean it."

He came back to her. She thought he meant to kiss her, and had already tilted her mouth for it, but Nick instead just looked.

"Everyone says that, Bess."

"I know," she told him without lowering her mouth, still tempting him to touch it with his. "But I mean it."

He kissed her then, soft and slow instead of hard and fast. "I believe you," he said, and left without looking back.

It wasn't until she was in her bed, showered and dressed in warm pajamas, that Bess allowed herself to wonder what he believed. That he could trust her? Or just that she meant it? And did it matter, in the end?

Chapter 33

Now

Vacations, when the boys were small, had been less than relaxing. Andy was fond of "big" trips to places like the Bahamas, the Grand Canyon, Yellowstone Park. Even when Connor and Robbie were too young to appreciate the nuances of beauty in the places they visited, Andy had insisted that if he was going to take a trip, he wanted to go somewhere he'd never been. By the time the boys reached high school, the yearly vacations had ended. Andy had apparently decided the sights he hadn't seen weren't worth the effort to share with teenage sons who didn't appreciate them any more than they had as children, but who were more vociferous about their lack of desire to go. He and Bess had gone on exactly one couples vacation, to an all-inclusive resort in Mexico. She'd gotten badly sunburned and he'd come down with food poisoning.

Neither of them had ever really talked about their reasons for not taking advantage of the beach house Bess's parents had finally inherited from her dad's parents. Andy, in fact, never spoke about the beach house at all, not even when Bess's parents died within a few months of one another and the house officially passed to her. Bess hadn't brought it up, either, though upon discovering it, both Connor and Robbie were more excited about it than they had ever been about Mount Rushmore.

Though they'd been to many different beaches in their lives, now both of Bess's sons took to the Atlantic water as if born to it. Within three weeks of arriving both had picked up as many work hours as they could, but when they weren't at work or asleep, Connor and Robbie spent their days toasting themselves on the sand. They met girls, of course, and Bess had expected no less. Both her sons had always been popular with the girls. They made friends and brought them home to hang out on the deck, eating the burgers she bought for them to grill. The beach house had become "the" place to hang out among the local crowd of young people working there for the summer.

Bess didn't mind, exactly. It had been the same at home, where their house was the place for all the neighborhood kids to play. She was the Popsicle mom, the one who kept a drawer full of spare toothbrushes for impromptu sleepovers. She'd always been the mom the kids could count on to pop corn and order pizza during monster movie marathons, and to give anyone a ride home who needed it.

She didn't speak of the relief it brought her to see Connor and Robbie recreating here the life they'd had at home. It was the surest sign, to her, that they were going to be all right, despite the upheaval she and Andy were putting them through.

The drawback to hosting the town's youth was, of course, the complete lack of privacy. So far neither Connor nor Robbie seemed to have noticed Nick never really left the house or the small patch of beach in front of it. Caught up in their own jobs and new friends, they didn't pay much attention to him. Bess, however, was constantly aware of Nick's presence as more part of the crowd than she was. He joined the boys occasionally for a few games on the video game player, or hung out on the deck at night, playing cards, but he spent just as much time in his small room with the door closed. He was as easily a part of the boys' world as he was of hers. It was only Bess who stood apart as one of the grown-ups now, and no longer one of the kids.

She didn't ask Nick what he did for hours in his room, but from the periodically changing gaps in the bookshelves she guessed he was reading a lot. She was reading a lot, too, and God help her, much the way she had as a young mother prayed for the day when both boys would be in school at the same time, she counted the minutes until they'd both be at work.

She spent three agonizingly long weeks in which Connor worked early and Robbie worked late, and the house teemed with newfound friends in nearly every spare moment between. But at last both sons were scheduled for the early shifts, though Connor was out the door before Robbie, who'd spiffed up Bess's old bike and had been riding it back and forth to work.

"What are you doing?" Robbie asked around a mouthful of cereal.

Bess looked up from the folder of brochures. "I'm making sure the house is winter-ready. It's never really been a year-round residence. If we're going to stay here full-time I need to make some changes."

"Yeah, like giving me the bigger room." Robbie grinned. "Conn'll be at college. He won't need it."

Bess laughed. "We could get rid of the bunk beds. That would give you a lot more room in there. We could get you a new bed and desk, if you want. IKEA usually has a great sale at the end of the summer."

Robbie nodded. "Yeah, okay."

Bess flipped through a few more glossy brochures from the local heating and cooling companies. The beach house had a furnace, and the windows had all been replaced less than four years before, when her parents had been considering moving here year-round. She looked around.

"This place is a lot smaller than the other house," she said.

Robbie got up to put his bowl and spoon in the dishwasher. "Sure, but it's just you and me."

He sounded so offhand, so matter-of-fact, it broke Bess's heart more than if he'd sounded upset. "Robbie? You okay with this?"

His shoulders hunched and he busied himself with something at the counter. "Yeah, sure. People get divorced all the time. I just want you and Dad to be happy."

Bess got up and leaned against the counter next to him. Robbie was polishing an apple, over and over, a gesture she recognized as a ploy to give his hands something to do so he didn't have to look at her. "You know you can talk to me about it, if you want."

"I don't have anything to talk about." He gave her a small, sideways glance and an unconvincing smile.

"Well," she said. "If you want to."

"I know, Mom."

Robbie had always been her snuggler, the son who brought her rocks colored with marker and weeds picked from the yard. He was the one who crept into bed with her after Andy'd left for work, to watch early morning cartoons, and the son who'd always told her about the girls he liked best. He had, at least, until a few years ago.

"I know you know," Bess said gently.

Robbie looked at her then, his smile getting bigger. "I know you know I know."

She laughed and rolled her eyes, shooing him with her hands. "Go to work."

"I'm going." He tossed the apple into the air and caught it, then leaned over to kiss her cheek. "I'll see you later."

"What time will you be home?"

"I'm done at nine." Robbie paused in the doorway. "But I'll be home later. I'm going out with Annalise."

Annalise was either the tiny brunette or the redhead who wore pigtails, but Bess didn't push for more information. "Have fun."

Robbie used his fingers to make two guns, pow pow! "See you, Mom."

He loped through the living room and thundered down the stairs, leaving behind sweet silence. Nick appeared at the top of the steps moments later, his smile saying more than words. Bess thought her heart would surely, one day, have to cease the skip and thump it always made when she saw him. Though apparently, not today.

They met in the living room with their hands and mouths. Two weeks had been too long a time to go with little more than secret glances to sustain them. Bess was already unbuttoning his shirt when they heard the sound of footsteps on the stairs.

She was expecting Robbie, coming back to retrieve something he'd forgotten, but Connor's face appeared above the railing. He took in the sight of them without expression, noting perhaps the distance between them that wasn't wide enough, or the mussed tangle of Bess's hair.

"Connor," she said, sounding too breathless. "What are you doing home?"

"I picked up an extra shift today so they're giving me two lunch breaks. I came home to get some grub." He fixed his gaze on Nick. "Hey, man. You don't have to work today?"

"Later," Nick said.

Without looking again at either of them, Connor went to the kitchen. Bess watched him pull out sandwich fixings and a bag of chips, and she glanced at Nick. Nick was watching Connor, too, his eyes narrowed. He turned his head to look at her.

"I'll be in my room," he said. "If you need me."

His voice dipped and scratched on "need," and Bess couldn't stop herself from glancing at Connor to see if he'd noticed. He'd hidden his face behind a copy of the local paper, and Bess looked back at Nick with a frown.

"Okay," she said, loud enough for her son to hear.

Nick smirked and ducked close to kiss her on the neck before brushing past her and down the stairs. Bess stood in the middle of the living room, breathing hard. Connor rattled the paper. Bess pretended she was dusting and straightening, an unnecessary task because the teenagers who'd adopted her house were polite enough not to leave a mess behind.

Connor finished his food and put the dishes away and left the paper on the table, then disappeared into his room, coming out a few minutes later with a backpack. Without saying anything to Bess, he headed for the stairs.

"Conn."

He stopped, but didn't look at her.

"What time will you be home?"

"I don't know," he said sullenly. "I'm going out after work."

"With who?"

"Friends."

"Do I know them?"

He looked at her then, Andy's blue eyes ablaze in his face, and Bess had to fight not to take a step back. "No."

She really didn't want to take a stand in this unspoken argument. She didn't want to fight with him about going out with his friends when that wasn't really what they'd be arguing about at all. "What about the car?"

"I'll bring it back after work."

"So I'll see you then, at least."

Connor glared. "Yeah, I guess so."

Bess sighed and waved her hand. "Have a good day."

Connor stomped down the stairs, ignoring her. Bess followed and watched through the downstairs window as he pulled out of the driveway and sped away. She waited until the car had turned the corner before she knocked on Nick's door.

"Come in."

He lay propped on the pillows, a paperback in his hands. Bess closed the door behind her. Nick lowered the book.

"He could have seen you," she said, referring to the kiss.

Nick's smile didn't wilt, but it became suddenly brittle. "Your kid's not an idiot, Bess."

"I didn't say he was."

Nick tossed the book onto the desk and swung his legs over the side of the bed. "You really think he doesn't know about us?"

Bess lifted her chin. "I told you I wanted to have them get to know you—"

"He knew from the first day," Nick said. "Maybe Robbie doesn't, but Connor does."

The uneasy feeling he was right didn't make it any easier for her. They stared at each other until Bess crossed her arms and Nick put his hands on his hips.

"You know I'm right," he said. "He knows I'm fucking you—"

"Stop it!" she snapped. "Do you have to be so crude all the time?"

"Excuse me," Nick said coldly. "Banging? Screwing? Laying pipe? What would you rather have me say? Oh, how about making looove?" He sneered the last. "Your kid's not a fucking idiot, Bess. Anyone who's around us for more than a day could tell we're fucking. You can smell it on us."

"Stop it," she repeated, more softly. "That's—"

"It's true," Nick said. "And you know it."

"It's more than that!"

He had her in his arms so fast she couldn't breathe. His mouth slid along her neck to the hollow of her throat. His arms pinned hers tight so she couldn't move. "And you'd feel better if your kid knew you weren't just fucking me? That it's more than that? That would make you feel better?"

She didn't try to get away. "I just think it's too soon for either of them to know anything."

Nick laughed against her skin. "Yeah. Right. That's it."

She pushed at him until he looked at her. "They're my children, Nick. They're more important to me than anything else in the world. Do I want to protect them? Hell, yes."

He blinked, without expression. "Do you think you'll ever tell them the truth about us?"

Bess drew in a hitching breath. "Which one?"

"Which truth?" Nick's lips quirked on one side. "Nice way to play it. Answer me." His grip tightened on her arms.

"You know I can't," she said, and no matter what else she'd said before, she knew she meant this, more.

Nick blinked again and let go of her. She stumbled back. He wiped his hands on his jeans, as if touching her had left something nasty on his fingers.

"We don't even know what's going to happen," she told him, moving forward as he moved back. There wasn't enough room for this dance, but she stopped just before touching him.

"Admit it," he said. "You don't give a flying fuck about what's going to happen. You don't care if I up and disappear back into the gray. You just care about scratching your itch and making sure nobody figures out your dirty little secret."

She turned her back on him.

"You won't ever tell them about us because you're afraid," he accused, as if she'd slapped him.

"Just…give me a little time," she said.

He laughed. "Right. Time for what?"

"Time to figure out how to tell them. Time to figure out if you're going to stay or go."

"I'm not going anywhere," Nick stated. "I know, because I've tried."

"I know, the boundary—"

"No. I mean I've tried getting back to the gray, back where I was before, and I can't do it."

This stopped her cold. "You did? Why?"

"Because you're never going to tell your sons or anyone else that I'm your boyfriend, Bess. You're never going to admit it to anyone. And Jesus," Nick said with a harsh bark of a laugh, "what if you do? Holy fuck, what's going to happen ten years from now when I still look twenty-one? They'll start coming after me with stakes and torches."

"No," she said, and touched his cheek. "No, I'm sure that won't happen."

She wasn't certain, but it seemed the thing to say.

Nick sat on the edge of the bed. "I thought when I came back that anything was better than being in the gray. I thought being with you… God, it was all I thought about, all I could think about. Being with you again."

He looked at her, but she didn't sit next to him.

"I thought it would all be better once we were together again, but this is worse. This is a worse prison. I can't go anywhere, I can't do anything. I can fuck you all night and all day, but I can't really be with you."

"That's not true!" Her voice broke. She reached to touch his hair, and he reached to pull her closer. He buried his face against her stomach, his arms wrapped around her legs. "You are with me. I love you."

Nick said nothing.

"I'll tell them," Bess said, resolved.

"What will you tell them?" He didn't look up at her. His voice was muffled against her. "Hey, kids, here's your new daddy, and by the way, he's been dead for twenty years."

"We'll start with letting them know we're together. We'll figure out the rest later."

He shuddered, then looked up at her. "You'll really tell them about us?"

"Like you said, Connor already knows. We don't have to tell them anything," she added, sitting next to him. "They'll figure it out. They don't need an announcement."

He smiled briefly. "And you're ready to do that?"

"No." She shook her head. "But it kills me to think you're unhappy."

He looked at his hands, folded in his lap. "This is all such a colossal mess."

"It will work out," she said, sounding more confident than she felt. "We'll find a way."

He snorted lightly. "Sure we will."

"Hey." She took his hand and waited until he looked up at her. "We will find a way for this to work. I'm not going to let this slip away from me again."

"You sound pretty sure of yourself."

"Nick," Bess said. "Trust me."

He leaned to kiss her, lingering at her mouth before putting his head on her shoulder and gathering her into his arms. "I do."

She hugged him back, hoping she wouldn't let him down.

Chapter 34

Then

If it had been their first fight, it had at least cleared the air. It didn't seem to matter too much what they called or didn't call their relationship. It seemed bigger than labels to Bess, anyway, something that could not be defined by a term.

This was love.

Oh, she'd thought she knew what that word meant a few times before in her life. Each time it had been different, and every time she fell in love with someone new she'd been convinced this time, this feeling, this version was "the one."

It took understanding that there was no "one" to realize what love really was.

She didn't tell Nick she loved him. She didn't know how. The three simple words that in the past had so easily fallen from her mouth, like marbles spilled from a jar, didn't seem adequate to describe the width and depth and breadth of her emotions when she was with him. Or without him.

He remembered her favorite brand of gum. Her favorite color, woven into the new beach towel he brought her. He knew how she hated the cages of hermit crabs in most of the souvenir shops and liked light sticks on the beach at night. He held her hand no matter who was watching, and kissed her, too, over and over and over.

Her love for him was not one whole thing but rather a myriad. Individual pieces, each with its important place, none of them useless. Everything from the sound of his laugh to the feeling of his hand on her back when they drifted into sleep with the sound of the ocean around them and soft sand beneath their bodies had a purpose and place within her love for him. She could do without none of it.

Yet she didn't say it.

The first time she went to sleep and woke up next to him, she thought maybe that would change things. That somehow that next step, of her not leaving after sex, would give their relationship a weight it might be able to bear. Not from Nick but from her. Sleeping in his bed and waking with him in the morning had seemed somehow more significant an admission than saying the word *love* ever could.

Eddie was right. Nick made her doubt herself.

Bess opened her eyes and stared at the dresser next to the bed. Behind her the slow, steady noise of Nick's breathing didn't change. It was early, especially considering they'd only gone to sleep a few hours before. They both had to work this morning, but she didn't feel like getting up yet. Getting up meant she'd have to shower, brush her teeth. Wash away the smell and taste of him.

Nick's hand slipped over her stomach and he aligned himself with her. A few hours ago their skin had been sticky with sweat from the effort of their lovemaking, but the night air had cooled them both. His cock stirred against her and Bess smiled but said nothing, not even when his hand slipped lower, between her thighs, to stroke her.

She let out a sigh when he shifted a little to nudge against her, then to push inside. Condoms seemed ridiculous after the night on the beach, when she was on the pill and neither of them was sleeping with anyone else. They'd taken a trip to the local women's health clinic for a few tests, at Nick's insistence and not hers.

He bit the back of her neck and thrust inside her harder. She was a little sore from the night before and hissed out a breath. He stopped, went slower. He stroked her clit until her hips moved again, and they tumbled into orgasm within seconds of each other.

"Good morning," he breathed into her ear.

"Morning." Bess gave him a smile over her shoulder. "I need to get ready for work."

"Me, too." He withdrew and rolled onto his back while she got up. He rose up on one elbow to watch her dig in her backpack for clean clothes.

Self-conscious, Bess pretended this was no big deal. In the shower she gave in to a series of giddy giggles she smothered under the water. She washed herself with his soap, his washcloth. She used his toothpaste and his towel. She stepped onto Nick's bath mat and used his toilet.

She'd never even stayed over with Andy like this. They'd always both had roommates and dorm rooms, not apartments. This...cohabitation...such as it was, made her think of houses with picket fences, a thought she tried to toss but couldn't.

Until the pancakes undid her.

"Can you grab the syrup?" Nick used his spatula to point at the fridge. "It's in there."

"You made breakfast?"

"Yeah. Sit down."

She did, after grabbing the syrup. He'd set the table with mismatched plates and cups, but he'd folded the napkins and place forks and knives on top of them. He'd even poured grape juice because he knew Bess didn't like orange.

"You cook," she said.

"Jesus, don't sound so surprised." Nick frowned and brought the platter of pancakes over and put it on the table. "I've had to cook for myself since I was, like, eight."

"That's not what I meant." She circled his wrist with her fingers to pull him closer for a kiss. "I meant you cooked for me. That's so nice."

"I'm not a complete asshole." Nick smiled. "See?"

He slid into his seat and stabbed the stack of pancakes, loading his plate and dribbling syrup overtop. Bess followed suit, her stomach growling. She cut the first bite and groaned with pleasure at the taste.

"Did you use a mix?"

"No. It's just as easy to make them from scratch if you have the ingredients." Nick shrugged as if it was no big deal. "Pancakes are eggs, milk and flour. Sometimes that's all we had."

They'd talked very little about his childhood, just a few anecdotes thrown in here or there, but it had been enough for her to know he'd had a very different upbringing than she had.

"They're good," she told him sincerely.

"They're better with bacon."

"They're good," she repeated, and when he glanced at her, she smiled.

He smiled, too. "Stop looking at me like that."

"Like what?" She blinked innocently.

He demonstrated, going dewy-eyed and fluttering his lashes. "Like that."

Bess laughed, ducking her head, embarrassed. "I can't help it."

"You're going to feed my ego."

"Oh, as if you need someone to do that," she teased, and held up her hands to fend him off when he got up to tickle her.

"Eat this pancake," he told her, forking a piece and holding it to her lips. "You can't be a smart-ass with your mouth full."

She took the pancake from the fork and chewed, grabbing his wrist again when he speared another bite and raised it to her lips. She licked the dripping syrup and thrilled at the way his gaze flared at the flicker of her tongue.

"You are one bad girl," Nick said.

Bess raised an eyebrow and licked the sweet stickiness from her mouth. "Oh, am I? I thought you liked that."

He snorted. "Keep doing that and both of us will be late to work."

As appealing as the idea was, Bess couldn't help a small wince. "All right, all right."

Nick sat again and stabbed his pancakes, but didn't eat. "I hurt you, didn't I?"

"It's all right." She drank some juice and wiped her mouth.

Nick's smile flickered and faded so fast she almost missed it. "I don't want to hurt you, though."

"I said…" Bess looked up, responding to what he said, but understanding, all at once, what he meant. "You won't, Nick."

He studied his food and ate a few bites while she watched. "My aunt and uncle weren't really related to me. My aunt was married to my mom's first husband. Who wasn't my father."

Bess ate a piece of pancake and washed it down with juice.

"They took me when social services took me away from

my mom. They didn't want to, really. I mean, they had four other kids and a foster kid. They didn't really have room for me."

"I'm sorry." She hated the trite response but had nothing else to say.

"They weren't mean to me or anything, but I always knew they didn't really want me there. When I turned eighteen they told me I'd have to start paying rent to stay there."

He laughed. "Four hundred bucks a month to share a shit-hole room and a bathroom with four other people? I moved out, got a job. I graduated from high school, though, and they didn't think I would. I'd go to college, too, if I thought I could afford it."

"What would you go to school for?"

He shrugged. "I think I'd like to be a social worker."

Bess blinked. "Really? That's my major. With a minor in psychology."

Nick smiled and finished his food. "No shit?"

"Really. You should check out the program at Millersville."

"No money."

"There are loans and grants, Nick." The idea of him going to school, her school, excited her so much she almost spilled her juice. "The campus is great and there are tons of work-study programs, too. You should really think about it."

"Huh," he said after a moment. "You think so?"

"Yes, I really think so."

He cocked his head to study her. "You're just trying to get me to go to your school, aren't you?"

It took her a second to see he was teasing her. "Maybe."

"Pffft." Nick rolled his eyes. "You're so transparent."

He had no idea, she thought. None at all.

"If you really want to do it," she said seriously, "you should."

Nick wiped his mouth with the back of his hand. "You know if I went there..."

"Yes."

He shrugged, making the moment casual even though she knew it wasn't. "We'd be able to keep seeing each other."

Her smile spread across her face as quickly as the syrup had spread over the pancakes. "Yes, we would."

"Huh," Nick said. "That would suck, wouldn't it?"

Bess threw a pancake at him. Nick was fast, but she was faster, up and away from the table before he could reach her. He caught her in the living room, when she had no place to go. He tackled her, pinning her arms from behind and goose-stepping her to the couch, where he forced her down and tried again to tickle her.

She shouted even as she wriggled, though not too hard. His hands on her were doing more than tickling. When he kissed her, her mouth was already open. Her hands were already reaching for him. She wrapped her legs around his waist, doing her best to pin him against her the way he'd pinned her before.

Their struggle didn't last long. The kissing lasted longer, until they were both breathless. Nick pulled away from her mouth to gaze into her eyes.

"It would be a lot of work," he said.

"School?"

He gave her a look.

"Hey, anything worth doing is a lot of work," Bess said. She pushed away to straighten her clothes and hair. "If you really want to go to school, Nick, you absolutely should."

She got up to look down at him, still half on, half off the couch. He shifted all the way to the floor, his back to the couch. She knelt in front of him.

"But make sure you're doing it for yourself," she whispered. "As much as I'd like to hear you say you'd be doing it to be with me, you have to do something like that for yourself."

She thought for sure he'd make some smart-ass comment, but all he did was kiss her again.

"Do you think I can do it?"

She looked into his eyes. "Absolutely."

Nick smiled. "I have you so wrapped." He held up his pinky.

Bess grabbed his hand and kissed it. "Shut up. I have to go to work."

The knocking on the door turned both their heads. Nick frowned, getting to his feet. He hadn't yet showered, but had pulled on a pair of sweatpants, so he answered the door with bare feet and chest, his hair mussed as if he'd just tumbled out of bed.

Bess, curious about who would possibly be knocking at Nick's door so early in the morning, peered out from behind him.

"Is Bess here?"

Nick stepped back to open the door a little wider as he looked over his shoulder at her.

She stared, mouth gaping, unable to speak as the young man on the porch saw her. She watched his face go from polite curiosity to resignation to anger.

It was Andy.

Chapter 35

Now

*N*ick was right. Of course he was. Connor already knew
Nick wasn't just a boarder. Robbie, on the other hand, did not.

They didn't make it an announcement. All in all, Nick was
more circumspect than she'd have given him credit for. Once
she'd told him she wasn't going to hide their relationship from
anyone any longer, he seemed to respect her desire not to push
her love life in the faces of her sons. Even so, Robbie figured
it out, and if his discovery had happened more slowly than his
brother's, he was also far less discreet in his reaction.

"Mom?" He sat at the other end of the picnic table on the
deck, his face pulled into stunned surprise.

Bess looked at him, at his expression, and knew at once he'd
figured out what his brother had already known. What had
triggered it? Nick's hand on the small of her back as he moved
behind her to help clear the table. A small and subtle gesture
that couldn't be construed as anything other than what it was.

Bess looked at Nick, his hands piled high now with a stack of paper plates and napkins. She looked back at her son, whose betrayed stare caused her heart to sink. "Robbie—"

Without waiting for her to say more, he got up and strode off the deck, down the stairs and onto the beach. Bess watched him go, but before she could head after him, Nick handed her the stack of paper plates.

"I'll go."

"I don't think—"

"I'll go," he repeated firmly.

Bess nodded. Her stomach seemed to have dropped to her feet and tangled around her ankles, so she couldn't walk away. She watched her lover go to confront her son. She wondered if there'd be blood.

Robbie faced away from the house, his hands on his hips as he paced back and forth along the water. Nick took his time getting there. He wasn't quite as tall as Robbie, nor as broad.

"What's going on?" Connor asked as he came through the sliding-glass doors, his polo shirt already half over his head. He pulled the shirt off, tossed it onto a lounge chair and stretched.

"Don't leave that there," Bess said sharply. "Put it in the laundry."

Connor gave her a look. "Sure, Mom. I will."

"Now, Connor." Bess took the trash Nick had handed her into the house, where she shoved it into the can beneath the sink.

Connor found her struggling to tie the bag and pull it from the container, but she'd shoved so much trash in it the plastic was sticking to the sides. He pushed her aside gently, and finished it for her. Bess washed her hands at the sink.

"Why are Nick and Robbie down at the beach together?" He put the full bag by the door.

Bess handed him an empty one. "Nick's talking to him."

Connor laughed low as he tucked the new bag into the can. "Yeah, Robbie's always been a little slow."

"I don't find that funny, Connor." She crossed her arms.

He straightened and looked her in the eyes. "I didn't think you would."

She stared at him. He stared back. Neither of them broke eye contact, neither looked away.

"I'm with him," Bess said without a tremble or trace of hesitation in her voice. "And I hope you boys can understand that. I'm not sure if I can expect you to. But I hope you do."

Connor leaned against the counter, his arms crossed in imitation of hers. "What about Dad?"

"Your father and I tried to make our marriage work. But it didn't." Bess shook her head. "It doesn't mean we don't love you and Robbie."

"Mom," said Connor with a trace of disdain. "I don't need the sunshine fairy glitter story, okay? People break up all the time. I'll be fine. Robbie'll be fine, too."

It didn't relieve her to hear him say it, even if he was convinced it was true. "I don't want you to think my relationship with Nick had anything to do with me and your dad."

Connor snorted, unfolding his arms and no longer resting against the counter. "Yeah, whatever. It's not any of my business."

He turned to go, but Bess's words stopped him. "You're right. It's not any of your business. But I should have told you and your brother the truth right away instead of lying about it. I'm sorry."

Connor paused, his shoulders hunching for a moment or two before he straightened again. He didn't turn to look at her. "Forget about it."

"I'm sorry, Connor," Bess said sincerely, knowing it would

do no good. Whatever chasm had opened between her and her oldest son was inexorably widening. "I love him."

"You love him?" He turned around to face her. "After what, three weeks? You love him?"

She couldn't very well admit it had been longer than that. "Like I said, I'm not sure I can expect you to understand."

"And you want me to believe it had nothing to do with you and Dad breaking up, but you *love* him?" Connor's voice got thick. "That's a fucking *joke,* Mom! A joke!"

Bess flinched, not at the language but the vehemence behind it. "Connor—"

He held up his hands. "He's, like, two years older than me! What's he doing with you, anyway? What's he after?"

Bess had never imagined her son might assume Nick was trying to scam her. "He's not after anything!"

"Yeah? So why doesn't he work? Where's he get his money? Is he your…what—your hired stud?" Connor's mouth twisted as if he'd bitten a lemon. "Don't tell me you love him, please. I'm a big boy. I can handle the fact you've got yourself a cute little fuck buddy—"

Bess hadn't spanked her boys when they were young, and though her hand itched to slap the nasty words right out of his mouth now, she slapped the counter instead. Hard. Her hand stung, but Connor stopped.

"You don't know anything about it," she said in a voice colder than she'd ever imagined having to use with her own child. "Don't think you're so smart, Connor Alan, because you're not."

Connor blinked rapidly, to Bess's dismay, and his eyes shone bright as though he fought back tears. "You should've just told us the truth right away, Mom."

"What would you have done, Connor? Would you have be-

lieved me then, or would you have jumped to the same con-
clusions? I can't explain it to you, it just is. I know it's not easy
for you, or your brother." She swallowed, hard. "It's not going
to be easy for me and Nick, either. But you can't choose who
you love, honey, it just happens."

"You can choose who you don't love," Connor said, with
an insight Bess wouldn't have imagined him to possess.

"I don't want to choose not to love Nick," she answered
honestly.

At least it was on the table, so to speak. In the open. Bess
drew in a deep breath, her stomach settled now that the worst
seemed past.

Connor scowled and stalked away, calling over his shoulder,
"I'm out of here."

The worst hadn't passed, after all. Bess had assumed Connor
meant out of the kitchen, but when he came back a few minutes later with his backpack and a duffel bag, her stomach
leaped and jumped again.

"Where are you going?" she cried as he passed the kitchen
and headed for the stairs.

"I'm going to crash at Derrick's place. He's looking for a
roommate. Maybe I'll stay there for the rest of the summer."

"Maybe— Connor, wait." Bess followed, but he didn't stop.
He thudded down the stairs two at a time. His duffel battered
the wall and knocked off a large, framed photo collage that
had hung there since Bess's childhood. The picture hit the
stairs behind him and the glass cracked. Connor didn't stop.

Bess didn't, either. She followed him out to the carport,
where they both stared at the Volvo. "You're not taking my
car."

He hadn't seemed to think that far ahead, but adapted
quickly. He pulled his cell phone from his pocket and dialed

a number. "Derrick. Can you pick me up, man? Yeah. Thanks."

Boys communicated differently than girls, and that was it. Connor disconnected the call and put his phone back in his pocket. He slung the duffel over his shoulder and made for the street.

"Connor! What about work?" Bess hurried after him.

"Me and Derrick can work the same shifts. I'll ride with him."

"And you can count on him for that?"

Connor stopped. Turned. He set his duffel on the sidewalk. Bess recognized his sulk from his toddlerhood.

"Yeah," he said. "I think I can trust *him*."

And he couldn't trust her. Bess winced. "You've known him only a few weeks."

Connor raised an eyebrow, looking so much like his father she wanted to scream. "Yeah? Apparently a few weeks is plenty long enough."

He turned away from her. Bess spun on her heel and started walking back to the house. She'd been prepared to let him go at the end of the summer, but she let him go now.

Back in the house, she found Nick in the kitchen, putting detergent in the dishwasher. He closed the door and switched it on, turning as she came into the kitchen. He took one look at her and enfolded her in his arms.

"Connor," was all she said.

"That bad?" His hand stroked her hair. "Shh. Bess. It's okay."

"Where's Robbie?"

"Down at the beach, I guess."

Bess tilted her head up to look at him. "What did you say to him?"

"I told him the truth."

She knew him well enough now to smile instead of grimace. "Which was?"

Nick smoothed her hair off her face and kissed her. "I told him I'm crazy in love with his mother and I plan on keeping her the happiest woman alive for as long as I can, and if he had a problem with it he might as well punch me in my face now, because I wasn't going anywhere."

"You didn't!"

"I did."

Bess studied him. "Did he?"

Nick grinned. "No. I thought he might, and damn, your boy's big. I was sure I was gonna get my ass kicked. But…no. Robbie's a good kid."

There was an irony there, in Nick calling Robbie a kid.

"He is," Bess said. "Connor walked out on me. He says he's going to live with somebody he works with."

"So let him. He's old enough."

Bess chewed the inside of her cheek and pushed gently away from Nick. She left him in the kitchen and went to the bedroom, where she sat on the edge of the bed and fought tears. When he appeared in the doorway a few minutes later and sat beside her, and when he took her hand, she stopped fighting.

She cried for a while, more because it felt good to weep and have Nick's shoulder beneath her face when she did it. When he pushed her gently onto the bed and cuddled her, holding her tight, that felt good, too. And when he stroked her hair. Being with him, just being, felt good.

It was different, this time around. All of it. In so many ways she couldn't begin to name them all.

Bess turned in his arms to face him. "I'm not sorry."

"Okay." He smiled and kissed her, but didn't ask what she wasn't sorry for.

"For anything," Bess said. "Not back then. But more...I'm not sorry about now."

Nick's brow furrowed. "Not sure I get you."

"I mean..." She shook her head, willing the words to come easily and knowing they probably wouldn't. "I'm not sorry about the way things happened back then. Because if things had been different then, I don't think we'd have this, now."

Nick frowned. Bess felt the tension in his body, but he didn't pull away. "We might have."

"No." She shook her head again. "We wouldn't have, Nick. You know it."

He didn't say anything for a minute, and Bess didn't try to fill the silence. When he spoke at last, his voice was low and deep. It held the currents of the ocean in its cadence, and the cries of the seabirds. It was a sad and lonely sound, but a beautiful one, too.

"I waited for you. But you didn't wait for me, not long enough, did you? Yet all those years passed with me waiting, and here you are. Here we are."

"Here we are," she whispered.

"Maybe you're right," Nick told her, still in a voice that reminded her of the sea. "Maybe things wouldn't have worked with us."

"We'll never know," Bess said.

"We don't have to know," Nick replied. "Because no matter what might have been, this is what is. This is what we have. It's what I have, Bess."

She kissed him, and held him tight, and together they listened for a while to the sound of the ocean outside.

"You might not be sorry, but I am." Nick said the words into her hair when Bess had nearly fallen asleep. Her eyes opened, but she didn't speak. "I'm sorry I didn't tell you the truth back then, when I had the chance. And I'm sorry I didn't come for you like I said I would."

"You had no choice. I don't blame you."

"But you did, didn't you?" His mouth moved in her hair, his breath hot on her scalp.

"Yes," she admitted. "I did blame you. For a while. But then I stopped."

"And then you came back." He sounded as if he was smiling. "And here you are."

"Here we are."

He sighed. There was more silence, but it wasn't awkward. "I just wish I knew…for how long."

She pushed herself up on her elbow to look at him. "Why can't it be forever?"

"There's no such thing."

She touched his cheek. "Then I'll take as long as I can get."

But as she settled back down into the comfort of his embrace, Bess, too, wondered how long that would be.

Chapter 36

Then

"What are you doing here?" Bess moved around Nick, who stepped aside to let her pass.

"What are *you* doing here?" Andy asked, glowering.

"I was just on my way to work." It wasn't a lie, but it wasn't quite the truth.

"Missy told me you'd be here." Andy glared over Bess's shoulder at Nick, who lounged in the doorway, smiling faintly. "Who's that?"

"If Missy told you to come here, she told you who I am," Nick said.

Andy's mouth worked, but he ignored Nick and looked at Bess. "What the hell's going on?"

The world had begun to spin, and Bess put a hand on the porch railing to keep herself from spinning with it. "Nick, would you get my backpack?"

Both of them looked at her as she gazed at the ground. She

felt them looking, but couldn't face either of them. After a heartbeat, then another, Nick said, "Sure," in a voice that told her he was no longer smiling.

He was back with it in a minute and thrust it into her hand. She glanced up then, but Nick wasn't looking at her. He was glaring at Andy. A quick glance at Andy showed he was glaring at Nick. She closed her fingers around the backpack's straps and slung it over her shoulder.

"I have to get to work," she said to Andy. "You can walk with me, if you want."

She turned to Nick. "I'll talk to you later, okay?"

He shrugged. "Whatever."

Stung, Bess recoiled, but then lifted her chin. "I'll see you."

"Whatever." Nick flashed her a smile that sent icicles straight down her spine. Then he shut the door in her face.

Bess unlocked her bike from the railing and started walking it without bothering to see if Andy followed. He did, after a minute, with the bike as a barrier between them.

"What the hell's going on?" he repeated, and when she didn't answer he grabbed her arm.

Bess jerked away from him, but stopped walking. "Why are you here, Andy?"

"Because I wanted to see you." He reached for her again, but when she twitched out of reach he stopped. "I wanted to find out what's going on. I figured I'd surprise you. I guess I fucking did."

"Yeah." Bess started walking again. Her backpack slapped against her side as she walked, and she paused to put it in her bike basket before continuing.

"I called your house but your cousin said you were with Missy. So I called her."

"I'm sure she was thrilled to be woken up so early."

"She wasn't."

Bess gave him a glance. Andy didn't look shamefaced at all, but he didn't look so mad anymore, either. "You stopped calling me," she stated.

"I thought you were mad at me." He gave her a sad little grin that did nothing to win her sympathies.

"So you just stopped calling? What were you trying to prove?"

Nick lived closer to the shop than Bess. The trip wasn't going to take long, and she wanted to finish this conversation before she got to work. Even this early, there were joggers and dog walkers out and about. She didn't want to make a scene.

"I wasn't trying to prove anything. God, Bess, would you stop and look at me?"

"I have to get to work, Andy, I don't have time to fight with you now."

"You don't have time, or you just don't want to?"

She stopped then. "I don't want to. I don't want to fight with you about this."

"So it's all my fault? I drive four hours down here to see my girlfriend and find her in some other guy's apartment, but it's my fault?"

"I didn't say that!"

Andy scowled. "You didn't have to."

"Don't put words in my mouth, Andy." Bess pushed her bike across the highway and toward Bethany's main square. To her left was the tall totem pole that had stood there for years. It appeared to be giving her a disapproving look. She didn't blame it.

"I'm not putting words in your mouth. Stop and talk to me!"

"I don't want to talk to you!" There it was. The truth. She hadn't meant to shout it but felt immediately better for it. "I don't want to talk to you about this, Andy. Not now."

Not ever, maybe.

"I drove four hours—"

"What do you want? A medal? You drove four hours to get to me when you wanted to, but oh, when I asked you to earlier in the summer there was no way you could make it!"

She stopped and faced him, her fingers clenched so hard on her bike handles her knuckles had gone white. Andy wore a hangdog look she wanted to believe but didn't. Bess bit her tongue against the accusations she didn't want to hurl.

"I came for you," Andy said, as if that should make it all better.

Bess couldn't decide if she wished it did, or was glad it did not.

"Maybe you should have come sooner."

At last Andy flinched. "Are you fucking that guy?"

"What made you decide to come find out? I asked you a dozen times to come down here. You always had an excuse for why you couldn't."

"I'm sorry!"

She did believe him, this time. "Jesus, Andy, I broke up with you and you didn't even notice!"

He blinked and swallowed hard. Bess was amazed to see she might have actually hurt his feelings. Shame and a secret, guilty pleasure both took up residence in her guts.

"You broke up with me?"

"Didn't you get my message?"

"Yeah, but I thought Matty was fucking with me. I didn't know it meant you broke up with me." Andy blinked rapidly.

"And yet you still didn't call," Bess said. "Wow. You must've really cared a whole lot."

"Are you with him now? That other guy?"

"His name's Nick. And…I don't know if I'm with him."

Andy's face turned bleak. "You're sleeping with him."

"Andy, does it *matter?*" she asked. "You've been screwing around on me all summer and maybe before that! Did you really think I wouldn't find out?"

"I haven't been!" Yet his guilty eyes told her the truth.

Bess sneered. "Oh, please. I'm not stupid. At least admit it, Andy. You've been screwing around."

"It didn't mean anything to me," he muttered, caught, not quite ready to admit to wrongdoing.

"Well, it meant something to me." Bess looked at the ground, surprised to see the splash of a tear hitting the dust on her sneakers. She hadn't realized she was crying.

"So you decided to get back at me? Or…what?" Andy sounded genuinely confused.

Bess looked at him. The edges of his face had blurred, but it was still the face she'd loved for so many years. "I didn't do it to get back at you, Andy. It just happened. And, yes. I've been sleeping with him. I'll tell you the truth, even if you couldn't tell me."

Andy flinched again and looked away. He scuffed at the sidewalk and didn't follow her when she started walking again. He caught up to her in the alley, though, behind the shop, where she locked her bike and prepared to unlock the door.

"So that's it? We're just…done?"

Her tears had dried as she walked, and she gave him a dry-eyed stare. "Yes. I think so."

"Why do you get to decide that?" Andy ran both hands through his hair, front then back. His fists clenched as he stomped in a small circle. "How fucking fair is that?"

"Why do you care?" she cried, hating this scene. Hating him. Hating herself, too.

"Because I love you!"

His shout stung her like a wasp. "I have to go to work," she stated.

"I thought you loved me, too." He probably didn't mean to sound so petulant, but he did.

"I did, Andy!" Bess cried. "I did!"

"But not anymore?" His eyes turned pleading, a look he knew damn well she couldn't resist. Eddie appeared on a bike of his own at the end of the alley. He rode closer and Bess wanted a hole in the ground to open up and swallow her. No, to swallow Andy.

"I don't know," she answered as honestly as she could. "A lot's changed this summer."

"Oh, a lot like that guy?" Andy sneered, the pleading gone from his face. "Funny how that works."

Faced with his anger, Bess found it easier to keep hold of her own. "Yeah, funny how it does." She unlocked the door so Eddie could get inside, but she didn't go in herself. She expected Eddie to push past her, but though he sidled by the bristling Andy, he stayed on the steps with her.

"A-are you all right, Bess?"

"Yeah, fine, Eddie. Go on inside."

"Who's this?" Andy sneered harder. "Hey, buddy, this isn't any of your business."

Eddie, bless him, didn't budge. "Is he th-threatening you?"

"Hey, get lost." Andy jerked a thumb down the alley. "I told you this isn't your business."

Andy wasn't threatening her, but it touched her deeply that Eddie was afraid for her. More so that he was willing to defend her. She smiled and touched his shoulder.

"Don't tell me you're screwing him, too!" Andy snorted.

"Shut up, Andy."

Eddie still didn't move. He angled his body slightly in front of hers. "I think you'd better get lost. *Buddy.*"

"Or what?" Andy, who stood a good three inches taller than Eddie and probably weighed at least twenty more pounds, puffed up. "What're you going to do? Make me?"

"Stop it, both of you." Bess put her hands out to keep them apart, though in fact, neither had actually moved. "Andy, you're being ridiculous."

"Tell me something, Eddie. That's your name, right? Eddie? Tell me, how long has Bess been banging that fucker with the long hair?"

Eddie's cheeks turned dusky. "Just go away, man. She doesn't want to see you, can't you tell that?"

"How long?" Andy asked again. He danced closer, trying to intimidate them. Bess knew he'd never lift a hand against her, but Eddie couldn't know that. Under her palm, his thin shoulder trembled, but he didn't move.

"All summer?"

"Eddie, don't answer him."

"Why not? You don't want me to know, right? You want to blame me, but you don't want to admit that you're just as bad as I am!" Andy's voice rose.

Eddie moved forward the tiniest bit.

"Oh, yeah, fucker, just come on at me. Come on." Andy gestured. "I'd love to punch someone right now. Come on."

"Don't, Eddie. This isn't your fight." The force in her voice stopped them both. "Andy, that's enough. Eddie, go inside."

After a second, Eddie did as she'd said, and went in. Andy glared, breathing hard. Bess crossed her arms over her chest and stared him down.

"I came all the way here to see you," he told her again, as if he hadn't already said it before. "Can't we at least talk about things?"

"Fine. We can talk about it. But I have to work now." How

she'd be able to concentrate, Bess wasn't sure, but she had no choice. "I'm done at five today."

Andy nodded. "I'll pick you up."

"Not here. Let me go home first. Pick me up at seven."

Andy looked as if he was going to protest, but it felt good, that small bit of control. Bess breathed a little easier. He ran his hands through his hair again.

"What should I do until then?"

"Umm, you're at the beach," Bess said. "Why don't you go hang out or something?"

"All day?" He grimaced, showing what he thought of that.

"Andy—" she sighed "—I really don't care what you do, okay?"

He nodded, and for the first time since he'd knocked on Nick's door, gave her a sorrowful look that seemed sincere. "We'll work this out, right?"

"I don't know."

"We'll work this out," he repeated, as if saying it over and over would make it true.

"Somehow or other it will all work out, Andy, yes. But who knows how?"

"I know," he said, with enough confidence for both of them.

Bess, instead of answering, turned and went inside the shop.

Chapter 37

Now

*B*ess waited two days before she sought her son. She had a legitimate reason for going to the Office Outlet. She needed a wireless router for her laptop at the beach house, as well as a new printer to replace the one she'd left behind at the other house.

None of that made it any easier to walk through the doors.

She sloughed off the eager young man in the red polo shirt and earpiece that made him look like one of the Borg from Star Trek, who accosted her as soon as she entered the printer section. "Sorry, I'm just looking for my son. Connor Walsh?"

The smarmy salesman's grin vanished, replaced by a jerk of the thumb. "He's stocking in stationery."

"Thanks," Bess said, but he was already off in search of other prey. She found Connor bent over a carton of boxed, mono-grammed stationery. "Got any *B*s?"

He looked up, then straightened. Did she imagine the shad-ows beneath his eyes? Mother that she was, she searched his face for signs of malnutrition, his clothes for wrinkles. Connor kept his expression blank.

"I didn't get there yet."

"I came in for a printer and a router. Can you help me find some good ones?"

He wasn't giving her an inch. "I think Roger's the one in that department."

"Connor. C'mon." Bess sighed. "I trust your opinion and I'm sure you can use the commission."

"I'm doing okay." He set aside the box in his hands.

Bess waited. He finally gave in, though his expression showed he wasn't ready to forgive her. That was okay. She could live with it. She followed him through the aisles to the row where the routers hung in their plastic blister packs and boxes.

Connor showed her the choices and explained which would be the best option for her laptop, an Apple iBook that was a few years old. He helped her pick out a printer, too, an inexpensive model without many bells and whistles, but which suited her budget.

"You know, I get a discount," he said sullenly. "I can hold these for you. Buy them tonight. I can drop them off at the shop with Robbie."

"Would you?" Bess made sure to keep her voice neutral, like this wasn't a big deal. "You could come by the house, too, if you wanted. Have dinner with us."

Connor nodded. He turned the router box over and over in his hands without looking at her. "Maybe. If I can get a ride."

She stopped herself from offering to pick him up. "How's the roommate situation?"

He shrugged. "Fine."

Which could mean it was fine or mean it was awful, and

she'd never know, because Connor was determined not to tell her. "Connor—"

He held up a hand and looked around to make sure nobody was paying attention to them. "Mom. Don't."

Bess bit back the offer for him to move home. Maybe two days wasn't long enough. "Okay. So you'll get those things and bring them by the house?"

"I'll drop them off with Robbie."

She didn't push it. She handed him a wad of cash. "Here."

"This is too much."

"Take it," Bess said, in a voice that allowed for no argument.

Connor hesitated, then tucked the money in his pocket. "Thanks."

"Connor," Bess said softly, and waited until he looked at her. "I'm sorry."

He shrugged, mouth pulled down. He was a boy trying hard to be a man, but he was still her son, and it twisted her up inside to know she'd done this to him. She'd dug this chasm between them with her own selfishness. Her need.

He shrugged once more, his only answer. Bess patted his arm and headed out of the store before she embarrassed them both. She meant to go right back to the house. Back to Nick.

The sign for Bethany Magick caught her eye again as she drove past, and Bess pulled into the alley without thinking twice. Inside the shop, Alicia looked up from her paperback novel and her place behind the cash register.

"Bess, hi!"

"You remembered me." Bess smiled, moving forward.

Alicia came around the counter. "Of course I remember you. Any luck with those books?"

"Luck?" Bess laughed self-consciously. "I have to admit, I haven't really had the chance to read them yet."

The shopkeeper grinned. "C'mon, girl. It's beach season. You're supposed to be out there, soaking up the sun and reading books."

"I know, I know." She held up her hands.

Alicia was right. What use was a beach house and no job if she didn't take advantage of it? Once she started getting busy with Just A Bite, she'd look back on these few months and wish she had all the free time back. Then again, she would remember how she'd spent all the free time, and doubted she'd regret not reading more.

"Just out of curiosity," Alicia said after the barest of pauses, "why the sudden interest?"

Bess cocked her head quizzically. "What makes you think it was sudden?"

The woman laughed. "I could sort of tell. You didn't have that New Age look about you. I figured something had to have triggered your sudden interest in the other side."

"I'm not sure, really." The lie tripped off her tongue without effort. "It just seemed interesting."

The shopkeeper nodded as though that made sense. "Sometimes it happens that way. I got my first taste of my interest in the metaphysical from an Ouija board."

Bess had been studying the display of smooth rocks in the bins across the front of the counter, but looked up at once at Alicia's revelation. "Really?"

"Yep." She nodded again. "I was at a party one summer back when I was in college. This girl and guy were doing it and I swear I felt a chill all the way up and down my spine. It was the first time I ever really believed in spirits."

Bess's own spine tingled with a chill. "So then what?"

Alicia shrugged. "I started studying. Decided to learn more about Wicca…discovered I had a real talent for the runes. It was a pretty life-changing experience, now that I look back on it."

The spit in Bess's mouth had dried, but she managed to say, "Do you remember the name of the guy? And the girl?"

"I didn't know the girl," Alicia said, "but the guy's name was Nick."

Bess let out the breath she'd been holding. "What would bring a spirit back?"

Alicia's laughter faded, though a faint smile still remained. "Strong emotion, probably."

"Like love?"

"Yes. Or anger, or hatred. But love, too."

Bess looked again to the piles of smooth, tumbled rocks. "Do you believe in an afterlife?"

"I do," Alicia said gently. "Do you?"

"I didn't." Bess looked up. "I mean, I wasn't sure. I never thought about it. I wasn't sure I believed in God."

"And now?" Alicia broke off a twig of rosemary from the pot behind her, and the shop filled with the fresh, pungent scent. She handed it to Bess.

Bess ran the feathery sprig through her fingers and lifted it to her nose. "I'm still not sure. But if there is an after-life…wouldn't it be a better place for a spirit than being stuck here?"

"I've heard people refer to spirits who remain here after they should have gone as being imprisoned," Alicia said. "But then again, some choose to stay, for whatever reasons. I'm not entirely knowledgeable about exorcisms or cleansing rituals, but I've known people who've shared space with spirits for years without harm. My neighbor swears she's got a ghost in her apartment, but it never does anything but rearrange the pillows on her couch."

Bess smiled faintly. "That's not exactly the sort of thing I was thinking about."

"Let me do a reading for you." Alicia came around the counter. "C'mon. I'll do a three-rune draw. A quickie."

"Oh, I don't know—"

"It won't tell you the future," Alicia said gently. "Usually, readings don't even tell you anything you don't already know. But it can help clarify what you do know. Put things into focus."

"I guess I could use that." Bess laughed and followed her to the back room, where Alicia motioned toward chairs and a small table. The she lifted a velvet bag, the contents of which clinked as she did so. "Pick three. Put them faceup on the table."

Bess did.

"This is Nied. It represents the past," Alicia said, pointing. "But it's reversed, so that means you made a mistake. But the next rune is Dagaz, which shows me you're dealing with the results of choices you made in the past, some for the better and some for the worse, but you're letting go of them. You're growing. The choices you made work together to make the whole. Even the negative has added up to the positive present. And this final one, the future…" Alicia trailed off, studying the runes, then looked up at Bess. "This is Uruz, and it's upright. It can represent strength. What I'm getting is that you're going to have to make another choice, one you're not sure is a mistake or not. You'll be uncertain, but in the end, you'll prevail. You have the strength to do the right thing."

Bess bit down hard on her lip and couldn't answer for a minute. Then she nodded. She looked up at Alicia and smiled. "Thanks. This helped a lot."

"I hope so," the woman said. "You can come back sometime when we can do a longer reading, if you want."

Bess stood. "Thanks. I might do that."

But she really didn't need to, she thought as she waved good-bye and headed out of the shop. Headed home. Alicia had been right. She didn't need the runes to tell her what she should do.

At home, her cheerful greeting did nothing to dispel the dark and quiet of the house. On the deck, a candle burned. Nick's shadowed form hunched in one of the deck chairs. The breeze swayed the candle flame, but didn't blow it out.

Bess let herself out the sliding-glass doors to the deck, where she slipped onto the chair behind him and put her arms around him. Her chin fit just right on the curve of his shoulder. She breathed him in, the scent of sand and sea.

"Hey," she said.

"Hey." He half turned his head to let her kiss his cheek. "Did you get what you needed?"

"Connor's going to buy them with his discount and leave them with Robbie."

"Okay."

"Have you been sitting out here a long time?"

"Just a few hours."

Bess heard the smile in his voice and pinched his sides lightly. Nick squirmed, laughing, and turned to pull her across his lap. She didn't fight him.

"Are you all right?" she asked.

He didn't answer for a few minutes. "Yeah, I'm okay. It's just…"

He trailed off. She waited. When he didn't speak, she stroked his face. "What?"

"It's the ocean," he told her. His eyes looked far away, past her shoulder, over the deck railing. Across the sand.

"What about it?" Concerned, Bess put herself in his line of vision.

Nick's gaze cleared, but slowly. "Nothing. It's just loud to-night. Isn't it?"

Bess tilted her head to listen. "It sounds fine to me."

Nick shook himself lightly. He came back to her, bit by bit. His smile didn't quite chase away the chill sweeping over her, but it helped.

"You want to go for a walk with me?"

Her stomach was rumbling, a familiar faintness washing over her at the lack of food. "In a few minutes, okay? I want to grab a snack."

"Sure, sure," Nick said absently.

She kissed him. He kissed her back, but his embrace was distracted and incomplete. Bess tried not to let it bother her. She got off his lap and went inside, where she rummaged through the cabinets for something that would satisfy her but not take too long to make. She settled for a package of peanut butter crackers and a glass of milk. By the time she went back out on the deck, Nick was gone.

Bess looked over the railing, but the beach was too dark for her to see far. She opened her mouth to call his name, but closed it just as quickly. Instead of yelling, she took the stairs to the sand.

He stood at the edge of the water, looking out. When Bess came up beside him and slipped her hand into his, he didn't move. His hands, for the first time, were cool.

"It just goes on and on, doesn't it?" he said without looking at her. "It doesn't end."

Bess looked out, trying to see what he saw. "It does end, Nick. Somewhere, the water ends."

His fingers curled in hers. "I wasn't talking about the water."

And because she was a coward, Bess didn't ask him what he'd meant. She was pretty sure she already knew.

Chapter 38

Then

A day had never passed so slowly for her, but finally five o'clock arrived, and Bess was out of the shop as soon as Ronnie came in. She didn't even bother saying goodbye, and when Eddie tried to catch her attention on her way out, she brushed him off in her haste to be gone. She felt bad about it, yes she did, but not bad enough to stop and listen to what he had to say.

She pumped the pedals of her bike fast and faster, and didn't bother locking it to the railing of Nick's porch, but let it fall when she leaped off it. In three steps she was at his door, pounding. He didn't open it at first and she thought he wasn't home. She pounded again anyway, bruising her knuckles.

When at last he pulled the door open, the sight of him framed in the doorway struck her like a punch to the gut. Bess lost her breath for a second or two, then found it again. She said his name softly. Then louder.

Nick didn't move.

"I have to talk to you," Bess said.

He shook his head but came out and closed the door behind him. Leaning against the railing, he lit one of his cigars and blew sweet smoke toward her. "So talk."

There was a wall as solid as brick between them, even if she couldn't see it. Looking at Nick's face was like staring at stone.

"I didn't know he was coming, Nick."

"Yeah, I figured that part out."

It didn't seem he was going to give her an inch. Not a fraction of one. He looked at her through a plume of smoke, and she could read nothing in his eyes.

"He says…he loves me."

Nick's eyes narrowed and he turned his face to the side and spat a fragment of tobacco off the side of the porch. "I bet he does."

"Nick," Bess said softly. "I'm sorry."

She was sorry that Andy had shown up unexpectedly. That she hadn't had the courage to make sure he knew she'd broken up with him. Now everything was a mess, tangling around her ankles and threatening to trip her up.

Nick's shoulders hunched slightly, but when he turned to look at her, his back was straight. "Don't bother."

"What?" She took a step toward him but kept herself from raising her hand to touch him. "I—"

Nick finished his cigarette, tossed it to the wooden floor and ground it out with the toe of his shoe. "I said don't bother, Bess. Go on to your boyfriend. I have stuff to do."

"But that's not what I came—" Nick pushed past her, knocking her with his shoulder. Bess stumbled back against the railing. "Hey!"

He didn't turn at the door, just shoved it open. She followed him. The door banged into the wall hard enough to bounce back. It caught her elbow, but Bess ignored the sting and went after Nick into his kitchen.

"Don't walk away from me when I'm talking to you!" The instant she spoke, she knew the words had been a mistake.

Nick had reached for a glass from his cupboard to fill under the tap. When she spoke, he turned, water sloshing from the tumbler. It hit the faded linoleum floor and dripped from his fingers.

"Don't tell me what to do." In contrast to Bess's voice, risen into not quite a shout, Nick's had gone low and fierce.

"I'm sorry." She shook her head, trying to get herself under control. "This isn't going the way I wanted it to."

"No shit."

"Don't be like that!" She didn't want to yell, but the words surged out of her and she was helpless to hold them back. "Don't be such a prick!"

When the glass shattered against the kitchen wall, it left behind a splatter of clear liquid and the glitter of splinters against the paint. The sound echoed in her head, but it wasn't until she felt the chill of her palms on her heated cheeks that Bess realized she'd clapped her hands over her ears. In the next few seconds the edge of the doorway hit her between the shoulder blades as Nick backed her up against it.

"But that's what I am," he breathed into her ear. "Or did you forget?"

He'd backed her up like this so many times before. Had breathed in her ear just this way. This time, he didn't press his body to hers, or kiss her. He didn't touch her, but Bess shrank from him anyway, as if he'd reached to pinch her.

"Go back to him," Nick said. "Since he loves you so fucking much."

It was the perfect time to run away, but Bess didn't go. She turned her face just enough to speak into Nick's ear, the way he'd done to her. "I didn't come here to tell you I'm going back to him."

"But you are going to see him. You didn't tell him to take a walk, did you? Didn't tell him to get the fuck out of your life?"

"No," she said quietly. "I owe him an explanation, don't I?"

Nick pulled away enough to look at her face. "I don't know. Do you?"

"He said he loves me." It was an inadequate argument, and she knew it, but while her morals may have been slippery enough to justify being unfaithful, they didn't allow her to be purposefully cruel.

"Yeah?" Nick moved away another inch. "And what about me?"

"What about you?" Bess asked.

He said nothing.

"Nick," she said, and put a palm on his cheek. "What about you?"

He gave his head an infinitesimal shake, and Bess took her hand away. Her throat tight, she fought back tears. She didn't want him to see her cry.

"If you have feelings for me," she said, "now is the time to tell me."

Nick shook his head and took another step back. He looked into her eyes, his face as smooth and expressionless as if they were strangers. Worse than that, as if they'd never even met.

"I don't have any feelings for you."

Bess blinked hard. It was not what she'd wanted him to say. Not what she believed he'd say. His answer flayed her open, and she no longer cared if he saw her tears.

"I don't believe you." She forced out the words in a voice as shattered as the glass he'd thrown against the wall.

Nick's only answer was a solid, unyielding stare that pushed her as physically as a fist. Bess backed through the doorway into the living room and swiped at her face. She lifted her chin and took a long, deep breath, but it did no good. She swiped harder at her cheeks.

"He's waiting for me," she said. "I came here first. Don't you want to know why, Nick? Don't you want me to tell you why I came here first instead of going to him? Don't you want to know what I came here to say?"

Nick shook his head. Then he turned and disappeared into his bedroom. He didn't slam the door, but the click of it shutting was as definite an answer as if he'd shouted it out.

Chapter 39

Now

"I've got to go meet Eddie to talk about the plans for the shop." Bess leaned over Nick from behind to wrap her arms around him and kiss his neck.

He nodded, not paying attention. His hand moved the computer mouse relentlessly, clicking and scrolling. "Okay."

"What are you looking at?" She tried to read the text on the screen, but it was hideously tiny and in a combination of awful colors that made her eyes ache.

"Nothing." Nick clicked back to a search engine. The cursor beat like a heart in the empty search box, but he didn't type anything in it. "What time will you be home?"

"I don't know. Not late. Want me to pick up a movie or something?"

"Sure." He was still staring at the computer.

It wasn't like Nick to be so blandly accommodating. Bess nuzzled his cheek. "Are you okay?"

"Yeah, sure. You go." He half turned to kiss her, his hands covering her arms, which were looped over his shoulders.

The kiss threatened to deepen, and Bess, laughing, pulled away. "I really have to go. Eddie's waiting."

It was the wrong thing to say. Nick nodded, his mouth thinning, but he made no comment. Instead he turned his attention back to the computer, letting her go and dismissing her at the same time.

Annoyed, Bess pulled away. "Want me to bring anything for you?"

"No."

"Are you sure?"

He looked at her then, with a frown. "I don't need anything."

"Okay, I was just asking." She tossed up her hands and left before the two of them started arguing.

She'd lent Connor her car for a couple days until he could get his own. Andy, it seemed, was going to buy him a car. It was just the sort of grand gesture Andy was so fond of making, the kind of generosity that had once so impressed Bess but now only irritated her because it was part of a game she couldn't afford to play.

And one she wouldn't play, she told herself as she pulled out one of the bikes from its place in the shed to one side of the carport. She didn't need to buy her boys' affections. Andy didn't either, if he'd only take the time to think about it, but Bess wasn't going to try to point that out to him. If he wanted to buy Connor a car or Robbie a new pair of skis, she was going to let him. After all, it wasn't like she was going to be rolling in cash anytime soon.

And, Bess thought as she pedaled streets that had started becoming familiar again, she didn't really care about the money. After all, if she'd decided to go back to social work, she'd hardly have been raking in the bucks, either.

Besides, working with Eddie to get Just A Bite up and running had been the most fun and rewarding job she'd ever had.
From getting the bank loans to writing up the business plan,
Bess had learned things about herself she'd never known. She
was going to be her own boss, and she was ready for it.

By the time she got into town, she'd thought of half a
dozen more ideas to share with Eddie. She parked her bike in
the back of Sugarland, locking it to the bike rack, and paused
as a feeling of déjà vu washed over her.

The same bike, the same alley, the same Dumpster. She looked
at her hands and their familiar pattern of freckles and lines. A
hot breeze pushed tendrils of hair against her cheeks, and that,
too, felt the same. Even her denim skirt, cut to just above the
knee, and the white Keds she wore, could have been the same.

With nothing to prove she wasn't twenty years old, Bess had
no reason to believe she wasn't. This idea slipped over her like
butter melting, oozing into her every crack and crevice. The
faint sound of the ocean, the louder cries of gulls, the laughter
of people passing and the purr of cars inching their way around
the square. It was all the same, and Bess closed her eyes. When
she opened them, what would she see? The past? What would
she do if she did?

She would go to Nick, she knew. This time she'd go to him
and tell him the truth of how she felt about him. She wouldn't
wait. Wouldn't lie to herself or to him. If this was the past, as
it felt so surely it must be, that's what she'd do.

Yet even as she opened her eyes at the sound of the back
door opening, Bess knew she hadn't been transported back in
time. She couldn't change the past, didn't have a second
chance. She could only sing the second verse of a song to
which she didn't know the lyrics.

Robbie came out with a bag of garbage for the Dumpster,

and the sight of him pushed away the eerie, liquid feeling of being caught in a memory.

"Hey, Mom. You okay?"

"Yes. Just hot. It's hot out here today, huh?" Bess smiled brightly, blinking against the sunshine. As soon as she said it, the words became truth. She was hot. The bike ride had left her panting and sweating, more than she'd thought. "I need to get something to drink."

"Mom? You okay?" Robbie grabbed her arm as Bess stumbled a little bit. "C'mon inside."

The back room was barely cooler than the alley, but sitting in one of the metal folding chairs and sipping from a jumbo paper cup of icy soda, Bess started to feel better. Robbie watched her, his blue eyes shadowed with concern. His hair had gone sun-streaked, turned from wheat to gold, a forceful reminder of just how far the summer had gone and how close it was to ending.

"Hey, Bess. You okay?" Eddie came out from the front of the shop.

"She got overheated." Robbie answered for her. "I gave her something to drink."

Eddie patted Robbie on the shoulder as he eased by him to sit across from Bess. "Good job. Hey, can you take over the register for me?"

"Sure." Robbie gave her a last, cautious glance before he left.

"I really can't tell you how glad I am I hired that kid," Eddie said. He scooted his chair closer to Bess's and put a hand over hers, flipping it up so he could press his fingertips to the inside of her wrist. "Your heart's beating too fast. Drink slowly."

"Do I look that bad?" Beneath Eddie's fingers Bess's pulse

skipped, and she gently pulled away. She sipped the cold, sweet drink and felt the world solidify under her feet.

"You look like you've seen a ghost, that's all."

"Not just seen one," she said before she could stop herself. Eddie gave her a bemused grin. "Huh?"

"Never mind." Bess smiled at him. "Are you ready to go?"

"Yeah." He stood and held out his hand.

Bess took it, though she didn't really need help getting up. The sugar and caffeine had chased away the lingering wooziness. Eddie's hand in hers was solid. Real.

"Whoa," he said with a chuckle as the floor tipped under her again. His other hand came around to support her beneath the elbow. "Are you sure you're okay?"

"It's hot out there." Bess straightened. "I rode my bike, and I guess I'm not in the sort of shape I used to be."

"Your shape looks pretty good to me," Eddie stated.

An uncomfortable throat-clearing sound turned both their heads. Robbie, cheeks the color of brick, held out a pile of mail to Eddie. "Kara brought this in from the mailbox."

"Thanks." The moment past, Eddie took the sheaf of envelopes. "Me and your mom are going to talk about the shop. I've got my cell if you need me, but Kara knows how to handle pretty much everything."

Robbie rolled his eyes. "Yeah. I know."

He laughed. "Don't let her give you a hard time."

"As if I had a choice," Robbie said, but good-naturedly, before disappearing back into the shop.

The exchange had given Bess the chance to drink a bit more soda and gather her wits about her. When Eddie turned back to her, she was able to give him a smile. "Ready?"

"I'll drive. You're not walking that far in this heat." He held up a hand, though Bess hadn't protested. "I insist."

"I'm not going to complain about being chauffeured." To- gether they walked to Eddie's car, where he opened her door for her, waited until she'd slid into the passenger seat, then closed it. The gentlemanly gesture sent a tingle through her she tried to ignore. She watched through the front windshield as Eddie crossed in front of the vehicle in loping strides that emphasized how long his legs really were.

"What?" he said as he slid into his seat and fitted the key in the ignition. He paused to look at her before putting the car in gear. "Did I miss a spot shaving or something?"

"No." Bess shook her head and looked out her window so he wouldn't see her stupid grin.

They chatted about lots of different things on the way to the restaurant. Talking with Eddie was so easy there was never a lull in the conversation. Never a dull moment, either, because his sense of humor made jokes out of even potentially boring subjects like mortgages and lines of credit. The jokes couldn't disguise the fact that he really knew what he was talking about.

"I feel bad," Bess said on the way into the Rusty Rudder. She hadn't waited for Eddie to open the car door for her, but she couldn't stop him from getting the door to the restaurant.

"Still? Maybe you just need something to eat."

"No." She shook her head as Eddie gave his name to the hostess, who led them to their table. "I mean, yes, I do."

She was suddenly starving. "But that's not what I meant."

Eddie waited until they were alone before asking, "What, then?"

Bess laughed at his concerned look. "Just that you really know what you're doing, and I'm only along for the ride."

He waved a hand and pulled a face. "Oh, stop."

"It's true." They paused in their discussion to order a bottle of wine. "You're the one with the business plan and everything. You know all about price points and stuff. It's all a bunch of gibberish to me."

"But you're the one who came up with the idea, which is brilliant, by the way. Have I told you that lately?"

Bess laughed and blushed. "Yeah, a few times."

She looked up to see Eddie smiling at her. His hair had grown longer and shaggier over the past couple months and fell over the rims of his glasses. Eddie's hair would be coarse, Bess thought suddenly, with heat flaring higher in her cheeks. It would feel coarse under her fingertips. Not like Nick's, which was as fine and smooth as satin. At the thought of him, she ducked her head to study the menu.

"Well, it's true." Eddie looked over his menu and set it aside. "I know what I want."

"I can't decide." Bess scanned the rows of entrées, salads and sandwiches.

"What looks good to you?"

She looked up. "Is that how you do it? Pick what looks good to you?"

"Yes," Eddie said with a smile that sent warmth tingling through her all the way to her toes. "That's how I do it."

Silence fell between them, but only for a few seconds, because the waitress arrived with their wine and her order pad ready. Eddie ordered a steak, and Bess, feeling bold, stabbed her finger down onto the menu and ordered the first thing she hit.

"Lobster tail— Oh, no," she said with a laugh. "That's too extravagant."

"Order it," Eddie said firmly. He raised his glass.

Bess nodded at the waitress, who moved away, then raised her glass, too. "What are we celebrating?"

"It was killing me, waiting until now to tell you, but we got the loan." Grinning, Eddie leaned across the table to clink his glass with hers.

She hadn't thought about how tense waiting to hear about the loan had made her until she heard the news and her shoulders suddenly felt as if they rose a good six inches. "Oh, Eddie, that's great!"

"It is!" His grin got impossibly wider. "We can really do this. We'll run Sugarland until the end of the season and start checking into the renovations right away. And I have an appointment with a Realtor about the property next door. She said she's keeping an eye open for any other stores looking to sell, too. Then it's just a matter of getting it all ready to go by the end of May."

"That's less than a year away." Bess drank some wine, trying to process it all. "It's really going to happen!"

"It's really going to happen," Eddie said.

They toasted again. Bess brought up a few of her ideas for menu items, and he listened to every one. Even the most ridiculous. Dinner was served and they ate as they talked more about what sorts of hours they could both put in. Whether they wanted uniforms, or a logo.

"So much to think about," Bess said as they walked back to the car. "It was just a silly idea a couple months ago, and now…"

"Now it's the real thing." Eddied stopped with his hand on the passenger side door.

They were standing very close. The day that had been so stiflingly hot had turned to a chilly evening, but that wasn't why Bess shivered. It wasn't the wine, either, though she'd had her share.

"Have I told you lately," Eddie said, "how glad I am you came back to town?"

"Me, too." She stared up and up into his eyes, the twinkling blue behind his glasses that had become so familiar. "How come I never noticed what nice eyes you have?"

Eddie's mouth curved upward. "All the better to see you with."

Bess laughed, but wasn't sorry she'd said it. "We should get going."

He looked down the street, then back at her. "I thought maybe we could go down to the Bottle and Cork. There's live music tonight."

"I haven't been out in a long time," Bess said. "To a bar?"

"You have your ID, don't you?" He winked.

"Oh, as if that will be a problem." Bess scoffed, but followed where Eddie's gaze had gone before. She'd never been to the Bottle and Cork, but had heard it advertised on the radio. "Who's playing?"

"Does that really matter?" Eddie held out a hand in such away it would have looked ridiculous for her not to take it. "C'mon. It'll be fun."

Still she hesitated. Nick was at home, waiting for her. With a start, she realized she hadn't thought of him in hours. Hours without his face in front of her eyes.

"Robbie and Kara can close up the shop, if that's what you're worried about." Eddie tugged at her hand.

"No."

"Are you feeling weird again?" His grin faded, replaced by a look of such genuine concern that guilt plagued her.

"No, I'm okay. A little tired." Bess shrugged and looked again with longing toward the invisible but alluring Bottle and Cork.

She *hadn't* been out in ages. So long, in fact, she couldn't recall exactly when it had been. The taste of beer, smell of smoke and heavy bass beat of "Rump Shaker" were her last memories of club hopping, for her cousin Angela's bridal shower. Angie'd gotten married what, twelve years ago?

"We can go home, then." Eddie popped the lock with his key-ring remote. "If you're tired."

"No," Bess said firmly. "I'm okay. And I don't really have to get up early or anything."

"Ha." He pointed a finger. "Yes, you do. You have to take all the paperwork to the copy place and get it out to the bank on time. Partner."

She laughed. "Fine. I do have to get up early. Even so, it's not that late. Sure, let's go."

Eddie clicked his key remote again, beep-beeping the car lock. He offered Bess his arm and she took it. The Bottle and Cork was as crowded as she'd expected for a Thursday night in prime beach season, but that didn't matter. The opening band was a rip-roaring hootenanny playing everything from washtubs to wooden blocks shoved in the front of one of the members' pants. It wasn't the sort of music Bess normally liked, but with Eddie beside her clapping and whistling, she felt no self-consciousness about doing the same.

She didn't need alcohol to feel slightly drunk, either. Not with the crowd moving like one solid entity and Eddie beside her with an arm around her shoulder to keep her from being jostled. Not with the sheer pleasure of being out with someone who made her laugh, doing something she enjoyed.

Last call took her entirely by surprise, since she hadn't been drinking more than a couple of sodas. Last call was pretty serious business, though, because the crowd around them eased as people swarmed to the bar to get the last drinks of the night. The band had finished playing an hour or so before, replaced by a DJ who spun an odd assortment of country and western and heavy-metal tunes.

"Want to head out before the crowd does?" Eddie had to lean in close to holler over the rumble of bass and shrieking guitars.

Bess nodded. The walk back to the car took longer than she'd thought, but that could have been because she was measuring each step and thinking how much she didn't want to take the next.

"I had a great time," she said in the car.

"My ears are still ringing." Eddie laughed. "But it was a lot of fun. Thanks for going out with me."

"Thanks for asking me."

The conversation lagged more on the way home than it had earlier. Bess knew it was her fault. Eddie's jokes still earned her laughter, but she didn't offer any anecdotes of her own. She stared out her window a lot, at the hotels and motels and restaurants, and then at the long, dark stretch of highway bordered by nothing but dunes and grass. They'd just passed the tall concrete tower that had been used in World War II when she noticed that Eddie had stopped talking.

Once Bess realized he'd gone silent, it seemed too awkward to say something. The longer they went without speaking, the more awkward she felt, so that by the time he pulled into her driveway, her palms had begun to sweat.

Eddie turned off the car, but made no move to get out or to open her door for her this time. He turned in his seat, though, and reached to touch her shoulder. Her hair had fallen out of its ponytail so often during the night she'd finally given up, and Eddie's fingers twisted the ends a little.

"Something on your mind?" he asked quietly.

"I had a really great time tonight," Bess said. She hadn't turned to face him, and that felt awkward, too.

Through the windshield she could see the small, high square

window of Nick's room. Uncovered by a blind or a curtain, it gleamed like a dark, staring eye from the shadows of the carport.

Eddie leaned forward to peer through the glass. "Either Robbie's not home, or he's already asleep."

Bess looked to the single light showing faintly through the kitchen windows. It came from the lamp in the living room, the one she'd left on. "What time is it?"

"Late." Eddie put a hand over the numbers on the radio. "But he works the late shift tomorrow, so maybe he went out with some friends."

"Maybe." For the first time in her son's life, Bess wasn't worried about where he was or what he was doing. "He's fine, I'm sure."

Eddie's hand hadn't moved from her shoulder. Now it slipped a little down her arm. His fingers brushed the small bump of her T-shirt sleeve under the soft knit of her sweater, then further down to the scalloped hem of the sleeve. His fingers loosely curled around her hand and turned it palm upward so his fingers could find the steady throb of her pulse on her wrist.

"Your heart's beating too fast again," he said.

Bess couldn't lie and pretend she was surprised when Eddie kissed her. Her instant immobility had nothing to do with surprise and everything to do with the sudden hot flash of emotion rippling through her.

And lust, she couldn't forget that or pretend not to feel it.

Eddie's lips were warm and soft on hers. He didn't push or try to get her to open her mouth, and when she didn't kiss him in return he pulled away with a small smile.

"I'd be lying if I said I was sorry I did that," he murmured. "But I am sorry if you didn't want me to."

"It's not that, Eddie." Her voice was hoarser than she'd anticipated, and Bess paused to clear her throat.

Whatever he heard in her tone made him sit back in his seat. "You don't have to explain, Bess. It's okay."

"I'm just not...ready...for anything like this, that's all." She looked at him.

"It took me twenty years to get this far," he said. "I think I can wait a little while longer."

"Oh, Eddie." Bess stared down at her hands, linked in her lap. "We're going to be partners. I don't think—"

"Don't." She looked at him. He was smiling, but serious, too. Eddie shook his head. "I know you have reservations, and I don't blame you. And maybe I shouldn't have kissed you. But don't try to think of an excuse not to give this a chance, Bess. If it's not something you want, just tell me flat out."

It was something she'd have wanted, under any other circumstances, but when she opened her mouth to tell him so, something dark and vaguely man-shaped moved in the shadows of the carport, and she drew back.

"I'm sorry, Eddie, but this isn't something I want."

The lie was surprisingly easy, made easier by the way she made sure not to be looking at his face when she said it. She heard his intake of breath, though, and the soft sound of his mouth clamping.

"I'm sorry," Bess repeated, and got out of the car.

There was nothing in the carport, nobody waiting for her, but she felt Nick's presence there just the same. The air smelled like him. Bess didn't turn to wave goodbye to Eddie when he pulled out of the driveway.

She didn't go inside, either. Instead she went around the house, over the dunes and onto the beach, where she could let the ocean air push away the smell and taste of everything else.

Chapter 40

Then

"I didn't want it to end this way."

It was the last thing Andy had said to her, spoken as he slid behind the wheel of his car and prepared to leave. They'd talked and talked until the sun came up and it was time for her to go to work again. It was the first time she'd ever called to say she wouldn't be in, and Bess didn't even bother saying she was sick. Being a model employee had been good for something, because Mr. Swarovsky didn't question her.

She and Andy had argued. Laughed. Both of them had cried. He didn't try to kiss her or anything, which was good because she wouldn't have let him.

"You still love me," he insisted.

"Why do *you* still love *me?*" she asked. "When you know I've been with Nick all summer?"

"Does he love you?" Andy murmured, and to that, Bess had to say no.

He hadn't asked her if she loved Nick.

"You don't want to break up with me," Andy said. "If you did, you'd have done it instead of just letting it slide."

That only proved he didn't know her as well as he thought he did, and Bess, this new Bess, the one who propositioned boys, told him so.

"So let me get to know you all over again." This suggestion came with an expression so sincere she didn't have the heart to tell him it was too late.

Because, in the end, it really wasn't.

She'd thought she loved Andy. She knew, now, without hesitation, that she loved Nick. Neither felt the same, not in depth or width or breadth, yet neither could be denied or dismissed. Bess had thought there could be room in her heart for only one man at a time, room for something this all-encompassing just once. She'd never thought to feel it twice, or at the same time for two different people, in two different ways.

Love couldn't be turned on and off like a light switch. Couldn't be shrugged out of like a jacket that had grown too heavy. Love was complicated and deeper, something Bess had always believed she understood until the day she stood with Andy at his car and watched him drive away from her. The day he told her he'd be waiting for her to change her mind.

All at once, she no longer knew what love was. Did loving someone mean doing what he wanted and she didn't, because it would make him happy? What was the point of love if she made herself unhappy so she could bring him joy? Was that love? Or was there something else, some secret, a trick to it that made it all work?

Bess had three weeks left in the summer. Andy would be waiting for her when she went back to Pennsylvania, to school. Nick hadn't waited at all. He'd made the choice easy for her, and still she couldn't decide. She hadn't said yes to Andy, but Nick hadn't given her the chance to say yes to him.

Good news spreads fast, and bad news faster. Bess shouldn't have been surprised to hear about Nick's parties. As summer drew to a close, it was tradition for the pace to increase. Hookups, breakups, drinking, smoking. Relationships that would have taken a full month to begin and end now were encapsulated into a week. It was end-of-season desperation, even for the townies. Bess shouldn't have been surprised by what Missy told her, but as it turned out, she was.

"You'll never guess who I did it with." Missy's eyes gleamed as she leaned over the counter. "Right on the kitchen table."

Sugarland was empty for the moment, though Bess had no doubts it would fill shortly. The tourists had end-of-season desperation, too, and had been consuming twice as much popcorn and ice cream, as though their aching bellies could hold on to summer and chase away the inevitable winter.

The question was, who didn't Missy "do it" with? Bess thought uncharitably, but not without reason. She swiped at the counter with her wet cloth, forcing Missy to leap back or risk getting her elbows soaked with soapy water. "Darth Vader."

Missy snorted. Since she'd barely spoken to Bess for the past month and a half, this must be news of the highest importance. "Don't be a bitch."

Bess slapped her cloth into the small sink by the soda machine and turned, hands on her hips. "You know something? I'm getting fucking tired of being called a bitch."

Brian, who'd been set to work refilling the slushy machine, and was making quite a mess of it, laughed. "Amen, sister."

Missy raised overtweezed brows in an expression that made Bess really feel like a bitch. "Sorrry."

"Just tell her you fucked him, Missy," Brian said. "Everyone else knows about it, and it's not like she won't figure it out."

The color seeped out of the world, little by little. Missy smirked. Bess heard a ringing buzz in her ears and had to remember to take a breath.

"You didn't," she said. "He wouldn't."

Missy's smirk became a full-on, cat's-got-the-cream grin. "Me and Ryan broke up."

Nick wouldn't have, anyway. Not with Missy. Would he? Bess put a hand on her stomach, where a sharp pain had suddenly lodged.

"Go away, Missy," Brian said, stepping between Bess and the counter. "You know you're being a bitch."

Missy gave a pretty pout, maybe thinking she'd provoke Bess into a confrontation. Maybe just being Missy. "C'mon, Brian, Bess doesn't care. I mean, it's not like they were really together."

The "really" tipped it, finally, for Bess. They hadn't "really" been together. It had only been fake, a sham, something to pass the time. A joke. Was he even now laughing about her the way he'd laughed about the others?

"Missy, you are such a cunt," she heard Brian say behind her, but Missy's outraged squawk did nothing to soothe her.

The concrete steps at the shop's back door were rough but sunwarmed on her bare thighs, and Bess welcomed the heat because it meant she might be able to stop shivering. She didn't even try to fight the tears, as if they'd be fought with any hope of winning, anyway. She buried her face in her hands and sobbed, not caring who might hear or who might make fun. She didn't care anymore.

She had no right to feel betrayed. Maybe she deserved to be. Maybe this was punishment for her weakness, her lying, her unfaithfulness.

Missy's smirk rose in her mind and she sobbed again, not
wanting to believe two people she'd thought were friends
could both be so deliberately cruel—or worse, care so little
for her that she hadn't even factored into the equation. Except
she knew that wasn't true; Missy might have had her eye on
Nick for a while, but it was the fact he'd been with Bess
instead of her that had made her pursue him so strongly. But
why had *he* done it with *Missy?*

Bess didn't want to know. Couldn't let herself think about
it, or else she'd hate him, and she didn't want to hate him.

The back door opened. Eddie sat down quietly next to her.
Bess didn't move, her face still buried in her hands against the
bony knobs of her knees. Her shoulders hitched with a fresh
flurry of sobs. Her tears had already soaked the hems of her
shorts and splashed onto the concrete steps.

Eddie put his arm around her.

He didn't remind her she was getting what she deserved, or
say he'd told her so. He didn't tell her Nick was a prick and
Missy a slut, or make her feel stupid. Eddie made no commentary on the situation at all.

He simply wrapped his arm around her and stroked her hair
while she sobbed onto his shoulder, and when she'd gone on
for so long she eventually had to stop, he gave her a handful
of tissues and a cold drink of water with ice, just the way she
liked it, and he left her alone on the back steps to compose
herself before she went back to work.

And eventually, she did.

Chapter 41

Now

They had the house to themselves again, but the quiet had become too much. They shared the couch, Nick buried inside one of the books she'd brought home from Bethany Magick and Bess working on some ideas for Just A Bite. It seemed like a natural enough progression, that the constant sexual tension should of course fade. That they should, in time, become like every other couple, settled into individual tasks.

She hated it.

"Hey." Bess closed the laptop and put it on the coffee table, then tugged the book from Nick's hands to set that down, too. "Robbie won't be home for a few hours."

Nick looked at her. "Yeah?"

He didn't reach for her, and Bess stayed her hand from reaching for him. "Yes."

"Let me guess. You want to get busy." Nick's quirking smile shot relief through her.

"I thought we could," Bess said.

He didn't move, so she leaned forward to brush her lips against his. He opened his mouth for her at once and, encouraged, she slid onto his lap to tip his head back. She cupped his face as she kissed him. She took her time. She kissed him deeply and slowly, until his hands tightened on her hips and his crotch bulged beneath her.

"That's better," she whispered against his mouth as she pushed her body down on his erection.

"I aim to please," he murmured, his hands sliding under her shirt to press her bare back.

It wasn't the first time he'd allowed her to take charge, but it was the first time it felt he was merely going through the motions rather than enthusiastically participating. He was inside her. His hands were on her. His mouth beneath hers moved, his tongue stroked. He whispered her name, and he shuddered as she rode him. When she came with a low cry, Nick held her close.

But when she looked into his face, he was gazing out through the glass, toward the sea.

He said nothing as she untangled herself from him and got off the couch, or when she rearranged her clothes. He got up after a minute and zipped his pants, ran his hands through his hair. He was still looking out and not at her.

"Where are you going?" She didn't like her own petulant tone, but Nick didn't seem to notice.

"For a walk."

"Want me to come with you?" She was already beside him, reaching for his hand.

He looked down at their linked fingers, then at her face. "No. Not really."

It took her a second, but Bess dropped his hand. Nick, not smiling, not frowning, turned his gaze back toward the glass.

He walked slowly toward it, pushed the handle of the door, stepped through.

She followed him. "Nick."

He paused at the top of the stairs, but said nothing. Bess stayed in the doorway. After a moment he started down the stairs toward the sand.

"Nick, wait!"

"I'm just taking a walk," he snapped, turning at last to glare at her. "Fuck, is that okay? Can I do that?"

"I just thought…" But she didn't know what she thought. Or what to say.

Once again, she'd begun to doubt.

"What? You thought you'd check up on me? Or what? You know I can't fucking go anywhere."

His voice was too loud and Bess glanced automatically toward the houses on either side. Nick saw the look and spat into the sand.

"You don't have to worry about me," he said in a voice thick with derision. "I'll be back to service your every desire in a while."

Bess drew back at the tone. "That's not what I was going to say."

She went down the stairs, but he drew away from her at the bottom, and she didn't touch him. Nick turned his face, jaw clenched, and Bess struggled to keep her voice from shaking. "What's the matter, Nick?"

"Nothing."

"Something is wrong. I can see it." She moved forward. He stepped back.

"I just want to take a walk, by myself. I just want to be alone for a little while, without you hanging all over me."

"I thought you liked me hanging all over you." Her sad attempt at humor didn't bring a smile from him, and her stomach turned over in dismay.

"Yeah, well," Nick said. "Do I have any other choice?"

She recognized the look he gave her. She'd seen it before, a long time ago. Knowing he was pushing her away on purpose didn't make it any easier to bear. She licked her lips, and for once his gaze didn't flicker to the motion of her tongue.

The breeze lifted his hair from his forehead. It brought the sound of the ocean to them both, but it was Bess this time who turned to face the water.

"Go then, if you want," she said. "Don't let me keep you."

He made a disgusted gesture and turned. Bess watched him, but she didn't follow.

Chapter 42

Then

*I*t wasn't the last party of the summer, but it was the last one Bess would attend. She'd already packed her car. The beach house had been cleaned and stood silent, empty of the stream of relatives who'd spent their summer vacations there. Tomorrow she'd be back in Pennsylvania, in the small, ugly apartment she'd rented instead of staying in a dormitory. Tomorrow everything that had happened here would finally be over.

Eddie, who never came to parties, but had asked her to come to this one, shadowed her. He wasn't so bold as to try to hold her hand, but Bess would have let him, if he had. She hadn't forgotten the comfort of his arm around her shoulder, or the way he'd stroked her hair without saying anything when silence had been exactly what she'd needed.

Brian's apartment was nearly bare in preparation for his own departure on the morrow, which was why he was having a party tonight. Nothing to break or stain, he'd told her earlier during their last shift together. And with charging everyone a two-dollar keg fee, he might actually make enough money to pay for his gas back to New Jersey. Bess admired his ingenuity.

She had a beer in her hand when Missy pranced across her line of sight, and to give her credit, Bess didn't throw it. Missy pretended she didn't see her, and that was just fine. Bess wasn't there to fight.

She wasn't sure why she was there until she saw Nick. He stood against the far wall of Brian's miniscule apartment, his baseball cap pulled low over his eyes. It was almost exactly the same way he'd looked the first time she'd seen him.

She still wanted to get on her knees for him, wanted him so much it made her shake. More now, even, then the first time she'd seen him, because now she knew just how good it would feel. Like a junkie, she wanted him even though she knew it was bad for her. It seemed she'd risk anything for that few moments of high.

"You okay?" Eddie touched her elbow, his gaze following hers. "Do you want to leave?"

"No. Not unless you want to." Bess smiled at him and was glad to see he didn't duck his face away or blush the way he always had.

Eddie shook his head, his gaze steady. "No. But if you want to leave, just let me know."

He was protecting her, and Bess wanted to hug him for it even though she didn't feel she needed protecting. "I'm okay, Eddie. Really."

He nodded solemnly. "Okay."

The party swelled, the music got louder. The beer flowed. Eddie disappeared into the crowd to get her another drink, and didn't come back right away. Bess spotted him in a circle of girls in the kitchenette. Younger girls, too young to be drinking, and too drunk to care. To them, Eddie must have seemed quite a catch, not that Bess any longer disagreed, and so when he didn't come back after another five minutes she took it upon herself to grab another beer.

She hated the taste and smell of it, but drank it anyway. It left fur on her tongue and the back of her throat, and made her wish for some water. Getting a drink of water meant fighting the crowd, and she didn't feel like doing it. Cool air might do the trick, as well, and she sought it on Brian's back deck. It didn't quite overlook the ocean, but if you hung over the railing and strained your neck around the corner and knew just where to look, you could catch a glimpse of the beach. At least you could in the daytime.

Nick was there, of course, because that was how the universe worked. Bess saw him right away, knew him by the slope of his shoulders and the smell of the smoke, even though she couldn't see his face.

Two beers hadn't made her drunk, but allowed her to fake confidence. When she put her hands on the railing next to him, Nick didn't startle. He turned to face her, and though she wanted to see something on his face other than impassivity, all she saw was the cherry, glowing tip of his Swisher Sweet.

"You're leaving tomorrow." He wasn't asking.

"Yes."

He drew in a drag and tossed the butt into the can of sand Brian had put on the back deck for smokers. It smoldered there briefly and winked out. Watching the ember die, Bess didn't look up when Nick spoke again.

"Back to your boyfriend, huh? Bet he'll be glad to see you."

Bess didn't reply, understanding from experience the power of saying nothing and the helplessness of being granted silence.

"Because he loooves you."

She didn't have to see his face to hear the sneer.

They battled with silence while the music from the party drifted out to them, punctuated by the hum and buzz of conversation and the occasional hint of the ocean's roar.

"Don't you know that love's a bunch of shit?" Nick asked finally, the first to break.

Bess had thought victory would taste sweeter. "Keep on telling yourself that."

She looked at him, and he looked back.

"Good luck with it," Nick said, not meaning it.

"Good luck with Missy," Bess said, not meaning it, either.

"Missy? What the hell's that supposed to mean?"

At last he wasn't staring from a face of stone. He actually looked shocked, a sight that gave Bess too much pleasure. She shrugged.

"She told me about you two."

Nick shook his head, then took off his hat and shoved it in his back pocket so he could run his hands through his hair. Agitated, he pulled his package of smokes from his shirt pocket, but didn't light one.

"Seriously, Bess, what the hell? Told you what?"

"She says you did it on the kitchen table." Bess kept her voice even, as if she didn't care.

Nick scowled. "She's lying."

"Really?" Bess crossed her arms. "Usually when Missy tells me she fucked somebody, she's telling the truth."

"Not this time." He put the small cigars away.

Bess kept her spine straight and her gaze steady. "She says you did."

"I say we didn't." He turned and gripped the railing hard enough to shake it. "Christ, Bess. You know I wouldn't—"

"She broke up with Ryan." That fact had been confirmed without a doubt by beach gossip.

"I don't care." Nick looked at her over his shoulder. "If she says I fucked her—"

"On the kitchen table," Bess interrupted.

He whirled and grabbed her by the upper arms. "She's a lying bitch, Bess, and you know it."

"I don't know it!" she cried, and he stepped back. "She says you did! And you know what, Nick? It doesn't really matter!"

"It should!" he half shouted.

"Well," Bess said after a moment. "It doesn't. Because you're both supposed to be my friends, and either way, one of you is lying to me."

"It's not me." He could only go two steps in either direction, but he paced anyway.

"It doesn't matter," she repeated, lying. "I don't care."

They faced each other, and he was the first to look away. His voice stopped her at the door.

"I can't believe you're going back to that asshole."

Bess turned to look at him. "Not that it's any of your business, and not that you care, but I haven't decided that yet."

"So it's him by default?" Nick's laughter pricked her like a dozen thorns. "I bet he'd be thrilled to hear that."

"Don't flatter yourself," she said. "If I decide to get back with Andy it will be because I want to give things with him another chance."

Through the sliding-glass door Bess could see people milling around in Brian's bedroom. They'd want to come out on the deck in a minute, and there wasn't space for all of them. She gripped the door handle but didn't pull it open.

"Is that supposed to make me feel better?"

"I thought you didn't feel anything, one way or the other!" Bess snapped.

Nick's laugh sounded shaky, or perhaps it was her wishful imagination. "What do you want me to say?"

"I don't care what you say," she said, "but give me a choice. Give me a reason to decide, one way or the other."

She waited a minute, then another, expecting and receiving his silence.

"Yeah," Bess said. "I thought so."

She didn't wait any longer for him to speak or for her heart to break. It was too late for either event to make any sort of difference to her.

Chapter 43

Now

"Bess?" Bess looked up to see Eddie in the carport, gazing at her with concern. He glanced past her, his eyes narrowing, then back at her. "Are you all right?"

"Fine." She didn't look back at Nick, but Eddie stared past her with the same assessing expression.

"You sure you're okay? I heard shouting."

Bess lifted her chin. "I said I was fine."

He'd heard them, she knew he had. Maybe not the entire conversation, but enough. She saw concern in his eyes, not censure, but she felt guilty just the same.

"I came by to see if you wanted to have dinner with me. Talk about the shop."

Bess opened her mouth, but no words came out. After the last time? He'd kissed her and she'd told him she didn't want something like that from him, yet he was still interested?

"Just to talk," Eddie said, as though he'd read her mind. He gave her a broad, warm smile. "Honest."

Bess glanced over her shoulder, but the dunes blocked her view. Not that it mattered. Nick was right. He couldn't go far, even if he wanted to. She looked back at Eddie, and made a choice.

"Yes, okay. That would be great."

He didn't take her someplace fancy, but that was fine. The small, blues-themed barbecue place smelled like heaven and was casual enough for Bess to convince herself this wasn't any sort of date. She'd expected things with Eddie to feel awkward or strained, but he opened the door for her the way he always had. And still she felt compelled to apologize.

"Don't be sorry," he told her as they sifted through piles of paperwork.

"It's not that I don't like you, Eddie—"

He held up a hand to stop her. "Bess. Don't make it worse."

She laughed self-consciously. "Sorry."

"Don't be sorry," Eddie insisted, laughing with her.

"I just…"

"I know," he said, with the same easiness with which he'd put an arm around her shoulders so long ago. "It's okay. Robbie told me you were seeing someone. I guess I just didn't want to believe it."

"Eddie…"

His gaze shifted a little bit. "Bess, it's not my business. I didn't know he was back in town, that's all. I guess I shouldn't be surprised."

Bess swallowed hard. "Robbie told you who it was?"

"Nick Hamilton," Eddie said, too casually. "Guess he didn't fall off the face of the earth, after all."

"Did Robbie say anything else?" Her chair seemed to tilt,

or perhaps the entire floor did, and Bess gripped the table to force away the sudden vertigo.

"Not really." Eddie's expression shifted once more to concern. "Are you okay?"

She nodded and drank some water. Forced a smile. "I just want *us* to be okay, Eddie. That's all."

"Can I tell you honestly that I'd rather be in your life as your friend than as nothing at all?" he asked her, and Bess sat for a long, long moment before she could reply. Nobody had ever said such a thing to her.

"Yes," she answered. "You can say that."

"Good." Eddie nodded and bent back over the pile of forms and documents they needed to sign to get Just A Bite off the ground. "Because it's true."

Chapter 44

Then

When the phone rang in the middle of the night, Bess knew who would be on the other end before she even lifted the handset from its cradle.

"Did you decide?"

She had, weeks ago. "Yes, Nick. I did."

She expected silence, but this time didn't get it.

"I can't stop thinking about you."

She'd been wrong, before, when she thought she'd finished with him. When she thought her heart had broken, irreparably. It broke again now.

"It's too late," she said through tears. Darkness made it easier to do so.

"Don't say that, Bess."

"I already did."

"Shit," Nick said. "But you didn't mean it."

"No," she agreed, an answer also made easier by darkness. "No, I didn't."

"I miss you," he stated. "A lot."

"Don't sound so surprised," Bess told him. "It's annoying."

Nick laughed. She hadn't forgotten how much she liked to hear him laugh, given that he wasn't prone to it. "I'm sorry. For a lot of things. I told you, I'm a prick."

"You don't have to be so proud of it, you know."

"I'm not proud of it."

She believed him, against her better judgment. "Why are you calling me at two in the morning?"

"I couldn't sleep."

In the background she heard a sudden flare of giggling and the bass thump of music. "Right. Do you usually sleep at parties?"

"Only if they're boring. How'd you know it was a party?"

"I can hear it," she said.

They were both quiet for a minute.

"Are you...happy?" he asked, and broke her heart all over again.

"I'm not with Andy, Nick," she said, unable for one minute longer to make him think she was. "And, no. I'm not happy."

"I can be there in three hours."

"You don't know where I live."

"Brian gave me your phone number. You think he wouldn't tell me where you live, too?"

"He doesn't know my address."

"Bess," Nick said, so seriously there was no question of her not believing him, "I'll find you."

It was without a doubt the most arousing thing anyone had ever said to her.

"That sounds vaguely stalkerish."

"It's only stalking if you don't want to be found."

"Next you'll tell me you're calling me from the gas station across the street," she said, feeling giddy.

"Ah," Nick replied. "So there's a gas station across the street."

"You don't have to guess," she told him. "I'll tell you how to get here. Drive fast."

"As fast as I can," Nick said. "I'll be there in three hours."

Three hours passed, then six, but even though she waited up all night, even though she cut all her classes the next day, even though she sat by her window, looking at every car that passed, hoping it was his, it never was.

Chapter 45

Now

*W*hen she pulled into the carport, the thump of music and the rich, smoky scent of the grill greeted her before anything else. She climbed the stairs into chaos. Someone had set up a portable laser show on the coffee table, and it shone its shifting pattern of red circles on the walls and ceiling.

Her living room overflowed with teenagers, most of them with plastic cups in their hands. The music rumbled her guts and hurt her ears. Her kitchen was a disaster, with open boxes of pizza and bowls of chips and pretzels all over the place. Her footsteps crunched. She saw no sign of a keg or suspicious bottles, but that didn't mean all those cups of soda were virgin.

This had Nick stamped all over it, but it was Connor who appeared from the deck with a broad grin on his face. "Mom!"

"Connor, what the hell's going on here?"

"Party," he said unnecessarily with a wave of his hand. "Just some friends. It's a going away party for me."

Bess leaned in but though his eyes were suspiciously bright, she couldn't smell liquor on him. "Where's your brother?"

"He's around." Connor reached past her to snag a can of cola from the ice-filled sink. "Do you want to know where Nick is?"

"I want you to turn down the music before the neighbors call the police," Bess said, ignoring the last question.

Connor popped the top on the can and drank around a grin so wide she was surprised he didn't spill all down his front. "He's out on the deck."

Bess eyed her oldest son. "Is he?"

Connor swiped his mouth with the back of a hand. "Yeah. He is."

Suspicious, but not certain of what, Bess pushed through the crowd of lounging, laughing kids and toward the sliding-glass doors. Robbie stopped her halfway there.

"Mom!"

"Nice party," Bess said, as someone bounded by her, chasing a beach ball. "If anything gets broken, you and Connor are paying for it."

Robbie grinned sheepishly. "They're mostly Conn's friends. But we're not drinking or anything."

Bess rolled her eyes. "Do you think I'm stupid, Robbie?"

"No." He shifted his feet, stepping in front of her when she tried to move past him.

Bess stopped. "What's going on?"

"Nothing." He'd never been the sort of liar his brother was, hadn't inherited Andy's effortless guile. He shifted again when she moved.

"Robert Andrew," Bess said. "Is there a keg on the deck? Do you know how much trouble I can get into if you guys are drinking underage?"

"No, there's no keg. Some people have been drinking out on the beach, but not up here."

Maybe she'd been wrong about the guile. Bess recognized his trick. Offer a little bit of truth to distract from the greater dishonesty. "What's going on, really? Drugs?"

He shook his head. "No."

"Robbie," Connor said, clapping his hand on his brother's shoulder. "Annalise's looking for you."

Bess clearly saw the war on Robbie's face. The girl he'd been crushing on all summer, or protecting Mom? The battle was fought but briefly, and he headed off into the crowd in the direction Connor pointed.

More kids crowded the deck, some of them sitting on the railings in a way that made her motherly heart quail. She wasn't quite uncool enough to tell them to get down. Someone stood at her grill, flipping burgers she knew hadn't come from her freezer. At least Connor or his friends were providing their own food.

It took exactly three heartbeats before she saw him, his mouth open under the onslaught of tongue and lips of some blond girl wearing a skirt so short everyone around her could see all the way to her panties. Nick, legs spread so the girl's ass dipped between them, had one hand on the back of her neck and the other on her thigh. It was the girl from the beginning of the summer, from the day he'd tried to leave the section of the beach in front of the house and couldn't.

Bess stood, unmoving. She meant to simply turn around and leave him to it, but he opened his eyes and broke off the kiss to smile at her.

To smile.

Bess turned on her heel and went inside, where she yanked the stereo cord from the wall. "Get out," she said without having to shout, and there was no doubt everyone in the room heard her. "All of you. Go home."

There were mutters and looks, but nobody argued.

"You, too," she said to Connor. "Take your brother."

"Where am I supposed to go?" he asked, querulous.

"I don't know," Bess said through gritted teeth, understanding now his humor from before. "Why don't you get in that pretty car Daddy bought you and find a place to hang out for a few hours. Just…go, Connor."

He wasn't laughing now. He looked out to the deck, where the news of the busted party had spread. Connor swallowed hard, his mouth turning down.

"Mom—"

"Go, Connor," Bess said. "You got what you wanted. Now go."

He went. Within fifteen minutes the entire house had cleared. Even the blonde had gone, though whether dismissed by Nick or just following the crowd, Bess didn't know.

She heard the sliding-glass door open and close.

"Not so nice when it's you, is it?" he asked.

"Is that why you did it? Because you think I'm fucking Eddie?"

"Yes. That's why I did it."

She turned to him. "Well, thank you for being honest. I'm not fucking Eddie."

"But you'd like to."

"Oh, Nick." Bess sighed, and covered her eyes with her palm for one minute. "It's so much more than just that."

"I know it is," he said after a minute. She felt his breath on her face and took away her hand. "And that's really why I did it."

He kissed her, or she kissed him. It didn't matter which. They went together into her bedroom, where he hesitated until she took his hands and put them on her body.

His tongue slid along her throat and down to the opened V of her blouse. When he found her nipples, already tight and hard, he moaned against her skin. His hands slid up her skirt and cupped her ass, grinding her against the bulge in his jeans.

His urgency moved her, but Bess put her hand on the back of his head, lightly, until he lifted it. Nick licked his mouth as he looked into her eyes, but he didn't move away when she cupped his face in her hands and brushed his lips with hers, so softly it was more breath than caress.

"I love you," she told him. "I think I loved you from the first time I saw you, and I have loved you for twenty years when I didn't know where you were. I won't stop loving you, no matter what else happens, Nick."

He shuddered, but didn't pull away from her. His eyes closed, though, and his mouth thinned, as though her truth was too painful to hear. Bess stroked her thumbs along his cheekbones, then down to his mouth. She'd already memorized every feature, every curve and line and scar, but she did it again now, slowly with her fingertips, knowing this was the very last time.

When she pulled his shirt off over his head, his skin bumped at once into gooseflesh. She warmed him with her breath. Along his collarbone, down one arm and then the other, across his chest. Down his belly when she got her knees and tugged open the button and zipper. Along his cock when she pulled it free and helped him step out of his jeans.

She took him in her mouth, her hand at the base of his erection. He put his palms on her hair, not pushing or pulling. She sucked him gently, then harder, the way she knew gave him the most pleasure. His voice broke on the single syllable of her name.

Her mouth and hands moved on him until his fingers tightened in her hair and her name became a plea. Then she got off her knees. She took off her clothes while he watched, his eyes gleaming.

When she stood naked in front of him, she said, "What do you see, now?"

His hand passed over the hair lying unbound across her shoulders. She saw him catalog the curve of her hips and belly, the small silver lines that marked her as a mother. The lines at the corners of her eyes had never had a weight before, but under his gaze she felt them now.

"You."

It was a sweet lie, and one she didn't contradict.

"I still see you," Nick said, his voice low.

She held out her arms and he pulled her onto the bed, where they lay facing each other, their legs twined and hands linked. "Tell me what happened."

"I meant to come to you right away, but I was at the party. I'd been drinking." His laugh rushed like lace-topped waves around her. "If I hadn't been, I don't think I'd have called you."

She held him closer.

"I wanted to get in the car and drive, just drive. Just get to you. That's all I could think of, was getting to you. But I knew I had to sober up first. So I went out, to the beach. I thought if I walked awhile that might help. And it was cold, you know? The water was cold. I thought if I splashed some on my face...well, if I took a swim. That would help. I thought I'd only jump in, get wet. I thought it would only take a few minutes and I could be on my way. To you."

His voice snagged like a burr on silk. Heat leaked from the corners of Bess's eyes and slipped between her lips. Salt water. Always salt water.

"I was stupid," Nick whispered.

"You didn't know," she whispered back.

"It took my feet out from under me. And all I could think of was how you were waiting, and I was going to fuck it all up again. How I was going to let you down."

"Shh," she soothed. "I don't blame you for any of it."

They lay in silence for a long time.

"I have to go," he told her at last.

"I know you do."

Nick shook his head, his hair moving on the pillow. "I want to go. I'm sorry, Bess. I'm so sorry, but I do."

Her throat had gone so tight she was certain she wouldn't be able to answer, but she managed just the same. "I know that, too, Nick. I know."

Bess had become the ocean, always breaking against the rocks but never staying broken. Her love was the ocean, too, endless and always changing, yet forever the same.

He moved on top of her and inside her, and she held on to him as tightly as she could for as long as she could, but the pleasure wouldn't be held back no matter how she wished not to feel it. Pleasure was an ocean surrounding and filling her, and they swam in it together without holding anything back.

She wanted to sleep in his arms, but that was a selfish wish and one she put aside.

"It's time to go, love," she told him.

"I don't know how."

Bess kissed him. "I know how."

She took him down to the water, which had gone cold in anticipation of the winter. Wavelets frothed around their ankles. She held his hand. She led him a few steps farther, and the cold water splashed to their knees. Her teeth chattered when the waves began to swirl around their thighs, but Bess didn't turn back. With Nick's hand in hers, she dived deep into the cold, black water, and she let it take them both away.

Chapter 46

Now

$\mathscr{D}$rowning wasn't as easy as she'd expected. Her mouth didn't want to open. Her lungs didn't want to take in water instead of air. Her body fought to live.

Nick's mouth pressed on hers in a kiss harsher than any he'd ever given her. Her mouth parted, but instead of his tongue's swipe, air pushed itself down her throat and into her lungs. Her head broke the surface, gasping; her arms and legs beat at the water.

She swam until the waves turned her upside down and she scraped along the bottom with sand in her hair, her eyes, her mouth. She swam until the ocean tossed her up onto the shore, where she lay panting, every muscle aching and her fingers and toes digging into the cold, wet sand, and she wondered if she was alive or dead.

"Mom!" She heard two voices shouting, felt the roughness

of more sand kicked across her as her sons both knelt beside her on the beach.

"Mom, are you okay?" Connor shook her, his voice quavering with fear. "Mom, Mom, please be okay."

He was crying, Bess realized. They both were. Both her sons were crying, and she put aside her own grief and pain to sit up and clutch them both against her, to reassure them she was all right. That she hadn't gone and left them before they were ready for her to do so.

She put aside her grief and let them help her to her feet.

"I'm fine," she said. "Go on in the house. I'll be right there."

They didn't want to, of course, but she told them to do it, so they did. Bess looked out to the ocean, always breaking and never broken, and she put aside her grief, not for her sons or for herself, but finally, for Nick.

She let him go.

From the deck, Bess watched the swirling lights of the beach patrol car cast the sand in alternating shades of red and blue. Connor had insisted on calling the police, and Bess hadn't resisted, though she knew there was no purpose. She'd told them the truth, that she and a man named Nick Hamilton had gone for a swim. The undertow had taken them, but she'd managed to swim to shore.

They'd asked her for more information, which she pretended not to know. If there were further questions, she supposed she'd deal with them later, but for now she sat wrapped in her old, wash-beaten cardigan and watched the officials wander to and fro, and finally, leave the beach marked with the tracks of their cars.

Even a crisis can't destroy the appetites of teenage boys.

When Connor and Robbie had asked her if she wanted to go with them for pizza, Bess said no. She also said no when they asked if she needed anything, including someone to stay with her. They took her at her word, trusting her with the unshakable certainty that mothers were always right, and they left her alone.

"Bess?"

Eddie's soft voice turned her head, but Bess didn't get up from the deck chair. She did, however, move over enough on the double lounger to give him room to sit.

"Robbie called me. Told me what happened."

Bess tucked her chilly hands into her pockets. Something smooth and rough tickled her palm. Her fingers closed around it.

"They said...you were with Nick." Eddie's voice went soft. "That he drowned."

Bess nodded. She pulled out the shell Nick had given her. It had scraped the base of her thumb, but brought no blood.

She waited for the questions she would be unable to answer, but Eddie didn't ask. He put his arm around her. He gave her his warmth, and her face found the solace of his shoulder.

She cried for a very long time, but when she was done, Eddie was still there, solid and real against her. He was her friend. More, if she wanted it from him, and though Bess wasn't sure she was ready for that, she was no longer fighting to make sure she'd never be.